The Mandibles:
A Family, 2029–2047

ALSO BY LIONEL SHRIVER

The Mandibles:
A Family,
2029–2047

Lionel Shriver

HARPER LUXE

An Imprint of HarperCollins Publishers

HarperCollins books may be purchased for educational, business, or sales promotional use. For information please e-mail the Special Markets Department at SPsales@harpercollins.com.

FIRST HARPERLUXE EDITION

ISBN: 978-0-06-246714-0

HarperLuxe™ is a trademark of HarperCollins Publishers.

Library of Congress Cataloging-in-Publication Data is available upon request.

16 17 18 19 20   ID/RRD   10 9 8 7 6 5 4 3 2 1

TO BRADFORD HALL WILLIAMS.
Although you had little time for fiction,
you'd have liked this book.
Who would have imagined that
a cantankerous misanthrope
would be so fiercely missed?

Collapse is a sudden, involuntary and chaotic form of simplification.

—JAMES RICKARDS, *Currency Wars*

The Mandibles:
A Family, 2029–2047

2029

Chapter 1
Gray Water

Don't use clean water to wash your hands!"
Intended as a gentle reminder, the admonishment
came out shrill. Florence didn't want to seem like what
her son would call a *boomerpoop,* but still—the rules of
the household were simple. Esteban consistently flouted
them. There were ways of establishing that you weren't
under any (somewhat) older woman's thumb without
wasting water. He was such a cripplingly handsome man
that she'd let him get away with almost anything else.

"Forgive me, Father, for I have sinned," Esteban
muttered, dipping his hands into the plastic tub in
the sink that caught runoff. Shreds of cabbage floated
around the rim.

"That doesn't make sense, does it?" Florence said.
"When you've already used the clean, to use the gray?"

"Only doing what I'm told," her partner said.

"That's a first."

"What's put *you* in such a good mood?" Esteban wiped his now-greasy hands on an even greasier dishtowel (another rule: a roll of paper towels lasts six weeks). "Something go wrong at Adelphi?"

"Things go nothing but wrong at Adelphi," she grumbled. "Drugs, fights, theft. Screaming babies with eczema. That's what homeless shelters are like. Honestly, I'm bewildered by why it's so hard to get the residents to flush the toilet. Which is the height of luxury, in this house."

"I wish you'd find something else."

"I do, too. But don't tell anybody. It would ruin my sainted reputation." Florence returned to slicing cabbage—an economical option even at twenty bucks. She wasn't sure how much more of the vegetable her son could stand.

Others were always agog at the virtuousness of her having taken on such a demanding, thankless job for four long years. But assumptions about her angelic nature were off base. After she'd scraped from one poorly paid, often part-time position to another, whatever wide-eyed altruism had motivated her moronic double major in American Studies and Environmental Policy at Barnard had been beaten out of her almost entirely. Half her jobs had been eliminated because an innovation became abruptly obsolete; she'd worked for a company that sold electric long underwear to save on heating bills, and then suddenly consumers only wanted heated underwear backed by electrified graphene. Other positions were eliminated by what in her twenties were called *bots*, but which displaced American workers now called *robs*, for obvious reasons. Her most promising position was at a start-up that made tasty protein bars out of cricket powder. Yet once Hershey's mass-produced a similar but notoriously oily product, the market for insect-based snacks tanked. So when she came across a post in a city shelter in Fort Greene, she'd applied from a combination of desperation and canniness: the one thing New York City was bound never to run out of was homeless people.

"Mom?" Willing asked quietly in the doorway. "Isn't it my turn for a shower?"

Her thirteen-year-old had last bathed only five days ago, and knew full well they were all allotted one shower per week (they went through cases of comb-in dry shampoo). Willing complained, too, that standing under their ultra-conservation showerhead was like "going for a walk in the fog." True, the fine spray made it tricky to get conditioner out, but then the answer wasn't to use more water. It was to stop using conditioner.

"Maybe not quite yet . . . but go ahead," she relented. "Don't forget to turn off the water while you're soaping up."

"I get cold." His delivery was flat. It wasn't a complaint. It was a fact.

"I've read that shivering is good for your metabolism," Florence said.

"Then my metabolism must be *awesome*," Willing said dryly, turning heel. The mockery of her dated vernacular wasn't fair. She'd learned ages ago to say *malicious*.

"If you're right, and this water thing will only get worse?" Esteban said, taking down plates for dinner. "Might as well open the taps full-on while we can."

"I do sometimes fantasize about long, hot showers," Florence confessed.

"Oh, yeah?" He encircled her waist from behind as she cored another cabbage wedge. "Deep inside this tight, bossy choirgirl is a hedonist trying to get out."

"God, I used to bask under a torrent, with the water hot as I could bear. When I was a teenager, the condensation got so bad once that I ruined the bathroom's paint job."

"That's the sexiest thing you've ever told me," he whispered in her ear.

"Well, that's depressing."

He laughed. His work entailed lifting often-stout elderly bodies in and out of mobility scooters—*mobes*, if you were remotely hip—and it kept him in shape. She could feel his pecs and abdominal muscles tense against her back. Tired, certainly, and she might be all of forty-four, but that made her a spring chicken these days, and the sensation was stirring. They had good sex. Either it was a Mexican thing or he was simply a man apart, but unlike all the other guys she'd known, Esteban hadn't been raised on a steady diet of porn since he was five. He had a taste for real women.

Not that Florence thought of herself as a great catch. Her younger sister had bagged the looks. Avery was dark and delicately curved, with that trace of fragility men found so fetching. Sinewy and strong simply from keeping busy, narrow-hipped and twitchy, with a long face and a mane of scraggly auburn hair eternally escaping the bandana she wore pirate-style to keep the unruly tendrils out of the way, Florence had often been characterized as "horsey." She'd interpreted the adjective as pejorative, until Esteban latched on to the descriptor with affection, slapping the haunches of his high-strung filly. Maybe you could do worse than to look like a horse.

"See, I got a whole different philosophy," Esteban mumbled into her neck. "Ain't gonna be no more fish?

Stuff your face with Chilean sea bass like there's no tomorrow."

"The danger of there being no tomorrow is the point." The school-marmish tut-tut was tempered with self-parody; she knew her stern, upright facade got on his nerves. "And if everyone's reaction to water scarcity is to take half-hour showers 'while they can,' we'll run out of water even sooner. But if that's not good enough for you? Water is expensive. *Immense* expensive, as the kids say."

He let go of her waist. "*Mi querida,* you're such a drear. If the Stonage taught us anything, it's that the world can go to hell in a snap. In the little gaps between disasters, might as well try to have fun."

He had a point. She'd intended to eke out this pound of ground pork through two meals; it was their first red meat for a month. After Esteban's urging to seize the day, she decided rashly on one-time portions of five ounces apiece, dizzy with profligacy and abandon until she caught herself: *we are supposed to be middle class.*

At Barnard, having written her honors thesis on "Class, 1945–Present" had seemed daring, because Americans flattered themselves as beyond class. But that was before the fabled economic downturn that fatally coincided with her college graduation. After which, Americans talked about nothing but class.

Florence embraced a brusque, practical persona, and self-pity didn't become her. Thanks to her grandfather's college fund, her debts from a pointless education were less onerous than many of her friends'. She may have envied her sister's looks, but not Avery's vocation; privately, she considered that fringy therapeutic practice, "PhysHead," parasitical humbug. Florence's purchase of a house in East Flatbush had been savvy, for the once-scruffy neighborhood had gone upscale. Indians were rioting in Mumbai because they couldn't afford vegetables; at least she could still spring for onions. Technically Florence may have been a "single mother," but single mothers in this country outnumbered married ones, and the very expression had fallen out of use.

Yet her parents never seemed to get it. Although they fell all over themselves proclaiming how "proud" they were, the implication that into her forties their eldest required you-go-girl cheerleading was an insult. Now their fawning over this shelter position was unendurable. She hadn't taken the job because it was laudable; she'd taken it because it was a job. The shelter provided a vital public service, but in a perfect world that service would have been provided by someone else.

True, her parents had suffered their own travails. Her father Carter had long felt like an underachiever in print journalism, being stuck for ages at Long Island's *Newsday*, and never snagging the influential, better re-munerated positions for which he felt he'd paid his dues. (Besides, Dad always seemed to have an edge on him in relation to his sister Nollie, who hadn't, in his view, paid any dues, and whose books, he'd insinuated more than once, were overrated.) Yet toward the end of his career he did get a job at his beloved *New York Times* (God rest its soul). The post was only in the Automo-biles section, and later in Real Estate, but having made it into the paper he most revered was a lifelong tribute. Her mother Jayne lurched from one apocalyptic project to the next, but she *ran* that much-adored bookstore Shelf Life before it went bust; she *ran* that artisanal deli on Smith Street before it was looted during the Stone Age and she was too traumatized to set foot in it again. And they owned their house, didn't they—free and clear! They'd always owned a *car*. They'd had the usual trouble juggling family and career, but they did have careers, not plain old jobs. When Jayne got pregnant late in the day with Jarred, they worried about the age gap between a new baby and their two girls, but neither of them anguished, as Florence had when pregnant with Willing, over whether they could afford to keep the kid at all.

So how could they grasp the plight of their elder daughter? For six long years after graduation Florence had to live with her parents in Carroll Gardens, and that big blot of nothingness still blighted her résumé. At least her little brother Jarred was in high school and could keep her company, but it was humiliating, having toiled on that dopey BA only to trial novel recipes for peanut-butter brownies with mint-flavored chocolate chips. During the so-called "recovery" she moved out at last, sharing cramped, grungy digs with contemporaries who also had Ivy League degrees, in history, or political science, and who also brewed coffee, bussed tables, and sold those old smart phones that shattered and you had to charge all the time at Apple stores. Not one lame-ass position she'd copped since bore the faintest relation to her formal qualifications.

True, the US bounced back from the Stone Age more quickly than predicted. New York restaurants were jammed again, and the stock market was booming. But she hadn't followed whether the Dow had reached 30,000 or 40,000, because none of this frenzied uptick brought Willing, Esteban, and Florence along with. So maybe she wasn't middle class. Maybe the label was merely the residue of hailing from a learned, literary family, what you clung to in order to separate yourself from people who weren't much worse off than you. There weren't many dishes you could prepare from only onions.

Mom!" Willing cried from the living room. "What's a *reserve currency?*"

Wiping her hands on the dishtowel—the cold gray water hadn't cut the grease from the pork patties—Florence found her son freshly washed with his dark, wet hair tousled. Though having grown a couple of inches this year, the boy was slight and still a bit short considering he'd be fourteen in three months. He'd been so rambunctious when he was small. Yet ever since that fateful March five years ago, he'd been, not fearful exactly—he wasn't babyish—but *watchful.* He was too serious for his age, and too quiet. She sometimes felt uncomfortably observed, as if living under the unblinking eye of a security camera. Florence wasn't sure what she'd want to hide from her own son. Yet what best protected privacy wasn't concealment but apathy—the fact that other people simply weren't interested.

Also somber for a cocker spaniel—though the forehead's perpetual rumple of apprehension may have indicated a drop of bloodhound—Milo was flopped beside his master, chin glumly on the floor. His chocolate coat was glossy enough, but the brown eyes looked worried. What a team.

Typically for this time of evening, Willing wasn't propped before video-game aliens and warlords, but the TV news. Funny, for years they'd predicted the demise of the television. Channels were streamed, but the format had survived—providing the open fire, the communal hearth, that a personal device could never quite replace. With newspapers almost universally defunct, print journalism had given way to a rabble of amateurs hawking unverified stories and always to an ideological purpose. Television news was about the only source of information she faintly trusted. *The dollar now having dropped below 40 percent of the world's . . .* a newscaster was yammering.

"I've no idea what a *reserve currency* is," she admitted. "I don't follow all that economics drear. When I graduated from college, it was all people talked about: derivatives, interest rates, something called *LIBOR*. I got sick of it, and I wasn't interested to begin with."

"Isn't it important?"

"My being interested isn't important. I swear, I read newspapers front to back for years. My knowing any of that stuff, most of which I've forgotten, hasn't made the slightest difference. I wish I had the time back, frankly. I thought I'd miss newspapers, and I don't."

"Don't tell Carter that," Willing said. "You'd hurt his feelings."

Florence still winced at that "Carter." Her parents had urged all their grandchildren to address them by first names. "Only" fifty and fifty-two when Avery had her first child, they'd resisted "Grandma and Grand-dad" as connoting a geriatric status with which they couldn't identify. They obviously imagined that being "Jayne and Carter" to the next generation would induce a cozy, egalitarian palliness, as if they weren't elders but buddies. Supposedly, too, the rejection of convention made them bold and cutting-edge. But to Florence, it was awkward: her son referenced her parents with more familiarity than she did. Their refusal to accept the nomenclatural signature of what they actually were— Willing's grandparents, like it or not—suggested self-deceit, and so was purely a gesture of weakness, one that embarrassed her for them if they didn't have the wit to be embarrassed on their own accounts. The forced chumminess encouraged not intimacy but disrespect. Rather than remotely nonconformist, the "Jayne and Carter" routine was tiresomely typical for baby boom-ers. Nevertheless, she shouldn't take her exasperation out on Willing, who was only doing what he was told.

"Don't worry, I'd never bad-mouth newspapers to your grandfather," Florence said. "But even during the Stone Age—everyone thought it was so awful, and some aspects of it were awful. But, gosh, for me liberation from all that noise was dead cool"—she raised her hands—"sorry! It was *careless*. Everything seemed light and serene and open. I'd never realized that a day was so long."

"You read books again." Mention of the Stone Age made Willing pensive.

"Well, the books didn't last! But you're right, I did go back to books. The old kind, with pages. Aunt Avery said it was 'quaint.'" She patted his shoulder and left him to the Most Boring Newscast Ever. Christ, she must have the only thirteen-year-old in Brooklyn riveted by the business report.

Checking the rice, she tried to remember what her weirdo son had claimed about the recrudescence of malnutrition in Africa and on the subcontinent, after both regions had made such strides. It was an outrage that the poor simply couldn't afford to eat, she'd bemoaned to the boy, when the planet had plenty of food. He'd responded obtusely, "No, it doesn't." He proceeded to recapitulate his great-grandfather's tortured explanation—something like, "It only seems like there's plenty of food. If you gave the poor more money, then the price would rise even higher, and then they still couldn't afford it." Which didn't make the slightest sense. Around Willing, she should monitor her grandfather's propaganda more closely. The old man was liberal by creed, but she'd never met anyone with money who didn't have conservative *instincts.* One such instinct was to make the morally obvious (if fiscally inconvenient) seem terribly complicated. Like, rice is too costly, then give people the money to buy it. Duh.

Willing seemed so subdued and unassuming at school, but behind closed doors that kid could get a bit full of himself.

"By the way, I've arranged to talk to my sister after dinner," she told Esteban as he reached for a cold beer. "So I hope you don't mind doing the dishes."

"Let me use real water, I'll do the dishes every night."

"The gray is real enough, just not especially clear." She didn't want to have this battle every evening, and was relieved that he changed the subject as the pork sizzled.

"Met this afternoon with the new group we're taking up Mount Washington," Esteban said. "Already identified the trouble-maker. It's never the weak, pathetic clients who give us grief, but these geriatric superheroes. Usually guys, though sometimes it's some tough, I-still-think-I'm-thirty-five old bag held together with Scotch tape and several hundred grand in plastic surgery."

He knew she didn't like him to talk about his charges with such contempt, but presumably he had to get the frustration out of his system beyond their earshot. "So who's the headache? Jesus, this meat's so full of water, these patties will be boiled."

"Must be the other side of eighty. Has that look, with these stringy biceps—spends hours in the gym and hasn't noticed that he's now doing curls with bar-bells made of balsa wood. Wouldn't listen to my safety drill. His only question was how we dealt with the fact that people 'keep to different paces,' and some climbers prefer to 'push themselves.' He's a type. They're run-ners, or used to be, though that was before their double hip replacements and five keyhole heart surgeries. You can bet they have money, and back before the dawn of time they did something with stroke. So nobody's dared to tell them they're fucking old. Usually their doctor or their spouse has laid down the law that they can't troop into the woods anymore without someone to scoop them up when they stumble down a gully and break their legs. But they never like the whole idea of trekking with a group, and they always look around at the other arthritic losers and think, *What am I doing with these boomerpoops?*—when actually they fit right in. They don't follow directions and they don't wait up. They're the ones who have accidents and give Over the Hill a bad rep. On a canoe trip, they're the ones who splash off solo and take the wrong tributary, and then we have to abandon the whole expedition to find them. Because they don't like following a guide. Especially a *Lat* guide. They're enraged that Lats are running the show now, since somebody has to—"

"Enough." Florence threw the cabbage into what was starting to look like pork soup. "You forget. I'm on your side."

"I know you get sick of it, but you've no idea the waves of resentment I get from these crusties every day. They want their domination back, even if they think of themselves as progressives. They still want credit for being tolerant, without taking the rap for the fact that you only 'tolerate' what you can't stand. Besides, we gotta tolerate honks same as they gotta put up with us. It's our country every bit as much as these has-been gringos'. It'd be even more our country if these tottering white cretins would hurry up and die already."

"*Mi amado*, that's too far," she chided pro forma. "Please don't talk that way around Willing."

As ever, Florence didn't have to ask her partner to set the table, fill the water glasses, and replenish the saltshaker. Esteban had been raised in a crowded household, and pitched in as a matter of course. He was the first boyfriend to convince her that just because she didn't *need* companionship, and she didn't *need* help raising her son, didn't mean she couldn't still *like* a man in her bed, and *like* for Willing to enjoy some semblance of a father—one who could take credit for the boy having become fluently bilingual. At once, Esteban was second generation, and spoke English with no trace of an accent; occasional insertions of Spanish were mostly tongue in cheek, a droll playing to stereotype that his elderly clients lapped up. He may not have gone to college, but that was a smart financial move, in her view.

As for the ethnic issue, it was not true, as her sister clearly believed, that she had latched on to a Lat to be hip (whoops! *careless*), to join what she could not beat, or to disavow her heritage out of a hackneyed liberal shame. Esteban was a forceful, responsible, vital man regardless of his bloodlines, and they had plenty in common, not least that their favorite emotion was disgust. All the same, the choice of a Mexican lover felt on the right side of history—open and melding and forward-looking—and she had to admit his background was a plus. Whether she'd still be so drawn to the man if he were a regular white guy was a question that didn't bear asking. People were package deals.

You couldn't separate out who they were and what they were, and the bottom line was that she found Esteban's nut-colored complexion, silken black tail braid, and wide, high cheekbones irresistibly sexy. In his otherness, he enlarged her world, and granted her access to a rich, complex American parallel universe that for battened-down rightwing paranoids like her sister Avery solely constituted an impenetrable, monolithic threat.

"Hey, remember the guy who moved in across the street last year?" Florence mentioned when Esteban returned to sweep up the bits of cabbage from the kitchen floor. "Brendan Somebody. I told you at the time it was a sign I'd never be able to buy a house in this neighborhood now. He works on Wall Street."

"Yeah, dimly. Investment banker, you said."

"I ran into him on the way to the bus stop this morning, and we had a pretty strange conversation. I think he was trying to be helpful. I get the feeling he likes me."

"Whoa, don't like the sound of that!"

"Oh, I'm sure it's more of that disgusting reputation for goodness and mercy that follows me around like a wet stray. So he told me that we should move 'our investments' out of the country—right away, today. We should transfer any cash into a foreign currency—like, what cash? I wish it weren't so funny—and get out of any, quote, 'dollar-denominated assets.' God, he was theatrical about it. Maybe that sort doesn't get much drama coming their way. He touched my shoulder, and looked me straight in the eye, like *this is totally fucking serious and I'm not joking.* It was hysterical. I have no idea what makes him think people like us have 'investments.'"

"We might if only your rich *abuelo* would keel over."

"Our seeing a dime of that inheritance would also entail my parents keeling over, so don't tempt fate."

Although Esteban was no gold digger, any reference to the Mandible fortune—of what size no one seemed to know—made Florence uncomfortable. A wealthy paternal grandfather hadn't appreciably affected her modest upbringing. Over time, she had devoted a great deal of effort to persuading a Lat boyfriend that she was not yet another lazy, cosseted, entitled gringo who didn't deserve her good luck, and whenever the money came up, that spoiled caricature reared its head again. It was touchy enough that she held the deed to 335 East Fifty-Fifth Street, and had resisted Esteban's offers to contribute to the mortgage payments. They'd been together for five years, but allowing him to build a claim to the equity would have meant trusting the relationship an increment further than felt fitting, given that a string of his predecessors had proved such spectacular disappointments.

"What do you think is going on that made the guy say that," Esteban asked, "out of the blue?"

"I don't know. I overheard on the news that some bank in Britain went bust a couple of days ago, but big deal. That has nothing to do with us. And yesterday, what, a something-something didn't 'roll over' something . . . ? You know I don't follow this stuff. And that was somewhere in Europe, too. After years of that 'orderly unwinding of the euro,' I'm *immense* burned out on their everlasting financial problems. Anyway, the news Willing was watching definitely said something about bonds. But I bet Brendan was just trying to impress me.

"Oh, and talk about super weird," she recalled, plating up, "Brendan asked if we were homeowners. When I said yes, though a tenant helped cover the mortgage, he said, 'Ownership might prove auspicious. The tenant you may regret.'"

With those where-were-you-then junctures—for people like his great-aunt Nollie, the Kennedy assassination; for his mother's generation, 9/11—it was all too easy to pretend-remember, to look back and impose the solid facts of what you learned afterward on the tremulous, watery past. So Willing resolved that later he would remember this night, truly remember-remember—right down to the sandy-textured pork patties, a long video powwow between his mother and her sister after dinner, and the dryout (by then, the protocol was routine). He would keep humbly in place the fact that he did not, at this time, understand the notion of a *reserve currency*. Nor did he comprehend what a *bond auction* was, although there'd doubtless been whole decades if not centuries during which both concepts were roundly regarded as boring and beside the point by just about everybody. Still, in the future he would make sure to give himself this much credit: during the 7 p.m. newscast, even if he didn't get it—this "US Treasury bond auction" with its "spike in interest rates"—he did pick up on the tone.

Since the Stonage, he'd had an ear for it. Everyone else thought that the worst was behind them; order had been gloriously and permanently restored. But for Willing, during his own seminal where-were-you-then occasion at the grand old age of eight, The Day Nothing Went On had been a revelation, and revelations did not un-reveal themselves; they did not fit back into the cupboard. As a consequence of this irreversible epiphany, he had learned to upend expectations. There was nothing astonishing about things not working, about things falling apart. Failure and decay were the world's natural state. What was astonishing was anything that worked as intended, for any duration whatsoever. Thus he'd spent his latter childhood in a state of grateful amazement—at the television aglow with supersaturated color (it turned on! again!), at his mother returned from work on a bus that ran on time or at all, at clean water flowing from the tap, even if he was rarely allowed to touch it.

As for the tone, he identified it while his mother was still chattering over cabbage in the kitchen. Neither his mother nor Esteban detected the timbre. Only Willing paid attention. Willing and Milo, that is; eyes alert, posture wary, ears lifted, the spaniel discerned a curious pitch as well. For the newscasters spoke with a strain of nervous excitement that was distinctive. People who delivered the news loved it when something happened. You could hardly blame them, since saying what happened was their job, and they liked having something to do. When events were bad, as they almost always were since good news was mostly about sameness, they'd get embarrassed by how happy they were. The worst of the anchors covered the happiness with big overdone fake sadness that didn't fool anyone and that Willing wished they would ditch.

At least tonight nobody had died, and whatever inscrutable occurrences were being reported had to do with numbers and clunky expressions that he bet most of the rest of the audience didn't understand either. So at least the newsreaders and their guests didn't pull their cheeks down and drop their voices into an artificially sorrowful minor key. To the contrary, everyone on the newscast seemed pleased, thrilled even. Yet the edgy gaiety was etched with a keen awareness that to the best of their abilities they should mask an exhilaration they would come to regret. The tone came down to: this is fun now, and it won't be later.

Chapter 2
Karmic Clumping

Avery Stackhouse was well aware that her sister was impatient with fleXface, since Florence liked to clean the kitchen while she talked. But in that event, the dishes always seemed to command the better part of her attention, and the distraction would squander a rare solitude: Lowell was teaching an evening class; Savannah was out with one of the boyfriends shuttling through her senior year so quickly that her mother had given up learning their names; Goog was prepping with his team for the big interschool debate on the proposition "Shortages and price spikes are caused by destructive national 'food security' policies, not by real agricultural shortfalls"—Goog had opted for the affirmative; Bing was practicing with his quartet.

Curling into a sumptuous armchair, she gave the living room a satisfied glance. In her young adulthood, fashionable décor had featured hard surfaces, sharp angles, and refraction, while color schemes were dominated by unforgiving whites. Deliciously, now softness, light absorption, and curves were de rigueur; even their walls were covered in dusty synthetic suede. This room was all umbers and toast, the furniture pre-worn leather and low-nap fur, so that lazing here with a glass of wine was like snuggling against a stuffed bear. The tacky blare of chrome had been replaced with the mute of pewter. Mercifully, affluent homes in DC no longer sported those dreadful sectionals, but had restored the dignified couch.

The Stackhouses had also banished the busy clunk of books that cluttered all three stories of her parents' jumbled brick house in Carroll Gardens. Nothing betrayed you as a fuddy-duddy like parallels of shabby spines junking up the walls. Once you'd read a book, why retain it in three dimensions, save as a form of boasting? Now that you could balance the Library of Congress on your fingertip, dragging countless cartons of these spent objects from home to home was like moving with your eggshells.

She unfolded and stiffened the fleXcreen to perch it on the hide-covered coffee table. The device was so thin that, before the distinctive bright colors of its second generation, some folks had thrown theirs away, mistaking the wads in their pockets for tissues. Since the diaphanous material would assume a screen size anywhere from a two-inch square to a fifteen-by-twenty rectangle, and you could fold a lower section onto a surface to become a keyboard, the fleX had replaced the smart watch, smartspeX, smart phone, tablet, laptop, and desktop at a stroke. Best of all, the fleXcreen didn't break—a plus its manufacturers were beginning to rue.

"Listen, are you settled?" Avery plunged in. "Because I'm dying to talk to you about this *farm* Jarred's bought."

"Yeah, Dad said something about it," said Florence. "But how can Jarred swing buying a farm?"

High resolution brought out incipient bags under her sister's eyes that wouldn't have been noticeable in person. Avery wasn't inclined to feel superior; flaws in her sister's visage were harbingers of her own in two years' time. Besides, a host of blotches, sprouting black hairs, and ghastly discolorations glared on her face as well. The device's forensic images so exceeded the benevolently blurred apprehension of the human face in ordinary life that video resembled a medical scan, which wouldn't tell you whether your sister was happy or sad but whether she had skin cancer. At least she and Florence had agreed to never go 3-D again, which was even worse: you looked not only malignant, but fat.

"Because Jarred never tapped the college fund for nearly as much as you and I did," Avery explained, "he convinced Grand Man that getting a down payment instead would be fair." A formidable man of formidable vanities, Grandfather Mandible had always seemed to savor the shorthand *Grand Man*—even more so once her children embellished it to *Great Grand Man*.

"Leave it to Jarred to cash in on dropping out of college," Florence said. "Twice. Still, I'm baffled. Jarred's never even expressed interest in gardening."

"He'd never expressed interest in seawater before he went on that desalination jag. He'd never fried an egg before he took that Moroccan cooking course. Jarred's whole life is a 'What doesn't belong in this picture?' puzzle where nothing belongs in the picture. An agrarian idyll doesn't fit, so it does fit. It's logical in its illogic."

"Is this how you bend over backwards getting your clients to make sense of their lives? I'm impressed. That was athletic."

"The truth is, Mom and Dad have been immense encouraging. They think the farm is great. Anything to get him to move out."

"Gosh, leaving home at the tender age of thirty-five—isn't that brave!" They shared a collusive laugh. They were the adults, and whatever their failings at least neither sister was the family's shiftless, self-indulgent fuck-up. "So where is this place?"

"Gloversville, New York, if you can believe it," Avery said. "Where they used to make *gloves* or whatever."

"Don't mock. Every town in this country *used to make* something. What does this place grow?"

"It's got some apple and cherry trees. Carrots, corn. I think he even inherited a few *cows*. One of those family farms, where the owners got too old and the kids wanted nothing to do with it."

"Those concerns always run at a loss," Florence said. "And he's in for a shock. Small-scale farming is backbreaking work. Nuts—I haven't talked to him in months."

"He's taken a survivalist turn. He's calling the property *Citadel*, as if it's a fortress. The last few times we've talked he's been pretty dark. All this End of Days stuff. It's so weird: I walk around the District, the bars are packed, property prices are skyrocketing again, and everyone's easing in the back of those driverless electric cars that cost two hundred grand. The Dow has the investment equivalent of high blood pressure. And meantime our little brother is holed up with these doomsaying downloads: *Repent, the end is nigh! The center cannot hold, we're all about to die!* The text he devours is secular, but the emotional appeal is evangelical Iowa. No wonder he's ended up on a farm."

"Well, a lot of people had that reaction to the Stone Age—"

"You crack me up. Nobody says that anymore."

"Call me a pedant, but blurred into 'the Stonage' it loses any of its as-in-bombed-back-into meaning—"

"You *are* a pedant. Just like Dad. Language is alive, and you can't put it in the freezer. But never mind. I don't think Jarred is having a delayed reaction to *the-Stone-Age*." Avery spaced the expression elaborately, as she might condescend to a moron who had to have it spelled out that "AC" was *air con-di-tion-ing*. "This idea of his—and it's hardly unique to Jarred, right? The conviction that we're teetering on a precipice, about to pitch into freefall? It's all projection. It has nothing to do with 'the world' or the terrible course this country has taken for which we're all going to pay. It has every-thing to do with Jarred's sense of personal precarious-ness. It's a pessimism about *his* future. But worrying about the collapse of civilization instead of the collapse of his hopes to become a desalination expert because the qualifications were too much trouble, well—the global prophecy makes him feel more important."

"Ever share this theory with Jarred?" Florence said. "He might not care to have his political opinions dismissed as being only about his relationship to himself. The stuff he gets fired up about—species extinctions, desertification, deforestation, ocean acidification, the fact that not one major economy has kept to its carbon-reduction commitments—it's not only in his mirror."

"But I see the same thing in my elderly clients all the time. They have different obsessions, of course: we're about to run out of water, or run out of food, or run out of energy. The economy's on the brink of disaster and their 401(k)s will turn into pumpkins. But in truth they're afraid of dying. And because when you die, the world dies, too, at least for you, they assume the world will die for everybody. It's a failure of imagination, in a way—an inability to conceive of the universe without you in it. That's why old people get apocalyptic: *they're* facing apocalypse, and that part, the private apocalypse, is real. So the closer their personal oblivion gets, the more certain geriatrics project impending doom on their surroundings. Also, there's almost a spitefulness, sometimes. I swear, for some of these bilious Chicken Littles, imminent Armageddon isn't a fear but a fantasy. Like they want the entire planet to implode into a

giant black hole. Because if they can't have their martinis on the porch anymore then nobody else should get
to sip one, either. They want to take everything with
them—down to the olives and the toothpicks. But actually, everything's fine. Life, and civilization, and the
United States, are all going to go on and on, and that's
really what they can't stand."

Florence chuckled. "That was a set piece. You've
said it before."

"Mm," Avery allowed. "Maybe once or twice. But
my point about Jarred stands. He's busy deepening
his well and stockpiling cans of beef stew because he's
experiencing a crisis of *psychic* survival. Once he gets
through it, he'll look around at his multiple first-aid
kits and whole cases of extra-long safety matches and
feel pretty silly."

"Uh-huh. But Jarred may not be the only one pro-
jecting. Your life's going swell, so everywhere you look
is sunny."

That *swell* was dismissive, and Avery didn't appreciate having the tools of her own analysis turned against
her. "Making a halfway decent living doesn't turn you
into a dimwit," she objected. "And the comfortably off
have problems, too."

"Uh-huh," Florence said again. "Name one." She
didn't even wait for an answer. "As for Jarred, the

trouble with his latest boondoggle is practical, not psychic. This 'Citadel' debacle sounds like a financial sinkhole. He's already in hock up to his eyeballs on credit cards—even with Mom and Dad putting him up. All those dead-end projects have been expensive. Grand Man better have deep pockets."

"Grand Man's pockets are flapping somewhere around his shoes."

Avery resolved to steer the conversation elsewhere. Whatever funds would trickle down from the Mandible estate was a prickly subject. Naturally Florence had never said so outright, but with the disparity in their incomes Avery wondered if when the time came she was expected to step aside and either sacrifice a substantial share to her siblings or decline her inheritance altogether. On the face of it, Avery didn't need the money. In other words, because she'd made intelligent decisions and prospered as a consequence, she deserved to be punished? That was the lesson the quote-unquote *progressive* American tax system should have taught her long ago. Oh, and Florence-as-in-Nightingale surely deserved the money more, since in her most recent incarnation she was so good and kind and charitable.

But they'd both been dealt hands from the same deck. Avery had decided to marry a somewhat older intellectual heavyweight who was now a tenured professor in Georgetown University's Economics Department; to co-purchase a handsome DC townhouse that had already appreciated in value; to establish a lucrative private practice; and to raise three bright, gifted children whom they were able to send to top-flight private schools. Meanwhile, Florence had decided to cohabit with an undereducated Mexican tour guide; to buy a tiny, ramshackle, but larcenously overpriced house in a Brooklyn neighborhood notorious when they were growing up for murderous turf wars between crack dealers; to raise a single kid born of a one-night stand who got sent to a public school where all his classes were taught in Spanish and who by the by was turning out a little strange; and professionally to plump pillows for schizophrenics. Avery wished desperately that her smart, savvy, ferociously hard-working sister—who was the real survivor of the family, not Jarred—would find a calling that put her talents to better use, and at least Esteban seemed a stand-up guy. But Florence's dismal situation—particularly awkward for the eldest— still wasn't Avery's fault. Surely circumstances Avery had gone to great efforts to arrange for herself shouldn't oblige her to feel so guilty every time they talked.

Yet the diversionary topic she raised next proved anything but neutral. "Hey, did you hear about the country-code kerfuffle?"

"Yeah, all the staff at the shelter thought it was hilarious that anybody cares. Though I'm sure this could keep Fox News foaming at the mouth for the rest of the year."

"Well, the country code for the States has been *one* ever since there were country codes, right?" Avery said. "For some people, it's symbolic."

"Symbolic of what? *We're number one?* If it means anything at all, the very fact we've been *one* forever is reason to give the dopey code to someone else for a while."

"You sound pretty exercised, given this is an issue that you supposedly don't care about. And it must mean something to the Chinese, or they wouldn't have put up such a stink about swapping codes."

"Sometimes the best thing to do when one party flies into a snit," Florence said, "is to give them what they want. Especially if it doesn't cost you anything but banging a few digits into a computer. This is the kind of concession you can make for free and down the road trade for something that matters."

"Or it's the kind of concession that sets a precedent for a whole bunch of other concessions down the road, in which case it does matter. One patient today said she felt 'humiliated.'"

"Most Americans live in America," Florence said. "They hardly ever enter their own country code. So unless she fleXts home from abroad all the time, your patient is never going to be actively 'humiliated' in the course of an ordinary day. It's just like that hoo-ha about *press two for English*. Is it any harder to press *two* than *one*?"

"Let's not get into that again. You know I thought reversing that convention was outrageous."

"It was a generous gesture that once again cost nothing. For Lats, that *two* represented *second-class*. It was a small change that made immigrants and their descendants feel included."

"What it made them feel is *triumphant—*"

"*Watch it*," Florence said. "There are red lines."

Florence's living with a Real Live Mexican had given her airs. She was now an honorary member of a minority so enormous that it would soon lose claim to the label. A watershed to which Avery was greatly looking forward. In her practice, she urged all her patients to embrace a sensation of specialness—but that very strong sense of identity, of belonging, of proud laying claim to one's own remarkable, particular heritage, was specifically denied the majority in this country, with a conspicuous host of achievements to be proud of. So maybe when white folks were a minority, too, they'd get their own university White Studies departments, which could unashamedly tout Herman Melville. Her children would get cut extra slack in college admissions regardless of their test scores. They could all suddenly assert that being called "white" was insulting, so that now you had to say "Western-European American," the whole mouthful. While to each other they'd cry, "What's up, cracker?" with a pally, insider collusion, any nonwhites who employed such a bigoted term would get raked over the coals on CNN. Becoming a minority would open the door to getting roundly, festively offended at every opportunity, and the protocol for automated phone calls would get switched *back*.

Esteban exclaimed off-screen, "What did I tell you? Should have opened the flood gates while we had the chance!"

Florence shouted over her shoulder, "Willing! Go to Green Acre and grab all the bottled water you can! Esteban will be right behind you—and bring the cart!"

"Okay, okay," the boy said behind her. "I know the drill. But you know I'll be too late. Everybody with a car is faster."

"Then *run*."

"Not another one," Avery said.

Florence turned back to the screen with a sigh. "The worst thing about a dryout is never knowing how long it will last. The water could be back on in an hour, or it could be off for a week. At least we've installed some rain barrels out back. The water's not potable, but it helps with the toilet. I've got some used bottles filled with tap, but it gets awfully stale. So I hope Willing and Esteban score. It's always such a free-for-all in the water aisle. We're lucky it's on the late side. Some people won't have noticed yet. Fuck, I hate to say it, but Esteban was right. I haven't had a shower in eight days. Should have grabbed one when I got home."

"Is it any clearer what the problem is? Not bloggy speculation. Real information."

"Real information, what's that?" Florence snorted. "Though even the bonkers-osphere doesn't contest that out west the problem is drained aquifers and drought. Here, it's more up for grabs. There may be supply problems upstate. Obviously, the Caliphate's sabotage of Tunnel Three hasn't helped. Lots of people claim it's decrepit infrastructure, massive leaks. And you know what I think it is."

"Yes, I know what you think it is." Being on camera, Avery suppressed an eye roll. It was fashionable to observe that in an age absent rigorous investigative reporting people believed whatever suited them. Their father made this clichéd point incessantly. Yet as far as Avery could tell, people had always conceived an opinion first and assembled supporting evidence at their leisure, as they might purchase an outfit and later acquire accessories to match. So naturally Florence blamed fracking. It *suited her.*

The front door slammed. "Hey," Lowell said.

"Hey! I'm talking to Florence."

"Well, wrap it up, would you?"

He was routinely self-important, but the irritability was odd. "When I'm good and ready!"

"That's okay," said Florence. "I've got to haul rainwater to the toilet. Bye, puppet."

Alas, at forty-eight her husband's quarter-inch stubble no longer looked hip but seedy, and his longish graying hair cut in once-trendy uneven lengths now made him appear disheveled. Avery should think of a way of telling him so, if not in so many words. For an economist, he'd always been flashy and downtown—a snappy, daring dresser with a loose-limbed swagger that attracted acolytes at Georgetown. That sleek dove-gray suit was cutting-edge—cuffless and collarless, with high-waisted slacks and a long tunic reaching just above the knee. His shoes this evening were bright pink. But it was risky to style your image around being young. Lowell looked like someone who thought he was young, and wasn't.

"Mojo, *yo*, turn on the TV!" Lowell commanded. The voice-activated household management system had recently developed a glitch, and was forever informing

Avery they were out of milk. Before she disabled the function, the program had kept ordering milk from the supermarket until they were drowning in it. Now the system was getting flakier still: after Lowell's instruction, she heard the dishwasher come on in the kitchen.

"Notice how everything goes wrong at once?" Lowell despaired. "It's what I was just explaining to that pea-brain Mark Vandermire. Same thing happens in economics. Little crap imploding all over the place at the same time makes it seem as if the failures are connected. But they aren't necessarily. It's just some sort of karmic . . . clumping."

"You may have another paper there. *Karmic Clumping* is catchy." She handed him the dusty television remote. "Fortunately we can override. Ellen's Mojo down the street won't switch to manual, and when it goes freaky they can't even boil water."

Lowell plopped despondently onto the sofa. Rather than turn on the news, he tapped the means for doing so against his knee.

"Want anything to eat?"

"Glass of that wine you're drinking. But I'm afraid if I ask Mojo for a BLT, it'll turn on the sprinklers. Or set the house on fire."

When she handed him the glass, he asked, "So— you up on the latest?"

"In that I don't know what you're referring to, probably not."

"The bond auction this afternoon."

"This is France again?"

"No, US Treasury. Look, *I* don't think it's a big deal.
But the bid-to-cover ratio was weirdly poor. Roachbar,
in fact: 1.1. And the yield on a ten-year note went to 8.2
percent."

"That sounds high."

"High? It *doubled*. Still, all I see is an accidental
confluence of arbitrary forces."

"Karmic clumping."

"Yeah. You've got France unable to completely roll
over a tranche of maturing debt—but Germany and the
ECB swept in right away, so it's not as if they're about
to close the Eiffel Tower for lack of funds. Messed with
some heads, that's all. As for Barclay's in the UK, the
official word is that Ed Balls's government can't bail
them out this time, but that's a strategic pose. I bet
they find enough ten-P pieces tucked into the crevices
of Downing Street sofas to keep the bank from going
to the wall. Then yesterday a couple of skittish hedge
funds in Zurich and Brussels reduced their dollar positions to basically zero and moved into gold. Let them.
They'll be using shiny rocks for paperweights when
gold drops right back down."

"It's up?"

"For now! You know gold. It's always ping-ponging all over the place. Unless you're really canny about playing the highs and lows, it's a ludicrous investment."

"Why do I get the nagging impression that you're not having this conversation with me? You keep arguing, one hand clapping. I'm not arguing back."

"Sorry. I did get into an argument, with that boomerpoop Vandermire. Because, okay, the bond auction today, it's—unfortunate. At the moment, foreign demand for US debt is low—but there are completely unrelated reasons for backing off US debt instruments in a variety of different countries that just happen to be coinciding. Here, the market is hopping; investors can find higher yields in the Dow than in dumpy Treasury securities. Interest rates aren't likely to stay anywhere near 8.2 percent and this is probably a one-time spike. Jesus, in the 1980s, Treasury bond interest careened to over *15 percent.* Bonds paid over 8 percent as recently as 1991—"

"That's not very recent."

"My point is, there's no reason to get hysterical!"

"Then don't say that hysterically."

"It's the panic over the interest-rate spike that's the problem. Imbeciles like Vandermire—oh, and guess where he was headed when I ran into him in the department? MSNBC. He'd lined up back-to-back interviews on all the main stations—Fox, Asia Central, RT, LatAmerica . . ."

"You jealous?"

"Hell, no. Those shows are a pain in the butt. With hyper-res, they slather on the makeup an inch thick. They can't wipe it off completely, and it stains our pillowcases. Besides, you never know whether under pressure you'll misremember a statistic and never live it down."

"But you're great at it."

His posture straightened on the sofa: compliment received. "The fear Vandermire will have peddled all night—it becomes self-fulfilling. Though he hardly sounds afraid. He's having the time of his life. It's like what you always say, right? This apocalyptic set—"

"I don't 'always' say anything. We had that *one* conversation—"

"Don't get your back up when I'm trying to agree with you. It's just, these people forecasting the end of the world, they never seem upset by the prospect, do they? Invoking ruin, heartache, and devastation, they can barely disguise their delight. What do they think actual collapse is like, a kid's birthday party where everyone dances in a circle singing, 'Ashes! Ashes! We all fall down'? And they seem to assume that they themselves will be immune, sunning by the pool while cities burn on the horizon. They're would-be voyeurs. They regard the fate of millions if not billions of real people as entertainment."

Lowell had that look on his face of wanting to write that down.

"Florence and I are worried that Jarred's going down a similar route. I think he's more into eco-horror, but same idea. Although to be fair I'd hardly characterize Jarred as delighted. He's been pretty morose."

"Well, Vandermire is ecstatic. He loves the attention, and he's on a high of having been supposedly right all along. 'Unsustainable! The national debt is unsustainable!' If I heard him say the word *unsustainable* one more time this afternoon I'd have punched him in the nose. The functional definition of *unsustainable* is that-which-is-not-sustained. If you can't keep something up, you don't. After all that noise twenty years ago about the deficit, the melodramatic shutdowns of government over raising the debt ceiling, and what's happened? Nothing. At 180 percent of GDP—which Japan proved was entirely doable— the debt has been *sustained*. It is therefore, ipso facto, *sustainable*."

"Don't let Vandermire get to you, then. If he's off the beam, he'll soon look as dumb as you think he is."

"His sort of loose, inflammatory talk is dangerous. It undermines confidence."

"Confidence, shmonfidence. What's it matter if a few rich investors get edgy?"

"Money is emotional," Lowell pronounced. "Because all value is subjective, money is worth what people feel it's worth. They accept it in exchange for goods and services because they have faith in it. Economics is closer to religion than science. Without millions of individual citizens believing in a currency, money is colored paper. Likewise, creditors have to believe that if they extend a loan to the US government they'll get their money back or they don't make the loan in the first place. So confidence isn't a side issue. It's the only issue."

The trouble with being a professor is that when you pontificate for a living it's hard to cut the crap once you get back home. Avery was used to it, though she didn't find Lowell's rants quite as enchanting as when they first got married.

"You know, most of the other doom mongers like Vandermire are also gold bugs," Lowell resumed. "Honestly, hanging on to a decorative metal as the answer to all our prayers, it's medieval—"

"Don't start."

"I'm not *starting*. But I don't know why George-town hired that jackass. He's meant to be a token of the faculty's ideological 'breadth,' but that's like claiming, 'We have academic *breadth* because some of our professors are smart and the others are nitwits.' The gold standard was put to rest sixty years ago, and nobody's missed it. It was clunky, it constrained the tools available to central banks to fine-tune the economy, and it artificially limited the monetary base. It's antiquated, superstitious, and sentimental. What the gold bugs never concede? Now that the metal has almost no real utility in and of itself, it's therefore just as artificial a store of value as fiat currencies, or cowrie shells."

Avery studied her husband. Maybe he'd refrained from turning on the news because he was afraid of encountering his bête noire Mark Vandermire. Or maybe he was afraid of the news itself. "You seem worried."

"All right—a little."

"But I know you. So here's the question: are you worried about what's actually happening? Because I think you're more worried about being *wrong*."

Kicking himself for that third glass of wine with Avery, Lowell got an early start the next morning with a muddy head. Skipping his usual compulsive glance at the one news website he marginally trusted, he decided to grab coffee at the department—even if it was mostly a sassafras-pit substitute; in Lowell's private view, the biggest agricultural catastrophe in recent years wasn't soaring commodity prices for corn and soy but the widespread dieback of the Arabica bean crop, making a proper latte the price of a stiff Remy. Driven more than ever to advocate for educated, creative, modern economics now that the likes of Vandermire would have everyone trading wampum with an abacus, he wanted to make progress on his paper on monetary policy before his 10 a.m. course, History of Inflation and Deflation. The class had hit Industrial Revolution Britain, nearly a century of persistent deflation during which the blasted country did nothing but prosper, which always put Lowell in a bad mood.

On his walk to the Metro, the sidewalks of Cleveland Park were busy for such an early hour. Though the sky at sunrise was clear, pedestrians had the huddled, scurrying quality that crowds assume in the rain. One woman quietly crying didn't surprise him, but two did, and the next weeper was male. While Lowell didn't by policy wear his fleX while strolling a handsome city whose sights he preferred to take in, his fellow Washingtonians routinely wrapped theirs on a wrist or hooked one on a hat brim. Yet it was very odd for so many pedestrians to be conducting audio phone calls. True, since the Stonage a handful of purist kooks had boycotted the internet altogether, and that atavistic bunch jabbered ceaselessly because talking was the only way those throwbacks could communicate. For everyone else with a life, the phone call was by consensus so prohibitively invasive that a ringtone was frightening: clearly, someone had died.

As he descended the long gray steps of his local station, the faces of scuttling commuters displayed an unnervingly uniform expression: wrenched, concentrated, stricken. He squeezed into the train as the doors were closing, barely wedging into the crowd. For pity's sake, it was only 6:30 a.m.

Here, too, everyone was *talking*. Not to each other, of course. To fleXes. *How low is it now? . . . Well, in London it's only . . . Hitting margin calls . . . Buy Australian, Swiss francs, I don't care! No, not Canadian, it'll get dragged . . . Bet POTUS has already been roused from his . . . Stop-loss . . . Crossed stop-loss two hours ago . . . Stop-loss . . .*

Even by Washington standards, Lowell Stackhouse was exceptionally averse to getting news everyone else was in on already, and after thirty seconds of this murmurous churn he'd heard enough. He whipped the fleX from his pocket, stiffened it to palm-size, and went directly to kind-of-trustworthy Bloomberg.com: DOLLAR CRASHES IN EUROPE.

Chapter 3
Waiting for the Dough

In the most ordinary of times, Carter Mandible would drive up to New Milford debating to what degree he felt guilty about dreading a visit with his own father. Why, most people his age would strain to extend themselves to the rarefied realm of ninety-seven, even if Douglas Mandible didn't subject his son to the additional trials of feeblemindedness. Rather, Carter sometimes wished that his father showed more signs of mental fatigue, which might excite his sympathy, and lay grudges to rest. One of those grudges being first and foremost that the old man was still alive.

Oh, Carter never actively wished that his father would die. He was entirely sure—he was fairly sure— that when the time came he would be felled by the customary measure of filial grief. Friends had warned that the loss always hits you harder than you expect. But that was a discovery for which he'd been more than ready for fifteen years.

It was also standard on the two-hour trip from Brooklyn—this leafy section through Connecticut was pleasant—for Carter to question his motivations for these visits. With an eye to the long view, you naturally dote on an elderly parent as a subtly selfish prophylactic: to be able to assure yourself, on receipt of that fatal phone call, that you'd been devoted. Sometimes being a shade more attentive than you're quite in the mood for can prevent self-excoriation down the line. After all, old people have a horrible habit of kicking it right after you ducked seeing them at the last minute with an excuse that sounded fishy, or on the heels of a regrettable encounter in which you let slip an acrid aside. To be dutiful without fail is like taking out emotional insurance.

Yet in Carter's case, the self-interest was crassly pecuniary. Did he keep in his father's good graces with monthly runs to the Wellcome Arms only to safeguard his inheritance from, say, a rash or spiteful late-life impulse to endow a chair at Yale? He'd never know. Worse, his father would never know, and might not ever feel confidently cherished for himself. A family fortune introduced an element of corruption. While

Carter might sentimentalize the ideal world in which he spent as much time as possible with Douglas E. Mandible because he loved his father, and enjoyed his father's company, and was resolved to make the most of his father's blessedly extended lifespan while he still could, the money was an inescapable contaminant, and it wasn't going to go away.

Or in theory it wouldn't go away.

For this was not the most ordinary of times.

While it was certainly usual for Carter to chafe that by the time he came into the legacy he'd be too old to spend it, this afternoon that exasperation rose to a frenzy. He and Jayne still lived in the same modest, increasingly disheveled Carroll Gardens row house— brick, not brownstone. It was finally paid off, but for years the mortgage was a stretch. He and Jayne did get to Tuscany in 2003—a first proper vacation, in their early forties! But they'd always planned on Japan. Now that Jayne was so fearful that she'd rarely leave the house, adventures farther afield than Sahadi's on Atlantic Avenue were out of the question. On one charge, newer cars would make it to Canada; this ten-year-old BeEtle couldn't get past Danbury. Once he got that post at the *Times* he was already sixty, by which time America's shrinking "paper of record," having already stooped to selling creative writing courses and colonial

knickknacks, was snarfing up desperate aging journal-
ists for pocket change. His pension was farcical. If they
might free up some equity by downsizing in the brief
window during which their youngest had pretended to
leave home, that meant finding someplace smaller and
meaner and more depressing. Great.

Yet a breezy, no-cares existence had been in the
pipeline all his life. The money was stuck further up
the system, like a wad of the disposable diapers you're
told never to flush. Meanwhile, awaiting his birthright
had suspended him in an extended adolescence. This
state of decades-long deferral presaged when his real
life would begin. He was sixty-nine. Real life would be
short.

What Carter craved was not so much furniture and
electronics, cruises and wine-tasting tours—whatever
he might buy—but a feeling. A sensation of ease and
liberation, of generosity and savor, of possibility and
openness, of whimsy and humor and joy. Granted,
he expected too much from mere money, but he'd be
happy to find that out, too. Relieved of this endless
waiting, he would embrace even a reputably adult
disillusionment. Because he still felt like a kid. And
now that theoretical Valhalla in which he and Jayne
could leave the heating jacked up to sixty-eight the
whole night through, or make an airy fresh start on a

wide-skied ranch in Montana where Jayne might get over the terror she associated with Carroll Gardens, well—in the last few days, that future had, very probably, gone to hell.

For this last week was the most historically savage of his experience, and that was counting 9/11 and the Stone Age. As for the latter, sure, the power went out, and there was looting of course, including of Jayne's chichi delicatessen on Smith Street, from whose gratuitous destruction she had yet to recuperate. Traffic lights going black resulted in a host of dreadful pile-ups. He could skip rehearsing all those airline disasters again, the train wrecks, the poignant human-interest packages about cardiac patients whose pacemakers began beating double-time, like an invigorating change-up in a Miles Davis recording. Parts of the country had no water, though that was good practice for the dryouts to come. Telecommunications and national defense systems ceased to function, even if in Carter's view America's vaunted "defense" had long put the country in the way of more munitions than it deflected. Understandably, then, for Florence, Avery, and Jarred, 2024 constituted the direst of calamities. But Carter hailed from a different generation—one raised locating phone numbers in scrawled paper diaries and tracking down zip codes in fat directories from the post office, painstakingly diluting encrusted Liquid Paper with plastic pipettes from tiny overpriced bottles of thinner and later upgrading with outsize gratitude to the self-correcting ribbons of IBM Selectrics, flicking through yellowed rectangles in the long wooden drawers of card catalogs and looking up articles in the *Readers' Guide to Periodical Literature* in the library. There was only so gravely he was likely to rate going without the internet for three weeks.

Albeit eerily invisible, eerily silent, this last week's turmoil was of another order. The Stone Age produced immediate, palpable consequences: the lights wouldn't go on, food rotted in the fridge, and none of the few stores remaining open carried milk. Throughout this latest mayhem nothing changed. A conventional number of cars on I-84 were doing the usual five miles per hour over the speed limit. The sky was mockingly clear. Exiting for a recharge, Carter didn't have to swerve around bodies littering the ramp, or duck to avoid gunfire. Its lot half-full, Friendly's was continuing to sell maple-walnut cones and SuperMelts. Strolling between chargers and convenience stores, none of Carter's fellow motorists appeared hurried or flustered. This whole placid commercial stretch testified to the fact that the folks most affected by the week's historical bad weather weren't temperamentally inclined to pitch rocks through plate glass. One such under-violent character was bound to be his father.

If you believed its literature, the Wellcome Arms was the most luxuriously equipped assisted-living facility in the United States. The high-tech gym was really a come-on for prospective tenants, promising retirement as renewal, as the unfettered free time to step into the trim, fit incarnation you'd always been too busy to manifest—until the shine wore off and residents were confronted with the odious exertion of using the machines. The joint actually kept horses, though Carter had never seen anyone ride one. Replete with water therapists and massage jets, the pool saw more traffic, since a proportion of the residents could still float. It went without saying that the home provided the medical facilities of a top-flight private hospital; given Wellcome's astronomical charges, it was worth the institution's while to keep its clients, however nominally, in this world.

Although Douglas Mandible would not commonly be parted from his fleX before the 4 p.m. close of the New York Stock Exchange, pulling into Visitor Parking, Carter spotted his father on the nearest tennis court. Douglas was once a hard-hitting, cutthroat singles player, who would risk stroke or seizure to retrieve a skittering down-the-line—in the same fashion that as an equally cutthroat literary agent he had pulled out all the stops to score celebrated novelists. Yet in advanced age he'd refined a very different game, whereby he ran this much-younger opponent (late seventies, Carter guessed) from corner to corner. Barely returning the shot, the other guy would blob his own right to Douglas's feet, and Pop could keep the ball in play without moving more than five inches in any direction. It was the same hyper-efficient, energy-conserving manipulation that Douglas could employ to effortlessly control his family without leaving his chair.

With a wicked crosscourt sharding out of the service box, Douglas dispatched the point in the spirit of simply having had enough. Carter didn't flatter himself that his father had cut the point short because he'd spied his son in the parking lot. Having given notice of this visit, Carter was right on time. Had Pop given a damn about not keeping his son waiting, he wouldn't have been playing tennis in the first place.

Douglas made a show of mopping his face and waved at Visitor Parking with the towel. His figure was closer to scrawny than sleek, but his bearing remained debonair. The mane of blazing white hair was more spectacular than the younger auburn version. In October, he sported a leathery tan. While spinal compression had shaved a good two inches off his height, that still left the patriarch a touch taller than his only son. Age had scored his long face with an expression of drollery once fleeting and now ceaseless. He would look dryly amused in his sleep.

"Carter!" The pumped joy in his voice was heartening, even if Douglas lavished the same elaborate glad-to-see-you on everybody. "I'm going to grab a shower. Meet in our library, shall we?" That trace of British inflection—*lie-bree*—was always deft enough that you couldn't quite accuse him of affectation.

Back in the day, Douglas Elliot Mandible had been an illustrious bon vivant and raconteur. Since Carter could remember, his father had been able to summon the names of obscure, long-dead authors and to reel off multiple lines from Philip Roth or William Faulkner verbatim—a facility the man had cruelly neglected to hand down to his son, who was more apt to launch into a point about some latest movie and then spend five tedious minutes trying to remember what the film was called. As a child, Carter took his father at face value: the literary eminence was fully formed, a given. But by adulthood, the sheer A-to-B of his father's flamboyant persona had grown confounding. How did anyone start out as a callow, superficially educated, and surely in any important sense rather stupid young man, and then ugly-duckling with no noticeable transition into a suave, lively, charming adult to whose parties celebrities and intellectual heavy hitters alike would eagerly flock? For not once had any of Douglas's copious, well-connected acquaintances ever taken Carter aside and shared, "For years, your dad would tell anecdotes in company that fell flat as pancakes. You don't slide into that kind of style like slipping on a jacket. You have to practice." So had Douglas sequestered himself behind closed doors for weeks on end memorizing long witty passages, the better to unspool them over the rims of two-onion martinis? Really, how did you make the journey from mouthy, naive, full-of-shit Yale undergraduate to one of New York's Great Characters, who could wear an ascot every day of his working life without looking ridiculous? Though perhaps the more pressing question now was how a redoubtable Manhattan mover-and-shaker had borne the indignities of extreme old age without appearing to have been humbled in the slightest.

Carter signed in at the office, whose Doric columns and classic New England white clapboard were meant to evoke a timelessness at odds with a clientele whose time was conspicuously running out.

"Your daddy gonna live forever, *sí?*" the portly receptionist quipped, to which Carter responded distractedly, "Yeah, afraid so." She shot him a look.

In truth, his natural impulse in encounters with strangers the last few days was to powwow over this "bancor" business and press them on what they presumed the game plan was in DC—since that's what happened after 9/11, wasn't it? All the social barriers fell, and you found yourself having heart-to-hearts with the clerk scanning your pretzels. We're all in this together, that was the conceit. Except we weren't all in this one together, and Carter stopped himself. A Lat minding the desk at an old folks' home was just the sort to have floated obliviously through the crisis, perhaps blissfully unaware that there was a crisis: *no assets.*

Douglas and his hapless second wife were allotted a whole compound—the better to absorb a goodly share of the effects from their liquidated estate in Oyster Bay. (Carter accepted a claret-red leather sofa from the excess, which from the moment it arrived made all their other furniture look tattered. They'd unloaded it on Florence.) That was the concept at Wellcome: to reconstruct as best you could the home you'd left behind.

Accordingly, the front door was thick, wooden, and beveled, with a heavy brass knocker, as would befit the entrance of a grand house. A male orderly in whites answered wearing plastic gloves. "Just getting Luella changed."

Chances were he was not referring to her outfit.

Carter padded the hallway's plush crimson carpet. The baseboards and notched cornices were a lustrous mahogany, the doorways topped with finely latticed panes. The bathrooms gleamed with alabaster and gold-plated taps. Such opulence lavished on people during the one period of their lives they were least capable of enjoying it seemed subtly obscene. Besides, as much as he would have relished the luxury of no longer worrying about the size of his Con Ed bill, he was suspicious of luxury in its conventional sense. For Carter, extravagance backfired. Taken to the max, the many-splendored thing merely demonstrated the limits to how wonderful a given whatnot got. A toilet with a heated seat and electric lid-lift might flush with a discreet hush, but you still pissed in it. Brass or plastic, a doorknob was a doorknob. It opened the door. He had never understood what fixtures that cost hundreds of dollars apiece were supposed to make you feel other than hoodwinked.

Douglas's appointments added a note of bygone class. The walls were decorated with framed dust jackets of novels by former clients. Through the French doors, the spacious library was lined floor-to-ceiling with literary properties Douglas would have sold to editors at auction, often for a great deal more money than the royalties they reaped. (If an author earned back his advance, went the Mandible Agency's ruling maxim, the agent had failed.) Oddly, though the physical book had only in the last few years made a wholesale departure, the room exuded the ambience of a historical diorama from the eighteenth century. All the effort poured into each volume—not only the effort of composing the text, but of choosing the font, selecting the paper, styling the diamonds under the chapter headings, and designing the cover, down to the touchy-issue size of the author's name—seemed both poignant and pathetic. But Carter resisted his father's sentimentality over a mere format. It made no more sense to get maudlin over hardbacks than it did to burst into tears over a mottled box of floppy discs. His grandkids had no idea what a microfloppy was.

"See anything that interests you, you're welcome to borrow it." Douglas closed the French doors behind him. He'd changed into one of the cream-colored suits he favored all year, though today's cravat was a seasonably autumnal rust. "But I'm fussy about my returns policy. Never did understand what about books makes people feel free to steal them. Casserole dishes, drat them, always come back."

Carter turned from the shelves. "Reading is an act of possession. You read it, you own it."

"So it seems! Most people assume what kiboshed publishing was the Stone Age. Suddenly nobody dared buy anything online anymore—"

"Actually, hackers had pretty much killed the online marketplace altogether way before the Stone Age—"

"—but supposedly readers had already made the leap to digital, and wouldn't go back to the textual equivalent of the ox cart," Douglas powered on; it was always fruitless to interrupt. "In truth, piracy had already brought the industry to its knees. Well before 2024, no one was *buying* books, in any form. The end of internet commerce was simply the coup de grace. What's left to download may be plentiful and free, but it's one big slush pile. Browsing is like falling into a sewer."

Carter had heard this shtick. Douglas would be mortified to realize how often he repeated himself now. Never retelling anecdotes to the same parties was a point of pride.

"By the end of Shelf Life," Carter said, "all Jayne made a profit on was the coffee. Watching Amazon go down in flames, I broke out marshmallows."

"I never told you"—Douglas had told him—"but I lost a small fortune on Amazon. Call it trading with the enemy, but I was holding some serious stock."

Reference to his father's portfolio was awkward at the best of times. Carter didn't want to seem too interested, but Douglas would never be persuaded by a contrived indifference. Carter had always to indulge the conceit that of course Pop's investment decisions were none of his business—which was horseshit. While he and his sister saw eye to eye on little, they agreed on this much: their father's unfettered day trading with their inheritance was worrisome. If Douglas seemed pretty together, they might only be alerted to the fact that he'd lost it by the discovery that he'd lost the money, too.

Douglas unstoppered a crystal decanter on the liquor cabinet. "Noah's Mill?"

"Early for me. And I'm driving."

"I thought nobody drives anymore, either."

Carter accepted the bourbon he thought he'd declined. Given the visit's agenda, he'd drain it. Driverless cars having virtually eliminated DWI, cops weren't on the interstate prowl anymore. "Our BeEtle has a driverless function, but I don't use it. I'm like you—a dinosaur."

"To paleontology, then!" Clinking Carter's cut-glass tumbler against his own, Douglas sank into a leather armchair by the window. Even five-inch tennis must have worn him out. "It was a splendid life while it lasted. At least Enola had a good run."

"But Nollie refuses to write for nothing. Which means an *esteemed* novelist like my sister writes nothing." Carter added unctuously, "Such a terrible waste."

"As her former agent, I can only approve."

"I never have sorted out how much she raked in," Carter fished. "She didn't have another bestseller after *Better Late Than*."

"We're all entitled to our financial privacy." Not the most promising preface for their pending confrontation, and the short *i* in *privacy* was annoying.

"So how's Luella?" Carter asked, though he didn't care.

"Oh, same, same. In remarkably fine fettle, I'm told." He sounded dismayed.

Leaving Carter's mother, Mimi, at sixty for a thirty-eight-year-old assistant might have given Douglas a second lease on life, but in due course the joke was on him. Oh, Douglas and his floozy girl Friday had a good stretch together—or so Carter was informed, since Nollie buddied up to their father after the divorce, while for years Carter avoided the couple's sumptuous new estate in Oyster Bay out of loyalty to their mother. But the willowy, elegant interloper—who was trendily Afri-merican to boot, which seemed to a liberal New York family like cheating—was stricken with dementia in her late fifties. Douglas kept the condition under wraps for years. But at length he came upon his second wife naked in the shower, a mechanism she didn't know how to turn on and whose purpose escaped her. That proved unfortunate, since she was also smeared head-to-toe in a smelly, sticky brown substance she could no longer identify and was trying to eat. Were it not for Luella, Douglas might have lasted a lot longer on Long Island. An irony that Mimi never ceased to savor: when Douglas dropped a thirty-six-year marriage like a hot brick, his wife was running the Dementia Research Foundation, and at ninety-five she was still on the board—stubbornly of sound mind, if only for revenge.

Relieved of his wife's day-to-day care by Wellcome staff, Douglas now modeled his marriage on the relationship of master and pet. He fed Luella treats, to which she responded with the human equivalent of a tail-wag—when she remembered to chew and swallow, and didn't remove the chocolate to melt it on the radiator. He did continue to talk to her; Carter had heard the running commentary when the two were in the next room. But then, lonely people talked the same way to their dogs.

"Ever wonder if this family is cursed?" Carter mused, still standing. Assuming the chair beside his father would have demarcated the point at which they were really going to talk. "I'm a newspaper journalist, and now Jayne complains that she can't find any news-print to clean the windows. As for Nollie, the career novelist is over. And, Pop, you were a king! But of one of those island nations swamped by sea-level rise that aren't even a dot on the map anymore. There *are* no more literary agents. Even diesel engines: they've sunk without a trace. Everything we've done has vanished."

Reference to diesel engines was strategic. The bulk of the Mandible money was amassed by Carter's great-grandfather Elliot, a Midwestern industrialist. Douglas had added to the pile a bit, but he'd always lived high, and Mimi extracted a fair whack of his agency earnings in the divorce. The inheritance from Mandible Engine Corp. was protected from marital depredations by a trust. So if Carter hadn't earned the cash to which he should soon be entitled, neither had his father. It pleased him to underscore that Douglas was a mere fiduciary caretaker, another undeserving beneficiary of capitalistic injustice.

Douglas expressed a sudden frustration with preparatory social niceties by rising with some difficulty for another finger of bourbon. Bad sign. He never drank before 8 p.m. "Since you *were* a journalist, you've been following the news?"

"Insofar as it's possible, with no in-depth coverage, no fact-checking—"

"The end of the *New York Times*," Douglas said patiently, "was not the end of the world. We all miss it, Carter. But it became a shadow of its former self."

"Meaning when *I* worked for it."

"Tetchiness doesn't suit you. Aren't you over seventy?"

"Not yet."

"But old enough to realize that the end of the world takes place on rather a larger scale. As you must have begun to appreciate. Quite a week!"

"Well"—Carter took a deep breath—"with the stock exchange shut down, I guess you've had something of a vacation."

"If having the federal government deny you access to your own accounts—scarcely different from being locked out of your own house—well, if that's your idea of a *vacation*, yes. It's been all beach umbrellas and boat drinks."

"And do you know, ah—I mean, ballpark, what kind of a hit you've taken?" His father played his financial cards close to his chest. Carter had no idea of the size of the portfolio, down to the number of zeros.

"Use your head. Trading closes automatically once the market dives a set percentage or point drop. The SEC hasn't deigned to re-open the Exchange since the Level 3 circuit breaker kicked in on Thursday. It doesn't take much imagination to picture what will happen to the market when they do. I'm sure the SEC has pictured it. So whatever the values at which stocks left off are academic. The question is not what they *are* worth, but what they *will be* worth three seconds after the bell. Imagine all those investment-bank computers primed at the starting line—with which my poor fleXcreen can't compete. Of course, one could argue that the value of assets to which you are denied access, perhaps indefinitely, is zero." Reseated at a jaunty angle, Douglas had assumed a whimsical demeanor. He seemed almost pleased.

"*One could argue?*" said Carter. "Or that's what you're saying?"

"One could also argue," Douglas continued with an infuriating mildness, "as a contingent on the web is already promoting, that this is an extraordinary and irrational hysteria from which the market will promptly bounce back. After a historically unprecedented dip, about which academics like your son-in-law will produce miles of trying analytical text, the dollar and the market may both more than recover. In which case, the next month or so could provide a once-in-a-lifetime opportunity to buy low and sell high. With a bit of leveraging, investors swimming against the tide could easily grow their holdings by three or four times."

This was not the multiple choice for which Carter had made this journey: his father was (a) destitute; (b) rich and about to get a whole lot richer; (c) somewhere in-between. Thanks.

"They've put limits on withdrawals, you know," Carter said sulkily. "I can't get more than three hundred bucks from an ATM."

"They're afraid of more bank runs. By trying too hard to prevent them, more bank runs are exactly what they'll get—should they ever be so imprudent as to let you at your own money again."

"The Fed chief was emphatic. Krugman said the limits were for a few days, max."

"Anyone in a position of authority telling you something unpalatable is 'temporary' is a red flag. The quick fix of capital controls can seem so alluring: 'We'll simply make the rabble keep their money here. We'll pass a law!' The hard part is lifting capital controls, which becomes unthinkable the moment they're instituted. Who wants to keep funds in a country that confuses a bank account with a bear trap? The moment you remove the constraints, the nation is broke. So you can be sure that at least the freeze on making monetary transfers out of the US will stay in place for some time to come. Look at Cyprus. The capital controls levied in 2013 weren't entirely rescinded until two years later.

Know how long those controls were meant to stay in place at their inception? *Four days.*"

"But this is the United States. Here, they can't—"

"They can. And will. There's nothing the Fed can't do." Again, this cheerfulness. Douglas fished a steamer from an inside pocket. The family patriarch was once a two-pack-a-day smoker, and Carter blamed electronic cigarettes for the man's now-catastrophic longevity. The e-bacco emitted a teasing scent of French vanilla.

"Why do you seem to find this debacle so entertaining?"

"What does it matter if I'm entertained? After all, wasn't it interesting," Douglas supposed, stabbing the air with his stainless-steel wand like a Philharmonic conductor, "when the ECB, Japan, the Bank of England, and the Fed banded together to intercede the day after the rate spike, and all that doing '*whatever it takes* to support the dollar' backfired? Traditionally, investors bow to the inevitable when central banks move in. But rampant purchasing of US securities meant the Fed was conjuring up yet more money out of thin air to buy the bonds. Which is why the dollar tanked in the first place. Made the fire sale of the dollar infinitely worse. I love it when by-the-book remedies don't work the way they're supposed to."

"But you don't seem the slightest bit upset! Is it because you're practically a hundred? And there's not much time left for you? Because not only am I planning to stick around a few more years, but I have kids, and they have kids—"

"Right now, every major stock exchange in the world has halted trading. It's relaxing. You should enjoy the respite. Because Quiet Time won't last."

Finally Carter plunked into the adjoining armchair, doubling his chin on his clavicle with a scowl. He should remember: for the time being, he and his father were on the same side. "Economics isn't my bailiwick. I don't understand this 'bancor' business. The American news coverage is so hostile that I can't make heads or tails of it. Guests on CBS just start shouting."

"I suspect it's a good idea—if it was not a good idea for Putin to roll it out."

"At least these days Mr. President for Life keeps his shirt on."

"I'm intrigued by how a whole new international currency was ready to go. Not the sort of thing one works out on the back of an envelope."

"Maybe I'd expect a financial putsch from Russia and China," Carter said. "But this coup is by US allies, too. Okay, not Europe—and never mind them—but the Saudis, the Emirates, Korea—after the tens of billions we shifted to them after unification? Ingrates. Not to mention Brazil, India, South Africa. Even Taiwan! Everyone's ganging up on us! What's going on?"

"We should be grateful," Douglas said. "You do realize that without the bancor lined up as a replacement reserve currency, the fall of the dollar would plunge the entire world economy into a Dark Ages? We'd be buying eggs with rocks."

"But how can they simply announce that oil, and gas—the whole commodities market—is henceforth to be conducted in these goofball 'bancors'? It's our damn oil, too, and our damn corn." A New York Democrat really shouldn't be spouting this indignant, nationalistic bilge. Too much American twenty-four-hour news, all singing the same apoplectic tune. Besides, father and son had chosen parts at the start. Douglas had co-opted the voice of reasonableness and fairness, which left Carter to fume.

"A better question is how we've got away with shoving our currency down the rest of the world's throat for so long," Douglas observed. "It's been a multipolar world for decades. After the refunding of Social Security, the US defense budget won't buy a cap pistol. Why should commodities be traded internationally in dollars?"

"Big whoop, you call it a *bancor* instead of a *dollar.* Like this 'New IMF': semantics."

"Not just semantics. *New* means administered by a consortium of countries that presently doesn't include us."

"What, is it just, presto!" Carter flailed. "And the dollar is worth zip?"

"Theoretically, the US could buy into the bancor along with everyone else. But only by ponying up real assets to back it. That's the difference in a nutshell. To swap fiat currency for bancors, you have to fork over to the New IMF a strictly proportioned basket of real commodities—corn, soy, oil, natural gas, deed to agricultural land. Rare earths . . . copper . . . Oh, fresh water sources! And gold, of course."

"No way is Fort Knox moving to Moscow."

"I don't expect Washington to play ball. It's too humiliating. Though if it makes you feel any better? The likes of Indonesia and Pakistan may have leapt to embrace the bancor as an antidote to chaos, but this new regime is going to screw plenty of the very governments that are backing it to the hilt. There's modest flexibility built in, to avoid another euro debacle. Countries who've merely pegged their currencies to the bancor can appeal for devaluation. But the NIMF is bound to be stringent on that point. Since the whole idea of the bancor is to restrict the money supply. From the 1970s, the G-30 have all been churning out Monopoly money as if drawing from a board game with the combined components of several sets. It's going to ferociously mess with some heads that now you have to cover your expenses and pay your trading partners in a currency that has real value."

"The whole thing stinks to high heaven. Maybe Putin and his new friends were passively waiting for an opportune moment to pounce. But it's a hell of a lot more likely that they *caused* the crash of the dollar."

"Oh, that's certainly how the White House is playing it. Big conspiracy. Threat to national security. Nothing to do with a Congress that won't rein in entitlements. Nothing to do with the deficit, or the national debt, or a monetary policy modeled on the population's waistline. Only evil outside forces conniving to destroy the greatest country in the world."

Carter raked his fingers through what remained of his hair; the gene for male pattern baldness being handed down from the mother was a formula for father-son resentment. "I don't understand how this happened."

"Carter. I will let you in on what isn't a secret to any housewife who's bought a cucumber. The American dollar is worthless now not because of the rate spike, and not because of crashing on the international currency exchange, and not because of the bancor. It is worthless now because *it was worthless before.*"

"That's melodramatic."

"Not melodramatic—dramatic. In the hundred years following the establishment of the Federal Reserve in 1913, the dollar lost 95 percent of its value—when one of the purposes of the Fed was to safeguard the integrity of the currency. Great job, boys! Ever wonder why no one talks about millionaires anymore—why no one but a billionaire rates as rich? Because a man who had about ten grand in 1913 would be a millionaire a century later. Hell, everyone's a millionaire these days, every halfway solvent member of the middle class. And the majority of that currency decay is historically recent. Why, the dollar lost *half* its value in the mere four years between 1977 and 1981."

Never a science-fiction fan, instead Douglas now immersed himself in the more recently minted genre of apocalyptic economics, rehearsing debt-to-GDP ratios as he had once memorized Saul Bellow. (When younger, Carter had never imagined he'd grow nostalgic for being quoted to death from Seize the Day.) If Pop couldn't remember the age of his only son, the chances were poor that any of this pontificating tutorial was even ballpark accurate. What few scraps of his feverish reading that the old man did recall verbatim would be exaggerated for effect. Yet the last Loony-Tunes statistic was the limit.

"You might double-check that," Carter chided gently, in preference to what a load of crap. "In 1981, I was a junior in college. Why wouldn't I remember my own currency that steeply in freefall?"

"Because it's boring, son. The American government counts on your being bored by it. Why, I barely remember the fallout from Nixon going off the gold standard myself. I buried my head in books. Perhaps the wrong books, looking back, but it's too late now. The point is, when you've debased your currency that utterly, there's not much further left for it to fall. Besides the sheer dullness of it all, the dollar sliding to the penny hasn't been all that noticeable because every other government has been busy doing the same thing—running the printing press overtime on the justification that a junk currency advantages exports. The world is drowning in worthless paper. But America in particular has been getting away with murder—playing on the heartbreaking international belief in Treasury bonds as the ultimate 'safe haven.' Really, the blind trust bears all the irrational hallmarks of theology. What else, financially, is there to believe in besides the *full faith and credit* of the United States? So we've borrowed for basically nothing on the basis of a childlike credulity for thirty years. You know the Fed's been steadily trying to monetize the debt—"

"Cut it out, Pop. You're showing off." In the agency days, Douglas Mandible held forth about anastrophe, metonymy, and onomatopoeia—and now it was all arbitrage, margin calls, and open market operations. Day trading had infected his father's mind like a fungus.

"You try living to ninety-seven with a wife who can't recognize a fork. You'd acquire new expertise out of desperation, too. And it's not complicated. Why, I taught Willing about monetizing the debt the last time you brought Florence up here, and the kid got it right away. Though I have to say that boy's got a knack. Has that sharp-eyed, quick-on-the-uptake quality that was obvious in Enola by the time she was three."

Drawing on an inhuman self-control, Carter stifled, *Oh, give me a break!*

"So," Douglas continued. "You loan me ten bucks. I photocopy the bill four times, give you back one of the copies, and announce that we're square. That's *monetizing the debt*: I owe you nothing, and you're stuck with a scrap of litter. For years, the fact that one can swap dollars for tangible goods and services has been a miracle of God. Why do you think I'm invested in the market? In theory, stocks entail owning real things. Unfortunately, I didn't take into account that most of those stocks are denominated in dollars. And I've been as vulnerable as the next idiot to the bias that keeping the majority of your funds in American companies is erring on the safe side. So I do apologize. Had I any idea what was in the offing, I'd have diversified quite differently."

The apology was Douglas's first acknowledgment that the portfolio that may or may not have abraca-dabra-ed into a bunny rabbit was in the long run more his son's than his own.

"I was going to ask you." Carter's tone was defeatist; he already knew the answer. "I have a 401(k), and a small pension from the *Times*. Is there anything I should do, to protect myself?"

"There's nothing you can do, for as long as this asset freeze is in place—which is relaxing, too, isn't it?" At last Douglas gentled his diatribe with a note of paternal tenderness. "As for when the SEC says, 'Ready, set, go!'—I'd advise moving to gold, but that's what millions of competing investors will be trying to do at the same time. There's simply not that much of the metal on the planet, which is one of the main reasons it's been a staple store of value for five thousand years. When the SEC called time, gold was already at an all-time high. When and if the game resumes, it will go through the roof before you can say Jack Robinson. I'm afraid the same advice pertains to any of the commodities that back the bancor. It's too late," Douglas announced elegiacally. "I wouldn't bother."

It had long before grown dark, and the banker's lamp on the table between them cast a soft, protective glow. Once again Carter was struck by how nothing, or nothing tangible, had changed. He'd gulped a horrifying quantity of bourbon, and it was only mid-evening. He shouldn't drive in this condition, and hadn't the presence of mind to figure out the driverless function in the BeEtle now. He'd have to stay over. Jayne would be frantic. She wasn't accustomed to spending the night alone. His wife had determinedly *not* kept up with the news this week, and wouldn't be amenable to the idea that exceptional times required extensive consultation with his father. Jayne had become a firm believer in rising above news of any sort, all of which was bound to blow over if you ignored it resolutely enough. The head-in-a-paper-bag strategy worked a surprisingly high proportion of the time.

Douglas patted Carter's thigh. "What say we have a bite? There's the dining room, or Grace could whip up something here that isn't low-salt, low-fat, low-fun."

"This conversation hasn't done wonders for my appetite." Carter continued to slump. He didn't call Jayne, who if she had attended to the nature of this errand at all would only want the gist. Which he still hadn't grasped. A bit of bravery was in order—not his strong suit. "Have you been trying to tell me that we're—that you're wiped out?"

Douglas laughed. "No, no, no! It's not as bad as *that*."

Relief didn't immediately drain the surge of adrenaline. Heart pounding in his ears, Carter felt faint, and dropped his head. "You never tell me about this stuff. Like you don't trust me." Hard booze made Carter morose.

"Not at all! I simply haven't read you as interested in the nitty-gritty."

"I guess I haven't been. Now there's nothing *but* nitty-gritty."

"Quite. Some detail, then. I've steered clear of index funds, but only because I've got a piece of every company listed on the Dow." The same pride once attended acquisition of the complete works of W. Somerset Maugham. "That aspect of the balance sheet could be grim. But I hold gold ETFs, mining stock, even the title to bullion in a safe-deposit box in downtown Manhattan. I always keep 10 percent in cash—with which one will still be able to buy a loaf of bread *in* the country, and you don't have travel plans, do you?"

"No, the safari in Tanzania can wait for another year. No animals left anyway."

"Good. Since the next endangered species will be the American tourist. Otherwise, a good tranche of the portfolio is in Treasuries. The yield is piss-poor, and they'll drop in value now that the rate's gone up, but, worse comes to worst, one can always wait for maturity. Times like these, it's the principal you most want to hold on to."

"But you said buying American bonds was a sign of worldwide gullibility."

"That's right! So why should I be any different?"

They were rising to head to the dining room—if Carter didn't get some food into him soon he'd be sick—when a knock rapped on the library door. "Mr. Mandible, sir?" The orderly who'd been minding Luella poked his head in. "The president is about to address the nation on TV. The desk was sure you'd want to know."

Chapter 4
Good Evening, Fellow Americans

M om! Alvarado's on in a minute!"
"That's okay, sweetie!" his mother shouted
from the kitchen. "I'll watch it later."

This was another of those where-were-you-then moments, and it was ominous when they bunched together.
Back against Great Grand Man's heavy wine-colored
sofa, Willing nestled cross-legged on the floor, where
he always felt safer, more deeply seated. The thrum of
the announcer's *in a few moments . . . has made only
one other address to the nation . . .* rose up from the
wooden parquet and trembled in his palms. For once
he didn't feel self-conscious about the blare intruding
on Kurt in the basement. Alvarado was their tenant's
president also. Kurt should be paying attention: *Ladies
and gentlemen, the President of the United States.* That

was another sign that stuff was going roachbar. When they had to say it the long way—not only "the President" but "the President *of the United States.*" "The United States of America." That was the worst.

Milo barked. Just once, before huddling into the protection of Willing's thigh. Milo had never seemed too sure about Alvarado.

His mother was making a mistake. There were copies of everything. The duplicates seemed identical to the originals. Willing, too, could wait and listen to this speech later. On fleX or catch-up TV, the address would be indistinguishable from the image he was following now. But the copy would not be happening. He couldn't explain it, but that made it completely different. Forever after, Willing will have watched this address when it was happening. Those sounds again, the artificially downward music of the announcers' suppressed excitement, the forcing of their voices into darker, whispering tones when really they wanted to shout, assured him that later he would be glad and proud that he was watching this now and not after the fact.

Because big news got old fast. If you waited, somebody was bound to *tell you about it* before you learned it for yourself. They'd change the words around, too, and get everything in the wrong order. Willing hated being *told* what had happened. The telling people always seemed so smug and powerful, and they maintained their power by keeping their special knowledge to themselves for as long as possible. So they would feed you bits of information in sadistic dribs, like dog treats for Milo. You couldn't trust the telling person either. Even if they claimed to hand over all that they knew, they only conveyed the part that they liked or especially hated. Being told—it was not the way to find anything out.

Buenas noches, mis compatriotas americanos. Daré instrucciones en español inmediatamente después de esta versión en inglés. Pero esta noche, y sólo esta noche, presionen uno para inglés.

Good evening, fellow Americans. At the beginning of this century, extra-national terrorists hijacked our own airplanes to rupture the Pentagon and destroy the World Trade Center. More recently, in 2024, our vital internet infrastructure was cataclysmically paralyzed by hostile foreign powers.

Modern warfare comes in many guises.

During this past week, our nation has once again been under attack. No towering skyscrapers have tumbled. Both the physical and digital systems on which we depend continue to function. Yet the attack we are currently sustaining is potentially no less devastating than nuclear missiles hurtling toward our cities.

What has been targeted is the very medium through which we trade with other nations and conduct commerce with one another—the medium through which our labors are rewarded, our debts are repaid, our tables are laid, and our children are secured medicines for their ailments.

What is at risk is no less than the almighty dollar itself.

Coordinating their chicanery, countries that wish this nation ill have played on the cowardly compliance of our allies. In the last ten days, a sequence of carefully timed financial dominoes were toppled—designed to raise the cost of financing our national debt, which would translate into you the American taxpayer keeping less of your hard-earned income. Our currency was also sabotaged on the international exchange markets. Most perfidiously of all, world leaders who resent the power, prestige, and success of our great nation have cobbled together the so-called "bancor"—an artificial, pretender currency with no history as legal tender.

Make no mistake. The bancor is not intended as a harmless alternative to the dollar. It is meant to replace the dollar. In a move every bit as threatening as raising a gun to our heads, we have been informed that the crops and raw materials on which we rely for our daily lives and livelihoods must now be traded internationally in bancors. A gesture of exceptionally high-handed insolence: the United States Department of the Treasury has also been apprised that American bonds held by foreign investors must henceforth be redeemed in bancors, at an unfavorable exchange rate capriciously chosen by an International Monetary Fund gone rogue. American bonds sold to foreign investors must henceforth be denominated in bancors— which is a challenge to our very sovereignty as a nation.

Ironically, the parties behind this organized fiscal coup immediately suffered from it. The American dollar is the lifeblood of international banking, and the backbone of financial markets around the world. That is why, as most of you know, we suspended trading on the New York Stock Exchange last week to prevent precipitous loss of wealth. But trading has also been halted in the wake of the same shock to the system in London, Paris, Berlin, Moscow, Hong Kong, and every other major stock exchange across the globe. International finance is holding its breath. As with every other crisis for more than a hundred years, the world waits for America to act. And this brave country never sustains insult without reply.

Right before addressing you, the American people, this evening, I convened an emergency session of Congress. Almost unanimously, your representatives passed a bill deeming that, until further notice, for American citizens to hold *bancors*, either onshore or within the confines of our financial system, shall from this point onward be considered an act of treason. In the interest of preserving not only our present prosperity, but our future prosperity—in the interest of maintaining our integrity, our capacity to hold our heads high as a nation—Americans and American entities are also forbidden from trading in bancors abroad.

For the time being, and only for the time being of course, capital above the amount of $100 is not to leave the country. These controls are temporary, their duration destined to be brief, and they will be lifted the moment that economic order is safely and securely restored.

As with military confrontations, fiscal warfare demands weaponry, and the fashioning of weaponry requires sacrifice. As we mobilized our forces and our industries to defend the cause of liberty in World War Two, so must we mobilize our resources to defend our liberty today. Rest assured that the greatest burden of this sacrifice will be borne by the broadest shoulders.

Using the powers vested in your president by the International Emergency Economic Powers Act of 1977, I am calling in all gold reserves held in private hands. Gold-mining operations within our borders will be required to sell ore exclusively to the United States Treasury. Gold stocks, exchange-traded funds, and bullion will likewise be transferred to the Treasury. In contrast to Franklin Delano Roosevelt's gold nationalization of 1933, when FDR made his bold bid to rescue our suffering nation from the Great Depression, there will be no exceptions for jewelers or jewelry. All such patriotic forfeitures will be compensated by weight, albeit at a rate that does not reflect the hysterical inflation of gold stocks in the lead-up to this emergency. Hoarding will not be tolerated. Punitive fines of up to $250,000 will be levied on those who fail to comply. Retaining gold in any form beyond the deadline of November 30, 2029, will thenceforth be considered a criminal offense, punishable by no less than ten years in prison.

All gold exports from our shores are henceforth prohibited. In retaliation for outside agitators' attempts to fray the very fabric of our flag, all foreign gold reserves currently stored with the Federal Reserve are hereby confiscated, and become the property of the American government.

Lastly: it is the intention of a conspiracy of foreign powers to yoke the government of this illustrious land with an intolerable and infeasible encumbrance from the interest on its debt. That debt was borrowed in good faith, and in due course, under any but the most extraordinary circumstances, would have been repaid in good faith. But when our probity is returned with malice and betrayal, continued good faith counts only as credulity and weakness. Both sides need to honor an agreement for any contract to remain in force. What's more, this great country will not so honor its obligations as to destroy its very existence in the process. A nation conceived in liberty cannot conduct its daily business on its knees.

As of this evening, myself, the secretary of the Treasury, and the chairman of the United States Federal Reserve have declared a universal "reset." In the interest of preserving the very nation that would meet its obligations of the future, we are compelled to put aside the obligations of the past. All Treasury bills, notes, and bonds are forthwith declared null and void. Many a debtor has wept in gratitude for the mercy of a wiped slate, the right to a second chance, which for individuals and corporations alike all fair-minded judicial systems like our own have enshrined in law. So also must government be able to draw a line and say: here we begin afresh.

Thus let us strike into the future, our step lightened, our hearts gladdened—confident in the endurance of the greatest country on earth. God bless you. And God bless the United States of America. Good night.

The moment it was over, the address was available all over the web, but sometimes too much access discouraged you from taking advantage of it; all urgency evaporated. So Florence was content for Willing to summarize the speech—with remarkable thoroughness for a thirteen-year-old—as she hung out the wash in the utility room off the kitchen. That low-water cycle always left the light loads dingy.

"That's a lot to digest." Florence eyed her son, at attention beside the washer, arms straight, hands flat to his sides, dark eyes burning forward, quite the little soldier. She'd no idea how she'd raised such a sober-sided boy, ready to take on the weight of the world at a scant eighty-six pounds. "You're not worried, are you? You look worried."

"I'm worried," he reported.

"Listen." Abandoning the socks in the drum, Florence knelt more than need be with his height at last shooting up. "From what you've told me, we've nothing to worry about. You see any gold lying around that we have to give the government? Even if we had some, they'd pay us for it, that's what you said."

"If the government can make us give them anything they want, what else can they make us give them? If they said they need all the dogs, would I have to give them Milo?"

She laughed. "President Alvarado is never going to take Milo. He's a nice man. Esteban and I voted for him, remember? And that newfangled money, well—I wouldn't know a 'bancor' if it bit me on the butt. Do we ever take 'bancors' to Green Acre to buy cereal? No. So no one's going to arrest you, or Esteban, or your mother for carrying around some nonsense currency that really has to do with complicated financial dealings between countries. As for this . . . 'debt renunciation'?"

"That's what the commentators called it."

"Off the top of my head, I bet that 'reset' you told me about will keep our taxes down. That's good for us. That way we keep more of my salary."

"The president borrowed money from people and now won't pay it back. That doesn't seem careless. That seems kind of boomerpoop."

Florence stood briskly and spanked her hands. "First off, this president borrowed hardly anything. He inherited the debt from other presidents, who couldn't stop *rescuing* jerkwater countries that only ended up hating us for our *helping hand*. Also, most of that money is from the Chinese, who are big cheats, and the real boomerpoops, since they almost certainly knocked out our whole country's internet five years ago. Fuck them."

"Nobody caught them. Nobody came up with any proof."

"That makes the operation even nastier. Not owning up? But you'd have to be an *idiota* not to know who did it." Florence caught herself. "Sorry, I didn't mean you're stupid."

"But the Chinese won't like this. If they could take out the internet before, they could do it again."

"No, they can't. All former vulnerabilities have been secured." Florence was uncomfortably aware of reciting this received wisdom with a slight singsong.

"That's what people say. That doesn't mean it's true."

"Willing, I've no idea how you got to be such a cynic by the age of thirteen."

He glowered. "They could do worse than knock out the internet."

"Stop it. You're letting your imagination run away with you. The point is, none of what you told me the president announced on TV has anything to do with us, okay?"

"Everything has to do with everything else," he announced grimly.

"Where did you get that?"

"From the universe."

"Jesus, my son's become a mystic. Lighten up. Let's have some ice cream."

Given that he was eternally free to watch the other two-thousand-some channels streamed *en español*, Florence knew better than to believe that Esteban was watching the second delivery of the address in Spanish to "maintain his fluency." Still jubilant over Dante Alvarado's narrow victory in 2028, he was basking. During this first honeymoon year, for hardcore supporters like Esteban, America's first Lat president could do no wrong.

The other slightly-less-than-half of the country was if anything more sullen than in 2008, but also more prone to keep their mouths shut. This time around, no dyspeptic "birthers" could object that the Democrat was born outside the country. Its passage greatly assisted by Arnold Schwarzenegger's failed bid for 2024, the Twenty-Eighth Amendment nullified the arcane constitutional requirement that presidents be born on American soil. (Florence wasn't the only one who attributed the Terminator's surprise defeat to the eleventh-hour incumbency gimmick of nominating Judith Sheindlin—a.k.a. "Judge Judy"—to the Supreme Court. The Court's sessions had been livelier since, and shorter.) Dante Alvarado being unabashedly born in Oaxaca had helped to get him elected. The fact that many DC press conferences and congressional debates were now conducted in Spanish was an enduring source of pride for Esteban's community. Although some Democrats regarded Alvarado's decision to deliver his inaugural address in January exclusively in his native language as gratuitously provocative, Florence didn't care. The broadcast of that soaring, historic speech on the Washington Mall had provided a welcome opportunity to brush up on her own Spanish.

Besides, back in 2024 she'd put herself on notice that Florence Darkly was a racist.

At 5:08 p.m. that fateful Saturday in March, she and Willing had been shopping in Manhattan, taking advantage of the blowout spring sale at the sprawling Chelsea branch of Bed Bath & Beyond. They'd just got through checkout when the store's lights went off. Out on the street, the sidewalks were jammed with people shaking out fleXes in frustration; checking for connectivity on her own fleX was as compulsive as it was futile. A blackout was one thing—the whole area seemed to have no power—but that didn't explain the absence of satellite coverage. People poured out of the subway stations; the trains had stopped. The stoplights out, an accident at West Nineteenth Street had brought traffic on Sixth Avenue to a standstill. The cacophony of horns was strangely comforting: signs of life.

Clutching her son's hand, she hadn't yet entered the world in which refusing to relinquish their new wicker laundry hamper was ridiculous—though its being weighed down with other bargains stuffed inside made the bulky object especially awkward. As they negotiated their way through crowds milling toward hysteria, her struggling with the white elephant must have been conspicuous. When a muscular Mexican attempted to take it away from her, she assumed he was undocumented and a thief, using the pandemonium to hustle. She yanked the hamper back.

The man promised her in soothingly correct English that he was only trying to help. He said no one he'd spoken to seemed to know why suddenly nothing worked, because the very devices with which you answered such questions had ceased to function. He warned her that, clutching the hamper with one arm and a child with the other, she risked being trampled. He asked where they lived; she was reluctant to tell him, but didn't want to be rude. He said he also had to get home to Brooklyn. He suggested they take the Manhattan Bridge, whose pedestrian ramp would be less popular than the Brooklyn Bridge one, sure to be mobbed. He hoisted the loaded hamper on his shoulder. At first they didn't talk. He terrified her. But as he prowed through crowds across Eighteenth Street, then down Second Avenue to Chrystie, she had to admit that she'd never have carried their chattel so far on her own, nor would she have as expertly navigated the most direct route to the pedestrian entrance at Canal Street without an app. He was right about the choice of bridge. They weren't jostled so badly that they were ever in danger of being pushed over the rail into the East River.

On the ramp, they all agreed that the hardest part was not knowing what had happened. On every side, other pedestrians volunteered their sure-fire theories: Halley's Comet had hit New Jersey. The government was conducting a security drill. There'd been another terrorist attack. Harold Camping's notorious prediction that the Rapture would arrive on May 21, 2011, was only off by thirteen years, nine months, and fifteen days.

When they finally curved down the ramp to their borough, she begged to assume the burden and proceed with her eight-year-old's help. Their Mexican escort claimed to live in Sunset Park, six miles west of East Flatbush, and his continuing in the wrong direction didn't make any sense—unless he planned to accost her.

Yet by now it was dark, obliteratingly so. Only individual fleXpots penetrated the blackness. Behind them, Manhattan could have been a mountain range. Traffic perfectly gridlocked, since driverless functions and onboard computers relied on the internet, most cars had been abandoned, though families huddled inside a few sedans, doubtless with the doors locked. So the Lat insisted not only on seeing them home, but on depleting his fleX to light the way. By the time the trio was trudging up Flatbush near the park, his fleX went dead, and they had to switch to Florence's. The avenue was lined with other pilgrims and the waning glow of their small devices, like penitents with luminarias. The whole trip on foot was nearly ten miles and took four and a half hours. So by the time they turned onto Snyder, Florence assumed the hamper and let their protector carry Willing, who fell asleep in his arms. Later the man would explain that of course he'd been scared, as everyone was scared, but that the surest way to keep his head was to concentrate on the safety of these two strangers. His name was Esteban Padilla, and by the time they reached East Fifty-Fifth Street, dog-tired, fully in the dark again because Florence's fleX was shot now, too, in need of locating candles and matches in the kitchen on their hands and knees, Florence was a lot less of a racist and in love.

Last November's election meant so much to her partner that she'd kept a slight queasiness about the new president to herself. Oh, she was thrilled by the symbolism; after all the acrimony over immigration, a Lat in the White House was the ultimate emblem of inclusion. Yet the man had a baby-faced softness only emphasized by the palatalized consonants of a Mexican accent, which in Alvarado's case sometimes seemed a bit put on. (When he spoke to white audiences during the campaign, his pronunciation crisped right up.) It wasn't only that he was fat—what the hell, three-quarters of the country was fat—it was the kind of fat.

He had a momma's boy puffiness that might make foreign heads of state regard him as a pushover.

Pulling down bowls, Florence debated asking Kurt
to join them for ice cream. She was always of two
minds about how much to enfold their basement tenant, a part-time florist, into the family's social life. He
was sweet about bringing back aging bouquets that
would have been thrown away, cheering their home
with freesias. And she liked him well enough, which
she wished he would simply register and then relax.
After all, he was polite, solicitous, intelligent, well spoken, and eager. (Overeager? And eager for what? To
be *liked*, obviously, and even being liked *well enough*
would have sufficed.) Yet his outsize gratitude for
every common kindness was exhausting. The fact that
he never complained made their lives easier, but he'd
every right to complain. Tall for the low ceiling downstairs, he perpetually hit his head on the crossbeams,
which she should have cushioned with foam appliqué.
An amateur musician, he would only practice the sax
with no one else home, while upstairs, even Willing's
light, stealthy tread translated into elephantine pounding from below. Did Kurt Inglewood even plead with
the family to keep the TV low? No, no, no. So what

tilted the balance this evening toward three bowls not four made Florence feel sheepish.

Roughly her age, trim and nicely proportioned, with a long, sharply planed face, Kurt should have qualified as handsome. A guy with a middle-class upbringing who'd struggled from one unsatisfying, low-paid job to another just as Florence had, Kurt would have come across as a charming and competent striver waiting for one decent break when he was younger. But one of the corners he'd cut for years was dental care. Decay had blackened an engaging smile into a vampiric leer. Absent fifty grand's worth of implants, fillings, and bridges, he'd be single for life. Now in his forties with those *teeth*, he'd tipped tragically, unfairly, and perhaps permanently into the class of loser—an ugly, dehumanizing label that she had narrowly escaped herself. She encountered no end of poor dental hygiene at the shelter, and maybe that was the problem tonight. She wouldn't have minded sharing ice cream with Kurt-as-Kurt. But it had been a long day at Adelphi, and she simply couldn't face that smile.

Florence dished up three scoops. Feeling that edgy gaiety of something major having happened even if she couldn't tell yet if it was good or bad, she impulsively put a chunk of peppermint chip in Milo's dog dish.

They convened in the living room with spoons, and Esteban turned off the TV.

"So what's your take on the address?" she asked Esteban as they lounged with dessert on the sofa.

"*Está maravilloso*," he declared. "Those decrepit Republicans—they're always carping about how Alvarado is weak and spineless. This'll show them. Talk about standing up for this country! That's the nerviest set of policy decisions I've heard from any president in my life. They can't call him a pussy now."

Florence guffawed. "They might call him some other things. Like a grifter."

"Only people get hurt deserve it," Esteban said confidently. "Bunch of Asian assholes. Who gives a shit."

Densely silent since their conversation in the laundry room, Willing emerged from his stewing with a prize-winning non sequitur: "We could always move to France."

"Oka-ay . . . ," Florence said, stroking her son's neck with a forefinger as he sat rigidly on the floor. His ice cream was melting. "And why would we do that?"

"Nollie lives in Paris," Willing said. "It might be safer. The president said they won't let dollars out of the country. He didn't say they won't let people out. Yet."

Florence glanced at Esteban and shook her head like, *Don't ask.* "I suppose you might visit your great-aunt someday. You two seemed to get on well during her last trip to New York."

"Nollie does what she wants. Everyone else does what they're supposed to," Willing said. "Jayne and Carter say she's selfish. That might be a good thing. It's the selfish people, a certain kind of selfish, who you want on your side."

Florence assured her son that there were no "sides," observed that he was overtired, urged him to bed, and finished his ice cream, now turned to soup. After he'd brushed his teeth, she murmured in the boy's door-way that no one was moving anywhere, and that lots of events that seem strange and scary up close end up looking like the plain ups and downs of regular life later on. The Stone Age seemed like the end of the world, didn't it? And it wasn't.

Yet later her own sleep was troubled. The disquiet was subterranean. Bedrock was shifting—what had to stay the same in order for other things safely to change. In 2024, Florence came to appreciate the vast differ-ence between something bad happening and the very systems through which anything happens going bad. Even if the president's somber decrees had no concrete impact on the day-to-day in East Flatbush, the edicts seemed to challenge her life at ground level—not so much the trifling to-and-fro of what she earned and what she spent, what she did and where she went, but who she was.

Walking to the bus stop the next morning, Florence crossed to drop the Con Ed bill in the mailbox—a payment method that felt as primitive as lighting a fire with flint. So history could reverse. Now that any transaction involving vital infrastructure or finance had to be conducted offline by law, trashy, space-eating paper bank statements and utility bills once again littered domestic tabletops. The checkbook, too, had been salvaged from the dustbin of the past, hair-balls and used dental floss clinging between its leaves. But at least the necessity of scrawling on a rectangle "Two hundred forty-three and 29/100s" alone justi-fied mastery of the formation of letters by hand. Close to losing the skill altogether, she'd been forced to void the first Con Ed check at breakfast because it was illegible. So she'd tutored Willing on printing the al-phabet, since they didn't teach handwriting in school anymore. Most of his classmates couldn't write their own names. This was progress? But that was an old-fashioned concern that kids considered drear.

As the envelope fluttered into the blue maw, she frowned. If "internet vulnerabilities" *had* been fixed, why did we still have to pay electric bills by check?

The "gentry" encroaching ever farther east into Brooklyn took private transport. As usual the only white passenger on the standing-room-only bus, Florence strained to pick up any reference to Alvarado's address. The Afri-mericans spoke their own dialect, only partially discernible to honks, infiltrated by scraps of mangled Spanish. Among the Lats, the only rapid urban Spanish she could confidently translate concerned the latest music rage, beastRap, comprising birdcalls, wolf howls, lion roars, cat purrs, and barking. (Not her thing, but when artfully mixed, some of the songs were stirring.) A screeching seagull tune with an overlaid rhythm track of pecking seemed to generate more excitement on the B41 than the wholesale voiding of American bonds. Yet once the news filtered down to the street, gold nationalization wouldn't go down well with this crowd, many of whose toughs were looped with gleaming yellow chains. It was hard to picture these muscular brothers and *muchachos* lining up patriotically around the block to deliver their adornments to the Treasury. With the likes of that hulking weight-room habitué looming by the door—were the feds planning to wrestle him to the pavement and yank out the gold teeth with pliers?

A generation ago, this stretch of Flatbush Avenue north of Prospect Park was trashy with the loud rinky-dink of carpet warehouses, discount drug stores, nail salons, and delis with doughnuts slathered in pink icing. But after the stadium was built at the bottom of the hill, the neighborhood spiffed up. The "affordable housing" that developers promised as part of the stadium deal with the city was nearly as costly as the luxury apartments. Flatbush's rambunctious street feel had muted to a sepulchral hush. Pedestrians were few. The *bee-beep* of the private vans that used to usher the working class up and down the hill for a dollar had been replaced by the soft rush of electric taxis. The avenue was oh, so civilized, and oh, so dead.

Florence rather relished the fact that the commercial transformation of the once vibrant, garish area must have put the well-heeled new residents to no end of inconvenience. Oh, you could get a facelift nearby, put your dog in therapy, or spend $500 at Ottawa on a bafflingly trendy dinner of Canadian cuisine (the city's elite was running out of new ethnicities whose food could become fashionable). But you couldn't buy a screwdriver, pick up a gallon of paint, take in your dry cleaning, get new tips on your high heels, copy a key, or buy a slice of pizza. Wealthy residents might own bicycles worth $5K, but no shop within miles would repair the brakes. Why, the nearest supermarket was a forty-five-minute hike to Third Avenue. High rents had priced out the very service sector whose presence at ready hand once helped to justify urban living. For all practical purposes, affluent New Yorkers resided in a crowded, cluttered version of the countryside, where you had to drive five miles for a quart of milk.

Florence hopped off at Fulton Street and headed east with her collar pulled close. Fall had been merciful so far, and this was the first day of the season the wind had that bite in it, foretelling yet another vicious New York winter. The jet stream seemingly having hove south across the whole country for good, the anachronism *global warming* had been conclusively jettisoned in the US. She hung a left on Adelphi Street, whose traffic had grown lighter now that the underpass was closed off a few blocks farther up; ever since the horrendous collapse of the Brooklyn-Queens Expressway along Hamilton Avenue, not far from her parents' house, no one was allowed to come near it.

She assessed the intake line as pro forma: about twenty families, the ubiquitous strollers looped with as many bags as they could carry without toppling over. Several adults were smoking. These were some of the last holdouts who puffed on real cigarettes, despite their being far pricier than steamers. Ridiculous, since she'd never been addicted herself, but the sharp, toxic scent of tobacco made Florence nostalgic.

On a leafy street in Fort Greene, the Adelphi Family Residence was formerly a private apartment building willed to the city by a childless landowner—one of a torrent of bequests that had poured into public coffers as well as into private charities from the boomer generation, a hefty proportion of which had neglected to reproduce and had no one else left to be nice to. The tall, tawny-bricked building with period details was a big step up from the much-discredited and now-defunct Auburn shelter in the projects a few blocks away. To accommodate more residents, the apartments had been carved into stingier units with no kitchens and communal bathrooms, but there was also a cafeteria and nominal rec room (whose Ping-Pong tables never had balls). Funny, she and Esteban could never afford this tony a neighborhood in a million years.

Florence waved at Mateo and Rasta, the guards at the entrance, then threw her backpack on the lobby's security belt and did a stylish twirl in the all-body X-ray. (Mere metal detectors no longer cut it. Plastic gun replicas made from home 3-D printers had improved.) It was too bad that the lobby's intricate nineteenth-century tiling was obscured by posters—HOME IS WHERE THE HEART IS!; SUCCESS IS JUST FAILURE TRIED ONE MORE TIME!—though the cheerful admonishments helped to

compensate for the grimmer notice, VERBAL OR PHYSI-
CAL ABUSE OF STAFF WILL NOT BE TOLERATED.

Adelphi wasn't the vermin-infested hellhole teeming
with sexual predators that her pitying neighbors like
Brendon the Financial Clairvoyant no doubt imagined.
What depressed Florence about her job, then, wasn't
squalor, or even the poverty and desperation that drove
people here. It was the aimlessness. The collective atmosphere of so many people in one place having lost
any purposeful sense of traveling from point A to point
B—that milling-about-and-waiting-to-die fug that
penetrated the institution—disquieted her not for its
contrast with her own driving, forward-thrust story,
but for its reflection of how she, too, felt much of the
time. At Barnard, she'd never have imagined herself
mopping up vomit with the best of them, save perhaps
in a charitable capacity, in some brave, brief experi-
mental phase before getting on with her career. She
didn't understand how she ended up at Adelphi any
more than its residents did. She didn't know what could
possibly lie on the other side of this place for her any
more than they did, either. While crude survival from
one day to the next might be every human's ultimate
animal goal, for generations the Mandible family had
managed to dress up the project as considerably more
exalted. Motherhood might have provided a sense of

direction, and Willing did give gathering indications of being bright—but the smarter he seemed, the more she felt impotent to do right by his talents. Unlike Avery, she'd no problem with Willing being taught in Spanish, so long as he was taught. Yet every fact he volunteered, every skill he exhibited, either she had taught her son or her son had taught himself. The school sucked.

An armed security guard behind her, Florence assumed the desk in the lobby and processed the morning's arrivals. As ever, a handful of families imagined they could simply show up at the door and grab a bed. Ha! So she'd send them to the DHS intake in the South Bronx, along with a voucher for the van parked outside. Few would be back. Qualifying as homeless was an art, and God forbid you should mention a great-uncle with a spare room in Arkansas or you'd be on the red-eye bus to Little Rock that night. For the others who'd jumped the hoops, arriving with fattening sheaves of documents in sticky plastic binders, Adelphi had barely enough vacant units, and larger families would be crowded. The shelter operated at maximum capacity because two-thirds of the units were permanently bed-blocked. In theory, shelter accommodation was temporary. In practice, most residents lived here for years.

Florence ushered the new families to their quarters, parents clutching pamphlets of rules and privileges.

In the rare instance that the family hadn't lived in a shelter before, the environs came as a shock. Rooms were equipped with dressers missing drawers and mattresses on the floor, with the odd kitchen chair but seldom a table to go with it. Though Adelphi had a few OCD neatniks, most occupied units were piled thrift-shop high with clothes in every corner, the floors junky with plastic tricycles, broken bikes, and milk crates of outdated electronics.

So the intake always complained: *What, you telling me there a shared baffroom? Where Dajonda gonna sleep, she sixteen—ain't she get a room with a door? What do you mean we can't have no microwave? Them sheets, they stained. Lady in the lobby say these TV don't get Netflix! Melita here allergic to wheat—so don't you be serving us any of that soggy pasta. Not much of a view. From our old room in Auburn, you could see the Empire State Building!*

Florence always shimmered between two distinct reactions to this inexorable carping: *I know, I would hate to share a bathroom with strangers myself. Being homeless doesn't mean you don't value privacy, and if I had a teenage girl in one of these places I'd keep her close. The policy on microwaves is unreasonable, since warming up a can of soup hardly means the room gets infested. Homeless people have every reason to value clean linen, to hope for quality entertainment, and to expect their dietary requirements to be catered to. Me, I hate overcooked pasta. Overall, it makes perfect psychological sense that, brought this low, you would want to firmly establish that you still have likes and dislikes, that you still have standards.*

A millisecond later: *You are in the most expensive city in the country if not the world. You have just been given a free place to live, three free meals a day, free electricity, and even free WATER, while people like me working long hours in jobs we don't always like can barely stretch to a chicken. For reasons beyond me, you have seven children you expect other people to support, while I have only the one, for whom I provide clothing, food, and shelter. You may have to share a bathroom, but your old-style torrent of a shower beats my "walk in the fog" by a mile, so put a sock in it.*

Flickering back and forth all day induced an intellectual strobe that was fatiguing.

For lunch, Florence grabbed a cafeteria sandwich and retreated to the staff room, lively today. The locust protein filling was supposed to taste like tuna fish. It didn't.

"Fantastic," Selma was saying, propping her legs on a table; the calves were the circumference of industrial mayonnaise jars. "*Malicious*, as my boy would say.

I love the pitcher of all them rich folk having to cough up they big piles of gold. Had my way, wouldn't get no 'compensation' for it, neither. Somebody got to level the playing field. Whatever happen to that idea of them 'wealth taxes' a while back? Platform Colbert run on. That was the shit. What I'd have Alvarado turn upside down, this just the start."

"You didn't even vote for him!" Florence objected over her sandwich. Afri-mericans had been roundly hostile to Alvarado's candidacy.

"I abstain," Selma said fastidiously. "Don't mean *el presidente* can't be useful."

"Wealth taxes are double taxation," Chris mumbled, with the nervous cringing of being the only white man in the room—a pale, weedy white man at that.

"Careless," Selma said. "You loaded, tax didn't work the first time."

"What about the debt thing?" Florence threw out neutrally. For reasons she hadn't pinpointed, it nagged at her.

"Stroke a genius," said Mateo, the stocky Guatemalan on a break from guarding the lobby. "I declared bankruptcy six years ago. Registered the vehicle with my sister, so even kept the car. Now I got credit cards coming outta my ears. Sorted everything out *bien bonita*. No reason the country can't do the same thing."

"You loan money to folks can't pay it back, joke's on you, right?" Selma agreed. "'Sides, I don't see why the gubment ever pay anything back. Pass a law say, 'We don't got to.' Presto. No more loan."

"But the majority of the people who've loaned the federal government money"—Chris trained his eyes on his teabag, which he only dipped twice; he liked his Lipton weak—"are other Americans."

"*Mierda*," Mateo said. "I heard it was all the chinks."

"Yeah," Selma said. "And they want they money back? *Come and get it.*"

"You know, the American military isn't what it used to be," Florence said cautiously.

"Bull." Mateo punched the air. "We got the pow-ah! Biggest army in the fucking world."

"Actually, the Chinese have the biggest army in the world," Florence said.

"But never mind the Chinese," said Chris. "It's our fellow Americans—"

"Ain't nothing 'fellow' about 'em," Selma said. "'Cause you mean rich Americans. With them *port-fo-li-os.*"

"Not only." Chris added a disgusting amount of milk to his tea. "Our pension funds are invested in Treasury bonds. They're always part of a balanced *port-fo-li-o.*"

Selma eyed him for signs of mockery. "City don't come across with our pensions?" She smiled prettily. "We gonna burn the place down."

Chris said quietly, "Then you may have to."

Is it true?" Florence pressed Chris after the other two had returned to work. "That the debt is mostly from us?" The *us* jarred. You always had to cite which *us*.

"From what I've read." Chris fluttered his fingers to the side, a routine gesture for if-you-can-believe-anything-you-read-now-that-there-is-no-more-*New York Times-Economist-FT-Guardian-LA Times*-or-*Washington Post*. "And the feds aren't only reneging on the interest, but the principal. My dad gave me a ten-K Treasury bond when I graduated from college. As of last night? That money's wiped out. And my family's not rich. This is going to be . . . explosive. Those guys don't get it."

"They get something," Florence said. "Selma and Mateo are both married. I know that partly because they have a traditional way of showing it. But this morning, when they came to work? *They weren't wearing their wedding rings.*"

Riding the bus home, contrary to policy Florence tugged out her fleX; many of these passengers could only spring for smart phones, and the distinctive sparkle of metallic mesh could make her a target. But she couldn't resist a scroll through the news sites. Sure enough, they bannered wall-to-wall outrage. By international consensus, the US was now a "pariah nation." All over the globe, there were riots outside American embassies, several of which had been overrun and looted. Her country's diplomatic service had ceased operations until further notice. American ambassadors and staff were evacuating their posts under armed guard.

Meanwhile, Florence detected much joshing and shoulder punching on the bus about earrings, studs, and chains, all noticeably less on display. The one tenet of Alvarado's address that had sunk in with the hoi polloi was the part about the gold, a form of wealth they understood. But in neither Spanish nor a host of street dialects did she detect a single comment on the "reset."

Come to think of it, throughout her afternoon, on coffee breaks, when pairing up with colleagues to do spot checks on residents for cleanliness and contraband, banter had featured no further remark on the renunciation of the national debt. Menial Adelphi employees were on low enough wages to pay no income tax, and plenty would qualify for working families' tax credits, which entailed getting what were perversely called "refunds" for taxes they'd never paid in the first place.

When you weren't responsible for paying the interest on a loan, maybe you didn't regard yourself as responsible for the loan itself, either. Neither her fellow passengers nor her colleagues at Adelphi felt *implicated*.

In the scheme of things, Florence paid pretty minimal income tax herself, though it sure didn't feel minimal, what with Social Security, Medicare, and state and local on top, while meantime Wall Street shysters connived to pay practically nothing. As for a pension that may or may not have been eroded by Alvarado's address, its monthly stipend was far enough in the future to be abstract. Even if the Social Security Administration didn't go broke again, the official retirement age was bound to keep moving forward, to sixty-nine, to seventy-two, to seventy-five, like a carrot tied before a donkey's nose. The sole rescue in her decrepitude for which she held out any hope was trickle-down from Grand Man's fortune—about which she kept her trap shut at Adelphi. (In college, her one reservation about adopting her mother's surname, Darkly, in a failed bid to cheer her more fragile parent out of a chronic depression, was that rejecting *Mandible* might alienate her grandfather in a way that could backfire later on. Fortunately, the redoubtable old man had never seemed that petty.) Otherwise, she belonged to a generation widely betrayed, one with no reason to believe that anything but more betrayal lay in wait. Still. Something. Something was bugging her.

She didn't think about being American often, though that may have been typically American in itself. She didn't regard being American as especially formative of her character, and that may have been typically American, too. The Fourth of July was mostly an excuse for an afternoon picnic in Prospect Park, and she was relieved that next year Willing would be old enough that he wouldn't be too disappointed if they didn't go all the way to the suffocating crowds along the East River to watch the fireworks. For years now it had ceased to be controversial to suppose that the era of the "American Empire" was fading, and the notion that her country may already have had its day in the sun she didn't find upsetting. Plenty of other countries had flourished and subsided, and were reputed to be pleasant places to live. She didn't see why being a citizen of a nation in decline should diminish her own life or make her feel personally discouraged. She was duly condemnatory of various black marks on the US historical game card—the slaughter of the Indians, slavery—but not in a way that cut close to the bone. She hadn't herself massacred any braves or whipped Africans on plantations.

This was different.

She felt ashamed.

Chapter 5
The Chattering Classes

I told you I didn't want to do this."

Avery eyed her husband warily at the kitchen counter as he poured himself a girding glass of French Viognier. After he'd put up such a stink about this dinner party, she wasn't about to let him know how much that bottle had set them back. The exchange rate with the nouveau franc must have been ghastly. To cover her tracks, she had buried the wine shop receipt in the outdoor trashcan.

"We haven't had anyone over in two months," she objected, "and it's coming up on Christmas."

"Notice we haven't been invited to one holiday bash this year? It's understood: if you're raising a glass, you're getting plastered by yourself, with the door locked."

"But you're the one who keeps saying this is temporary."

"I do think this is temporary. But for the time being, we're surrounded by people who think they've been ruined."

"According to you, if only everyone would stop freaking out and act normal, the economy would settle in no time. Since I never go this long without having people to dinner, that's what I'm doing: I'm 'acting normal.'"

"It sends the wrong signal," Lowell grumbled. "This town is roiling with suspicion that certain-someones got their cash out of the country in advance. Or worse, have made a fortune at everyone else's expense. It's not a good time to live conspicuously high on the hog."

"Fine, we're not having pork," Avery said brusquely. "And there's nothing highfalutin about the menu."

This was not entirely true. Avery had her standards. People thought you couldn't get bluefin tuna anymore, but you could—for a price. After all that ruckus about the bees and patchy pollination on the West Coast, tossing shaved almonds in a salad was like scattering gold leaf. Since the jet stream's burro-belly sag over North America had frozen Florida's crops *again*, the lemons and the avocadoes were from Spain; the guy stacking them reverently in the produce aisle said shipments from Europe were so extortionate that Wholemart might stop stocking citrus altogether.

Worst of all, like most cooks of her generation, Avery listed the primitive necessities of life as fresh water, shelter, clothing, and extra-virgin olive oil—preferably oil pressed in Cyprus; all the Italian stuff was fake. But when the liter went through the scanner at checkout, she objected that there must have been a mistake. Perhaps weary of this interchange multiple times a day, the surly clerk assured her that the bottle had scanned correctly, and asked if she wanted to have the olive oil put back. Embarrassment won the day, and Avery shook her head no, she'd take it. That receipt went into the outdoor can, too.

"It's not only the risk of ostentation," Lowell said. "I'm not in the mood. I ran into a guy from Administration today, and he said to be prepared for a big drop in enrollment next semester. Parents are pulling their kids out of school. They can't cover the tuition—if they ever could. Lucky I got tenure. When it came through, I took it as a compliment. Now it's a lifeline."

"Therapists, I'm afraid, don't get tenure," she warned him, grating ginger. "Four more cancellations today. Those patients may never be back."

"They'll be back." He smoothed a hand over her rump, wrapped in a tight little black number for the evening. "If only to get counseling over, 'Oh, why on earth did I sell my GM stock after it took such a dive? Had I simply held my nerve, I'd be sitting pretty!' Like my wife"—he gave her buttock a squeeze—"who can't help but sit pretty."

"Thanks. Listen, I do want credit: when you were so tepid about tonight—"

"Not tepid. Violently opposed."

"When you were so 'violently opposed,'" Avery revised, "I cut the guest list to the bone. It's only going to be Ryan and Lin Yu, Tom and Belle."

"My, two out of the four I can actually stand. Good odds, as dinner parties go."

"It's in your interest to stay on Ryan's good side. Mark Vandermire's a passing clown who got lucky, and given your positions you were always going to hate each other. But Ryan is your boss."

"He's only head of the department, in defiance of my seniority, because he threatened to take his marbles to Princeton. They should never have capitulated to blackmail."

"That's because Ryan Biersdorfer is a rock star. Economics doesn't have many rock stars, so you have to make nice."

"Your husband's not a rock star?" He'd have tried to say this lightly, but it came out wounded.

She looped her wrists around his neck, keeping her ginger-hairy hands from soiling his shirt collar. "My husband's more like a jazz musician. Much more careless."

Lowell left to check on the kids upstairs. Hopefully with that butt-patting banter and grousing about the guest list, he'd pulled off a reasonable facsimile of the grumpy yet affectionate husband on an ordinary Saturday evening when he wasn't up for company. Everything he did and said lately felt fake—like cover, or distraction. Yet he did believe fiercely: *this too shall pass*, and more rapidly than anyone expected. Look at the Stonage: the country sprang right back. GDP took a hit in '24, but the market recovered lickety-split. So: all that hair-tear for basically nothing. Same cycle, all over again.

He rapped on Savannah's door, then poked his head in. "You consider joining the grown-ups tonight?"

"Nah." His seventeen-year-old was sprawled on the bed, hunt-and-pecking on her fleX. Savannah was one of those girls who managed to make brown hair seem exotic. He trained his eyes away from her long bare legs; she was a knockout, she had powers, but he was her father. Which made him fortunate. He'd hate to be one of the teenage boys she turned to jelly.

"I want to finish this application. I can ask Mojo for an omelet."

"Better make it yourself. Mom's turned Mojo off for the night. She didn't want it to bury the guests in the backyard or something."

"There's a new Netflix series about that, you know. About a murderous Mojo run amok."

"Oldest sci-fi plot in the book. Goes back to *2001: A Space Odyssey*."

Savannah frowned. "Why would science fiction be set in the past?"

"Because when the novel was written, 2001 was in the future. Like *1984*—which seemed far away when Orwell wrote it, but then the real 1984 came and went, and it wasn't nearly as horrible or alien or sad as he predicted. Plots set in the future are about what people fear in the present. They're not about the future at all. The future is just the ultimate monster in the closet, the great unknown. The truth is, throughout history things keep getting better. On average, the world's population has a higher and higher standard of living. Our species gets steadily less violent. But writers and filmmakers keep predicting that everything's going to fall apart. It's almost funny. So don't you worry. Your future's looking sunny, and it'll only get sunnier."

She looked at him with curiosity. "I wasn't worried."

Well, that makes you a colossal idiot popped into his head before he could stop the thought. "What's the school?"

"Risdee. I can draw. But they want you more than anything to be able to talk about drawing. I'm not sure I'm so good at that."

"Visual art stopped being about making anything a long time ago. It's all about talking. The talking is what you make."

"Doesn't 'visual' art have to be something you see?"

"I guess text is something you see."

"Not anymore," she said. "Nobody at my school reads anything. They use ear buds, and get read to."

"Sounds slow," Lowell said glumly.

"It's easy. It's relaxing."

"They do *know how* to read."

She shrugged with a smile. "Not all of them."

"You have to be able to read even to work for the post office."

"Not really," she said with an air of dreamy mischief. "Hand scanners can read aloud addresses, too. Careless, huh?"

Lowell rolled his eyes. "Good luck with the application."

He shut the door. Not long ago, he'd been pleased that Savannah had fostered the marginally practical ambition to become a fabric designer, and of course she was pretty enough—no father was supposed to think this way anymore—that some guy was bound to scoop her up and take care of her come what may. But at this exact point in time, Lowell was leery of quite so airy-fairy a profession as crafting new prints when the world was already chockful of paisley. More pressingly still, last he checked a degree from the likes of the Rhode Island School of Design cost about $400,000—before room and board. The 529 Plan that Avery's grandfather established when Savannah was born, meant to cover Goog's and Bing's higher education as well, was currently worth about ten cents.

When Lowell stopped by Goog's room, Bing was on the bed, too. Indoorsy and pale, Goog managed to thrust his chest out when seated on a pillow with his back to the bedstead. Didn't a normal fifteen-year-old slump? As ever, his chestnut hair was neat, his clothing tidy. The boy seemed always to be putting himself forward for inspection, and Lowell worried that the kid conceived of himself too much in relation to adults.

They both clammed up when their father made his appearance. But if they were up to something, Lowell would hear about it. Goog had the same garrulous, eager-to-please, desperate-to-impress quality that he had evidenced from the moment he learned to talk. He couldn't keep a secret for five minutes. Bing could—but for all the wrong reasons. Soft and a touch overweight, their ten-year-old was chronically frightened. He'd make ideal prey for pedophiles: warned that if he blabbed he'd get into terrible trouble, Bing would hush-hush the story with him to the grave.

"You boys planning to stay upstairs tonight? Because you can come down and join us if you want. Though I'm not sure Mom has quite enough fish."

"Oh, yuck!" they said in unison. They didn't realize it, but given the outlandish prices and poor availability of anything but the farmed varieties, which tasted like pond scum, these boys had been trained to hate fish.

"Mom said we could have grilled cheese," Bing said.

"Who's coming?" Goog asked.

"Mom's friend Belle Duval—you remember, the cancer doctor—"

"Oncologist," Goog corrected scornfully.

"The *oncologist*." God forbid you should insult Goog's vocabulary. "Her husband, Tom Fortnum, is a lawyer with the Justice Department. Also, my colleague Ryan Biersdorfer and the woman he lives with, Lin Yu."

Goog squinted. "The guy who did that ten-part documentary on inequality."

Lowell's middle child was keenly alert to the proximity of fame and influence. It required an unearthly
maturity to keep from getting irked that the kid's celebrity radar didn't blip around his own father. Hadn't
Dad been on TV, too?

"What made Ryan's name was a book, believe it or
not. One of the last big bestsellers. It predicted that
American low-skilled wages will soon be so abysmal
that the Chinese will outsource their jobs to us." Lowell
tried to discipline the derision from his voice. "One
of the things that makes an economist popular with
regular people is a proclivity for hyperbole. Which
means . . . ?"

"A tendency to exaggerate," Goog said promptly.
"But how could you get more hyperbolic than what's
really happened? Olivia Andrews has taken a leave of
absence from school because her father shot himself in
their kitchen. I don't think you guys have been exaggerating enough."

"Sounds like you two should come downstairs, then.
Join the conversation."

"I don't wanna listen to a bunch of economy stuff,"
Bing said.

"Then maybe you were born into the wrong family."

"Yeah. Prolly was."

"Tonight, Bing?" Lowell said. "I'm with you. You guys stay up here, I might sneak away and join you. Ryan is a bigmouth showoff. I bet you know the type at school. When you grow up, nothing changes."

He turned toward the door, but Goog piped up, "Dad, can I ask you a question?"

That boy could never get enough attention. Alas, *bigmouth showoff* was a label that might apply to his elder son. "Sure," Lowell said coolly.

"A friend of mine at school. He said his mother had a bar of gold she bought a while ago in Dubai. Where I guess you could buy it like, you know, shampoo, without a paper trail. His mom had to explain to him about Dubai because he walked outside when she was digging a hole for the bar in the backyard. Isn't that against the law?"

"Right now, yes. But your friend is a knucklehead. He shouldn't have told you that. He needs to keep his piehole shut."

"Well, he made me swear not to tell anybody."

"So why are you telling me?"

Goog looked hurt. He'd be the only teenager in DC upbraided for sharing secrets with a parent. "'Cause I wonder what to do. Whether I should report it to somebody."

"Like the police?"

"Yeah, that's what they told us to do in assembly."

"That," Lowell said, "is sinister. And the answer is no, you do not want to report that gold to the police, or even to a teacher. Keep a lid on it. Your friend's mother could be fined and even thrown in jail."

"But what about the law?"

"I don't care. There have been places and times where everyone rats on everyone else, and nobody trusts anybody. They were bad places, and bad times. This is the United States, and we don't operate that way, got it? If I had some gold I wasn't handing over to the feds, would you turn me in?"

"Are you hiding any?"

"Given this discussion, I wouldn't tell *you* if I were." The levity fell flat.

"But if people who surrender their gold get a roach-bar price from the Treasury, like you said . . . And then the *recalcitrant*"—Goog gave the recent addition to his vocabulary an emphatic flourish—"not only get away with hiding their gold but can get a better price for it on the black market, or overseas . . ." Lowell was bursting with pride that his son had mastered the basics here without any help. "Doesn't that mean that the people who follow the rules get punished?"

"As your father, I shouldn't be letting you in on this rather ugly fact of life, but people who follow the rules are almost always punished."

On that mournful note, Lowell headed downstairs, where the guests had arrived.

Word of warning," Ryan advised. "It slows down security something fantastic."

Avery was a bit exasperated that their company didn't sink into the plenitude of seats in the soft chocolate living room. Everyone remained standing with their wine, instinctively encircling the dark, striking man in a trendy bronze-weave tie. He employed the flamboyant hand gestures of a VIP accustomed to holding court. Receding hairline, true, but Ryan Biersdorfer exemplified that good looks were 50 percent conviction. He was neither as smart nor as entertaining as he thought he was either, but since he did think he was, other people did, too.

"We flew out of Reagan last week, since I had to give a lecture in Zurich," he continued. "The lines were staggering. I'd say add two hours. Even in 'Fast' Track."

"Naturally," Lin Yu said. "Business travelers are the worst offenders."

Half Chinese, Lin Yu Houseman had reaped the best of both worlds—with the smooth, purified lines of a classic Asian face, but a Westerner's slender nose and wide eyes, which women in China were once eager to endure plastic surgery to mirror. (Avery had read that the younger mainland set now considered eyelid augmentation pandering and undignified.) Barely thirty, she combined that hint of the orient that fifty-ish men like Ryan found sexy with a relaxingly straight-up American accent. Intellectually as well, she'd melded the diligence of an Asian upbringing—she'd been one of Ryan's star grad students—with the earnest political passion of the East Coast liberal. Avery would have admired the young woman more had she parted ideological ways with her partner-cum-mentor even occasionally.

"But you should see the scene," Ryan said. "It's almost worth the aggravation for the theater. They're searching every bag, not only the belongings of an unlucky few."

"Thank God that, ever since the Shaving Cream Bomber, you can't check luggage anymore," Avery noted. "Or security could take a week."

"Right now, the TSA couldn't care less about bombs!" Ryan said. "But they are checking the inside sleeves of suitcases, and sometimes ripping the linings out. They're prying into the folds of every wallet. They're authorized to do hand searches, too; they slide their palms into your pockets, right next to the groin— unsavory, to say the least. You don't only take off your shoes but your socks. They examine the heels for signs of tampering, and pull out the insoles. You could haul a rocket launcher through Reagan, and nobody would blink. But don't try slipping out with an extra ten bucks!"

"It's amazing how many cheats they're catching," Lin Yu said gleefully. "You wouldn't believe how brazenly corporate fat cats are trying to walk onto planes with briefcases bulging with cash. It was so gross. Stacks of thousand-dollar bills everywhere. All these supposedly upstanding citizens, and it looked like a drug bust."

"Except the bills scattered around the X-ray machine aren't necessarily illicit," Tom said. "I mean, we can at least presume that it is *their* money."

"We can presume nothing of the kind," Lin Yu said. "That's wealth that this entire country helped to create."

Tom took an it's-going-to-be-a-long-night breath. "According to that reasoning, no one owns their money. The funds in your bank account actually belong to everybody."

The pleasantness of Tom's tone sounded forced. Wearing an outdated suit jacket with a collar, he was a rumpled, easy-going, good-humored man, more inclined to defuse tension with a joke than to ratchet it up by getting personal. Ordinarily, his gentle Maryland accent—that would be *Murrelun* accent—further beveled his tactful opinions, but events this fall had put even the laid-back on edge.

"Morally, your money does belong to everybody," Ryan said. "The creation of capital requires the whole apparatus of the state to protect property rights, including intellectual property. Private enterprise is dependent on the nation as a whole for an educated workforce, transportation networks, and social order. No country, no fortune."

"Yadda, yadda," Lowell said. "We've all read *Fair Game*." (Liar. In his resentment of the fuss made over it, Avery's husband had never brought himself to read past a few pages of the introduction.)

"I'll grant you this much." Tom was making an almighty effort to remain affable, for which Avery was grateful. " 'Kay, for the last several years inflation has bounced between 3 and 4 percent. I realize that to experts like you folks, I'll sound dumb as a coal shovel. But the figure I tripped across the other day came as a shock to *me*: with 3 percent inflation, the dollar *halves in value* every twenty-three years. That's from Fed money printing. So when I don't control what 'my' money is worth, maybe it isn't really mine in the first place. At best, it's a loan. Which Krugman can zap into ashes while it's still in my pocket, like a superhero."

"I'm afraid that's a layman's reading, Tom." When amateurs trod on his patch, Lowell rarely heeded Avery's admonition that he would better beguile his companions by acting humbly receptive, not haughtily authoritative. "And too simplistic. Inflation has to be kept positive, to prevent deflation, which is the real bogeyman. Most of that 3 to 4 percent hails from rising commodity prices, not loose monetary policy. In fact, increasing the monetary base has had all sorts of benefits for our economy. Everyone got so excitable about quantitative easing back in the teens. What happened? Jack. Most of the cash seeped, profitably for everyone, to emerging markets."

"Look, I won't argue about money supply, which is outside my purview." Tom was now sounding testy. "I was trying to make a point about these airport searches. Because in the *olden days*, meaning *two months ago*, you could take what was, by popular conceit, delusional or otherwise, *your money* out of the country or back in again, as much and as often as you wanted. So I don't see why y'all are getting het up about these terrible, criminal businessmen"—*tear-ble, crimnal bidnessmin*—"who have the gall to try and transport their own cash overseas, when in October the same behavior was perfectly legit."

"I thought there was a limit," Avery said. "Like on those Customs forms—"

"Lotta people misunderstand that, hon," Tom said. "Before Alvarado's Renunciation Address, you only had to report carrying over ten thousand dollars on a FinCEN 105. So long as you declared it, carrying more than ten grand over the border wasn't illegal, and they sure as hell didn't take it away from you, either."

"Hold it—are they confiscating the cash at the airport?" his wife Belle asked in horror—very restrained horror, since Belle Duval would remain contained and understated in the midst of an asteroid collision. Her attire was typically subtle: a creamy faint-pink top with a beige pencil skirt, a thin white scarf adding a subdued dash. Her voice was quiet; her makeup was quiet; her not-quite-blond hair may have been recently touched up with highlights, but the do itself—soft and neat— was quiet as could be. Yet Belle's was a smart quiet, her reserve an attempt to withhold judgment.

"Yup, all smuggled goods are impounded," Lowell said. "I gather these confiscations of cash are getting immense emotional, too. Fainting. Shouting matches."

"Worse," Ryan said. "One guy lay on the floor and sobbed. They had to carry him out. A woman in front of us—big enough you wouldn't want to cross her—got into a fistfight with one of the agents. Before they took his wad off him, another guy tried to set the money on fire. Meanwhile someone at the next machine over was ripping up thousand-dollar bills—which is also a federal offense, and just compounded the charges."

"Anything but let someone else have it," Lin Yu said. "Gosh, makes you think that wealth doesn't have an improving effect on people."

"Currency seizure is making a fortune for the feds," Tom said. "It's basically an 'airport departure tax,' except they get to charge whatever a passenger is packing. Minus that hundred-dollar allowance, of course. So gracious of them to let you keep a little something for a hot drink."

Avery basked in Tom's soothing provincial accent: *eh-uh-paht depah-chuh* taxes, *hunner-dollah allownse*. So many *Warshingtonians*, as Tom would say, were blow-ins from elsewhere that friends born in the region were blessedly anchoring. Tom made her feel she lived somewhere in particular.

"Call it a tax, then," Lin Yu said. "Probably the first taxes the douche bags have ever paid."

"You have a doctorate in economics," Belle said to Lin Yu, politely but firmly. "You must know that's not likely the case. People of means pay the vast proportion of federal income taxes—"

"I've always admired that 'airport departure' gambit," Lowell said, keeping conversation light as he poured another round of wine. "Popular in Africa. You have to pay to be allowed to leave. Like being held hostage. It shows a healthy humility about the state of your nation: 'We know you'll fork over just about anything to get out of here.'"

"Pretty soon," Tom said quietly, "we may be willing to pay just about anything to get out of the United States."

Sharing her husband's wish that this early in the evening the gathering not get too dark, Avery intervened. "Think about it: no way are those TSA officers hanging around that much hard cash without picking an occasional twenty off the floor."

Lowell chuckled. "More than a twenty. I heard the New York airports are feeding frenzies. But what gripes me is that hundred-dollar limit. You can't get a taxi home from the airport with a hundred bucks."

"But why are so many people trying to get cash out of the country," Belle asked, "at the risk of having to forfeit it all?"

"Foreign exchange in the US is suspended indefinitely," Ryan said. "Since the initial crash, the dollar has been dropping, oh, two-tenths of a percent or so almost every day. The über-rich are frantically trying to bundle their booty to London or Hong Kong—anywhere they can convert it to another currency that will hold its value. Bancors, usually—whose value is going up slightly, to Alvarado's chagrin."

"But if the value of the dollar outside the country is so low," Belle said, "why consolidate the loss?"

"These are greedy people," Ryan said. "For whom anything is better than nothing."

"What's so 'greedy,' Tom said, "about wanting to safeguard some tiny fraction of the worth of money you may have worked hard to earn?"

"Oh, please," Lin Yu said. "Do you know anything about the people we're talking about? The only 'hard work' they do is poke at a fleX to check their hedge funds, or—even more debilitating—transfer the proceeds after some squillionaire parent dies. They're not digging ditches."

"It can be a mistake," Belle said carefully, "to throw the upper middle class and the 'über-rich' in the same boat. The moderately well off may not, as you say, dig ditches. But they often put in quite long hours and may still struggle to pay mortgages and tuition—"

"Not the poor little rich people routine!" Lin Yu cried. "I've heard the tear-jerk stories—about how all over DC the affluent can't afford childcare anymore. Well, the nannies are losing their jobs. I know where my sympathy lies."

"Ever notice, with these folks," Tom murmured in Avery's ear, "how *injustice* only applies to the hard-up? Nothing unfair can possibly happen to you if you own more than one pair of shoes."

Having recently earned her doctorate, Lin Yu worked at a nonprofit, the Real American Way (on the left and right alike, outfits trying to co-opt patriotism all sounded the same). Alas, the redistributive policies that RAW promoted—vastly higher property, inheritance, and upper-bracket income taxes; a blanket 2 percent wealth tax on all cash, investments, and tangible assets—were the very policies from which anyone in a position to give money away would recoil, and the organization was chronically underfunded. So on her do-gooder salary, Lin Yu was unlikely to have experienced a vertiginous drop in net worth during the last two months. Like Tom, Avery was queasy about these heedless opinions, which applied exclusively to other people and cost their advocate nothing. Those ready refills of imported Viognier notwithstanding, Lin Yu's hosts were another matter. Oh, Avery had no idea how severely their family's circumstances had been damaged; with his expertise, obviously Lowell handled that side of things, and she'd been too frightened to ask for specifics. Yet she could still feel the wind in her ears, as if riding an elevator in freefall. Making a note to herself that inviting Ryan and Lin Yu had probably been a mistake, she slipped away to sear the fish.

I was telling Avery earlier this evening how much it breaks my heart to see all these panicking bastards scrambling out at the bottom of the market," Lowell opined at the head of the table.

"*If* it's the bottom," Ryan countered from the foot of the table.

"That very anxiety is a trap," Lowell said. "Suckers slosh in when the market's frothy, and freak when it tanks. The key is to keep your nerve. I'll want credit for this later, Biersdorfer: the dollar's going to recover and then some. So will the Dow."

"A century ago," Ryan said, "the Dow only returned to its pre-Depression valuation after twenty-six years. In that long, you'll be in your mid-seventies."

"I've had it up to my eyeballs with this superstition that history is repeating itself at a tidy base-ten interval," Lowell said. "Whole sectors of the economy are hale, and with the dollar so devalued our exports will undercut Vietnam's."

Avery wished her husband wouldn't stab at his blue-fin so distractedly; that ginger dressing had come out smashing. And she thirsted for a change of subject. It was all her patients wanted to discuss as well, or the few who showed up: what had happened to their investments. So drear.

Ryan shook his head paternally. "You're kidding yourself, Stackhouse. Stocks are only headed further down. It took three solid years of unrelenting decline for the Dow to drop to its nadir in late 1932. From 381 to *41*, remember? You should get out while you can still rescue some spare change."

"Thanks for spreading the gloom, Biersdorfer. It drives prices knee-high, making this the time to buy," Lowell insisted. "I'm scarfing up every depressed large cap I can."

Avery's ears pricked up. "You're *what*?"

"Picking up bargains. Nothing you don't do at Macy's, my dear." *Macy's* came out with an incipient lisp. He'd had a fair bit of wine. Everyone had. The whole evening had been laced with the End of Days hysteria that drove Avery's younger brother to a muddy field in Gloversville, but which drove normal people to drink.

"I may not know the fine points of our situation," Avery said, hardly savoring her own tuna, "but gambling whatever pittance is left on more plummeting stocks is insane."

From the chair opposite, Belle caught Avery's eye. Trying times maybe, but it wasn't seemly to conduct marital spats about money at table.

Avery shot her friend a returning glare. Fuck decorum. She and Lowell had three kids in private schools who would all expect, and had a right to expect, Ivy League educations. The mortgage on this townhouse was massive. All that at stake, and what did her husband do? *Act* optimistic in order to *feel* optimistic, as if by playing the Pied Piper of Pollyanna he could lead everybody else, and history itself, into la-la land. Usually, he was determined to be right for the sake of his pride. Now he was desperate to be right for the sake of their survival. But really, really *needing* to be right rather than merely *wanting* to be right didn't affect *being* right, as opposed to fatally off the beam, by an iota.

"The slide has already slowed," Lowell told his wife.

"If you're so sure everything will turn out pink, why'd you order me to Chase in November to clean out our accounts? Remember, when they finally re-opened the banks?"

Lowell blushed. She was embarrassing him, in public, on purpose. "What I remember is you didn't do it."

"I wasn't going to spend all day in the rain in a line that snaked around an entire city block, when by the time I got to the counter they'd be out of cash anyway. But *you* were the one who made fun of everybody afterwards. The ones who stood outside banks in the rain."

"I only made fun of the people who lined up to pull out their money *after* the Fed promised to provide liquidity," Lowell said coldly. "And *after* Alvarado clarified that bonds may have been voided, but Federal Deposit Insurance remained in force. Before that assurance, it was rational to worry that some banks would fold."

"They 'provided liquidity' by printing money," Tom said quietly, to no one in particular. "And they'll cover FDIC claims by printing more."

"What I've found fascinating," Belle said, diplomatically directing the conversation elsewhere, "is the difference between the way Americans rallied around FDR, and how the public has responded to the gold recall from Alvarado. People are simply refusing to cough it up."

"I had one patient so indignant," Avery said, "that she wanted to go out and *buy* some gold, under the table, just so she could refuse to hand it over."

"Fortunately, most compliance doesn't rely on probity and patriotism," Ryan said. "ETFs, mining stocks, bullion on deposit—the Treasury neatly commandeered everything on the record in one fell swoop." He smiled. "Compensation was deliciously risible. A stunning laying of waste to what economic survivalists imagined was the ultimate safe bet."

"Yes, it was like the Darwin Awards," Lowell said. "*Species eliminates ninnies clutching arcane medium of exchange like teddy bear.* Man, that poor fool Mark Vandermire must be busted."

"On the QT," Avery asked the table, "anyone here slip a tinkling baggie into the rose bed?"

"Theoretically," Belle said, glancing at Tom, "I can see why some couples might withhold their wedding rings."

"I really thought Alvarado should have exempted rings," Avery said.

With a nod toward Ryan and Lin Yu, Lowell said, "The left would have squawked about sports stars and Wall Street wives keeping engagement rings the size of bowling balls."

"But all that government propaganda," Tom said, " 'bout how we been 'attacked' and we all have to 'pull together' and make 'sacrifices'—it hasn't worked. I loved the InnerTube video of that sumbitch flinging jewelry off the Golden Gate."

"Some of the pushback is anti-Lat," Lin Yu said. "Those videos are always of white people. It's significant that it's Alvarado's policy. They won't abdicate gold to a *foreigner.*"

"Americans have despised the federal government since way before Alvarado, hon," Tom said. "The main difference this time is they got good reason. At Justice, we been charged with going after gold scofflaws, and I got to say I'm uncomfortable with the job. I thought I grew up in a country where you could own gold, or silver, or mud, or *bancors*—whatever stuff you took a fancy to long as it wasn't, like, heroin. In a truly free country, you should prob'ly be able to buy heroin, too. This policy rubs me the wrong way. I don't relish being dragged into enforcing it."

"The US has confiscated assets en masse since the advent of income tax," Belle countered reasonably; she'd drunk noticeably less than everyone else. "And never mind lousy old money. Historically, Uncle Sam has taken your *sons.*"

"Speaking of which, there's a rumor going around," Lin Yu said, "and it's leaking from more than one department. I've heard the whole reason the administration has called in the gold is to give it to the Chinese. To buy Beijing off. To keep from having a war. To prevent, you know, even an invasion."

It felt a little awkward. Lin Yu was American born and bred, but she bore the countenance of divided loyalties. Badmouthing Lats or peoples of scale, of course, was beyond the pale. Yet ever since China replaced the US as the world's largest economy, suspicion or even outright loathing of the Chinese had achieved an unnerving acceptability. It seemed that no matter how right-on America grew, one group or another would be designated as okay to hate. In a pinch, you could round on the bigots themselves— which is why Avery was scrupulous about keeping it secret, even from Lowell, that she hadn't voted for Alvarado.

"I gather that's why we didn't only default on foreign-held debt," Belle said. "If American investors took an even worse hit, we were less apt to start World War Three."

"Not sure I'd credit that rumor about the gold, Lin Yu," Lowell said. "Beijing doesn't have that big a beef. Turns out the bancor was in the works for years—and Christ, where's all that American surveillance when you really need it? That's why Beijing started quietly buying shorter-term securities with their current account surplus. Their dollar holdings were in three-month T-bills by the end, and plenty of the bills had matured. The Chinese were ready to be welshed on.

Which is the best evidence yet for their having actively conspired to crash the dollar."

" 'Kay, but . . . ," Tom said. "Sorry for the cliché: Beijing does still care about face."

"Screw the gold. Let 'em have it." Lowell said. "What matters is the bancor. Now, I still think it'll prove another euro. These ideology-driven currency unions never work, and we could be back to the dollar as the world's leading reserve currency in a couple of years. But meanwhile prohibiting American companies from holding bancors is catastrophic. Corporations can organize shell companies, but small business is being crucified. How are they supposed to import bancor-denominated commodities?"

"Alvarado is playing a game of brinkmanship." Everyone turned to the doorway. It was Goog. "He figures if he can deprive even American allies access to the US market, he can strangle the baby currency in its crib. But the American market is smaller comparatively than it used to be. So the question isn't whether we can live without them, but whether they can live without us."

Lowell clapped. "Bravo! Chip off the block. A bit cynical, kiddo. But I like that line about 'strangling the baby currency in its crib.' Classy."

"We're doing 'American entities should be allowed to trade in bancors' in Debate Club. I'm affirmative. In the new year, we're doing 'The United States will never be able to borrow again.' Dad says I should take the negative. Dad says Argentina defaulted in 2001, and came back a roaring success only four years later. Dad says pretty soon everyone was 'bending over backwards' to loan them money—some of the same banks, hedge funds, and companies that had been burned. Dad says America's going to bounce back even faster."

Tom said, "Yeah, well, you want to win that debate, hon, best leave off the *Dad says*." Everyone but Ryan laughed.

Goog's visit relaxed the table somewhat, and they let him show off a bit more before Lowell shooed the boy to bed. It was obvious: Goog's know-it-all loquacity could abruptly get on Lowell's nerves because his son sounded just like him.

Given most of the evening's conversational fare, Belle's segue into how terrifying even simple surgery had become in a world of failing antibiotics qualified as light relief. She said that chemotherapy, which weakened the immune system, had become much more perilous with the prevalence of antibiotic-resistant bacteria, and at the very point at which designer drugs could be perfectly tailored to the individual patient.

"These bespoke drugs may be miraculous, but they're exorbitant!" she said. "Medicare is groaning under the strain. Alvarado may have declared a 'reset,' but the entitlement burden will simply run the debt back up again in no time."

"How do you run up a debt if you can't get a loan?" Avery asked. "Maybe 'Deadbeat Nation' will refurbish its reputation in only a few years, but there's no way anyone's going to loan America a dime right now. So unless our taxes double—which for us would mean giving the IRS more than we earn—I don't understand where the money for those individually tailored chemo drugs of yours is going to come from."

"They-will-print-it," Tom said emphatically.

"Tom, I'm sensing a running theme here," Lowell said, no longer disguising his annoyance.

Tom took another hefty slug of wine. "I happen to have given this some thought. Your wife's dead on: for a right smart number of years to come, nobody's gonna loan us a sou. So the deficit'll be covered by cash conjured up from ether. 'Cause foreigners want dollars like a hole in the head, the funny money's gonna flood our own country and nowhere else. Am I right, or what? You're the *expert*." This time the deference was sour.

Lowell said, "Well, that's only one direction the Fed could go—"

"Bang," Tom said, "inflation shoots through the roof."

"It *doesn't matter*," Ryan announced at the far end of the table, where he'd been brooding silently for half an hour.

Tom guffawed. "Tell the Germans in the 1920s that it 'didn't matter'—"

"Tom, in the field," Lowell said, "nothing could be more hackneyed. The Fed can always raise interest rates—"

"I am *tired*"—Ryan was more like drunk, actually—"of listening to some bloodless Keynesian technocrat who thinks an economy is a widget you just got to tighten a few screws on, and not made of *people*—most of whom are a whole lot harder up than the pampered fussbudgets around this table. And I am *tired* of listening to this whining and carping and hand-wringing from a bunch of spoiled, affluent white folks worried about where their next side of smoked salmon is coming from and how much it's going to cost."

"He doesn't mean he didn't like your appetizer," Lin Yu directed to Avery with a nervous smile.

Ryan thumped the table and the silver rattled. "This whole package. The debt renunciation, the stock market crash, the gold recall, the poor barracuda corporations who aren't allowed to hold bancors . . . The decimation of fat-cat pensions, the incineration of the bloated portfolios of the über-rich . . . It's the *best thing that ever happened* to this country, you hear me? It'd got out of control, you hear me? The preening rent seekers sipping another esoteric flavor of martini, wracking their brains over how to waste another billion dollars today, casting about for whatever else they could *possibly* still want. Sucking the country dry while everyone else scrapes by, terrified of turning on their central heating when it's fifteen below. That's not what America was ever meant to be, you hear me? *We hold these truths to be self-evident: that all men are created equal.* So screw the plutocrats. The upper echelon in this country is *wiped out. Finished.* Which I think is fucking great. What's kid-speak for 'fucking great' again? Right, *malicious.* I think it's fucking *malicious.*"

"Ryan and I agree," Lin Yu chimed in.

"What a shock," Avery whispered to Tom.

"This moment," Lin Yu said. "At long last, it's the great leveler. In fact, Ryan and I are thinking of co-writing another book. We thought we'd call it *The Corrections,* and distribute it free online. What we're going through, it's better than a revolution. More like a divine intervention. At long last, we have a shot at real justice in this country."

"What," Tom said incredulously. "By *making everybody poor?*"

"Better everyone is somewhat less well off than we keep tolerating the grotesque economic disparities of the last thirty years," Lin Yu said. "As Americans, we can return to first principles. This is a chance at reboot and rebirth. A chance for transformation and redemption. An opportunity to eschew corruption, and cronyism, and inequity, and division, and re-create this country from the ground up. To be the *United* States again, to *live* in a united state. To restore this nation to the egalitarian utopia the founding fathers envisioned. We should all be proud to be participating in this watershed."

"*Are* you participating?" Tom charged across from her. "'Cause participating means losing something. Losing a *heck of a lot*. Waking up and finding your pension—sorry, *fat-cat pension*, as I gather even the pensions of firemen and schoolteachers are called—waking up and finding your savings for retirement have been halved overnight. But you can't have much of a pension, hon. Or savings; more likely you're drowning in student loan debt, which any runaway inflation in the pipeline would marvelously melt away. Only way you could have taken an investment hit would be through Ryan there. Who"—Tom swiveled to the foot of the table—"mysteriously don't count hisself as rich—'scuse me, *über-rich*, apparently the only color *rich* come in. Sorry for raising an awkward subject, old boy, but you must've cleaned up right smart after *Fair Game*."

"Not that my finances are any of your business—"

"Why not?" Tom said. "You regard everyone else's finances as your business. Fact is, you made a killing from sticking your nose into other people's bank accounts."

"Hardly a killing," Ryan said disdainfully. "Internet piracy was already approaching its zenith. For the handful of the upstanding, Amazon was discounting at 70 percent. As for what small royalties I did recoup, my ex-wife walked off with half. Calling me wealthy would be absurd."

"Always loved it," Tom said, "you having used a treatise on the evils of the rich to join the club."

"For pity's sake, darling," Belle said. "You don't get rich by *writing* anything."

"It's a slippery category in any case," Lowell said. "*Rich* means anyone who makes more money than you do."

"I didn't mean he flies his own jet," Tom said. "Point is, our friend Biersdorfer here is worth something. But last time we all get together for dinner? Him and I jawed about how he'd got out of the market. It was 'over-heated,' he said. Fucker's all in rental property, he told me. And for now, hard assets are safe. They'll weather currency depreciation, they'll weather inflation. And he sure as heck wasn't holding any Treasury securities. Know how you can tell? *He's not pissed off.* So no wonder Ryan and Lin Yu think this whole debacle's so fabulous. It don't affect them!"

"You have any bonds, Tom?" Lowell asked softly.

"Yes, we did. And I feel personally betrayed. By my employer. By my country. It don't seem like any triumphant return of the true American spirit to entice people to loan you money and then pull out your empty pockets with an embarrassed little grin. 'Renunciation' my ass. Regular people call that *stealing*. You realize that beyond the standard five-K deduction for market losses, they won't even allow you to take the defaulted principal off your *taxes?*"

"Oh, and why should you?" Ryan snarled. "All investment entails risk. Any bond can default, which you know going in."

"Not *US Treasuries.* That's how we've got away with paying such miserable interest for decades: *safest investment in the world!* Which makes reneging on repayment disgraceful. I don't blame folks from Turkey to Nicaragua for burning KFCs and McDonald's. Over here, we got ever reason to self-mortify. Those two bombings of federal buildings near the Mall? Perfectly understandable." After what had to be his second bottle of wine, that came out *perfickly unnustannable.* "What I don't understand is why this whole town's not burnt down."

"Because," Belle said, "the people with the 'broadest shoulders' who lost their shirts aren't the rioting sort." She gestured to Tom and Ryan. "Why, look at you two. Standing red-faced by your chairs, hands lifted at your sides, quick-draw? But neither of you has thrown a glass or a punch. You've got to worry about the state of American manhood. Maybe this really is the end of the empire. Now, let's all help Avery clean up."

Collecting plates that rattled loudly in the silence, Avery was chagrined; she had never hosted a dinner party that had grown so uncivil. Yet later she would look back on the fractious evening as positively elegiac—indeed, as profoundly civilized. In a few months' time, even if you were so rash as to invite other people to dinner, you wouldn't be sure whether your friends really wanted to see you, or if they just wanted a free meal.

Chapter 6
Search and Seizure

Since Florence didn't think of herself as someone who would own any gold, it had taken her days to realize, with a sudden stab, that she did.

After her Barnard graduation, Grand Man had convened a blowout lunch for the extended family in a top-floor restaurant on the Upper West Side. The paterfamilias tinged his glass after dessert. He thought it fitting, he said, for his grandchild to possess some small token from his own grandfather's estate—the majestic Second Empire mansion with a broad, canopied front porch in Mount Vernon, Ohio, of which Florence had inherited a few digitized sepia snapshots. Stocked in her imagination with crystal, starched linen, and sterling cutlery, the imposing home of her great-great-grandparents, long ago torn down, emblemized the very opulence she philosophically deplored. Yet those faded archival photos of Bountiful House, lovingly transferred from smart phone to tablet to speX to fleX, always filled her with a mournfulness that was hauntingly familiar. For years, Florence had been disquieted by a recurrent dream, in which a big blue swimming pool shimmers barely out of reach—on the other side of a locked gate, restricted by a prohibitively stiff entry fee, or useless without her swimsuit. She would awake both stirred and melancholy.

In dreams about those alluring pools, she was never allowed to dive into the deep end, but the gift with which her flamboyant grandfather bestowed her that afternoon fostered the sensation of dangling a toe in the water. The box was the size that held stationery in the days when people sent thank-you notes, its sturdy cardboard mottled, its corners soft and gray. Only the ribbon was new. Grand Man apologized that the contents were of no practical utility whatsoever, and he was right. Nestled in brittle yellowed satin, inside lay two matching miniature goblets, about four inches high— for schnapps or port perhaps, though chances were good that no one had drunk a drop from either. The stems were the deep cobalt glass of European cathedral windows. Engraved with ELLIOT IRA MANDIBLE on one and DORA ROSE MANDIBLE on the other, the cups were gold. And not merely plate. Funny how you could tell: a thin, crass coating refracted light; the butter of pure metal invited light inside. Grand Man had no idea what the goblets symbolized; maybe they acknowledged a wedding anniversary, or expressed civic gratitude. Elliot Mandible had given away a fair portion of his fortune, albeit not nearly as much as he kept.

The finely wrought pair was a rare tangible connection to a past that Florence had otherwise repudiated. Like so many of the absurd objects that wealthy people both manufactured and attracted, the goblets were merely money reconformed. They were never intended to be folded unassumingly into the conduct of daily life, but would always be aggressively given things. Thus they displayed a particular ostentation on the part of the benefactor, for the set was a present that never stopped presenting itself. The goblets were silly and all for show. The world in which they existed didn't vary a jot from the world in which they'd never been crafted in the first place.

Consequently, Florence adored them. Such a grindingly pragmatic person, she treasured the midget stemware for the very fact that it was of no earthly use to anybody. She'd tucked the goblets tenderly into their aged box each of the dozen-some times she'd moved, and currently stored them on the highest shelf of what was farcically dubbed the *master* bedroom, slipped so close to the wall for safe-keeping that you couldn't even see them without climbing on a chair. She was indifferent to the cups' value in metallurgical terms. They were precious because they were hers. Thus the prospect of pitching those artisanal heirlooms into a US Treasury grab bag, where the cobalt stems would shatter, and the cups would await smelting into lumps, all for the sake of "patriotism," whatever that was, struck Florence as not simply anathema, but out of the question.

She first remembered the Bountiful House goblets in the shelter's staff room; a dirty espresso glass by the sink dislodged the memory. She fretted for the rest of the day, and rushed for the bus the moment her shift ended. Back home, she scuttled upstairs, stood on an armchair, and slid the keepsakes from the shelf, dusting the cups before resting them in the mottled box stashed in her dresser. All the while she felt oddly watched, jumping at creaks from the hallway so slight that they must have been imagined. Using what lay at hand, she pulled a spare blanket from under the bed, wrapped the box multiple times around, and stuffed the bundle back under the bed in the very middle, surrounded by duvets and guest pillows.

Someday this lunacy was sure to pass, and one could again prop a couple of shiny yellow knickknacks on a high shelf without being fined a quarter of a million dollars—the very thought of which sent her pulse into the stroke zone. Once the "abdication deadline" of November 30 uneventfully came and went, she was able to think about something else.

Until, that is, a rude knock thumped the front door one weekend in January, a few days after Willing's fourteenth birthday.

"Mom," Willing said placidly, as if this happened every day. "It's the Army."

"You're joking." Oh, word was out about the house-to-house searches, but Florence had assumed the police, National Guard, and US Army units drafted into the operation would stick to neighborhoods ritzy enough to make their efforts worthwhile.

There were two of them. The bigger and taller white fellow was dressed in regulation combat fatigues, but by force of sheer sullenness managed to look slovenly. His heavy face conveyed an impression of both stupidity and cunning; perhaps it was the tiny eyes. His slight subcontinental companion stood officiously upright, and neither's bearing was apologetic. At a glance, contrary to cliché, there was no Good Cop.

"Can I help you?" Florence said coldly, keeping the screen door closed and allowing the front door open only a few inches. It was in the teens, with a skim of snow on the porch, and she'd splurged on putting up the thermostat to fifty-eight.

"Don't need no help," the big one said, spinning the laminated ID around his neck with a contemptuous flick. "Comin' in, lady." He opened the screen door himself.

Florence barred his way. "Excuse me, do you have a warrant?"

"Got better than a warrant," the lout said. "Got a law. Let's move, Ajay."

"I don't allow guns in this house," she insisted.

"Ain't that a shame. 'Cause the US Army don't leave M-17s on the porch like shoes outside a mosque."

Armed also with metal detectors, the two trooped into the foyer uninvited, neglecting to wipe their boots on the doormat and getting black snow on the rug.

"Why are you wearing that camouflage when we don't have any trees?" Willing asked, studying them from the stairs. "If you don't want people to see you in this neighborhood, your uniforms should look like aluminum siding."

"That smart mouth's not doing your mom any favors, kid," the big private said.

"I am giving you a final opportunity before we search the premises," the smaller soldier said in a mincing Indian accent, "to declare any gold, even in very small quantity on a larger object, that you have failed to turn in to the federal government. The penalties will be less severe if you surrender hoarded material. If we find it instead, you will be subject to criminal prosecution."

"What the fuck are these assholes doing in our house?" Esteban had a deadly authority problem.

"They're ransacking every inch of this dump," the first soldier said, "if members of the United States Armed Forces get called *assholes* one more time by some hothead Lat who obviously got no real loyalty to this country."

"Tear up our house, I'll sue you to kingdom come, Army or no," Esteban said.

"Know how many times a day I hear that? About a hundred. Good luck, bozo."

"I can do you for racial abuse," Esteban said.

"I did say *Lat*," the big guy said. "Not *spic* or *wetback* or *mexdreck*."

"Mention versus use," Willing said. Florence had no idea what he was talking about.

"You have anything to declare, ma'am?" the Asian repeated.

"I'm *declaring* that I will photograph any unnecessary destruction of the 'premises,' which I will report." Though Florence had a rather unexamined idea of herself as brave, her hands were shaking. No goblets, however charming, were worth ten years in prison.

As she groped for the best way of introducing an epiphany of "just remembering" some "old family trinkets," they started in the living room, where the Asian pulled out all the leather cushions of Grand Man's wine-colored sofa from Oyster Bay. It was the household's only quality piece, and may have given the soldiers a misimpression of the family's circumstances. After shoving a hand into all the crevices, the soldier made a display of pretending to find a lump, and slit one of the cushions with a box cutter, clearly carried for the purpose of ruining the citizenry's most treasured appointments.

"Is *my* government paying for that upholstery's repair?" Esteban asked sourly.

"That's what they make duct tape for, sir," the soldier said, pulling out stuffing.

The gratuitous slashing of that sumptuous sofa suffused Florence with a distinctive rage: the suppressed, fist-in-mouth kind of fury that it isn't in your interest to give in to. So, fine, she wouldn't berate these soldiers, and she wouldn't use profanity. However stiffly, she kept her body still; her bite was clenched, but her expression remained impassive. Yet now she could not bear to reward them by proving herself another lying "hoarder" and letting them waltz off with her beloved graduation present—with which she could easily picture these creeps toasting her degradation with cheap whiskey later this evening.

The big one trod methodically over the floor, as if to check for hollow-sounding boards. But the thin wooden parquet was laid over flimsy framing, and it all sounded hollow. When they dragged the furniture about, the feet scored scratches in the flooring, and they didn't put the furniture back. After removing the prints from the walls and piling them on the ravaged sofa, the soldiers knocked on the Sheetrock with a pretense of forensic diagnosis, though the walls all sounded hollow, too. They pulled books from shelves, flipping them with an air of incredulity that anyone would keep these things for anything but carved-out caches.

When they moved to the kitchen, the big one emptied a canister of flour onto the counter and stirred, as if planning to make homemade pasta. The self-important Asian fellow pulled out the pots and pans and piled them on the floor, while his partner poured out the tub in the sink, splashing greasy gray water all over the clean cookware at his feet. They even went into the refrigerator, as if gold might keep better there; when Midas appeared not to have touched the vegetable drawer, they settled for two cold chicken legs. Out the back door, they went over Florence's sad excuse for a garden with their metal detectors, getting terribly excited around the rosemary bush, the only herb that she'd been able to nurse through the winter's biting cold. Hacking at the hard ground with her own shovel, they did manage to sever the roots of the plant, but the corroded key ring that had set their detector ticking, shinier versions of which the Chinese manufactured by the shipload, was unlikely to make a substantial contribution to settling the national debt.

Once the defenders of the free world hit the second floor, Florence grew silently hysterical. Gripping Willing's hand, she followed in horror as the duo made a beeline for the parental bedroom. The Asian emptied the jewelry box on her dresser, poking impatiently through broken watches, hair ties, ChapSticks, and a few rhinestone pieces from a brief bling period that Florence no longer wore. After tossing a confetti of socks, bras, and panties onto the floor—"You wouldn't believe how many folks actually hide shit in their *underwear drawer,*" the big soldier said scornfully—they began to drag out all the spare duvets, blankets, and pillows from under the bed, unfurling as they went. Florence broke into a cold sweat, and her heart beat in her teeth. Maybe it wasn't too late to make a "declaration" and escape a prison sentence. Before they reached the middle, she blurted out, "Wait, there is one thing, maybe I should have—"

"No, Mom," Willing interrupted, meeting her eyes with a shake of his head. "I checked that necklace you were so worried about. I even did a scratch test, with one of the free kits the cops were giving away on Jay Street. It's only brass. I know he was trying to seem nice and everything, but Esteban was pulling a fast one on your birthday."

"What's this about a necklace?" the lunk asked warily.

Willing pointed at the junky-looking pile the Asian had amassed, then separated out a pretty collar with a tiny dangling opal. "That one."

The heavy soldier picked it up, bent the metal, and dropped it. "You're right, kid. Piece of shit."

Right then, the Asian reached the middle-most blanket under the bed and unwound the wadding with a flourish.

Nothing clattered out. Which was fortunate, since Florence was on the brink of throwing up, and flushing the toilet midday would have been a waste of water.

As rapidly as the soldiers had rampaged into their house, they seemed to weary of the pillage. They tromped downstairs and let the screen door slam, leaving the front door open to ensure that the interior dropped another ten degrees.

It didn't make any sense. They'd sifted through the flour, but hadn't poked one head into the attic, or taken even a cursory stroll through Kurt's lodgings in the basement, when either space could have stored all the gold in Tutankhamen's tomb.

Lightheaded from adrenaline, Florence shuffled through the sofa stuffing to close and double-lock the door. As he pushed furniture back into place, Esteban was fuming around the living room to which she'd exiled him, lest his temper incite the soldiers to further destruction. Peering out the front window to confirm that the men had moved on to ruin someone else's day, she turned to Willing, who had resumed his perch of choice on the third stair. When searching his face, she often found herself looking for clues as to who his father was. It was that bling period.

"How did you know . . . ?" she whispered.

"I know about everything," he said, "that I need to know about."

"It was you," she said. "The creaks, while I was wrapping them up."

"You picked a roachbar hiding place."

"And you chose a different one." He nodded. "Wasn't that taking a big risk?"

"Not if it was a good place. Mom. Think about it. All these houses. All the closets. All the floorboards and boxes. When stuff made of gold is so small. It's impossible. The house-to-house searches are ridiculous. Except not really."

"Except not really."

"They're trying to scare you. If they scare you bad enough, they don't have to find it. You'll give it to them. Even with you: it almost worked."

"¿Qué estás conspirando?" Esteban said, pausing in his reshelving of splayed Steinbecks. *"Tenemos mucho trabajo aquí."* He and Willing often chattered together in Spanish, in which Florence was less fluent than her son, and the lingual bond bred a distinctive intimacy. But Florence and Willing generated an intensity that even a live-in boyfriend of five years couldn't rival, and Esteban sometimes seemed jealous.

"Es mejor si no lo sabe," Willing said.

"You going to tell me where you've stashed them?" Florence asked quietly.

"No. It's better you don't know, either."

"So when those boomerpoops come back I'll be petrified no matter where they look."

"They won't come back," Willing said confidently. "The government will figure out that they aren't scaring enough gold out of people to pay the soldiers and policemen to do the scaring. The government can't borrow money anymore. For now, that means they won't waste it."

"*For now.* You're such a weird boy."

"It's more complicated than that. But yes. For now. Later there's going to be a different problem. The government will have lots of money. But it won't be worth anything. Which is the same as having no money." He didn't often, but Willing smiled, slightly. He seemed pleased with himself.

"Kiddo, a little internet is a dangerous thing."

"That's right," he agreed. "A *little* internet is immense dangerous. A *lot* of internet is dangerous in a different way. Dangerous to other people. Not to you."

At the time, the Army raid had seemed high drama. In short order, there was grander theater to be found in the grocery store.

Sunday afternoons, Florence laid in supplies for the week, Willing wheeling the rickety metal cart to drag the haul home. A few years before, they'd often strolled a block and a half up to the commercial drag on Church Street to, say, pick up a bargain baggie of cinnamon sticks from a street vendor for two bucks and take in the bustle of blazing fabric in which busty women from Jamaica were clad, but lately they didn't bother with the detour. Now that the enterprises had been replaced by Pilates gyms, yoga parlors, and pet groomers, Florence actually missed the check-cashing outfits, African hair-braiding salons, pawn shops, and candy stores with three sticky sour balls stuck at the bottom of a single jar that were obviously fronts for dealing cocaine. The shaved-ice carts on corners long before cleared off, with their lurid syrups of cobalt, chartreuse, and hot pink, the area had been literally drained of color.

Naturally, she carried more cash to the supermarket as the years went by, what with routine inflation, crop failures, energy price spikes, and the relentless rise of demand from Asia. Her modest cost-of-living adjustments from Adelphi never reflected the steep increase of her expenditures on food.

But this was different.

Oh, make no mistake, by Christmas, Florence had learned to ignore any merchandise that was imported. Their family was already accustomed to doing without fripperies like Greek olives, Italian Parmesan, Japanese rice vinegar, and even Mexican dried chilies (to Esteban's dismay). Soon the imports disappeared from the shelves anyway. According to Brendan, their neighbor the investment banker (*former* investment banker; the entire financial industry had melted overnight), the country's international trade had come to a virtual standstill. Exporters couldn't deposit bancors in American banks but had to employ clumsy intermediaries offshore. With capital controls still in place, importers had to get every transfer of dollars abroad approved by the Department of Commerce, which was overwhelmed. Yet by February something was going funny with domestic goods.

"I specifically remember buying a cabbage for twenty dollars in October," Florence told Willing, hefting a poor specimen of same. "This is smaller and crappier, and it's twenty-five dollars. From the same store. Do the math: at that rate, what will a cabbage cost next October?"

"Forty dollars," Willing said readily. "But never mind. I'm sick of cabbage."

"Well, so am I! But look around you. What else are we going to buy?"

For an urban grocery, Green Acre Farm on Utica Avenue was well stocked, having been given a flashy makeover after the watercress-and-wasabi set began systematically displacing the Caribbean immigrants who previously dominated the neighborhood. But now the piles of zucchini ($24/lb.), 7 oz. bags of spinach (formerly 10 oz.; $15 each), and snap peas ($31/lb.) might as well have been museum exhibits. Florence settled on a ratty bunch of kale ($18) and the lone bag left in the quick-sale section, a brown-tipped head of Boston lettuce she didn't especially want.

By April, that cabbage was ahead of schedule. It was $30.

Florence's fellow shelter employees were obsessed with the cost of meals. Though masking-tape labels on brown-bag sandwiches in the staff-room fridge bristled with exclamation marks, filching grew common; Selma decked a cleaner cold over a bologna on rye. And the topic of fast-food prices was incendiary. They competed on breaks over who could cite the most outrageous markup of the week. "Thirty-five forty-nine for a chicken and bacon wrap at Subway!" Mateo reported. "Threw the bag at the lady and walked out. Said she must think I Howard Buffett or something, and Buffett don't eat no wraps."

"Notice Taco Bell chuck the plastic menu behind the registers?" Rasta said. "Now it all digital. So they can raise the price of the enchilada/tostada combo every week without climbing a ladder."

Her pantry frugally stocked to begin with, Florence was hard- pressed to know where to economize. They ate no prepared foods, and little enough meat that she feared for her hair. Strictly speaking, the store-brand dry dog food was an indulgence, but Willing would have scraped his own plate into Milo's bowl rather than let the spaniel go hungry. So she stopped buying fresh herbs, and spurned condiments. Sadly, she foreswore ice cream. She made Willing eat cooked rice with milk for breakfast instead of corn flakes, and bought white long-grain rather than the more wholesome brown rice because processed grains were, however insensibly, cheaper. You'd think there was a limit to how much pasta a person could bear, but apparently not.

Compounding the crisis, her flexible-rate mortgage had risen two solid points, and to cover the payments she should really raise her tenant's rent. Letting out the basement was illegal; the neighborhood was zoned for single-family occupancy. Having signed no formal lease, Kurt relied on her good graces not to boost his rent by caprice. Thus far he'd kept up with his payments, but she worried about his part-time job at the florist's. In this economy, if there was anything that people could live without more readily than periwinkles she would like to know. Though she didn't think of herself as a soft touch, the prospect of asking for money he couldn't possibly spare was hateful.

One Sunday afternoon in May, they made their traditional trip to Green Acre Farm; now that they purchased so little, they left the cart at home. On the weekly shop they'd usually walk the dog, but Willing insisted on leaving Milo at home as well. He claimed that tying the mutt outside the store risked an unscru-pulous passerby getting sticky fingers of the most grisly sort: "Someone might eat him."

Florence was further nonplussed on their return journey when Willing said, "I saw that notice you left on the dining table. Your mortgage payments have gone up. This could be a problem."

"Look, buddy—not only is that my business—"

"It's our business. Mine and Esteban's and Kurt's. We live in the house, too."

"When I was your age, I didn't even know what a mortgage was."

"I told you: I know what I need to know. Maybe when you were fourteen you didn't need to know about mortgages."

"Well, I don't want you to worry"—ever a wasted admonishment—"but, yeah, it's a bit of a problem."

"Interest rates rise with inflation. Your mortgage payments will keep getting stiffer."

"And why's that, Mr. Expert—?"

"Nobody wants to lend good money and get paid back with crummy money." Willing's bored monotone implied this was obvious.

"But there's always some inflation. Interest rates don't always go up because of it. In fact, we need infla-tion. The alternative is supposed to be sort of terrible."

"That's what they want you to think."

One of her few concerns about her only child was that he inclined toward *smugness*. "All right. *What*. Since I've heard we need regular inflation, like at least 2 or 3 percent, my whole life."

"I know you have. You've been brainwashed." He sounded so cheerful. "We could easily get along with a small, steady, predictable rate of *de*flation. Inflation is a tax. Money for the government. A tax that people don't see as a tax. That's the best kind, for politicians. But inflation isn't inevitable. Starting in 1300, the British pound pretty much maintained its value for six hundred years. And that was during the Empire, when English people practically ruled the world. Great Grand Man said what's happened to the pound is a 'tragedy.' All these expressions we have, they're from that currency: *In for a penny, in for a pound. Penny wise and pound foolish.* Even the word *sterling*. It means 'excellent' and 'valuable.' But the actual money, he says, is now 'a joke.' That's because of inflation. I told Great Grand Man that *I* thought when your money is a joke, then people think you're a joke. And now the dollar is a joke, too."

"Do you feel less valuable as a person because the dollar is less valuable?"

"In a way. I haven't worked it out yet. But what's going on may not only have to do with what we can buy. It may also have to do with how we feel. Like, smaller. Maybe I feel smaller. You might not realize it, but maybe you feel smaller, too."

"I feel smaller because with the cost of groceries, I'm losing weight!" It wasn't a boast. Florence was under no illusion that she needed to slim down, and the wan quality she met in the mirror expressed the very sensation of becoming less substantial that her son seemed to share.

"*So,*" Willing introduced jauntily, "do you think now that we've bribed the Chinese with all that gold they'll leave us alone?"

"I think Beijing got what they wanted. Even if the handover was embarrassing for the United States."

"Great Grand Man says unless the gold was used to go back to a 'modified gold standard' instead, or to buy into the bancor, giving it away doesn't matter much. Just sitting there, he said, it was 'merely pretty.'"

"Well, I sure don't miss it," Florence said.

"I don't mind Spanish. But I don't want to have to learn Chinese. I've never liked the sound of it. Too high pitched. Too up in the nose."

"The Chinese aren't going to invade New York, if that's what you mean."

"Maybe not with an army," Willing said. "But haven't you seen the packages on the news? They're all over Midtown. In Saks, and Lord and Taylor. At Tiffany's, there's a line of Chinese out the door. Along with some Koreans, and Indonesians, and Vietnamese."

"They can get good deals here. It's the exchange rate."

"I *know*," Willing said scornfully. "I hate it when you tell me things I *know*. I just meant—there are lots of different ways to take places over."

"You have to be careful, talking like that. You don't want to sound racist."

"Great Grand Man says we should be grateful. Without foreign tourists, no one would be buying anything. We'd already be in another depression. Great Grand Man says for people from outside the country, everything here is practically free."

"Well, nothing's free for us! I couldn't believe how much plain old *bleach* had gone up today." They'd sprung for the gallon size, since it would only cost more next time, and the bag with the bleach was cutting into her shoulder.

"Prices aren't going up," Willing said authoritatively.

Florence snorted. "Could have fooled me!"

"They have fooled you." Willing's stride had developed a swagger. "It's the mistake people always make. They think things are getting more expensive.

Actually, everything costs the same. Prices aren't going up; the currency is going down."

"Come on. I see why the exchange rate would affect imports. Not stuff we make and grow here."

It was now an established role reversal, Willing speaking to his mother patiently, as to a child. She thought she was indulging him; he thought he was indulging her. Somehow, it worked: "Leave aside that America doesn't make anything. Tax take is way down. The deficit is big. The government can't borrow money because no one believes they'll pay it back. The Renunciation was a short-term cost-cutter: it eliminated payments on the debt. But the Federal Deposit Insurance Corporation had to pay out immense amounts after the smaller bank failures. The big banks had to be bailed out. Lots of pension losses had to be covered by the Pension Benefit Guarantee Corporation. Unemployment insurance is going up. And that's on top of Medicare, Medicaid, and Social Security, which are already more than half the budget."

"You want me to believe that at fourteen you know the difference between Medicare and Medicaid? Most people my age can't keep those programs straight."

Willing explained contemptuously, "Care is for old people, aid is for poor people. It's not rocket science. But you *said* you wanted to understand!" He never liked his line of reasoning interrupted. "They're in a corner. They can't borrow. They could raise taxes. But the rich already pay high taxes. And now their investments are gone. The rich aren't rich. So the only people left to tax are people like you and Esteban. Who can't buy cabbage. Blood from a stone, as Great Grand Man put it. What else is there to do? Photocopy the money."

She eyed him. "Such a mile-a-minute. And you used to be so shy."

"I was never shy. I was waiting to have something to say." Willing stopped and turned to her on the sidewalk with a characteristic formality, though they were almost to East Fifty-Fifth Street. "Mom, listen. It may be lucky you work for the city. I researched this. The city gets some funding from the federal government. That means your employers have access to the fake money. That's why you got such a big raise in March. And you'll keep getting raises. That's part of the problem. Lots of government payouts, like salaries, pensions, and benefits, are pegged to inflation. Meaning they have to keep printing more and more money to meet the budget, *because* they keep printing more and more money. It's what Great Grand Man calls a *feedback loop*. The whole thing snowballs, gets a life of its own. Nobody quite catches up. So your paychecks

might not get bigger fast enough. I checked the cabbage, at Green Acre. It's thirty-eight dollars now."

"Nuts," Florence said.

"Another thing," Willing said, as if going down a
list. "As your salary rises, you're going to get hit by
higher tax rates. They won't move the brackets."

"But that's not fair! What a drag."

"*Fiscal* drag," Willing corrected mirthlessly. "See,
people getting what's really happening the wrong
way around, like you have—it's how governments get
away with it. The 'everything's getting so expensive!'
thing—it makes the problem seem to be coming from
the outside. Like they can't control it. Meanwhile, they
think they're controlling it. If they secretly do control
it, that might be dishonest. But not so bad. I don't think
so. Twenty to thirty-eight dollars in seven months. I
think we're in a driverless car. But with no onboard
computer. Because the really big mistakes were made a
long time ago. You can't unmake them. You just have
to pay for them. That's what Alvarado got wrong. You
can't get out from under a debt by making a speech.
You have to pay, one way or another." Willing's tone
had grown dolorous. "I think we've started to pay."

They resumed walking the rest of the way. "So when
do you do all this talking with Great Grand Man?"

"We don't *talk*," Willing said. "We fleXt. It's clearer that way. For things that are complicated. Or that seem complicated when they aren't."

Florence was still unsettled by her son's earlier assertion that "the rich aren't rich"—especially if she could safely assume that he'd appropriated this generalization, like so much of his dissertation, from Douglas Mandible. Ideally, she was perturbed because a reversal of fortune might force her elderly relative in his final years to curtail his pleasures. But she couldn't kid herself: that wasn't it. "Never forget where information comes from, puppet. I wouldn't accept everything your great-grandfather says as gospel. He's liberal on social issues, but wealth always pulls people to the right—because they can't help wanting to keep it. Everyone has an agenda."

"That's why I *triangulate*," Willing said obscurely.

"I've been distracted, and haven't contacted him in a while. Is Great Grand Man okay?"

"I think he may be sad. But that's not what we fleXt about. I know he's immense old, but he doesn't seem old in fleXts. And he has time on his hands. Since Luella has the mind of a doorstop."

"Don't be unkind. It's not her fault."

"I could call her a doorstop to her face. She wouldn't care. I don't see why we don't shoot people like that. It would be better."

"Willing, don't talk like that."

He sighed. "It's people like Luella who help to explain what's happened. She's an expensive doorstop."

"Wait till you're old and addled. You'll want us to shoot you, too?"

"*Yes.*"

"Oh, that's what everyone says. They don't mean it, or they don't have any idea what it's really like to be old. 'Just shoot me!' It's a casual, cheap assertion that only healthy people with no imagination make."

"Great Grand Man says he'd rather be dead than end up like Luella. And he's older than she is."

"So if I get like that, you're going to shoot me?"

He said somberly, "If you want me to. I don't think it would be easy."

"I'm relieved to hear you say that."

Before dinner that evening, Florence and Esteban folded laundry in their bedroom—where they still kept the hamper that Esteban carried from Manhattan the first day of the Stone Age. Not everyone could find a laundry hamper romantic.

"Have you noticed how Willing's become more talkative?" Florence mentioned. "He's been so pulled into himself, for years. Now he's got this almost *prophetic* thing going. He exhorts. Holds forth. It's charming and creepy at the same time."

"You admiring, or complaining?" Esteban victoriously matched a stray sock with an orphan from an earlier load.

"Both, I think."

"Not a bad household resource, our own oracle."

"The soothsayer routine won't go down well with his classmates."

"Have faith," Esteban said. "Bet he keeps the I-bring-you-tidings-of-whatever to himself at school. He's not a social *bobo*."

"I'm not so sure. During these sermons of his—he seems oddly driven."

"If he's 'driven' to do anything, it's to protect you."

"From what?"

"Maybe he *can* sense something coming. We Lats have a feel for mystery, for the unseen. And you're so no-nonsense, so hard-nosed, so what-you-see-is-what-you-get."

"You admiring, or complaining?"

"Both, I think." He swept her onto the bed, and messed up her piles. To avoid confirming his rigid characterization, she didn't object.

"Mom, when you have a minute?" came from the doorway. Fair enough, they'd not closed the door, nor had they gone far. But Willing was disconcertingly un-embarrassed by sex. Maybe his mother's *no-nonsense, hard-nosed* education on the matter had made it seem ordinary.

When she'd straightened herself up and given Esteban a kiss that promised more later, Florence allowed herself to be drawn into her son's bedroom. He kept it tidy, aside from a flutter of papers on his desk and spread over the bed, all covered in equations, columns of figures, and what looked to the casual eye like astrological charts. If they read at all, Willing's generation read on fleX. How frustrating for the modern parent, to no longer be able to infer anything about a teenager's interior life from a telling shelf of books or revelatory stacks of niche-interest magazines.

Her son shut the door and announced gravely, "I would like to give Milo away."

"What on earth?" Florence exclaimed. "You love Milo."

"That's why I want to give him away." Willing's air was military.

"It flabbergasts me that you'd sacrifice the only thing you own that you adore."

"I don't own Milo. I've taken responsibility for him. So I have to act in his interest. In the long run, entrusting Milo to someone else's care is in my interest, too.

I won't kick myself for not doing what was necessary while I had the chance."

"Okay, sweetie, I know you've mixed a lot of hazy, ominous hocus-pocus with dire premonitions from Great Grand Man, who's old enough that his mind may not be at its best. But this is a serious decision, and you're going to have to explain better."

"I see multiple-choice scenarios," he said methodically. "They're all sappy. Willing takes Milo to Prospect Park. He releases the dog from the leash. Milo looks up expectantly. 'Go on!' Willing urges. Milo pants and looks trusting. Willing throws a stick. Milo races after it. Willing stalks from the park, looking stricken yet resolute. The dog catches up, with the stick. Willing kicks the dog. Milo looks hurt—mostly by betrayal. Tears stream down Willing's face. Willing kicks the dog harder, and then starts to throw rocks. At last the dog gets the message. Milo drags toward the woods, head hung low. The pet shoots a final backward glance at his master, with a look of incomprehension, of undying love. Cut.

"Or," he continued, "Willing spikes a last meal for Milo with poison. It is a piece of steak. The only steak his mother has bought for years. Milo eats the meat ravenously. The boy looks mournfully on. He holds his pet for the next hour as it whimpers and goes into convulsions. At last, Milo goes slack in his arms. Poignant scene in backyard, Willing insisting on digging the hole himself.

"*Or*," he rounded up triumphantly, "short and sweet. With no warning on an ordinary summer evening on the front stoop, Willing raises a mallet over Milo's head and bashes in the skull. His expression is strangely pitiless." Willing looked up as if expecting applause for his performance. "I warned you," he added. "Nauseating."

Florence wasn't sure what about the recital was most disturbing, the detached third person, the violent imagery, or the Disney schlock.

"What am I supposed to construe from that," she said, "aside from the fact that I've been too gullible in having faith that you're not using drugs?"

"We won't be able to feed him."

"Oh, honey," she said softly. "Maybe you shouldn't come shopping with me. You've taken our situation too much to heart. It may be challenging to make my salary stretch through the month, but we can still afford to feed Milo."

"I know we can. But by the time we can't, no one else will be able to feed their pets either, and you won't be able to give any dog away."

"Where do you get this stuff?" Florence puzzled.

"I don't only consult Great Grand Man, if that's what you're worried about. But I don't mean give Milo to just anyone. Definitely not to the ASPCA, which sooner or later will be a death camp. Brendan. Across the street. He has two little kids. He likes Milo. Milo is a good dog for small children. He's friendly, never rough, and he doesn't bite."

"Why Brendan in particular?"

"Brendan has money. Real money. You told me. He gave you a heads-up. Which means *he* had a heads-up."

Utterly bewildered, Florence did insist that Willing wait a week to think about it. He waited the week. He remained adamant. At length, she concluded that this was an opportunity to teach him a lesson. If he had to evoke storm clouds of omens and portents, then maybe Chicken Little should pay a price when the sky doesn't fall after all. He'd be sorry, but they could always get another dog.

For once signaling a normal, healthy emotional disposition, Willing didn't want to give Milo away himself. To Florence's surprise, Brendan was not only grateful for the gift of such an agreeable, affectionate pet, but he didn't question why her son might decide to divest their household of a four-legged dependent. Shortly thereafter, too, Brendan and his family moved out, saying cursory good-byes to neighbors and explaining only that they were going "abroad." Which was odd, since it was still illegal to take more than $100 out of the country. Until the restriction was lifted—a repeal of the controls was expected any day now—no one was going "abroad." They took Milo with them. Rather than despondent and regretful, the better to learn his lesson, Willing seemed relieved. At least Milo, he announced, was safe.

Chapter 7
The Warrior Queen Arrives in Carroll Gardens

"Your mom and dad was meant to be checked out by eleven a.m., *comprende*?" The receptionist at the Wellcome Arms no longer wore her name badge. Her sleeves were jammed above the elbows. She was chewing gum. And she was rude.

Carter had detected the same fraying of propriety in New York. Police shuffled their beats in open collars and dirty shoes. Doormen didn't open the door for frail tenants or offer to carry groceries, and their livery looked slept in. Sometimes the changes were subtle—a maître d' didn't see you to your table, but jerked his head irritably to indicate you could sit anywhere— but the touch-and-feel transformation of daily life was substantial. The voiding of some rules seemed to have opened the floodgates to the voiding of them all.

"*Checked out?*" he said. "This isn't a hotel."

"Is a business, *chico,*" she said, smacking. "A for-profit business and not a charity, which I'm immense tired of explaining to you people, wanna know the truth."

"I can't imagine there's a long line of applicants for my father's compound, is there?" Carter dropped the pen from a height. The formality of signing in now seemed daft. "You should be grateful for residents who've hung on as long as my father, thanks to whom you still have a job."

Surfaces revealed that a cutback in staffing had already begun. The baseboards were lined with black dust. Carter's shoes didn't squeak as he strode the marble hallway, where the reek of urine was piercing—despite half the doors along the corridor listing open, the units unoccupied. Out the back door leading to the premier-class compounds, the lawn was six inches high. The previous June a riot of pansies and marigolds, the borders were now plain dirt. He didn't hear any horses. He wouldn't be surprised if they'd been shot.

The front door of Douglas and Luella's compound also lolled agape. Alarmingly, framed book covers bound in bubble wrap were propped along the hall; none of these decorations would fit in the car. The crimson carpet was trod flat and specked with sod.

Carter found his father once more in the library. The shelves were bare. Douglas stood staring aimlessly, surrounded by towers of cardboard cartons. His cream suit was rumpled, and he wasn't wearing an ascot—an affectation that may once have grated, but whose absence was worse. He didn't look natty and trim but feeble and underweight. His posture had collapsed. At last, Douglas Elliot Mandible looked every day of ninety-eight.

Carter asked with a sweep of his arm, "Pop, what's all this?"

"The library, of course."

"Well, clearly we're in the library," Carter said patiently.

"I haven't turned into Luella, son. The books, not the room."

"If you're of such sound mind, then you also remember what I told you. A few clothes, your medications and toiletries, *maybe* a handful of keepsakes. Small keepsakes, not the sort that would fill a U-Haul."

"I assumed you'd be renting a vehicle appropriate for the task."

"I came up in the BeEtle—into which you, Luella, and a small amount of luggage will barely fit. We don't need to incur any unnecessary expense right now, and our house is already crammed with crap. You can download everything in these cartons onto a chip the size of a ladybug. It's the ideal time to join the modern world."

"But these are signed first editions! If it's money we need, this library is worth a deep six figures!"

"New York is awash in old print books, Pop." Carter tried to say this kindly, but exasperation got the better of him. "Your generation's left behind truckloads of hardbacks, and younger people don't want them. So collectors have their pick. More to the point, what collectors? Do you know one real person who'd part with cash right now for stained wood pulp? If not, all these boxes stay behind." The sternness was unabashedly parental. Yet having at last been granted the status of full adulthood was not as gratifying as Carter once had hoped.

Tipping backwards toward his armchair by the bay window, Douglas fell more than sat. "Chucking a collection of this quality into a Dumpster is sheer barbarism."

Carter kneeled at the chair. "What's important about these objects you *can* take with you. You read them, right? They're in your head."

"All that's left in my head is grief and muddle."

As his father grew weepy, Carter laid a hand on his shoulder, which felt too narrow and too sharp. "Jesus, have they been feeding you?"

"Not much. Not since the eviction notice. Forget asparagus and béarnaise. It's a few hard rolls they all but throw at you, and some sort of dog-foody ham. Which I might have tolerated, had the staff not raided my bar. All they left is a liqueur—some dreadful benefaction, orange peel macerated in gasoline."

"Since when do the orderlies help themselves to your property?"

"I've overheard grumbling about their wages not keeping up, so they've started to steal. Speaking of which, the one thing you must find room for in that midget car of yours is the Mandible silver service." Douglas tapped a rectangular mahogany box on the long central table. Carter was familiar with its contents; the curlicue *M* on each heavy piece of cutlery was distinctive. "It could come in useful, for the metal alone— unless the feds confiscate silver next. For weeks, I've not let it out of my sight. I sleep with that box under my pillow, and I can't tell you how uncomfortable it's been."

"If you'd told me this joint was going to the dogs, I'd have rescued you sooner."

"Best to put this off as long as possible for your sake, son. I fear the novelty of caring for Luella is apt to wear off quickly."

"You're seeing Mimi again. Mimi, see me. Don't think I don't know it!"

Speak of the devil. Luella had wandered in wearing what might once have been a stylish frock, but the hem was shredded from her having torn at it, and the sky-blue fabric was encrusted with food. The bloop of her stomach echoed the bulge of an adult diaper at the rear. Carter had grown accustomed to this decayed incarnation of his father's second wife, but fifteen years earlier the shock had been profound. Sure, he'd resented the way the younger woman moved in on her employer in 1992, making herself oh, so indispensable in every department. He'd suspected at the time, too, that his father's financial situation had made the twenty-two-year age difference easier for Luella to excuse. But when Douglas first remarried, Carter had conceded that the woman was a looker: an unapologetic five ten, slender and stately, with plumb posture, impeccable nails, and a sharp eye for clothes. He could hardly blame his father (though of course he had). Even at seventy-something she hadn't entirely lost her figure— just everything else.

"That woman has airs," Luella added, with the occasional cogency grown more disconcerting than the nonsense. "But *I* descend from the Warrior Queen of the Ivory Coast, Nana Abena Pokuaa! Who ruled the Baoule Kingdom of the Akans for thirty years! Dirty fears! *I* am royalty, and *Mimi* is common. Lemon ramen! From traders and shopkeepers. Raiders and peepers!" She leaned accusingly into Douglas's face. *"Don't think I don't know it."*

"She's intermittently convinced I'm seeing your mother again," Douglas explained. "Which is thrilling, because in that event she seems to know who I am. Otherwise, whatever greeting-card part of the brain that conjures up rhymes remains intact."

"Hi, Luella," Carter said pointlessly. "Today, we're going on a trip."

"Trip, flip, conniption fit. Today, hooray!" She giggled girlishly, placing a shy hand to her cheek, then tonguing the air as if trying to catch a fly. This rapid flicking and licking motion was one of Carter's least favorite of Luella's ticks.

"Is it going to be hard to get her in the car?"

"She can throw tantrums with no warning," Douglas said. "But maybe we'll get lucky. I'm sorry about the state of her, but after we missed the first payment the orderlies went on strike. I don't have the strength to change her dress more than once a day. Are you certain Jayne is up for this?"

"Oh, Jayne's a trouper," Carter said reflexively. But what he'd wanted to say was, "Does it matter if Jayne is 'up for this'? What's the alternative—leave your wife in a basket on somebody's doorstep?"

Because in truth Jayne was beside herself. Getting it all over with at once, Carter had delivered a one-two punch: that inheritance they'd been counting on for their retirement? There wasn't one. His father hadn't fled the market fast enough to save his shirt. The bonds could have been claims on the Brooklyn Bridge. The gold and gold stocks were confiscated. Most of the cash was absorbed by debt, since years before some idiot had talked Douglas into investing on margin. The Wellcome Arms sucked up the tiny remaining liquidity to the tune of $27,500 per month. Surprise number two: guess who's coming to dinner.

Jayne wasn't an ungenerous person, but she was private, and since her breakdown found the company of other people stressful beyond measure. She seemed to have lost the simple facility of concocting spontaneous topics of conversation, while at once suffering an unholy terror of social silence. Before friends arrived for a drink, she would grill Carter for an hour on what on earth they might talk about—a waste of preparation, since socializing didn't work that way, and none of these premeditated topics would ever arise naturally. In a panic, she would insert them arbitrarily and bring any small, successful interchange in its infancy to a halt. For Jayne, the prospect of having to interact with live-in guests in perpetuity was horrendous.

Besides, for any woman of sixty-nine to adopt Luella, barely older than Jayne herself, meant confronting daily her greatest fears for her own future. As for Douglas, he'd never really *noticed* Jayne, who was a sensitive, intelligent, intuitive person but even in her less phobic days never especially loud. Her character was built on too small a scale for Douglas, who'd therefore blithely accepted her hospitality for decades, and blithely dispatched it in return, while paying little heed to who exactly was filling his glass or whose glass he might be filling. Penniless at ninety-eight, her father-in-law might never have seemed less intimidating, but neither in-law could draw on a long shared history of mutual warmth.

In short, they were looking at disaster, of the worst sort: not a single cataclysm like 2024 from which assorted parties might recover, but an ongoing, borderless nightmare ended only by death. Within the week, Carter could be clamoring to go first.

What about Medicaid?" Jayne had raised immediately, groping for any way out of this. "If Douglas is destitute, he qualifies for state nursing home care."

"Six months ago, you'd be right," Carter said. "But I told you: they've changed the rules. If you have immediate living relatives with assets, Medicaid won't pick up the tab. Our 401(k)s and pensions have been slaughtered, but we do own this house."

"How about Nollie? Why are your father and his deranged wife all our problem?"

"You know my sister's in France."

"Make her come back from France. You're the one who's been visiting New Milford for years."

"That's right, because it's the decent people who always get fucked. Nollie didn't only end up in Europe out of pretension. That ocean between her and the family is a firewall. It's got her out of weddings, funerals, birthdays, and Christmases for decades—not to mention slogs to the Wellcome Arms."

"But she must have some resources squirreled away. From that supposed 'international bestseller'? Even from afar, she could cover the bill for a nursing home. Maybe not one as opulent. But with so many seniors insolvent, cheaper facilities must have places going begging all over the country."

"Nollie and my father have both been cagey about the scale of her royalties. Though she can't be pulling in much now. With fiction a free-for-all, everybody writing it and nobody reading it—and absolutely nobody buying it—what do you want to bet she'll cry poverty? Whatever her real finances, it's a plausible line."

Jayne started unloading the dishwasher so she could have plates to slam. "I've never forgiven her for completely shutting down the discussion when you finally brought yourself to hazard that *maybe*, just *maybe*, a childless, solipsistic old woman and a younger brother with three children and four grandchildren shouldn't split an enormous inheritance fifty-fifty. I mean, what was she going to do with that money, buy an island and install it with another toy boy to service her dried-up loins? When poor Florence has to take in a tenant—"

"That doesn't matter now," Carter cut her off. In truth, the depth of that sibling rift was now a source of chagrin. The acid argument over whether he was morally entitled to substantially more than his sister when Pop died, because after all he had *issue* and she did not, now seemed like an evil version of "*The Gift of the Magi.*"

"Douglas should have changed his will as soon as it became obvious that Nollie was a barren spinster—"

"That terminology is beneath you. And I did bring it up with Pop, only because you insisted, and you remember—it was very awkward. He shut me down. He said we got college funds for the kids and grandkids, and help with our down payment, none of which Nollie got, and that was enough; he didn't want to 'play favorites.' But we've talked about this ad nauseam, and it's a moot point now."

"I don't care if the money's gone," Jayne continued obliviously, crashing silverware into a drawer. "Your sister's greedy, take-no-prisoners position still means something. That huffy, 'But it's my half to do with what I want!' All that righteous indignation over how it was your choice to have children and she 'shouldn't have to pay for it' just because she was too self-absorbed to become a mother herself—"

"Enough!" Carter cried.

It was staggering how the enmity over who-would-get-what could survive beyond the point at which there was nothing to get. Perplexingly, Jayne's feelings about his inheritance had always run higher than his own—as if avarice once removed grew the sharper for the prize lying a few more tantalizing inches out of reach. Yet in no other context had Carter known his wife to be grasping. The ferocity with which she'd coveted the legacy may have derived from her father-in-law's disregard: she might as well get something out of a relationship that otherwise made her feel inadequate and uninteresting. Or perhaps the rapacity was a product of her powerful partisanship in respect to the ongoing tensions between her husband and sister-in-law. Alas, spousal bias has a blunt, crude quality, and misses all the nuance. Jayne took sides in a subtle, conflicted rivalry—Carter's simultaneous resentment and admiration of his sister combined into a unique emotion he couldn't name—and reduced it to plain antagonism. Thus she often forced him to defend his sister when he'd have preferred to carp.

He did take exception to Jayne's implication that in not fighting Nollie harder for a fairer share of his inheritance, he had failed to support his family. Jayne was left an only child after her younger sister committed suicide in adolescence (a tragedy, yes, but one whose psychic statute of limitations might have run out by now—not that you'd get his wife to relinquish the trauma, which seemed to confer the special-protection status of landmark architecture). According to Jayne, only assurance that their one remaining offspring would be well provided for by Mandible Engine Corp. had made her parents feel free to spend down their savings in retirement. It would have been unseemly to object to the couple's availing themselves of their own earnings, so he and

Jayne had held their tongues as the two went on vacations in Bali and took out a reverse mortgage. When the pair died in a ballooning accident in Morocco a few years ago, his in-laws left nothing behind but debt. Somehow this, too, was all Carter's fault.

He and Jayne had been married for forty-three years; they had grandchildren. Be that as it may, he'd let slip about the Mandible estate while they were still dating. Subconsciously, he may have dangled the money as a lure. Their union had stood the test of time, but sometimes he sympathized with his father—having to live with that worm of a question mark over what about your companionship was really so entrancing.

"She's a vain, selfish woman," Jayne said summarily, banging a final sauté pan home, "who for once in her life should be forced to pitch in."

While Carter was still debating how to coerce his older sister into behaving like the member of a family, that very evening his fleX tringed. Behold, Nollie proposed not so much to help solve a problem as to become another one.

"You would not believe the anti-Americanism in this country," his big sister began. "And I thought it was bad before. I no sooner open my mouth—"

"I thought your French was so perfect that no one could tell," Carter said dryly.

Once fine and silky, now listless, his sister's dyed butterscotch hair had thinned further, exposing glimmers of scalp. At seventy-three, she still pulled off an imperious manner and youthful boisterousness. From a lifetime of sarcasm, the left-hand crease around her mouth was slightly deeper than the right. Yet her slight, wiry build hadn't prevented the inexorable jowling that befell their mother. Nollie's neck—the one part of the human body that never lies—had striated, with an incipient puffiness under the chin. No doubt his sister was conducting a similar assessment of her brother's image, with the same bittersweet mingling of triumph and sorrow. Carter had been passably handsome in his day; Nollie was once a stunner. Funny, he had dully accommodated himself to the sagging of his own cheeks, the weediness of his own locks. He found any disintegration of his domineering older sister's appearance a shock. You always imagine you'll savor these icon-cum-nemeses' undoing. You're always wrong.

"I said nothing of the kind," she said. "You're always imputing all manner of posturing to me merely because I live in Paris. My accent is slightly better than the average American's, meaning it's short of ghastly. I never said my nationality was undetectable. I wish. They've always hated us for being crass, and for ruling the world. Now they hate us for *not* ruling the world. Now we're two-faced thieves who brought the entire international monetary system to the brink of collapse, and only Putin and Co., with his brave bancor, rode to the rescue. It's become weirdly personal. The French are taking it out on expats because there aren't any American tourists now that a baguette costs the equivalent of fifty bucks. Last night a woman in the *supermarché* dumped a pot of crème fraîche on my hair."

Nollie had always been wildly opinionated, and Carter wouldn't be surprised if she was assaulted by crème fraîche because she wouldn't keep her views to herself even in a supermarket. In her time, Enola Mandible had been quite the performer, speaking to countless literary festivals in the wake of her sole big success. He'd seen her speak once at the Ninety-Second Street Y, addressing that kind of soft crowd that you didn't have to win over—that was already pleased as punch with the main attraction and yearned only to grow more so. So she could toss out perceptions that for any halfway intelligent person constituted run-of-the-mill dinner-party fare, but that scanned to her band of pumped fans as life-altering revelations. Likewise she could crack the odd lame joke, and because writers had a well-earned reputation as stuffy and tedious, these pre-delighted folks thought she was hilarious.

"That's all very interesting," Carter said. "But we have to talk about Pop—"

"Sure we do, but we can talk face-to-face. That's the point, Carter. I'm coming home." Nollie hadn't referred to the United States as *home* for decades.

"Coming home where?" Carter asked warily.

"Well, with all your extra bedrooms . . . I thought, you know, as usual, I could stay at your place."

"No can do. That's what I'm trying to tell you. Pop and his batty sidekick are moving in here. He can't pay for that larcenous feedlot anymore. I sure hope you weren't counting on it, because the Mandible 'fortune' is finished."

"Jesus fuck! I hope you mean—it's depleted?"

"I mean it's *gone.*"

The silence, hardly Nollie's preferred form of communication, spoke volumes: she had been counting on it. Of course she had. They all had. "I guess I shouldn't be surprised," she said glumly at last. "Why should our family be any different." It wasn't a question. "Christ, are there any rich Americans left?"

"If so, they're keeping their heads down. So if you do come back here, don't complain and keep your mouth shut. Which doesn't come naturally to you, so you're going to have to be mindful. The whole country is convinced that the 'über-rich' have walked off with the store. The truth of the matter is that to be robbed, you have to have something to steal. So the folks who've been really burned are necessarily the people whom *nobody* feels sorry for."

"Maybe we shouldn't expect sympathy," Nollie said, rousing, "when we never deserved the money any-way—"

"Can the pious poppycock with me, sister. Jayne and I had been thinking about decamping to a ranch in Montana once the Mandible ship came in. Now we're crammed into the same old shit box in Carroll Gardens, looking at second careers as full-time geriatric nurses."

"Well, you do have those two other bedrooms—"

"Pop can't sleep with Luella, who needs her own room, because she apparently suffers from 'nighttime agitation.' So Jayne will need her Quiet Room more than ever."

"Oh, right, I forgot. Jayne's *Quiet Room*."

"Don't be snide. You take up a lot of space yourself, friend. If you need a place to crash, why not make up with Momma? That apartment's the size of a football field."

In the divorce settlement, Douglas was awarded the appointments that hailed from Bountiful House, but their mother retained the couple's four-bedroom on West End and West Eighty-Eighth Street. Alas, Mimi's fury that Nollie applauded their father's "rediscovery of desire" in 1992 proved to have the shelf life of radioactive waste. Nollie had hardened in response, and wouldn't care to admit it even now, but being disowned by her mother and banished from the home where she grew up had been deeply wounding. The feud helped to explain her flouncing off to Europe a few years later—on the proceeds of a scarcely fictionalized novel that recapitulated the Mimi-Luella-Douglas triangle in terms sure to keep their mother's grievance fresh.

"We're not getting into *that*," Nollie said. "Besides, she'd see right through any rapprochement contrived to secure me a free bed. She's old, she's not an idiot."

"Maybe you should stay in France."

"I can't. For an American, anywhere in Europe is physically dangerous. We're being assaulted. And not only with crème fraîche."

"Stay in nights, then. It's sure to blow over."

"Besides, this country's hardly one big wine-swilling *soirée*. At any given time, half the population is on strike, and what good is a great train system that never runs? They're apoplectic that they can't all retire at fifty-two. They all expect their child benefit, their gold-plated pensions, their token-pittance healthcare charges, their truncated workweek, and two solid years of unemployment at a salary most lawyers don't earn—all of which is a *human right*. Along with so many holidays and vacations that the fuckers put their feet up for a third of the year. Oh, and *everyone* wants to work for the government; most of them *do*. Your basic all-cart, no-horse. So the whole country plops into the hay wagon and wonders why it doesn't move."

"It's got to be better than here," Carter said.

"Furthermore, the whole Muslim thing is out of control," Nollie bullied on obliviously. "If I walk down the Champs-Élysées, I'll get thumped for being a deadbeat. If I walk anywhere less central, I'll get thumped because I'm not wearing a trash bag. Even in France, they've given up on the assimilation shtick, and gone for slavish appeasement instead. Whole tracts of the country are effectively no-go areas for actual French people. It's the same all over Europe now, so there's nowhere to go."

"I'm getting a feel for how popular you must make yourself over there."

"Oh, it's just like the US. Everyone's resigned. America is now Greater Mexico, and the Continent is an extension of the Middle East."

"Look—do you have any money?"

"Some," Nollie said carefully. "Fortunately, in bancors."

"You can't hold bancors in this country."

"Boy, land of the free! But officially, you can't do a lot of things. At least the exchange rate is wildly in my favor—and more wildly every day. What the hell is happening over there? Every time I check, the dollar has sunk again."

"I was going to say—I don't want to speak for her—but if you have *resources*, it's possible that Florence could put you up. Her tenant isn't paying nearly market rent, and he's turned into another of her charity cases. And you and Florence always seemed to get along." Which is beyond my understanding, Carter did not add.

"I like that kid Willing," Nollie considered. "I don't like many kids. Funny, he fleXted me a few months ago. Wanted to know how hard it was to immigrate to France. I told him to forget it, but the question, if peculiar, showed pluck. Anyway, it'll take me a few months to wrap things up here, so there's time to explore the options."

"Think about it. And, you know"—Carter had to push himself—"it'll be good to see you."

Recap: he had failed to tempt his sister into any support of their father and his pet wife, either fiduciary or logistical. Typical. Nollie had done as she pleased her whole life. The concept of duty was foreign to her, and it was only the people who acknowledged duty, and who had regard for duty, who got saddled with it.

Carter allowed himself a last walk-through of his father's compound to say good-bye to a host of objects that had furnished his childhood, discreetly taking memorial snapshots with his fleX. Darkened from hours of absorption in all that future landfill in the library, the padded leather four-seater and its companion armchairs displayed a workmanship the world would never see again. Ditto the claw-footed, curly-maple dining table, from which he and Nollie had been exiled during raucous adults-only dinner parties with the wits and scholars of the day; they probably didn't make wits and scholars of that quality anymore either. Surfaces were dotted with treasures, the overtly useless but pricey detritus that one gave the well-off, like the ornate clock in the shape of an open book whose tiny numbers were too poorly positioned to tell the time, and whose battery had run out in the 1980s. Presumably staff would hold a giant stoop sale once residents of his father's ilk had cleared off, but they wouldn't raise much. Carter had contacted a few estate sales agents about liquidating his father's effects, but they must have been drowning in similar requests; none of his messages was returned.

Back when imagining Douglas's overnight impover-
ishment would simply have been a game of emotional
sudoku, Carter would have supposed that the effect of
perfectly removing the money from the equation of
their relationship would be, say, "considerable." He'd
not have anticipated that it would be more like "earth-
shattering." It turned out that the fortune Douglas had
just lost wasn't merely a large element in their dealings
with each other; for all intents and purposes, it had
been the only element. Horrifyingly, that lurking lucre
had controlled everything that Carter did in his father's
presence, and everything he said.

The surprise of sudden penury wasn't only the scale
of the change, but its character. In retrospect, wealth
had contorted Douglas Mandible's very nature. It
made him suspicious, cynical, and aloof; it made him
secretive, manipulative, and superior. It exaggerated a
father-son hierarchy that in Pop's advanced age should
have been breaking down. These days, Douglas was
staggeringly expressive, needy, and direct.

As for Carter: before the elephant left the room, he
had no idea how much he resented it. Dancing around
the money for decades, being exaggeratedly deferential,
dithering about whether to ever allude to the money
or to elaborately avoid its mention, questioning himself
over why he really made these obeisant pilgrimages to

New Milford, however fleetingly *looking forward to his own father's death*—the whole package had made him feel venal. Vulgar. Unworthy, scabrous, and morally bankrupt. And he'd resented his father personally— for the man's complicity in making Carter feel like a weak, dissembling worm, and for his crude abuse of power (take that sadistic delay before the Renunciation Address, when Douglas had toyed with him, dragging out the verdict on what was left of the investments, so clearly enjoying himself: the scene returned to Carter in a rush of revulsion). So while he might have expected to be consumed with fury that Pop hadn't better protected the family piggy bank, Carter's far more dominant sensation was relief.

For it was impossible to be angry at the poor guy. Deprived of his mighty financial cudgel, Douglas Mandible was just a very old man with a host of heartbreaking vanities, no influence, and scads of dead friends. Carter felt he could see his father clearly for the first time. There was no colossal edifice to rage against—just a half-broken man who needed his help. Obviously, Douglas could still be exasperating, and the practical consequences of Pop's insolvency were cataclysmic. But in the main, to his son's astonishment, on every visit here this year Carter had been flushed with tenderness, sometimes to the point of tears. (Cleansed of ulterior motives, he had continued to visit, had he not? Perversely, the divestiture bestowed a gift: he'd woken one morning to discover that he was not a monster. He hadn't even realized that he'd felt like a monster. That's how monstrous he'd become.) In the face of Pop's blubbering apologies about having mishandled the estate, he'd repeatedly intoned that the events of last fall were unforeseeable, most other Americans of means had suffered the same fate, and the fortune's annihilation was not his father's fault. Whether or not Carter quite bought into the lyrics of this lullaby, he was finally able to like his father, and to like himself, too. Freed to be genuinely kind—kindness to a purpose was not called kindness—he was also newly at liberty to act brusque, testy, bored, cross, impatient, and inattentive if not oblivious, *like a real person.* Only now could he appreciate how much a desire to please imposed distance, created falsity even when a putatively pleasing assertion was perfectly true, and ruined your sense of humor.

Affectionately, Carter remembered to slip the mahogany box of silver into a battered canvas book bag from long-defunct Barnes & Noble. He carried it nonchalantly to his backseat, making sure to lock the car again before returning for the luggage.

To Carter's consternation, Douglas had hung on to an enormous 1940s leather suitcase plastered with decals from exotic destinations and designed for ocean voyages with swarms of porters. No wheels! No porters, either, since Wellcome's staff had grown sullen with residents whose accounts were in arrears. At seventy, Carter shouldn't be hauling awkward loads this heavy, not with the arthritis in his knees and an iffy disc in his lower back. But muscular Lat orderlies observed his difficulties from the reception steps with contemptuous detachment.

Lugged at last to the BeEtle, the cursed case wouldn't fit in the trunk. Under the merciless gaze of those orderlies, it was humiliating to deconstruct his father's packing job and stuff the white suits, ascots, monogrammed boxers, and finely stitched cordovans into the canvas shopping hold-alls stuffed under the front passenger seat for trips to Fairway. Jammed between stashes of adult diapers, which Carter had prudently pilfered from the compound's cupboards, the appurtenances looked like thrift-shop donations. He could not picture Jayne ironing all that linen.

Luella had wandered off. The two men spent half an hour finding her, snagged and whimpering on the perimeter's barbed wire. Troublingly, rather than help disentangle his wife's dress, Douglas shuffled back to the car. Thrashing, she re-ensnared herself almost as fast as Carter could release the fabric, crying, "Phasers on stun, Captain!"

Carter clapped his hands once she was free. "Let's go, Luella! Here, girl, get a move on!" As she heeled, he could see how his father had fallen into the pet thing.

Yet at the car she balked, less like a dog than cattle with a whiff of the abattoir. "Never, won't, can't, not!" she screamed, whipping her arms back and forth. Like toddlers, Luella commonly located her sole sense of agency in the negative.

"Best let her exhaust herself," Douglas advised from the passenger seat. Sure enough, after a few minutes' flailing, Luella plopped in a heap on the gravel, and Carter was able to lift her into the backseat, eyes rolling back, limbs flopped.

"Are her immunizations up to date?" Carter asked, starting the car. "Because she scratched herself on that rusty wire. There might be a danger of tetanus."

"We can always hope," Douglas said.

On the gloomy drive to the city, Carter inquired, "Do you have *any* income streams right now? Pensions, annuities, corporate bonds?" Now that there was no money, they could talk about money.

Douglas's chuckle lapsed to a cough. "There's always Social Security!"

"Don't mock. Plenty of people are barely hanging on because of Social Security."

"But where does the Social Security come from? Payroll intake must have plummeted."

"They have to come across with those checks, or there'd be a nationwide insurrection."

"At my age, I wouldn't frighten many bureaucrats on a picket line."

"You can still vote."

"For now," Douglas said. "I know we relics tend to see things bleakly. But I wouldn't count on anything anymore, and that includes the right to kick the bums out."

Handwringing about the end of American democracy seemed silly, and Carter didn't pursue it.

After a journey grown circuitous since the partial closing of the BQE, they drew into Carroll Gardens. "I thought this borough had become a shining citadel of the professional class," Douglas remarked. "Not as smart as I remembered."

Every block was blighted with closed commercial properties. Elite restaurants that nine months ago kept long waiting lists had dirty windows plastered with FOR RENT signs. Shops selling upscale trinkets like wind chimes for cribs were boarded shut. The city had cut back on street cleaning, and curbsides fluttered with trash. Panhandlers were not only more numerous, but older and better dressed. Begging always picked up during downturns, but their placards were distinctive to this one: RUINED BY MY OWN GOVERNMENT. ALVARADO CLEANED ME OUT—PLEASE GIVE. MY DAUGHTER *AND MEDICAID!!* REFUSE TO TAKE ME IN. I COULD BE YOUR GRANDMOTHER.

Carter hadn't renewed his garage membership, and street parking was encumbered by abandoned cars the cops were sluggish about towing away. Finding a space would take a while, so he dropped off his passengers and their bags in front. Alerted to their arrival by fleXt, Jayne was waiting on the stoop to greet them, her frozen rictus of welcome straight from a horror-movie reaction shot. She was flapping in one of the dark, ankle-length dresses in which she'd huddled since her breakdown—the masses of fabric with which aging women often concealed weight gain, though Jayne was a picky, neurotic eater and disturbingly thin. That tortured expression—what she surely imagined was a look of gladness, openness, and joy— would appear to anyone else like pain. The fact that she dyed her hair a severe jet-black intensified the suggestion of fraudulence. A pity. Jayne Darkly had been a beautiful woman, a truthful woman, and the snapshot was unfair.

But talk about giving the wrong impression: with an elegance that recalled what had originally attracted his father, Luella held the shredded hem of her dress daintily above her knee and stepped regally to the sidewalk. "What a pleasure," she said, touching her hands lightly to Jayne's shoulders and kissing her hostess airily on each cheek. "Why, I'm sorry to trouble you, but I could simply murder a cup of tea."

Jayne glanced at Carter in surprise, and he shrugged. "Don't get used to it."

Chapter 8

The Joys of Being Indispensable

When Lowell scheduled a "family meeting," the kids didn't know what it was.

"It means you all show up in the living room, at the same time, with no excuses, and shut up." The last few months, Lowell's sensitive parenting skills had frayed.

"But my debate team is strategizing on Thursday night," Goog objected.

"I don't give a hoot about your debate team, and pretty soon"—Lowell feared he was letting the agenda out of the bag—"you won't, either."

Since the stilted practice was never a part of the Stackhouse routine, the convocation was resentful. Goog scowled on the sofa with his arms crossed. Bing kicked at the footstool repeatedly. Savannah curled sulkily on the floor and buffed her nails, her body oriented toward the dark picture window as if no one else were present.

Lowell and Avery had discussed which parent would take the lead. To her credit, Avery had volunteered, conceding, "Whoever delivers the blow-by-blow they're going to hate." Lowell countered, "They'll hate both of us soon enough. Might as well act like a man. I get little enough opportunity." So Lowell remained standing, while Avery perched on the arm of a recliner, as if poised to tackle children who tried to bolt.

"When I was a boy," he started in—not the most propitious introduction, since when he was a boy any speech that began *When I was a boy* he immediately tuned out—"I had only the haziest notion of what my parents did for a living, and I didn't really care. I didn't care how they made sure there were always groceries in the fridge. All that mattered was when I wanted one, I could make a sandwich. I wasn't given carte blanche permission to do or buy whatever I wanted, but within reason I was privileged—although not nearly as privileged as you three. But all you kids must be aware of some big changes in this country since last fall, because we've raised you to pay attention. I'm afraid that means big changes for our family, too. Mom and I want you to know that we're not doing this because we're big meanies. We don't have any choice."

"What's with the drum roll?" Goog said. "In public-speaking class, they warn you against excessive build-up. With too much *da da-da dahh!* no matter what you say later, the audience is disappointed."

"You will be disappointed," Lowell snapped. "Starting next term, you and Bing will be enrolled in public school. We can't pay tuition at Gates and Sidwell anymore. Goog, you'll be going to Theodore Roosevelt High School in Petworth."

"But Petworth is—" Goog objected.

"Petworth is *what*?" Lowell would make him say it.

"Lat," Goog muttered, at least sounding ashamed of himself.

"And what's wrong with that?" Lowell's question dangled. "Bing, we tried to get you into Deal Middle School, which is closer and might have a more . . . *like-minded* student body. But they don't have any places for the fall. Too many parents like us are in the same situation. So for next year it's Tubman Elementary in Columbia Heights."

"Does Tubman have an orchestra?" Bing asked in a small voice.

"Come on, all my friends are at Gates, and Roosevelt is roachbar!" Goog exclaimed. "A lot of public schools don't participate in the interschool debate circuit at all! I bet Roosevelt doesn't even have a lacrosse team."

"No, Goog, no lacrosse, and no, Bing, I wouldn't take an instrument worth a nickel into that neighborhood these days, even if they do have an orchestra."

"I'm going to have to drive you to and from school, honey," Avery told Bing, who had been walking the four blocks to Sidwell Friends School. "Just for safety."

"How are you going to do that?" Savannah asked coolly, still facing away from the rest of the family and concentrating on her hands. "I thought you worked."

"Mom's practice," Avery said, curiously driven to the third person, "is part of the problem. Mom's patients can't afford their appointments anymore. Which means Mom can't afford the rent on her office."

The complete lack of involvement in the work world of parents that Lowell had initially addressed was already palpable in this living room. The particulars of what led them to withdraw their sons from private education were clearly the source of perfect indifference. Kids must universally be like this: all that matters is what happens to them.

"Maybe if you gave the kind of therapy that's actually useful," Savannah said, "that wasn't half-mystical hokum—people would still pay for it."

"What's useful to people," Avery said with admirable control, "changes."

224 · LIONEL SHRIVER

"As for you"—Lowell pivoted to his daughter—
"we're all very proud of you for getting into Risdee.
It's a big achievement. But I'm afraid you're going to
have to take delayed acceptance, and I can't make any
promises about next year, either."

She turned to eye him. He'd never seen her look at
her father with quite that disdainful a cast. She'd been
blindly affectionate as a girl, and Lowell recoiled from
the alien coolness. Maybe you couldn't know anyone
profoundly until they stopped getting their way. "This
is about funding, right? If I'm detecting the pattern
here. I can apply for grant support, then. If you're so
broke, I might qualify on the basis of need."

"Be my guest," Lowell said. "But good luck. College
endowments all over the country have been devastated.
That includes Georgetown, which hasn't even paid me
this month. Probably just an oversight, but it makes life
more difficult for now."

"What's an *endowment*?" Bing asked.

"A sort of savings account. When everything is
normal, schools can run off the interest and dividends."

"But *you* said the market would bounce back!" Goog
charged. "*You* said faster than anybody expected! *You*
said we were going to make a killing!"

"I could still be right in the long run—"

"'In the long run we're all dead,'" Goog quoted. "John Maynard Keynes. It's not going to help any of us to get a decent education in the *long run*."

"Most kids I wouldn't bother to explain this stuff to, but you're bright enough to get it," Lowell said. "The interest on our mortgage has doubled. With her current office rent, Mom's income is negative. Students can't afford to attend the university where I teach. Be honest—don't some of your friends have to transfer out of Gates, too?"

"Olivia Andrews was going to, but she got a scholarship. Because her dad killed himself."

"You trying to give me ideas?"

Goog shrugged. "It was a pretty successful gambit. Whatever works, right?"

"Sweetie," Avery intervened. "That's not funny."

"Neither one of you has ever believed in my talent," Savannah said. "You never wanted me to get an arts degree. Now you think you can browbeat me into something *practical*, like a degree in Mandarin."

"I don't want you to get a degree at all," Lowell said. "I want you to get a job."

"Doing what?"

"I don't care. Anything to contribute to the family coffers."

"If I flip burgers, I'm not giving the money to *you*."

How did this happen? Did they do something wrong? All this time, should they have withheld what these kids wanted and it was within their power to give, from an abstract dedication to building "character"? "If I have to flip burgers," Lowell said, "I'll give the money to you. Seem like a double standard?"

"Oh, sorry—back to the workhouse! This is *Dickensian*."

"Tell you what," Goog proposed. "You take out a loan on my behalf, send me to Gates. We'll work out a formula, how much of my salary after grad school I'll devote to paying you back. As my salary increases, we can boost the percentage."

"Nobody's going to give your dad a loan, sport," Lowell said. "Even if they did, the only terms available are 11 percent and rising."

"What's the equity situation, then?" Goog said gamely.

"We're paying interest-only. Nice try."

Goog lost his cool. "I can't believe this is happening!"

"You don't have to believe it for it to keep happening," Lowell said. "Reality's funny that way."

For all his purported fascination with his father's field, the boy didn't really credit the primacy of economics. Lowell attributed the discrepancy to Goog's particular brand of precocity: the boy's involvement in the many topics about which he held such fierce opinions was essentially rhetorical. He'd yet to make a visceral connection between a high school debate over some barmy balanced budget amendment and an interstate highway system so underfunded that hundreds of Americans per year were dying in pile-ups on I-85 from potholes alone—a connection that registered the very real possibility that one of those casualties could be you. Distinguished by the same precocity at Goog's age, Lowell wondered whether this purely rhetorical relationship to the pressing issues of his profession dogged him to this day. Avery constantly rode him for caring too much about being right. But maybe he didn't care about being right, actually and truly right, which would have mattered. Maybe he only cared about winning.

"When you have a bunch of kids," Savannah said, "you're not supposed to throw up your hands and say, 'Sorry, we can't make any money, you do it!' My art teacher says I'm *immense talented*, and you're not going to ruin my life!"

But when she rose to flounce out, Lowell grabbed her arm, at which she stared in incredulity. "The *family meeting* isn't adjourned. A few more announcements, *children.* This summer, there will be no Debate Camp, no Art Camp, and no String Quartet Camp, got it? No Science Camp, no Water Sports Camp, and no Survival in the Wild Camp—even if that last one might actually end up being worth the money."

He let go; she'd started to cry. Avery accused him of being a bully. Sure enough, he'd delivered the pronouncements with a trace of vengefulness. Taking away all their toys gave him a sick thrill.

"You're taking it out on them as a substitute for punishing yourself," Avery said quietly once they'd retired for the night.

"No-o-o," Lowell said. "I'm taking it out on them as a form of punishing myself."

"That's too convoluted for me, and I'm a therapist." She sounded tired.

"Look—do I want to throw the boys to the animals in public school? Of course not. Bing will be eaten alive. Goog? His broad general knowledge, his lucidity, the crafty way he inveigles himself into the good graces of his teachers—everything that makes that kid popular at Gates will make him a pariah at Roosevelt. And Savannah . . . It's one thing to take a year out from college to go to Europe and learn Italian. Quite another to loll around the house getting into mischief and losing your momentum. What a waste. Everything we've paid hundreds of thousands of dollars to have drummed into their heads will dribble right back out. And I feel as if we've failed them. But not the way you think. I mean they've never been told *no*. And now we expect them to learn about adversity, self-denial, and disappointment overnight."

"You can't fake adversity," Avery said. "When we had the means, we provided. Now we can't. Which, if you hadn't bought all those stupid stocks—"

"In 1919, Coca-Cola was a *stupid stock*," Lowell cut her off. "And you cannot invest, or run your fiscal life at all, in a manner that covers an infinite array of contingencies. The destruction of wealth in this country since October has been on a scale that's, well, fundamentally impossible. If you'd gone to any financial adviser a year ago and instructed him—"

"Or her," Avery said.

"Or *her*," Lowell corrected sourly. "*I would like you to protect my portfolio from the destruction of the world as we know it. Please choose mutual funds that invest with an eye to Judgment Day, the flooding of all the earth's coastal cities due to sea-level rise, nuclear war, and incurable plague.* He, *or she*, would have sent you packing, regardless of your net worth. To participate, at all, in any economy, down to getting paid and buying pork chops, means having faith that the rules of that economy won't upend. There *is* no insurance against game change. So whatever happens, you keep playing the game. That means when Apple is going for jack, you buy Apple. Exactly the way you always have. If that doesn't work out, because of reasons beyond your control the whole game is out the window, nothing else would have worked out, either."

"It's just, if we'd kept more in cash—"

"Cash is also an *investment*," Lowell overrode her brutally. "Historically, a very poor investment. One of the worst. You can't help making investments of some sort if you're going to have capital at all."

"But admitting to having made some mistakes can be a surprising relief—"

"I didn't make any mistakes! All those pension funds with pie charts of 62 percent equities and 27 percent bonds . . . All the investment accounts with their contrasting strategies of 'growth' or 'income' . . . The solicitous questionnaires from Morgan Stanley about the degree of 'risk' you'll tolerate—questionnaires that tend to play down the fact there's nowhere on the form to check 'zero' . . . The 'large cap' versus 'small cap' versus 'emerging markets' . . . The delicate tweaking, *Maybe we should move a little more into the energy sector and de-emphasize pharma* . . . Well, *all* those accounts have been flattened. The strategies didn't matter."

"What a waste of effort, then," Avery mumbled.

"Kept a lot of people occupied. But there's an upside: if no one was right, then no one was wrong, either. If everyone is screwed regardless of what they did or didn't do, then everyone is blameless. Including me. Unfortunately, that logic never seems convincing when I'm wide-eyed in the middle of the night."

Yet after a knock came on the master bedroom door, Lowell would feel sheepish about having embraced his new paternal role as the "big meanie" with such zeal. It was Bing—cradling a crumple of bills, the allowance he'd been saving for a new violin bow. "I want to help," he said, offering his stash up to his father. It was shocking, that only their eleven-year-old seemed to grasp the gravity of the situation. More shocking still—that three hundred and some bucks? Lowell took it.

If he seemed touchy, Lowell was getting it in the neck from more than one direction.

When his parents retired—from being *real* scientists; his father was a microbiologist at Tufts, his mother the sort of ingratiating zoologist who discovered a family of great crested newts on a building site and brought a $10 billion development project to a halt—they turned to their elder son for investment advice. Wanting to be of service (wanting to show off?), he dished out plenty. Did he at least get credit now for having steered them away from gold? No, his parents were in hysterics, because their impeccably proportioned portfolio—tactically diversified, judiciously spread between growth and income—had fallen on the floor like a nutritiously balanced plate of whole grains, green vegetables, and high-omega-3 fish fillets landing face down. Their both bending over backwards on fleXface to explain that they didn't blame him in the slightest didn't require his wife's professional psychological acuity to translate: they blamed him entirely.

To make matters worse, it was at Lowell's urging that they'd cashed in the sprawling family home in Brookline two years ago. The released equity and its investment income were meant to finance pseudoscientific jaunts abroad, which wouldn't amass meaningful data, but would encourage the harmless fiction that they kept a professional hand in. But the "cozy" apartment in Fort Lauderdale into which they downsized had only made sense as a sunny respite from the excursions to the Arctic or the Russian tundra that they could now no longer finance. They were left with that confining apartment as their only hard asset; stuck there, they hated Florida.

It wouldn't have done, he supposed, to remind them that throughout his childhood both his parents had stressed how little they cared about wealth, and how crucial it was to focus not on money but on work that interested you (a homily Lowell threw rather on its head, since what interested him was money). Yet his parents had always been packrats, why they were able on moderate salaries to build healthy reserves in the first place. Thus their pose of fiscal obliviousness was a lie, for he knew no other couple who talked more incessantly about money. This or that was *on sale*, the price of something else was *outrageous*, despite no claims all year an insurance premium had *soared* . . . Their every decision, down to purchasing fine, tender green beans versus fat, tough ones, was still determined by the better *deal*. Which is how they ended up in a pretty drab apartment in Florida: it was a *steal*. Caught up in money-as-game, they mistook their raffle tickets for the prize. Because the only thing that bargain hunting "won" was more money—which was solely valuable as a route to buying the *thin, tender* beans instead of the *fat, tough* ones.

Previous to the Great Renunciation, Lowell had veritably to put a gun to his parents' heads to get them to go out for a meal. Then assured that both sons were flourishing—Aaron was in IT security, and made a killing from the Stonage—Dave and Ruth claimed not to be scrimping in order to pass an inheritance to their

boys. Because for mortals gratification infinitely de-
ferred equaled *no* gratification, their inability to switch
economic gears in old age, to go ahead and splurge
since when else were they going to spend it, ultimately
implied the illusion of eternal life. Had Dave and Ruth
registered in the gut by their seventies that they were
soon going to die, they'd have ordered the tiger prawns
every night of the week.

As for his parents "not caring" about money, well—
recent events should have put that myth to rest. They
were *beside themselves.* But then, Lowell couldn't
think of a soul who did not have powerful feelings about
his or her capital, regardless of its amount; why, try removing two bucks from a beggar's hat and see what
happens. To truly pull off proper apathy about the stuff
would require so much energy, such contrived ideological zealotry, that the indifference would amount to
a kind of caring. That was one of the fascinating qualities of money: it excited the passions.

So! Having relied on their elder son's wise, benevolent investment counsel, Dave and Ruth had now to buy
fat, tough green beans from not pathology but necessity. Did Lowell feel guilty? Yes, *Avery.* Of course. But
this parental hardship—was it really his fault? Even a
tiny bit? NO! Naturally Aaron had likewise solicited
investment advice from his big brother—advice that

didn't depart substantially from the standard guidance of any large financial institution at the time, aside from the tip to steer clear of gold, *which had turned out to be dead right* (that the Emergency Economic Powers of 1977 were still on the books should have been known to any financial adviser worth his *or her* salt, yet when Alvarado availed himself of the legislation they'd all acted scandalized). Was the fact that a digital wheeler-dealer with a wife and two small children had gone from affluent to desperate in a heartbeat *also* Lowell's fault? NO!

More frustratingly still, now that Lowell's advice *was* important—now that it did indeed run contrary to the orthodoxy of the moment (*sell, sell, sell*—tantamount to, "Find tall building, jump")—neither his parents nor his brother would take it. The investors who would come out ahead were the ones who'd held their nerve. The only rational response to derisory valuations was to *hold, hold, hold.* That instead his relatives were lemming off the cliff and consolidating their losses made stoical Lowell Stackhouse want to cry.

Fuck it. He and Avery had their own troubles.

Now, Lowell hadn't always been well off. In graduate school at MIT, he'd lived on a meager stipend abetted with stints as a TA. Before his first proper academic appointment at Amherst, he'd done some down-and-dirty adjunct teaching—including at the odd *community college*—a wallowing in the trenches that had helped further to convince him that he knew what it was like at the bottom. But he had never been at the bottom. He'd been at the bottom of the top.

Accordingly, Lowell had never received a bill that he couldn't pay. He had long unthinkingly relegated folks who kept no cushion in their accounts, who spent merely because there was cash in their pockets, who reached out for payday loans to cover their electric bills, who were chronically in arrears and lived in fear of knocks on the door, to a remote category of the hopeless, the irresponsible, the feckless. As for debt, an economic wheels-greaser that ideologically he was quite big on, Lowell promoted getting into hock as a splendid idea for companies and whole countries, but paid off his Visa bills in full. His avoidance of credit was emotional. He didn't like the sensation of being beholden, of being in someone else's pocket.

Which made him a sucker for the sad-ass Protestant values that most of the country had gleefully abandoned. The international economy had punished the frugal and rewarded the profligate for most of his professional life. It was an odd lesson for a man in his position to have failed to learn. Look at southern Europe, in the end. The euro zone's Club Med took trillions, spent them, and didn't pay them back. It wasn't nice. It was smart. Economics doesn't reward nice. It rewards smart.

So Lowell felt pig-thick. With his spotless credit report, he should have borrowed up a storm, and then once the Renunciation hit he could have walked away. Whether through formal bankruptcy or by slipping quietly off-grid, that's what everyone else was doing. Which is why the First USA Visa he'd carried since 2001, and all the other plastic in his wallet, had just been canceled. Unless they ceased lending to insolvent citizens of Deadbeat Nation, the card companies would go under: one more lifeline, snipped.

Meanwhile, the "delay" of his salary from Georgetown in June segued into July. He simply could not get his head around the idea that an institution legally contracted to deliver a certain sum on a particular day of the month would ever simply: not do it. He appeared to believe that because the university *owed* him his salary, it would ipso facto *pay* his salary, in a confusion of *should* and *will* that bordered on dyslexic. He had made his living analyzing systems, assessing in what circumstances they worked well or less well. He had no expertise whatever in what happened when they didn't work at all.

Thus as the summer advanced, Lowell watched in horror as their liquid resources evaporated. They were fast approaching the point at which Avery would refrain from buying a cantaloupe not because they didn't feel like cantaloupe, or because the fruit had been suddenly found to concentrate toxins even more virulently than strawberries. Not because she wasn't up for making the bags too heavy when she hadn't brought the car. And that's right, Mother, not even because the melon wasn't a very good *deal*. No, pretty soon Avery would not buy a cantaloupe because *they did not have the money.*

Taking his cue from Georgetown, then, Lowell made a discovery that the "hopeless" had beaten him to long ago. What do you do when a mortgage payment comes due, and the requisite funds are not in your account? You don't pay it. You don't pay it in June. You don't pay it in July. By August, you'll have got with the program.

When Avery specialized, drawing a hard line between mental and bodily suffering had seemed glaringly misguided, since treating the whole patient meant addressing what a person *felt* in every sense. Having completed a grueling but powerfully driven, goal-oriented project, many patients post-chemo got depressed. Simply staying alive had abruptly ceased to qualify as a respectable prime directive. Accustomed to the energizing terror of mortality up close and personal, some patients missed being sick. Others contending with milder ailments like arthritis had strong feelings about whatever restrictions knee replacements had placed on their Extreme Running regimes, and yearned to air their despair about relinquishing an ambition to run one hundred marathons in as many days in their eighties. To a man and woman, all of her elderly patients had been surprised to be old—which Avery privately regarded as a serious failure to pay attention. PhysHead was an eclectic discipline, drawing on tai chi, a variety of talk therapies, yoga, dream analysis, weight training, and forced crying—whatever worked.

The last thing she'd considered when qualifying as a clinician was whether PhysHead was recognized by Medicaid and Medicare. For most of her career, exclusion from the programs was a blessing (government reimbursement rates were roachbar), but in 2030 it deprived her of the only clients who might have afforded her treatment. She shouldn't have taken the deluge of desertions personally, but a few bit so close to the bone that she acted unprofessionally. Perhaps betraying her own priorities, she'd cried after one formerly loyal patient, "I bet you're still budgeting for a case of wine every month!" To which the woman replied smoothly, "Two cases."

Lowell was so dominating that without the ballast of her own work she feared for the even keel of her marriage. Yet he was terribly sweet about helping her to move out of the office she'd rented for nine years, during which they glass-half-fulled about how maybe it was for the best, since the kids had to handle their own disappointments and could use some old-fashioned mothering.

A Washington summer was hot and sulky, more so now that Lowell had banned air-conditioning. They switched off Mojo as well, whose monthly maintenance was a killer, and the loss felt oddly intimate; now that you couldn't shout imperiously for home-cooked brownies, it was as if some long-abused domestic had stormed out. The kids were surly, with nothing to do, and understandably angry about having had all their plans for the season canceled.

"You might find," she told the boys in the breakfast room as they glowered at fleXes, "that in a public school you have more opportunity to excel. At Gates and Sidwell, the intake is so selective, it's harder to stand out—"

"I already excel at Gates," Goog grumbled. "Don't try and sell being thrown into a cesspool as some great opportunity."

"But these are extraordinary times, honey. As your father says, in even a few months—"

"According to Aunt Florence," Goog cut her off, "*she* graduated from college in the perfectly roachbar year. Everyone who graduated when she did was cursed, while students a few years behind her did okay."

Florence should really keep a lid on her questionable theories about why she'd underperformed, when the real problem was her vague, do-goody double major. "I don't think working at a homeless shelter means you've been 'cursed'—"

"Would *you* want to do it?"

"No. But Aunt Florence is more self-sacrificing than I am."

"Even if the country recovers, I could be part of a marked generation, too. We could all end up walking around with ash on our foreheads, like Cain."

"Tell Dad," said Savannah, gliding past in micro-shorts with that air she'd refined of seeming permanently aggrieved, "I'm not applying for any more of these booby jobs."

True, with foreign tourists overrunning the city, the upscale hotel and restaurant sectors were thriving. But teenagers had now to compete with forty-year-old former hedge-fund managers begging to wait tables.

"Why don't you and Goog consider going up to Citadel in Gloversville?" Avery suggested. "I talked to Uncle Jarred last week, and he could use some help harvesting vegetables and feeding livestock. I don't know how much he could pay, but more than I will for languishing around the kitchen making toast."

"God," Savannah said. "Not only am I some waster with no prospects for a college degree, but now I'm a farm hand!"

"Yeah, Mom," said Goog. "Tell Uncle Jarred that's what they make undocumented immigrants for."

"Actually, since the amnesty," Avery said, though she was not helping her own case, "most immigrants won't do that work, either."

"It wasn't called an amnesty," Goog said. At thirteen, he'd written *one* paper about the long-in-coming immigration reform bill of 2020—the very year used to promote it as a signature of clear sightedness—which qualified the boy as an expert.

"I'll go to Citadel," Bing said softly. "In biology camp, we learned to pull carrots. I thought it was careless. And somebody has to make some money or we can't go to the grocery store."

"You're a bit young to send into the fields," Avery said, ruffling his hair. "I could be done for violating child labor laws. But I like your attitude, sweetie."

"He's a scaredy-cat toady momma's boy," Goog said scornfully, "who knows full well you won't make him dig potatoes. He's just saying what you want to hear."

"*Scaredy-cat toady* is a mixed metaphor," Avery chided. The boys went through phases of being close, but ultimately when she christened her two sons, Avery created competing search engines. (She was attached to their names, of course, which seemed so fresh, quirky, and contemporary when she and Lowell chose them, and at this point she couldn't imagine the children called anything else. But perhaps it was the very products of trying too hard to be modern that were guaranteed to date. One of those engines had so decisively trounced the other, too, that she worried the boys would internalize the hierarchy as fated.)

Embarrassed to have time on her hands in a town that placed a premium on being overbooked, Avery sometimes dragged the kids out shopping to cool down. Yet many stores had also grown stingy with the AC, leaving her nostalgic for the days when shopping in America in July required a down parka. Only the luxury outlets, popular with foreigners, were jumping. Milling with a few other local families also seeking respite from the heat, Macy's and the like were nearly deserted. Shopping had become a spectator sport. It was almost thrilling, tracking how much a flimsy pair of shorts made in Sri Lanka went for this week.

Fortunately, the kids were bored with the museums by now, since strolls down the Mall were out. The iconic national thoroughfare was so often colonized by violent cost-of-living protests that the long lawn was brown and trampled. Municipal authorities were unable to keep ahead of the graffiti that defaced the steps of the Capitol—MEXDRECK SOLD US DOWNRIVER—or that smeared down the border of the Lincoln Memorial's reflecting pool: THE BUCK STOPS. The abbreviated aphorism was chilling.

Competing convocations on the Mall displayed a classic inconsistency. Jovial raves, with dancing and booze, celebrated the demise of the universally despised "über-rich," with banners declaring: STINKIN RICH NOW JUS STINKIN, OR FAT CATS BOWL EMPTY, BOO-HOO! Yet the very same people would return the next day for demonstrations of outrage that the wealthy had escaped unscathed, waving placards like WALL STREET GOT HEADS-UP ON THE BIG WELSH; REPATRIATE OFFSHORE TREASURE CHESTS! and BANKERS EAT CAKE! The double-think reminded Avery of the Middle Eastern response to 9/11 when she was fourteen: the same Muslims who told pollsters the World Trade Center was toppled by the Jews also wore Osama bin Laden

T-shirts in homage. Who says you can't have it both ways?

Even the armies of Asian tourists that flooded the Smithsonian in the spring were dwindling. Flashing arrays of hundred-dollar bills like geishas with cheap fans, too many girlish visitors in ridiculous shoes were getting beaten up. When word went out on the web that the Chinese were routinely distracting their assailants by tossing fistfuls of cash, for which locals would scramble in preference to kicking them in the kidneys, the rumor fueled still-larger crowds of rowdies, eager to turn a profit on racist attacks.

The closure of her practice might have desolated Avery more had her small business failure not constituted a single daub on a large and strangely exhilarating canvas. The tumultuous times shouldn't have been exhilarating, and she felt self-conscious about an excitement she made every effort to hide. Many Americans could barely feed their families. All the same, she was reminded of the vitalizing urgency that a brush against terminal illness had provided her patients. She felt privileged to benefit from the same energy, the same frisson of risk, the same casting aside of complacency, without also losing her hair. While the delay of Savannah's college entrance and the boys' demotion to public schools was a waste, Goog and Bing would later leap to the fore with high test scores, and all three would get back on track when the country got back on track. Meanwhile, they were getting a different kind of education that money couldn't buy.

As a point of pride, Avery hadn't unduly relied on a pending birthright as a backstop. Earning your own way was more reputable than counting on a handout from a long-dead industrialist. The Stackhouse assets had always manifested a moral purity that inherited wealth would soil, and she told herself that she wouldn't have wanted the tainted old money anyway. Be that as it may, the erosion of a chunk of change that might have arrived somewhere down the line recalled those thin, chafing blisters from poorly fitting sneakers, wearing away that very top layer of skin one can barely manage without. Yet should the abrasion continue, the next layer down will smart. The Mandible fortune in the background had offered an extra film of protection, without which her family was a degree more exposed.

Fair enough, they didn't eat bluefin tuna any longer, but they weren't starving. They had a roof over their heads, a handsome roof. Avery may have been haunted by Savannah's hurtful remark in June—about how if only her mother had specialized in a "useful" therapy her practice might have survived. But Savannah was right, in a way: yesterday's essential was today's extravagance. Under duress, people could live without tricep dips and personalized soul-searching. What a relief, then, that in an age of turmoil playing to her husband's very expertise, at least Americans would always need professors of economics.

When summoned to a meeting with the chancellor in August, Lowell assumed that Ellen Packer wished to apologize in person about the unconscionable delay of his salary. In straightened times, you cut the budget for the student union, and reduce the opening hours for the pool. You don't punish the faculty.

An ironclad grievance conferred a sense of clout, and he went back and forth beforehand over giving the woman an earful versus acting magnanimous. Feeling jaunty, Lowell wore his pink shoes, which he jittered up and down while Packer kept him waiting in the outer office. At no point did the chancellor's secretary look him in the eye, not even when the young man announced that the chancellor would see him now.

Ellen Packer was fat. Not pudgy or plump, but full-tilt, what're-you-lookin'-at fat, with a lack of apology that alone unsettled his expectations for this encounter. Of course, he'd never use the word *fat* in company, the judgmental adjective having joined the N-word and the M-word as not careless, period. Besides, more had changed in the last fifteen years than language. Plunked behind an equally massive desk, Packer's enormity was a political statement. Ever since the obese had obtained majority status, peoples of scale had won a sly advantage over punier contemporaries. After all, nouns like *weight* and *gravity* implied importance and seriousness; a paper that had *heft* made an impact. Folks like Packer deployed their mass to emphasize that they were forces to be reckoned with. Confronting those meaty arms splayed frankly on either side of her fleX, he didn't feel sorry for her. He felt intimidated.

"Professor Stackhouse, I don't see anything to be gained from beating about the bush," she announced after he assumed the hot seat before her desk. It was always surprising: her voice was high and musical. "I'd like to thank you for your long service to this university, and I hope you won't take this as a reflection of the administration's dissatisfaction with either your teaching or research skills. But I'm afraid we're going to have to terminate your contract."

Lowell was sufficiently stunned that his comeback arrived a beat too late. "That's impossible. I have tenure."

"Late last night, the board voted to revise Georgetown's bylaws. From this September, the university will no longer offer tenure, and previous promises of permanent employ are forthwith rescinded. Professorial salaries are consuming an unacceptable proportion of the budget."

"But tenure protects academic freedom—"

"Tenure is an anachronism," she interrupted. "What other occupation offers jobs for life?"

"There are procedures for removing tenured faculty," Lowell said, trying to keep his temper from flaring into self-immolation. "But the protocol is elaborate—much more so than a single visit to the chancellor's office. Rare cases almost always involve accusations of sexual harassment or racial insensitivity. Neither of which have I been charged with—unless you have some other *happy news* to convey."

"You're welcome to sue," she said casually. Previous to their 4 p.m. appointment, she must have conducted this conversation several times. "Though in your position, I'd think twice about incurring legal fees. The university has also consulted counsel. You'll find our *i*'s dotted. What's at stake right now is the very existence of this institution. Were you and other laid-off colleagues to prevail in court, there could be no university. So much for your restitution."

"But tenure aside—this is flat-out unfair dismissal."

"Unfair dismissal does not apply when the position you occupy has been eliminated. Off the record, I agree that, in a short-of-legal sense, your losing your job is unfair. Look around this town and you'll see similar unfairness on every corner."

"Given the nature of current events, I'm staggered by how you could fire anyone in the *Economics* Department."

"I concede the irony," she said blandly. "But if your discipline were a harder science, the nature of current events might be otherwise."

"Just because Economics includes a few outlier nincompoops doesn't mean we all have our heads up our asses." The acid was an indulgence. "Speaking of which—do you mind telling me which other faculty members in my department are getting the boot?"

"I shouldn't. That's confidential. But I suppose it will be common knowledge soon enough." She rattled off the names of a handful of his colleagues.

That was half the department. But Lowell mostly made a note of the names he didn't hear. "You're keeping Mark Vandermire? He's a rabble-rousing populist twit!"

"I'm not going to justify the thinking behind every very difficult decision. But with the gold recall and debt settlement with China, Professor Vandermire's research on precious metals continues to be germane."

"So ideology did play a part in this cull. So much for academic freedom."

Packer scrolled down her fleX. "Did you or did you not publish that the United States could 'readily manage' the national debt of 290 percent of GDP we were on track to hit in 2050? Or that the Fed had in fact 'under-used' monetary policy, which could afford to be 'more expansionist'? That inflation is a 'social good' that helps the poor by relieving indebtedness, and that 'sound money' is merely 'a fetish of the wealthy'? I'm not sure that my by-no-means-affluent neighbors would agree with you. Not now that they're paying twenty dollars for a Tootsie Roll."

"Vandermire fed you those quotes, didn't he?" They were the same snippets in which the weasel had been rubbing Lowell's nose for months. "But I stand by every one of those statements, since this calamity has nothing to do with the national debt, or monetary policy, and everything to do with the bancor! Besides, what about Ryan Biersdorfer? Are you telling me you're keeping him on because the university endorses his view that financial collapse is the best thing to happen to the United States since the frost-free freezer?"

"Between ourselves, I find his iconoclasm extreme. But his treatise *The Corrections* is getting a great deal of play internationally, and may help him to raise funds for Georgetown abroad. At least it's a positive perspective that seems to make some people feel better."

"That's how you're selecting your faculty now. By rescuing the academics who make students *feel better.*"

"I'm sorry, Professor Stackhouse, I didn't mean to involve myself in the internal conflicts of your field. I'm afraid we're going to have to bring this meeting to a close."

Lowell started to panic. He hadn't meant to get adversarial. "Listen, what if I accept a reduction in salary?"

"Then I'd say you were a poor economist indeed. This country has an annualized inflation rate of 80 percent—and that's the *official* figure. It's hardly the time for wage cuts, even if I were empowered to offer such a thing."

"Well, what about my back pay?" Lowell would have worried that he sounded sniveling, but his mind was clamorous with the mortgage, his kids, and Jesus Christ, how to break this to Avery.

"There you have an excellent case. The university is doing everything in its power to bring terminated faculty up to date."

Rolling her chair back in regal slow motion, the chancellor stood formally behind her desk. "I hope you appreciate the fact that I am choosing to conduct these painful conversations myself, though I might have delegated the unpleasant duty to an underling. I'd also like to apologize for letting you go at the last minute, right before the term resumes. The board had been desperately hoping that applicants from Asia and the subcontinent would make up for the devastating drop in domestic enrollment. But the highly publicized, often racially motivated violence downtown has led to a sudden wholesale withdrawal of foreign students, who pay much more lucrative levels of tuition. They now prefer the Ivy League satellite campuses in Delhi, Beijing, and Jakarta, where they feel safer. Our own satellite campuses are Georgetown's only sectors in the black. But their surplus can't supplement the shortfall in DC, because we're having trouble repatriating bancors. Which you of all people should understand."

With that lone nod to his competence, their meeting was adjourned.

Chapter 9
Foul Matters

Florence Darkly's skirting of poverty had always been contaminated by a hint of pretense. Throughout the string of punk jobs for which she was overeducated, she'd always known that in a pinch she could turn to Grand Man. Her grandfather had a parsimonious streak, but he was generous on birthdays, and open to well-reasoned appeals to make "good investments"—which is how Jarred copped a failing upstate farm that was starting to look a shade less wacky. Without Grand Man, she'd never have managed the down payment on the house, and at Adelphi she lied to co-workers about renting. Serving a population on the absolute edge, Florence was ashamed of the leg up. Advantage was separating. Having even limited access to wealth two generations away was like having secret powers. Those superheroes were always lonely.

But this last July, her parents had organized a conference on fleXface, breaking it to all three kids at once that Dad hadn't, after all, brought Grand Man and Luella back to Carroll Gardens simply to spend more quality time with his father during Douglas Mandible's final years. Receiving the news with grim stoicism, Avery made a great show of concern for their parents, who were the *real* victims of fortune-go-blooey. *Oh, no, what about that ranch in Montana?* (The overdone performance usurped Florence's traditional role as the considerate one. And it was a bit too easy for Avery to suppress *Fuck, so much for that kitchen extension,* given a lifelong affluence of which Florence could only dream.) Jarred spouted his standard bilge about governmental treachery; what the hell, he'd already snagged his farm. The great-heart legendarily oblivious to worldly prosperity, Florence alone was detectably dolorous. But honestly, someone had to find the annihilation of God knew how many millions just a little bit depressing.

Suddenly becoming mortal should have made her feel closer to the others in her "community," who'd never enjoyed surreptitious resort to a loaded old man in New Milford. Instead she felt frightened. It was hardly comforting to be all in the same boat when the boat was sinking. That whole helping-hand lark—turning to one another in times of tribulation—only worked when who was under the gun varied from week to week. It did not work when everyone had a crisis at once—at which point the *community* atomized into a large number of people in the same place, who wanted and needed the same things, and lacking the means of getting them might take what they required by deception or force. As the urban crime rate escalated across the nation, Florence marveled that it had ever been possible to walk down the road with a wallet, or to wear a fancy watch. Late in the day, she appreciated the miracle of civilization, whereby people paraded sacks of groceries, or jingled keys to a car, and were not immediately set upon. Even all those beggars in downtown Brooklyn: they were still *asking*.

Real poverty is about doing what you have to do as opposed to what you want. So while Florence didn't warm to her father's suggestion that she take in her aunt from France, Willing's forecasts were proving accurate: the mortgage interest continued to soar; her cost-of-living raises lagged behind roaring prices. Every trip to Green Acre Farm fostered post-traumatic stress disorder. She shunned ironing to avoid paying for the electricity. To skip showers, she cultivated the pirate-style bandana into a permanent affectation at work. For a time, Kurt had hung on at the florist; Asian tourist dollars spilled into Brooklyn, and restaurant bouquets kept the shop afloat. But news of muggings and racist gang murders discouraged moneyed travelers, restaurants suffered, and the florist closed. Kurt had missed paying his usual pittance two months running, and she couldn't bear to say anything. Besides, even if her tenant improbably kept current, his rent had been set in 2027, and no longer covered his share of the utilities.

She would have to replace Kurt with a relative who had "resources."

"I don't know," Esteban said quietly on the sofa, now duly repaired with duct tape. "Kurt's an asslick, but he keeps to himself. Family—they butt into your business. Can't see your aunt mousing around the basement, never saying a word about the tromping, yakking, and television overhead."

Esteban put a premium on privacy, since he kicked around the house all day. When he first lost his job with Over the Hill, he was almost relieved. On one trek he led in the spring, a ruined banker threw himself off the Palisades, plunging hundreds of feet and missing the Hudson River with a sickening crunch. Numerous other instances of older clients who'd lost everything scraping together the remnants of their savings to go out in style made leading expeditions stressful. It was hard enough to worry about elderly clients accidentally slipping down the mountainside without also worrying that they'd pitch themselves into oblivion on purpose. Over the Hill acquired a murky reputation, and no business could prosper long from a consumer base that was self-eliminating—not when said consumer base was both suicidal and broke.

Thereafter, he'd picked up temporary kitchen work in Manhattan, also enabled by bargain-hunting foreigners, for whom whole meals cost less than a soda at home. (Some subsequent violence insensitive tourists were said to have brought on themselves—as by singing loud, snide renditions of "The Star-Spangled Banner" while weaving drunkenly down Sixth Avenue.) Esteban hated the work; his people had served their time with piles of china smeared with Bolognese, and the grungy, invisible job seemed a generational demotion. Yet he hated idleness more. He'd stooped to loitering on corners for day labor, as his father had, but the competition was stiff, including from gringos, and when construction crews came shopping, he seldom got picked. Esteban had lost the hunched, I'll-do-anything-and-ask-for-nothing quality evinced by his father's generation of immigrants. He stood too straight. He looked people in the eye. He came across as a man who expected to be paid what was agreed on at the start, and who would raise a fuss if he were shafted. Who wants to hire that?

"My aunt is a writer, or was, so she must value her solitude," Florence said. "I don't know her well, since she moved to Europe in the latter 1990s and only came back to the US for book tours. She's incensed that novelists don't earn royalties anymore, so for the last ten years she's been on strike; even my dad doesn't think it's writer's block. But she did swing through New York on general principle about three years ago, when you were away on an expedition. She and Willing went on a marathon walk to Manhattan, just the two of them—which surprised me, since my dad claims Nollie 'hates children.' There's always been some friction between her and my dad, but I thought she was pretty cool—*careless*—when I was a kid. My dad was the play-it-safe sort; Nollie was the brave one. Mouthy, adventurous, always involved in torrid romances that blew up with a lot of shouting and breaking of stuff. She used to be a looker. Fit. But Jesus, she must be . . . seventy-three? Not the kind of woman you imagine becoming seventy-three."

"After *Over the Hill*, I can imagine anybody seventy-three," Esteban said. "Everybody I see just *pre-old*."

"Including me?"

"I keep waiting for you to turn sixteen"—he kissed her—"so that I can't be done for statutory. Now, you really want to swap a timid, no-problem suck-up for a crazy old lady you've barely seen since you were twelve?"

"I don't *want* anyone in this house but the three of us. But we need the money."

She dreaded Kurt's eviction. When she first took in a tenant, she hadn't considered that, for landlords with a conscience, renting was closer to foster care than commerce. She couldn't bear kicking someone out who had no place to go.

Steeling herself in the kitchen the next evening, Florence knocked delicately on the door to the basement. She hadn't laid eyes on Kurt since he'd missed the first rent payment. He must have been mortified. "Can I come down?"

"Of course, it's your house, Florence!" When she arrived downstairs, he was feverishly stuffing a pair of socks into the hamper. "Look, I'm super sorry, if I'd known you were coming, I'd have cleaned up."

"Cleaned up what?" Florence said, scanning the Germanic order of his domain. The bedding was cornered and smooth. The carpet was thin and a strangely depressing off-blue, but it was spotless. A grainy scatter on the counter beside the stove only stood out because every other surface was immaculate.

Kurt followed her line of sight, and immediately began sponging the counter. "Sorry," he said again. "I've been learning to make tortillas."

An odd complaint for a landlord, but the basement was *too* clean. Aside from one bag of cornmeal and a canister of salt, the shelves above the kitchen unit were bare. On a hunch, she sidled to the small fridge, and sure enough: only a juice bottle filled with tap water and a crumple of margarine foil. "Kurt, you've got to eat better than this."

"Oh, I'm not that into shopping, and I put it off." He was thinner. Sunken cheeks combined with the teeth to make him look ghoulish.

"And it's chilly down here!" Florence said. "It's November. Some warmth bleeds from upstairs, but I told you to make free with the space heater. It's very efficient, and I was assured it wasn't a fire hazard. Also . . ." She sniffed. "I don't mean to embarrass you, but that toilet needs flushing."

Kurt blushed, and did the honors. "I just know that, you know, water is . . ."

"Pricey, but a necessity. I warned you this was an illegal tenancy, but that means *I'm* breaking the rules. It doesn't mean you have no rights."

Kurt bent his head and clasped his hands. "Look," he said to the floor. "I'm surprised you didn't knock on the door a long time ago. You've been really, really decent, beyond the call. And I've been applying for jobs all over—"

"So has everyone else," she said gently, taking a seat at the small laminated table. "And since your job at the florist was part-time, I guess you don't qualify for unemployment. Do you have any family?"

"We've sort of, um, lost touch."

"The trouble is, I have family myself. An aunt, who's coming back from abroad and needs a place to stay." She left out the part about Nollie having "resources."

"I immense, immense understand," Kurt said hurriedly. "I'll get out of your hair like, tomorrow. And promise, soon as I'm back on my feet, I'll get you that back rent—"

"But where will you go?"

"If you could lend me a tarp, I hear the encampments in Prospect Park are malicious," he said with forced cheer. "Everybody singing, and playing instruments, and telling stories. Just like Woodstock! It could be a great experience. Something to tell the grandkids."

Florence thought reflexively, *You're not having any grandkids with those teeth.* "That's not what I hear the encampments are like. More like *malicious* in the old sense of the word. Central Park is even worse. And winter's coming."

"There's always, you know, city-subsidized . . . the projects . . ."

"The waiting list for social housing is closing in on a million applications." Florence was exasperated to find herself on the wrong side of this conversation, and tried to wrest back her rightful role. "But there's always the city's shelter system."

Though she'd rehearsed it, the suggestion was disingenuous. The shelters were overwhelmed. Lines in the morning were as long as the ones for the banks a year before. Adelphi tried to get the word out that all their rooms were taken by de facto permanent clients, even after the facility doubled the building's occupancy by forcing more than one family to share the same small units—resulting in the kind of conditions that in the old world of investigative reporters might have produced a lacerating exposé. Staff couldn't police the ban on food in the rooms and had given up. Rats and roaches scuttled through the halls. Toilets overflowed. Drains backed up. Meal portions in the cafeteria were stingy. Fights broke out over dinner rolls. And still they came. Yet who arrived had changed. The slept-in clothes were from L.L.Bean. The strollers were wide-bodied, with snap-up plastic covers for inclement weather and expandable side pockets for shopping and snacks; baby blankets were cashmere. These strollers

once went for thousands, and more than one bedraggled foreclosure victim camping on the sidewalk had
been mugged for their luxury transport. When she
turned this type away, she often heard railing about
how much they'd paid in taxes. If she informed this
latest brand of homeless that they had to register with
the DHS in the Bronx first, they weren't having any
of it, refusing to give up their places on line. Florence
was accustomed to stories from the homeless about
having once been nuclear physicists, too—occasionally
from educated but unbalanced former professionals
who'd suffered breakdowns a while back and dropped
off the map, more often from raving fantasists. But
the new homeless had been nuclear physicists in good
standing just last week. If they were demented, it was
with rage.

Florence stood and raked her hair. Kurt would all
too willingly shuffle out the door with his few belongings in canvas hold-alls and make his way to the park.
But in comparison with the shelter, this house had
space.

"There is the attic," she introduced reluctantly. "It's
not finished, but it's big enough for a mattress and chest
of drawers."

"Oh, man, Florence, no problem, and I promise, I'd
be so quiet up there, you'll never know—"

Florence raised her hand. "You misunderstand. You're six-foot-what? You'd die from a hemorrhage in five minutes. I was thinking we could put my aunt up there. She's barely over five feet. You could stay down here. But only if you give me a hand clearing all the junk out, cleaning up the dust and mouse shit, and making the space livable. And you'll need to accommodate more storage down here, for anything in the attic we decide to keep."

By asking him for favors, she was doing him one. Kurt had started to cry. Esteban was going to kill her.

All that time in Paris, and I never had a proper *garret*," Nollie said approvingly. Spruced up, woody, and aglow with strategically warm indirect lighting, the attic was cozy, although the new arrival was also being a good sport.

Short and bony, Nollie dressed like a kid, in worn, dated jeans; red Converse All Stars; a LIFE'S TOO SHORT TO DRINK BAD WINE T-shirt; and an enormous, beaten-up leather jacket that looked to have been around the world twice. Her ponytailed hair was thin to be kept that long. Her face was lined, but it was easy to discern the acerbic, smartass younger woman she seemed to believe she still was. She moved with an abrupt, angular authority: she was used to getting her way. Florence couldn't say her father hadn't warned her.

The septuagenarian clambered nimbly up the last three ladder rungs and slung the jacket onto the mattress. The sleeveless tee revealed the kind of arms that Esteban had mocked at Over the Hill: stringy and sinuous, with mean, hard-won muscles, but nonetheless sagging with the shriveled skin beneath the biceps that boomers tried so heartbreakingly hard to avoid. Standing in the middle of the attic, she clapped her arms at her sides, then raised them in an arc overhead until her fingers touched, barely missing the roof beams. "Check!" she announced. Florence didn't get it.

Nollie's having arrived with scads of luggage was a pain, yet also an indicator that if she could pay for extra baggage, she must indeed have savings. Willing helped hoist the cases through the hatch.

"I've got a few contributions for dinner," their new resident announced, tossing Willing a bag. "But first I need to earn it. Shake off the flight." With an impatient smile, she shooed them from the attic and retracted the ladder.

In the kitchen, Florence unpacked the lavish gifts: sausage, acorn-fed ham, smoked horsemeat of all things, exotic French cheeses. They'd have a feast.

"Fuck me, *qué es eso?*" Esteban exclaimed. The frame of the house had begun to quake, *poom, poom, poom.*

Florence and Willing crept back upstairs and stared up at the ceiling. "What do you think she's doing?" her son whispered over the rhythmic din.

"Home improvements, already?" Florence puzzled. "It sounds like construction."

They shrugged and slunk back down. The pounding lasted about half an hour—a very long half an hour—and proved especially grating for the fact that the pummeling was unexplained. "Christ," Florence muttered. "What have I done to us?"

In due course, Nollie reappeared downstairs, cheeks flushed, and wearing a fresher version of the same down-market uniform; she'd have passed herself off as in good trim for seventy-three if only she dressed her age. It was a generational blindness. Young people could pull off ill-fitting rags as stylish; Florence's niece Savannah would look sexy in a paper bag. Past cohorts had understood that beyond sixty or so you compensated for the shabbiness of your birthday suit by cloaking it as nattily as possible. Grand Mimi wore silk brocade, stockings, and tasteful pumps for trips to the post office. But the following generation dressed badly first as a political statement, later out of indolence, and latterly from delusion. Boomers considered old age one more conspiracy to expose, like the Pentagon Papers.

Florence gestured to the spread. "Nollie, this is so generous. But how did you get this stuff past Customs?"

"Oh, it's murder to get anything *out* of the United States," Nollie said. "You can get almost anything *in*." She flourished three bottles of red wine and a liter of brandy.

They'd invited Kurt, already sliding from freeloader to family. His insistence on being helpful put an extra burden on his host; with a repast of cold cuts, there was nothing to do. Florence no longer merely worked at a homeless shelter; she lived in one, too.

Oiled with alcohol, dinner was raucous, Nollie presiding. Florence tried to savor the enlivening of her aunt's strident views, which could soon begin to wear. She was starting to feel the strain of real generosity, as opposed to the more formal charity for which, after all, she was paid. Real generosity entails no recompense. It means giving up something you fiercely value and cannot replace. In this case, the sacrifice was of privacy, intimacy, and quiet. The addition of the garrulous old woman and obsequious ex-tenant to life upstairs completely transformed what it felt like to walk around her own house, even in the unlikely instance that those two kept their mouths shut. Newly self-conscious, she felt observed and judged; when making an ordinary request that Willing fetch Nollie a towel, a whiff of performance parenting polluted the instruction: *Look how I have raised my son to lend a hand.* Despite the evening's casual plates-on-laps dining style, she didn't dare plunge hungrily into the platter of meats and cheeses on the coffee table, but hung back to ensure her guests got enough prosciutto first. That was the biggest change: Florence checked everything she did and said now for whether it was *polite*—surely the very antithesis of what it was supposed to feel like to be home.

"The national debt was bound to come to a head eventually," Nollie held forth on her third glass of wine. "It was just hard to predict when. And prophets too ahead of their time are always ridiculed. Take population. In my teens, the species was allegedly reproducing itself into extinction. Last time I checked, the human race was still here. Now we're closing on nine billion—a tripling in seventy years. But what if the 'overpopulation' hysterics were right, just too soon? Same with debt. Twenty years ago, doom-and-gloomers were foaming at the mouth about excessive borrowing. Nothing happened then, either—until a year ago, when everything happened. Familiar with complexity theory? It helps to explain why everything can be fine for a long time and then go to hell all at once."

"I'm betting if we all had PhDs in 'complexity theory,'" Esteban said, "you'd tell us about it anyway." Nollie was the sort of know-it-all whom Esteban couldn't abide. After Over the Hill, he cut no one slack merely for being old.

"Complexity theory isn't itself all that complex," Nollie said pleasantly, not rising to the bait. "As systems become more complex, they grow exponentially more unstable. They can keep puttering along, getting messier and messier, until one tiny disturbance sends the whole shebang into meltdown. Like those towers of playing cards, where you add a single queen of hearts and suddenly it's fifty-two pickup. Or jugglers who can keep ten balls in the air, but not eleven. Feeding, watering, and employing nine billion people and rising is the ultimate complex system. You never know when adding that one last baby boy sends all the balls in the air to the floor."

"That's absurd," Esteban said.

"Is it?" Nollie said mildly. "*The straw that broke the camel's back* is complexity theory in a nutshell. Economics—same idea. Massively complex, massively unstable. It doesn't take much. See, that's the other rule: complex systems collapse catastrophically. Look out the window."

"This is nothing," Willing said.

The company turned to the boy.

"Care to elaborate?" Nollie asked.

"No."

Her son's obscure pronouncement was freaky, and Florence was relieved when her fleX tringed. "Dad! I guess you want to say hello to Nollie. She's right here."

"I guess, but I mostly wanted to ask if you've talked to Grand Mimi." Her father looked harried. But then, didn't he always.

"Not for a while, why?"

"I can't raise her. Fair enough, though I've imposed a fleX on her, she never turns it on. But my mother is one of the last holdouts with a landline. Which for weeks she hasn't picked up. Maybe she's been out, and the voicemail being full could be simple inattention. But now the line is dead."

"But the landline is dead in general. Telecoms don't maintain the network. I wouldn't worry too much. She has live-in help."

"When she first moved in, Margarita seemed energetic and capable, but that was fifteen years ago. She's pretty damned old herself."

"If you're that concerned, maybe you should stop by, then."

"I can't, that's the point," her father said irritably. "You have no idea what we're dealing with here. I say *we* loosely speaking. Your mother barricades herself in her Quiet Room all day, and I have to beg her to baby-sit just to run out for milk."

"Can't Grand Man take care of his own wife?"

"He's not strong enough. She can get violent. And he's become so passive. Without any investments to manage, Pop's lost all sense of purpose. He fleXts, noses around the net, but rarely leaves his chair. We tried leaving them on their own for an afternoon, and when we got back the house looked as if there'd been a tornado. You keep asking us over for dinner. Why do you think we haven't accepted?"

Florence sifted discreetly into the kitchen. "I'm responsible for a full-time job, a kid, an unemployed husband, and a tapped-out tenant, not to mention your sister—who as far as I can tell takes up a lot of room. Like, the whole house. It's not going to be easy for me to find time to go on another care mission. Couldn't Nollie stop by?"

"Good luck with that!" her father jeered. "Those two haven't spoken for thirty-five years."

Florence promised that someone would check on Grand Mimi. The call ended before she realized that her father hadn't tried to talk to his sister. Ever since taking his father and stepmother in, he'd churned in a sustained state of wrath, and some of that anger seemed aimed at Nollie. The put-upon posture was a pity. Having sidelined his own life to care for elderly parents, he came across as unkind.

When she returned to the feast, Willing was addressing his great-aunt with unnerving focus. "That can't be the real reason. You wouldn't leave France only because people don't like you. After all. You must be used to it."

"Ha!" Nollie said. "You're right there. I guess there was more to it. I have a penchant for being where the action is. I'm a writer. I like story."

"Mom says you don't write anything anymore."

She smiled. "You don't go out of your way to ingratiate yourself either, do you? As for writing, no, I don't see the point. But you don't lose a certain mindset."

"The United States is a bad place to be," Willing said sorrowfully. "You should have stayed as far away as possible."

"I've been an expat a long time," Nollie reflected. "I always thought I haven't bothered to get French citizenship because jumping the bureaucratic hoops was too much trouble. When the dollar crashed, I realized that my reluctance to swear fealty to France went deeper than laziness. It's weird, because I don't believe in nationalism. I've always dismissed patriotism as blind, mindless cheerleading. I don't have many friends left in the States, and I haven't been that close to our family. But I felt pulled back. I can't help—caring. It's been unbearable, watching this last year from afar."

"You're an American," Willing translated.

"I'll always be American to Europeans, and maybe I'm tired of fighting it."

Willing didn't appear to find the explanation satisfying. "I think you're crazy." He cut himself another slab of Camembert. "This cheese won't last, and then what?"

The following afternoon, Florence returned from work to find a large van double-parked in front of the house. A burly Central American was unloading cartons onto the sidewalk. Willing was schlepping the delivery inside. On inspection in the light of the streetlamp, the boxes were all addressed to Enola Mandible, c/o Florence Darkly. Scrawled on the side of the uppermost box: *BLT, PB—UK.*

"What's this," Florence asked Nollie, who was overseeing the operation, "first the cheese, now bacon, lettuce, and tomato and peanut butter?"

Her aunt chuckled. "*Better Late Than.* British paperback."

Florence hadn't read it. In her early teens, everyone seemed to be reading Enola Mandible's bestseller except for her own family. At a glance, *BLT* seemed to dominate the shipment: *BLT, HB—PORTUGUESE; BLT, TRD—SERBIAN; BLT, BK CLB—FLEMISH.*

"You know," Florence said carefully, "this house is already pretty cluttered."

"Oh, I left all the chairs and whatnots behind, even most of the clothes. But I wasn't about to leave the books."

"This is all books?" Florence was staggered that anyone would pay to transport anything so superfluous. Her father had regaled her with the story of Grand Man having packed up his library in the ludicrous expectation that Dad would store all those formal anachronisms in his house. But as she decoded the labels in black marker—VF = *Virtual Family*, AO = *Ad-Out*, C2G = *Cradle to Grave*, TIM = *Time Is Money*—she registered with astonishment that these were multiple copies of the *same* books, mostly in languages that no one in the household spoke, including Nollie herself, and which presumably the addressee had already read because she wrote them. The vanity of the consignment beggared belief.

"They'll have to fit in the attic." Florence felt awkward issuing an edict to an elder. "That's all the space we can spare you, I'm afraid."

"Oh, I think we'll manage. Uh-uh! I'll take that one." Nollie intercepted a box marked *Foul Matter*, and struggled it possessively up the stoop stairs herself. *Foul Matter* being the only good title of the lot, Florence was moved to inquire.

"It's a term of art for original manuscripts and their permutations en route to publication," Nollie said. "Invaluable material for literary critics, biographers, and doctoral students. Sold to a university library, those papers could be worth a great deal."

Willing and his great-aunt did miraculously cram the dozens of cartons in long, snug lines below the eves, though Florence was crestfallen that after her homey redecoration the space now looked trashy and cramped. But even more was she distressed by her aunt's glaring failure to have digested what had been happening in the United States. Maybe the woman really did need a good dose of the country up close—where "literary critics" comprised a few online cranks who deplored any screed downloaded by more than ten people, and self-published authors who talked up their own work under assumed names; where people were too resentful about having to relinquish their own dreams to read biographies about lucky predecessors who'd been allowed to realize theirs; where no student who could manage to remain in school would squander tuition on anything as trifling as *literature*, while universities were furiously selling off the very real estate that might improbably have accommodated the weak first drafts of an aging one-hit-wonder who'd exiled herself to France.

Florence had kept abreast of her sister's travails in DC, but it had been difficult to take them seriously. Avery's life had always seemed charmed. The younger sister was the mercenary, the materialist, the con-formist, the conservative, whose politics had grown only more rightwing. She'd never seemed to work that hard, yet milk and honey flowed effortlessly in her di-rection: the townhouse, the luxury cars, the sumptu-ous dinner parties, the three perky children who were nicely spaced and brimming with arty talents. Her barmy therapeutic practice had been backstopped by a husband with a solid academic post in an institution at the very heart of establishment Washington. Avery had chosen the safe route, the wide, well-paved road.

In short, her sister was rich—in Florence's circle, a permanent designation, one that stripped the so anointed of any right to pathos. Florence eked by from month to month, but people like Lowell kept money in jars all over the house. He may have lost his job, but people like Lowell got another one. If Florence had to repress a trace of satisfaction that at last her sister had troubles, too, she had to try harder still to appreciate that the troubles were real, that they were large, that they were insoluble.

"We're selling the house," Avery declared, without even saying hello. Nollie's preposterous shipment just installed in the attic, Florence was disappointed by her sister's cut to the chase on fleXface. She was dying to tell Avery about the delusional chutzpah with which their aunt expected her papers to be purchased by a prestigious university library.

"Well, it's not a bad idea to downsize, is it?" Florence supposed. "With Savannah soon off to college—"

"Savannah's not going to college."

"I thought you said she accepted delayed admission."

"The delayed admission is a fiction. And we're not *downsizing*." In contrast to her musing ruminations of yore, Avery's discourse had grown jagged and declarative.

"What's the point of moving if you're not—"

"If-we-do-not-sell-the-house," Avery spelled out staccato, "we-will-face-foreclosure. That is the 'point' of moving out."

Her sister's frustration made Florence worry that a certain humoring quality on her part may have infected their conversations hitherto—conversations into which she'd never have expected a word like *foreclosure* to make an appearance. Nonplussed, she said neutrally, "So what's the plan?"

"Fortunately, real estate has appreciated. But we've built no equity, other than the increase in value, a whack of which will be seized to cover defaulted interest payments."

"But you can use the profit as a down payment on something cheaper, right?"

"Florence, you idiot! You don't put a down payment when you can't get a mortgage!"

Had they been in the same room, Florence would have taken a step back. Whatever she said seemed to enrage her sister, and the next question would prove no different: "Why can't you get a mortgage?"

"I have no job! My husband has no job! We have no income, other than Lowell's pissy unemployment checks! What bank is going to give us a loan of, like, a million dollars?"

"You don't get unemployment, too . . . ?"

"Not if you were self-employed! Florence, you've really got to start paying attention here! I have three children. We're living on meatloaf. Goog keeps getting beaten up at school. He's a target because he doesn't speak Spanish."

"It might have been a good idea if you'd encouraged him to study—"

"In the *olden days* it wasn't *illegal* to learn *German* instead, the language of *Goethe* and *Günter Grass* and *Bertolt Brecht*, which he actually *likes*. And which, by the by, they don't teach at Roosevelt, either. They don't teach anything at Roosevelt, as far as I can tell, besides the lyrics to 'Guantanamera' and how to punch out a kid with just enough restraint so that he can come back the next day and you can do it again."

Florence decided this wasn't the time to take on her sister's racial insensitivities. "So could you rent for a while, then?"

"Landlords aren't going to leap at a couple without jobs, either. Maybe if we flashed the cash from the house. But it wouldn't last long, since new leases are astronomical. It would be better if we could cool our heels for a while until the economy recovers." Avery had disciplined herself into using a more reasonable tone, even a pleading one.

"Like where?" Florence asked warily.

"Somewhere urban, ideally. Where Lowell could jump on any university openings."

"What *are* Lowell's job prospects?"

"Right now?" Despite the suggestion of a snarl, Avery kept trying to control herself. "Abysmal. The irony has come home to me late in the day that economists are of very limited *economic* utility. And he's useless in every other regard, too. I have to do everything. I was the one who found a buyer for the house."

"Who can stretch to property like that, unless they pulled some fiddle before the crash? I heard tycoons with connections in Congress made out like bandits."

"Sorry not to play to your leftwing conspiracy theories. Who can swing a nice *American* house, really? Some guy from Shanghai. Asians are buying up everything. Not only residential real estate, but companies. Landmarks. Any day now it's going to be the Mao Monument in the middle of the Mall."

Florence sighed. "Talk about conspiracy theories! Dad says we went through the same thing in the 1980s with the Japanese—*Oh, those slant-eyes are taking over, they're buying up Rockefeller Center*—and now look at them."

"Florence." In the proceeding silence, there was a girding. "Would you mind. For just a little while. Would it be all right—if we stayed with you?"

In Florence's silence, a horror.

"We'd bring the cash," Avery continued. "We wouldn't be a burden. We could help with expenses. Help with other things, too. And everything's getting so weird. Maybe we should band together. Rally around, as a family. Florence. I already asked Dad, about our staying in Carroll Gardens, and he said"—she was choking up now—"he said no. He just kept railing about Luella."

Florence's mind was racing. The money would have been more tempting had Nollie not unobtrusively delivered an envelope of bills to defray expenses that very morning. "But this is only a two-bedroom, and full to the gills. With a tenant in name only. Nollie . . . You don't have to be in the city, do you? What about Jarred?"

"I asked Jarred, too," Avery said glumly. "He said maybe if I'd asked earlier in the summer, but then he hired some 'temporary' farm workers, and now they won't leave. With their families, and everything. It sounded creepy. Like, it wasn't exactly his idea. Halfway between having serfs and being held hostage. He said he actually pointed a rifle at them, and they laughed. They could tell he wouldn't use it. I couldn't take the kids up there even if he said the more the merrier. It doesn't sound safe."

"Why not turn to Lowell's family? Why is this purely a Mandible problem?"

"My in-laws also live in a two-bedroom, in Fort Lauderdale. Where my brother-in-law, his wife, and their two kids just moved in. They were all wiped out in the Renunciation—thanks to my husband's peerless investment advice."

"You're not doing your marriage any favors by blaming him like that." Florence was stalling for time. "He didn't personally default on the national debt."

"Sorry, but the urge to blame someone you can get your hands on is irresistible. These days, taking on the sins of the world is Lowell's only constructive function."

Once in a while, when you have a great deal at stake, like turning a small, quiet nightmare into a big, out-of-control one, your brain actually works. "Listen! Why not approach Grand Mimi?" The inspiration was such a relief that Florence felt weak.

"But I hardly know her . . . ," Avery faltered. "She's always been so remote . . ."

"Like you said, this is about family, about pulling together. And she's got two bedrooms gathering dust. She's, what, ninety-five, ninety-six? But not that out of it. She must have some idea what's going down. It's not that big an ask, even if she is kind of private."

As they discussed the proposal further, both sisters relaxed. It was a good plan. The Stackhouses would simply need to keep to themselves, and be respectful. The caretaker Margarita was a good-hearted woman, more companion than nurse, who would surely see as well that this was a Mandible emergency.

But when Florence mooted the idea at the dinner table, Willing was skeptical. "Why should she?"

"Because she's family," Florence reiterated, with a sentimentality she didn't quite buy herself. "We're talking about her grandchild, and her great-grandchildren."

"I don't get the impression she feels any connection to us. She's always looked at me like some floor lamp."

"Willing's right," Nollie said. "My mother can be one cold customer."

"She never talks to me," Willing said. "It's only, you know, *Do you want a cookie?*"

Grand Mimi paid her familial dues by giving a rather formal Christmas Eve cocktail party every year, and she did always seem glad when the kids skittered to their parents' sides for removal. Mimi could barely extend herself to grown grandchildren, and giving a hoot about yet another generation was a bridge too far.

"Maybe it's better if I clear off," Kurt said. "Make room for your blood kin."

"Even if I were willing to throw you out on the street," Florence said, "it's not going to help me to lose one houseguest and gain five."

"It's not going to help *us*," Esteban said testily. He was touchy about pronouns in relation to a house whose deed remained in Florence's name. With their dinners now crowded with two people neither of whom he cared for, he was touchy, period.

"Nollie?" Florence implored. "I told you my dad hoped you could check up on Grand Mimi, and you weren't keen on the idea. But now you could go with a mission. Best of all, not on your own behalf."

"I'd be the worst possible emissary with that woman, on anybody's behalf."

"Your appearance would have shock value," Florence pressed. "It would underscore that these are extraordinary times, calling for extraordinary measures."

Nollie shrank into herself, looking queasy. It was bizarre to see a woman of seventy-three afraid of her own mother. But with enough manipulative appeals to her lifelong "bravery," she relented.

Nollie mobilized in a spirit of gritty resolve. Attached to a reputation as intrepid, she insisted on taking the bus to the Jay Street subway stop, though in light of the previous morning's fat envelope she might easily have covered taxi fare. It was a Saturday afternoon, and after drilling her aunt with directions, Florence was glad for once that the woman dressed so shabbily. Public transport was getting chancy. Anonymous sneakers and jeans lowered the likelihood of her being accosted. Florence almost asked Esteban to act as an escort, but that seemed condescending, and if mother and daughter got into a heart-to-heart, he could be waiting for hours.

Yet Nollie came back more rapidly than expected. On the return journey, she did take a taxi—stepping out shakily, looking wildly up and down the street as she pocketed the change from the fare. As Florence turned from the window, Nollie let herself inside, bolted the top lock, and secured the chain. She headed straight for the cognac.

"So . . . ," Florence said. "How'd it go?"

Nollie burrowed into the sofa and tucked her feet under her thighs, cradling her juice glass. She looked like a six-year-old with progeria.

"Was she mean to you? Could she honestly be harboring a grudge over *Better Late Than* this many decades later?"

"I have no idea," Nollie said robotically.

Willing crept downstairs and sat on the third step to eavesdrop.

"You came back awfully soon," Florence prodded. "Was she not home, then?"

"She wasn't home." Nollie's rigid manner did not convey the experience of an unanswered doorbell.

"Would you . . . be willing to try again? Avery's family has to relinquish their house within days—"

"We can't try again."

"Nollie, what happened? This is pulling teeth."

Willing slipped to the doorway. "She likes story, she said. Stories are about *not* telling you what happened. When you blurt out the ending, it's not a story."

Nollie eyed her grandnephew. "I'm not sure I do like story. Real story. I think maybe I only like the fake kind. Or only real stories about someone else."

Willing turned to his mother. "See? She's still doing it. Carter says she's 'a hack.' Who only wrote 'one bare-all success that titillated literary circles back when there were literary circles.' But I think she's good at it. I think she's got the knack."

Florence blushed. "Nollie, please don't take my father's remarks to heart. Willing's quoting him immense out of context."

"I'm familiar with the context," Nollie said. "I know what Carter thinks of my work. And if I didn't, I'd be grateful to Willing for letting me know."

There already seemed a thread between those two, and now Florence appreciated how Esteban must sometimes feel: jealous.

"Go on," Willing said.

"I was taken aback by Manhattan." Nollie took a stiff swig. "All the panhandlers. Very aggressive, too. Threatening. When I lived on the Upper West Side, the bums were crazy. Now they're sane enough, but rancorous. I was surprised: rancor is worse. Crazy people are sealed in their own world, and their energy churns around and around, like in a blender. But this bile is straight arrow. It's aimed at other people.

"You folks are used to it. But for me . . . The families camped out on the meridians in the middle of Broadway. So many shops closed. Restaurants still open keeping their shutters down. The news reports in Europe—they don't include what it's like to walk down the street. Less like New York, and more like Lagos.

"I'd hopped off a station short, at Seventy-Ninth Street. I thought I'd go to Zabar's, show up with my mother's favorite smoked sable, as a peace offering. Zabar's has been at Eighty-First and Broadway for a hundred years. I've made runs there for whole-grain mustard and pop-up sponges since I was a kid. But the store has been vandalized. Someone slashed graffiti over the plywood, EAT YOUR SALMON. I thought that was almost witty. I decided to skip bringing a present.

"At my mother's building, there was no more doorman. Fortunately I brought the keys, which I've carried all over Europe since 1996." Nollie turned. "See, I didn't fight this assignment that hard, Florence. I've never been resigned to not seeing her again. We're both so willful, feasting on our grudges. But generating all that anger, year after year, has worn me out. And by now, the whole feud thing isn't only exhausting, but exhausted. It's been feeling a little stupid for quite a while."

"All grown up, at seventy-three," Florence said. "There's hope for us all, then."

"The floor was gritty. Mailboxes were listing open. Fifty-eight's had a copy of *Foundation Journal* jammed inside, but the issue was from back in September. The elevator was broken, so I took the stairs. Some guy walking down bumped into me, hard, as if on purpose. His clothes were disheveled, with one exception: an immaculate white fedora. I thought, *That's weird*, because when I was a kid my father had one just like it.

"When I rang the bell, I was shaking. I'd no idea how she'd respond to me, with no warning. I didn't want to give her a heart attack. And that was the other worry: what if she hadn't answered the phone because of a health crisis."

Florence said, "If Grand Mimi were in the hospital, someone—"

"I don't mean that kind of health crisis. The thing is, I wasn't shaking only because she might still refuse to speak to me. Or because she might be *indisposed*. Something felt wrong. After I buzzed, the peephole cover lifted. There was an eye. It wasn't my mother's."

Florence said, "Margarita—"

"The peephole cover dropped, and spun around, as if someone flicked it. No one opened the door. I tried the bell again, and heard laughter on the other side. Youngish voices. Then the man on the stairs came back, carrying a bottle of gin. He shouldered me aside and said, 'Got a problem, lady?' He took out a set of keys. I recognized them. Looped with a red ORGAN DONOR tag. They had to have been my mother's. That man didn't look like an organ donor, unless he was planning to donate someone else's."

Florence said, "Maybe she's had to take in tenants—"

Nollie ignored her niece's jive theory. "I know I get myself into trouble. I have a temper. My last ex, Gerard, told me I have to learn to rein it in. He said I've no idea how small I am, how old I am, how I'm not as strong as I think. Gerard said I had to learn to be *cowed*. But I don't have a talent for cowed. So when this man began to bully in the door, I demanded, 'Where is Mimi Mandible? This is my mother's apartment, and I need to check she's all right.' He repeated 'Mimi Mandible' as if that were the funniest, stupidest name he'd ever heard. I insisted he explain what he was doing there, and he said something like, 'Piss off, you old bag.' He shoved me, and I fell."

"Are you okay?" Florence asked.

"Achy, but nothing broke. While I was still on the floor, the man doffed the fedora with mock chivalry, and repeated, 'Mimi Mandible! Mimi Mandible!' before letting himself in. No one has ever found my mother's name quite so hilarious.

"At that point, I should have left, I realize that now. But I was so angry. Apartment fifty-eight is my home— and somehow having been banished from it for over thirty years makes it *more* mine. I thought, this place has already been taken away from me once, and twice is beyond the pale. Carter and I raced each other as kids on that staircase. I grew up on the other side of that door, which is full of my mother's things, her jewelry, her perfume, her beautiful shoes—and we wear the same size. Someday those should be my things, mementoes of my childhood and of my mother. For decades, I've held on to the idea that she picked the fight to begin with, and *she* owes *me* an apology. After living with Pop so many years, surely Momma of all people should appreciate the importance of a *book*, and how *art* has to take precedence over *feelings*." If Nollie was sneering, it was at herself. "Anyway, suddenly it all seemed so wasteful. Even *I* didn't care about my book, or any book. I had to get in there. In my imagination, I'd rescue her from that awful man who made fun of her name, and she'd cling to me, and weep in gratitude, and she'd forgive me."

"You used your keys," Willing said.

"Everything happened very fast, but I saw enough—and I wish I hadn't. The place was a wreck. Trash, dried-up sandwiches, hypodermics on the floor. Someone sleeping or high in the hallway was rolled up in one of Momma's Persian carpets. A girl naked below the waist wandered past wearing the shreds of Momma's mink; that girl looked right at me and didn't see me. It was freezing; the utilities must be shut off. And it reeked. Encrusted pieces of my parents' wedding china, the teal with the silver edge, were crashed around everywhere in shards. It looked as if they'd been using Momma's collection of art vases for football practice; chunks of them were rolling around the hall. Through the entrance to the living room, I could see more young people, mostly out cold. The cream upholstery was covered in what looked like vomit. Carter and I got into terrible trouble if we ever ate chocolate sitting on that set."

"Tell me you got out of there," Florence said.

"I only stood in the doorway a few seconds. Then the man in the fedora sauntered into the hall, down by the dining room, swigging from the bottle of gin. His eyes lit up, and he lunged toward me. I picked up a chunk of vase at my feet—the clear Deco one with the crystal jags; I always thought it was ugly—and I hurled it. I only hit his knee, but I think it hurt. Then I ran. When Carter and I raced on those stairs, I always won. I didn't even turn to see if the man gave chase, just powered to Broadway and flagged down a taxi. Finally fifty years' worth of all that tedious exercise proved good for something." The story, more than the sprint, seemed to have worn her out.

"We should call the police," Florence said.

"I already did," Nollie said flatly. "The dispatcher promised to send someone around, but I'm not convinced. She warned me that 'squatting' incidents were rife, and when I explained my mother was ninety-six I could hear her lose interest. The police were 'overstretched,' she said. They had to 'prioritize.'"

"Everyone at school," Willing said, "says contacting the police is a waste of time. They're mostly obsessed with protecting themselves."

"What have those people done with Grand Mimi, and Margarita?" Florence said.

"I'm not sure that bears thinking about," Nollie said.

"But how would strangers get in to begin with?"

Nollie shrugged. "Must be easy to dog two old women with their shopping. Don't you ever feel vulnerable, inserting a key in the front door? I sure will from now on."

"Nollie is right," Willing said. "We can't go back there. Not without a gun."

"Willing!" Florence admonished. "We don't carry guns in this family!"

"I should have swallowed my pride, back in the nineties," Nollie said, "and come to terms with my mother. I thought it was a matter of artistic integrity, refusing to regret writing the very novel that made my reputation. But it was ordinary stubbornness. The truth is, the portrayal of the mother in *BLT* isn't flattering. I sure wouldn't appreciate anyone publishing that *I* was 'as sexual as a dead mackerel,' for all the world to read. I never needed to unwrite the book, which is impossible anyway. All I ever had to say was that I was sorry for hurting her feelings, which would have cost me nothing." She rose to pour another finger. "I made a terrible mistake."

"The mistake," Willing said, "was not taking a gun."

Chapter 10

Setbacks Never Bring Out the Best in People

In theory, Avery accepted that material possessions were a trifling concern in an emergency, and all that mattered was the safety of her family. The competent characters in disaster movies didn't dither in burning buildings about how to rescue the couch. Yet expecting herself to feel blasé about abandoning a $6,000 armchair was tantamount to assuming you could go into Settings on your fleX and select "Become completely different person."

So she wearied around in the same circles. They could not arrive at Florence's narrow, depressing house with a vanload of upscale furniture. They could stash their things in storage, but the substantial monthly charges would add up. She'd heard through the grapevine that one neighboring family, also forced to sell to some opportunistic plateface—there, she'd said it, if only in her head—had gone through the whole rigma-role of storing their stuff, which was as much trouble as moving, only to default on the payments and lose everything anyway.

The Stackhouses might have held a giant yard sale or contacted a house-clearance company, but the District was awash in objects of every description, and it was a buyer's market in extremis. Nobody wanted your matching mango-wood side tables, though ears might prick up if you mentioned a five-pound bag of rice. In the encampments on the banks of the Potomac, the homeless were sleeping on top-of-the-line Posturepedic mattresses salvaged from curbsides. Getting their hands on rotgut might have been challenging, but street people could take their pick of cut-glass Waterford highballs from which to sip it; in the massive impromptu flea markets that had sprung up all over town, whole sets of crystal were going for ten bucks. Hauntingly, Belle Duval had once reflected on the disconcerting discovery of coming into means: that above a surprisingly low threshold of primitive needs, "there isn't that much to buy." Since the affluent purchased up a storm anyway, the high-end detritus flooding American cities pressed Belle's point: if it didn't line your belly or protect you from the elements, it was junk.

Thus the only intelligent option was to accept their purchaser's derisory offer for "contents," since their realtor advised that they could instead be charged for removal of effects. Emotionally, too, it was easier to leave everything than to cling to one side table and let its sibling go. Simply closing the door and walking away at least spared the kids a *Sophie's Choice* confrontation with their own belongings, and she'd been able to sell Bing on the notion they were going on an "adventure"—a line for which the older two, alas, were too savvy.

Yet once she accepted the inevitability of near-total divestiture, Avery felt surprisingly powerful—not only lighter and less encumbered, but strong, as if she were flinging desks and bed frames off her shoulders like an adrenalized survivor of an earthquake. She was moved to consider the dual meaning of the very word *possession*: an object of which you take custody, but also a wraith taking custody of you. Had she ever owned those mango-wood side tables, or had they laid claim to her?

Meanwhile, Lowell was hopeless. He stuck her with everything: Tossing partially used cleaning products. Choosing the five best pairs of socks from a drawer of thirty. Remembering that despite the historic upheaval, they were required to keep financial records for tax purposes going back seven years. Canceling the utilities. Finally getting through to the Salvation Army, only to learn that charities were swamped with donations of household goods, and their kitchen implements, gardening tools, linens, Christmas decorations, and most of their wardrobes were destined for the dump. Researching the few stations that still sold gas for their SUV en route to New York. Meanwhile, her formerly debonair husband huddled in his office banging on his fleX in a bathrobe, claiming that someone needed to submit a "counterargument" to Ryan Biersdorfer and "restore confidence." But a disheveled, unemployed academic wasn't going to restore anyone's confidence, least of all hers. It wasn't a time for *writing*.

In all, Avery was astonished that she wasn't more distraught. For necessity is the mother of self-reinvention. She woke early without an alarm clock. An impetus infused her final days on Thirty-Sixth Street NW of a sort that a determination to locate thick-cut veal chops had never furnished. Long insulated from misfortune by a successful practice and high-earner spouse, she felt as if she'd thrown off a quilt in an overheated house. A mildness had suffocated most of her adult life, and suddenly the late November air smacked sharp against her skin. Things seemed to matter again. It seemed to matter how she spent her time and what she told her children. Why, it was tempting to wonder whether, while the likes of the Stackhouses were musing idly over whether to cover the footstool in taupe or mauve, folks on the margins were living real lives, and making real decisions, and conducting real relationships, full of friction and shouting and moment—whether all this time the poor people had been having all the fun.

As the family piled out of the Jeep Jaunt (to streamline, they'd had to sell Lowell's sleek GMFord Catwalk), the atmosphere was jovial. Fierce hugs and joyous greetings recalled earlier visits when the kids were younger, and eager to spend time with their aunt and first cousin in New York City. Fresh from her sister's embrace, Avery could put out of mind that they hadn't arrived as guests but as indefinite parasites. Besides, ever since she married Lowell, Avery had been designated the sibling who had it easy, and the role reversal was liberating. Advantage in this country had conferred a distinct social *dis*advantage since she could remember.

They pulled their bags through the front entrance to the dark basement, from which some penniless tenant had been evicted; for reasons beyond her, the man hadn't been thrown out, but had shifted to the living room upstairs. The air was dank. One double mattress lay on the floor, next to two single airbeds.

The carpet—one of those blues that clashes with everything—was thin as felt. The bathroom didn't have a tub. A compact kitchen unit sported a small sink and stove, its mini-fridge decaled with nasty white and yellow flowers. The comedown was precipitous—from a roomy, leather-walled DC kitchen whose Mojo was programmed to prepare chicken cacciatore. Avery's initial elation fell away.

Which she was obliged at once to cover. "See?" she said cheerfully to the kids, who were surveying their new home with incredulity. "It'll be like a camping trip."

"I hate camping," Goog said.

"Mom!" Bing cringed from a skittering. "This place has bugs!"

"And it smells," Savannah said.

"We've had some trouble with moisture," Florence said flatly.

"Oh, don't mind Savannah," Avery said. "She doesn't understand that all basements get a little musty."

"Ours didn't," Goog said. "And ours had a pool table."

"Pity you didn't bring it, then," Florence said. "You could have slept on it."

Avery detected a practiced coolness in her sister, a refusal to be provoked that was new. In times past, she was a self-righteous hothead. Florence had mentioned being continually "under siege" at her shelter, where this nonreactive mode must have come in handy.

"The basement was moisture-proofed two years ago," Florence told Avery. "But when I tried to get the company to make good on the five-year guarantee, the website was down. Out of business."

"I know," Avery said. "I almost brought our robotic vacuum cleaner. But a crucial plastic tab is broken, the manufacturer's gone under, and you can't get parts."

"Real American tragedy," Willing said from the stairs to the ground floor. His inflection neutral, it was impossible to tell if he was being sardonic.

"What's *real American tragedy* is our ending up in this shit hole," Goog returned.

"Thanks," Florence said, with a glance at her sister: *Nice parenting job, puppet.*

"Tragedy is ending up on the street," Avery snapped. "And not having generous relatives who offer you refuge."

"If this is a 'refuge,' " Savannah said dryly, standing at a distance from the rest of the family like an indifferent onlooker, "does that make us refugees?"

"Yes," Avery said, "in a way, we are refugees."

"Nonsense, my dear," Lowell said from the stairs of the outside entrance, where he was struggling with their largest case. "This is the United States, not Yemen. In short order, you'll look back on overblown remarks of that nature and feel ridiculous."

"I don't understand why we can't rent somewhere decent," Goog whined. "We're not broke. You said you turned a profit on the house."

"No income?" Avery said through gritted teeth. "No lease or mortgage. Which any economics whiz kid should know, even if I hadn't already told you that ten times."

Abandoning their luggage, Lowell was scouting out the basement, brow furrowed—testing the stability of a small table, disconnecting a lamp and dragging it across the room, then searching on his knees along the wall.

"Honey," Avery said. "What are you doing?"

"Trying to find a socket. I have to set up a workspace. On the drive up, I got some ideas I have to get down."

Avery had tried to tolerate her husband's self-importance about "his work," some vital economic analysis without which the world would fall apart. The world having already fallen apart, her tolerance had morphed to contempt. In retrospect, it seemed pretty rich for her whole family to have none too subtly dismissed her PhysHead practice as quackery, when

Lowell's whole field had been exposed as far dodgier hocus-pocus; at the worst, Avery's cures merely overpromised, while Lowell's gang of charlatans had wreaked nationwide havoc. Yet she'd humbly done all the packing and cleaning, all the soothing of the children's anxieties and indignations; she'd leapt all the bureaucratic hoops for the sale of the house—while Lowell scowled over his fleX, pattering fervidly on his keypad, intermittently pressing the far-right Delete button for seconds at a time in melodramatic disgust. He reminded Avery uncomfortably of playing with her father's vintage BusyBox at Grand Mimi's when she was four—turning a crank that didn't drive anything, twisting a phone dial that didn't place a call, opening a drawer with nothing in it, and setting a clock that didn't tell the time.

"Lowell, did you lock the car?" Florence asked. "It's not only New York, but New York max. You can't leave anything unattended."

With a whiffley sigh, Lowell trudged back outside.

"I'm afraid we've run out of mattresses, not to mention floor space," Florence said. "So I thought Goog could double up with Willing upstairs. The bed's a single, but Willing's on the slight side."

"Oh, man!" Goog said. "It's so passé to be gay. I'd rather sleep in the car."

"Is that okay with you, Willing?" Avery knew territorial teenage boys well enough that she needn't have asked.

"It doesn't matter if it's okay with me," Willing said. Embarrassingly, he was right.

"Sorry these digs aren't what you're used to," Florence told her sister quietly. "I warned you it would be a squeeze."

"I'm the one who should apologize," Avery said under her breath. "The kids have been such boomer-poops—"

"It's been a shock for them," Florence said. "I've seen it repeatedly. Everyone adapts effortlessly to coming up in the world, and improved circumstances always seem well deserved. But going in the opposite direction feels unnatural. What's really poisonous is that it also feels unjust. There's a whole other class of people who've always had it tough, and they take adversity for granted. They may not think they deserve hard luck, but they accept it, it's what they're used to; there's no railing at the gods. But I've never met anybody whose life has taken a sudden turn for the worse who thought a reversal of fortune was just what they had coming to them. The outrage, the consternation, the fury, all of it impotent—well. Setbacks never bring out the best in people."

Lowell returned shaking his head. "I can't believe someone stole the *corn chips*."

What's that god-awful pounding?" Avery asked that evening as Florence stirred a couscous concoction at the stove.

"I finally asked her," Willing said from the kitchen doorway. "It's jumping jacks. Nollie does three thousand every day."

"She claims it takes thirty-two minutes, but it feels like a lifetime. Sweetie?" Florence directed to Willing. "We don't have enough plates. I think Nollie took one to the attic, though *don't* interrupt her until she's through *exercising*. I tried once. She took my head off."

"But she's seventy-three!" Avery exclaimed.

"You know boomers," Florence said, head down to the cutting board. "They're all crazy. Even Dad's turned from mild-mannered reporter to homicidal maniac. Mom barricades herself in her Quiet Room as if the house has been taken over by Al-Qaeda. Luella keeps trying to redecorate. Last week she shredded off all the wallpaper in the upstairs bathroom. So Mom's coming over tomorrow night as their 'envoy.' Otherwise all four have to come, and it's too much of an 'ordeal.' I'd be touched if Mom didn't want to put me out. I'm afraid she meant it would be too much trouble for her."

"Any word about Grand Mimi?"

"She's officially a missing person, but so are lots of people."

The cutting board commanded an intensity of concentration at odds with her sister's competence. Florence was an efficient cook who could chop tomatoes in her sleep. She made no eye contact. Avery felt awkward, and couldn't help but suspect she was being made to feel awkward, if not deliberately, then from a wrath that her sister was at a loss to control. She felt unwelcome.

"Hey." Avery touched her sister's sleeve. "I'm sorry it's worked out this way."

"I am, too," Florence said. "I mean, it's worse for you. Losing everything and all." She didn't sound as if she meant it.

"It's different from a visit." Avery looked at the floor.

"No, it's sure not like a visit!" The guffaw sounded like a sob. "What happened to the gray water in the sink?"

"In the plastic tub? I poured it out. It was disgusting."

"Don't do that." The muscles in her sister's jaw rippled. "It's for the dishes."

In which case, Avery had just rescued her family from cholera. "Listen—can I help with dinner?"

"Esteban!" Florence cried, ignoring the offer. "*¿Mi querida?* The table will barely fit eight! We need extra seating!"

"I don't want to sit at a kiddie table!" Bing wailed from the living room.

The children were all watching TV, and there'd already been an altercation over Willing's peculiar preference for the business report. Clearly, her kids were never going to spend much time in that dismal basement. Avery felt chagrined about her promises to keep out of Florence's way. She couldn't imagine preparing her family's meals on that Tinkertoy unit with daisy decals. The thought of which prompted her to lie, "I hope you don't think we expect you to cook for us all the time."

"Let's take things as they come, shall we?" Florence exuded that dense quality of keeping a great deal in, and for now Avery was glad for whatever was churning in that head to stay there.

Grateful for a task—was Florence refusing to delegate the smallest chore because it might make her sister feel useful and so less beholden?—Avery volunteered to help Esteban retrieve the coffee table from the living room, whose tatty thrift-shop mélange of fringed lampshades, baskets, crocheted pillows with little mirrors, and faded oriental throw rugs wasn't to her tastes. It shouldn't matter—*all that mattered was her family's safety*—but she missed the soft, supple, simple interiors that had taken years to design just so. This room might at least have looked snug, but that freeloader's pile of crap in the corner tipped it toward church-basement tag sale, and made others feel like intruders in the dwelling's only communal space.

They placed the coffee table adjacent to the dining table and set it with three extra places, though it was far too low. Kurt and Willing volunteered for the crummy seats, and Savannah joined them at the end, the better to be maximally distant from everybody. Avery scuttled downstairs to announce that dinner was ready. Hunched in his improvised office, Lowell made a show of having to finish some vital passage, keeping everyone waiting ten minutes while the couscous dish got cold.

Assembled at last, the convocation might have exuded the jubilance of a family reunion, were it not for the indefinite nature of the Stackhouses' presence here, awareness of which hung over the gathering like low barometric pressure—the dull, heavy weather with a glowering sky that could persist for days before coalescing into a cleansing but violent thunderstorm. The occasion was further adulterated by the oddball tenant—ex-tenant—who spoke little and whose gratitude was oppressive. Those teeth were enough to put Avery off her food. Why didn't Florence get rid of this guy? Her sister was either softhearted or attached to the idea of herself as softhearted, a conceit for which they all had to pay. Absent the scrounger who wasn't even a relative, and with Nollie pushed off more sensibly on Dad rather than on a niece—Avery found the old woman imperious, and imprudent with her opinions—they would all fit around this table, she and Lowell could find some peace and quiet in the attic, while the kids could have their own hang downstairs. The arrangement was so vividly doable that Avery grew annoyed. The extra social flotsam was what made her family's arrival seem such an imposition.

"Florence, this looks lovely." Avery stirred her serving, dismayed by the paucity of chicken. She might have overlooked the protein deficiency, save for the alcohol deficiency. The two bottles of wine she and Lowell brought were a contribution, not three loaves and five fishes to feed the five thousand. The dribs in juice glasses that Florence poured all six adults were the size of a measure of mouthwash, almost worse than no wine at all. The second bottle had been primly removed to a high shelf.

"It's too hot!" Bing cried. "It makes my mouth hurt!"

"The jalapeños are a treat," Florence said. "We don't buy much, only for flavor."

"Relief to eat something with kick," Esteban said. "This is malicious."

"Mom!" Bing whimpered. "It's like devils attacking my tongue with pitchforks!"

"We like spicy food," Willing said squarely, holding Bing's gaze and somehow managing to impart: *Here begins the phase of your life in which you will not always, often, or perhaps ever get what you want, and this is a phase that could last indefinitely.* Bing shrank from the look in horror.

Having arrived at the table with her private jar, Nollie was showering her plate with chili flakes. By her age, she might have outgrown the adolescent boast of some purportedly cast-iron constitution. The couscous had turned red, and looked roundly inedible. "This is a hell of a crowd to feed, Florence," she said. "I may need to top up the cookie jar donation."

"Me, too!" Avery said. "Don't think you have to carry this mob by yourself."

"When I was growing up on Long Island," Esteban said, "only ten people in a two-bedroom house would have seemed palatial. Place across from us in North Bellport, maybe a thousand square feet? Put up sixty-five Lats. They slept in shifts. Our house never had less than fifteen."

"So"—Nollie nodded at the company—"instead of our assimilating the illegal immigrants, the illegal immigrants have assimilated us."

"Nollie, you've been away," Florence mumbled in the abashed silence, "but no one says *illegal* now. It's not careless."

"I'm not *illegal* anyway," Esteban said tendentiously. "I was born in Brookhaven Memorial in Patchogue, New York. I'm American as you are, *mi tía*—"

"Thanks to our generous Constitution," Nollie said, eyes sparking—the woman loved to start fights—"you certainly are. Though for an *American*, you're pretty prickly."

Esteban appraised the old woman with an unforgiving glare. "Florence, bless her, is the exception. Otherwise, your whole family got an attitude problem. Still think you're special."

"This whole country has an attitude problem," Nollie returned equably. "It's you Hispanics who bought into the idea of America being special, and it's not my family's fault that you've been suckered."

"I wouldn't write off the United States just yet!" Lowell said. "See the Dow is climbing back up, Goog? What'd I tell you!"

"It's only going up in dollars," Willing said from the coffee table.

"What else is it supposed to go up in?" Goog jeered.

"In a hyperinflationary economy—"

"Whoa, hold on there, Willing," Lowell said. "*Hyperinflation* is a technical term. In my field, Philip Cagan's definition is broadly accepted: at least 50 percent per *month*. We're nowhere near that. In the 1920s, German inflation was 30,000 percent, and Serbian inflation was *300 million* percent. In Hungary, after the Second World War? It was 1.3 *times ten to the sixteenth*—literally beyond your imagination. No comparison."

"Sorry," Avery mumbled to her sister. "I think Lowell misses teaching."

"In a *high* inflation economy, then," Willing corrected, and it was difficult to tell who was more patronizing to whom, "all assets seem to appreciate, including stock. But the gains are false. In bancors, the market continues to drop."

It was a bit wicked: Avery rather enjoyed watching her husband get pushback from a fourteen-year-old kid. He'd trained their elder son to be a voluble minime, but Willing hadn't memorized the same script. Oh, no doubt her nephew had no idea what he was talking about—patchy knowledge could be worse than clean ignorance, and there was no more blind a zealotry than that of the autodidact—but he was doing a remarkably good job of ruffling Lowell's oft-preened feathers.

"When your country has its own currency, son," Lowell said, "you're not obliged to measure your gains in comparison to another currency. It's a closed system."

"It's only a closed system because the United States is barely participating in world trade," Willing said.

"We're engaged in a protracted tug-of-war over which currency in the world will reign supreme," Goog said. "It's a showdown between the dollar and the bancor."

"You don't call it a *showdown*," Willing said evenly, "when there's no contest."

Two years his cousin's senior, Goog wasn't giving ground. "The dollar is a historied currency that's stabilized the international economy for over a century, *Wilbur.* The bancor is an upstart pretender whose constraints are unworkably strict. We just have to hold our nerve. After all—look at what happened to *bitcoin.*"

"*Historied?*" Willing said. "The dollar's *history* is of becoming systematically worthless. A pile of paper versus promissory notes that can be exchanged for wheat, oil, gold, and rare earths? I know what I'd want in my wallet."

"It would be treasonous to have bancors in your wallet, *Wilbur.*" At first the misnomer Goog contrived that afternoon had seemed affectionate. Perhaps not.

"The bancor will go down in flames. You're the kind of credulous schmuck got stuck with trunks of Confederate bills at the end of the Civil War."

"*I'm* credulous?" Willing shot a withering glance at Lowell before leaning toward his cousin. "*Who's staying at whose house?*"

"Boys!" Avery and Florence said at once.

Florence cleared plates, and Avery leapt up to help. She was mortified her kids had scarcely touched their meal—yet still more mortified when, rather than scrape the uneaten food into the garbage, her sister stored the remnants in a glass refrigerator container. The practice was unsanitary!

When they returned with what used to be a half-gallon of ice cream, Goog and Bing really shouldn't have asked for a third scoop. Willing demurred from having any. Avery refused to believe he didn't want it. Twenty ounces would not feed ten people.

Kurt was opining earnestly to Savannah, "See, Republicans can't blame both evil foreign powers *and* a supposedly unqualified president—"

"Who cares what Republicans do?" Savannah looked so bored she was limp. "That's like worrying about, you know, Zoroastrians."

"Know who really can't afford for the Republican Party to get sucked into the bowels of the earth?"

Nollie said. "Democrats. When you're permanently in power, everything is your fault."

Nollie delivered verdicts with a last-word authority that made Avery want to kill.

"You also get credit," Florence said. "Like for changing Social Security's cost-of-living adjustments from annual to monthly. That's made a huge difference to our parents, and to Grand Man and Luella."

"Which Republicans fought tooth and nail," Kurt said.

"Republicans want to cut Medicare, of all things!" Florence said passionately. "To curtail unemployment benefits! Trim the Medicaid rolls! What kind of platform is that? No wonder they were slaughtered in the midterms."

So the old picket-line Florence was still in there somewhere; ineffectual railing against injustice wore Avery out. She vowed never to let slip here that she'd ever voted Republican, even if right now that meant shoving a fist in her mouth. Maybe it was fortunate there was so little wine.

"It's the usual GOP austerity blunder," Lowell said. "Because this is a time to pump up government expenditure. Invest in infrastructure, like a second New Deal. Reinvigorate America's industrial base, and reduce the need for imports."

It occurred to Avery that her husband needed to get out more. His familiar economics platitudes failed to connect with the rampaging crowds on the Mall, the encampments on the Potomac, the numerous cars on the interstate on the trip to New York with mattresses and bundles of clothing lashed on top, like a modern-day *Grapes of Wrath*. She had the same sensation listening to press conferences from the White House. The administration went through the motions of being the American government, and saying the things that American officials say, but the exercise had an air of imitation—the studied intensity of tots who cook pies with mud.

"By the way, everybody, Friday my mom gets paid," Willing announced. "That means we go shopping. Right away."

"What's the hurry?" Lowell asked.

"By the next paycheck, prices will be higher."

"A couple of weeks can't matter that much," Lowell said. "Aren't you being a tad theatrical, kiddo?"

"Obviously," Willing said, "Aunt Avery buys the groceries in your family."

"That's ri–ight!" Avery sang. "And everything e–else!"

"Prices go up every week," Willing said, "and sometimes every day. And it's not predictable. Some products stay the same, and then suddenly the cost of Ziploc storage bags will double. We don't use them anymore. We use glass."

As Goog, being a guest, went first in the upstairs bathroom, Willing stacked the unassailable facts like building blocks before him: (1) According to this country's customs, insofar as it continued to manifest a unified culture of any sort, caring for family was an obligation. The ties that bind might have frayed over the years, but they had not yet snapped. (2) Whether you "loved" each other was immaterial. (3) The Stackhouses had nowhere to live. (4) The basement could not accommodate mattresses for all five members of that family. (5) If everyone had to make sacrifices, Willing had to make sacrifices, too. That meant the fact that he found Goog's invasion of his small second-floor kingdom insufferable was so irrelevant that it didn't even get a number.

This being "his" room was a mere conceit, perhaps one he should be too old for. His mother owned the house. He had permission to sleep here, and now his mother had given his cousin permission also. But he had cherished a door he could close, as well as the protocol, however artificial, that for others to open it they had to knock first. Solitude was vital for his research. That sounded pretentious. So be it.

His dislike for Goog was thin, and so did not provide much entertainment. The boy's body was rounded. Not heavy, but the limbs had no articulation, no indentations and no sharpness. Everything he said he got from somewhere else. Which made Willing worry that he, too, was derivative. Perhaps he instinctively recoiled from another kid who recited received wisdom because he himself did the same thing. Willing did, of course, pride himself on *triangulating*. But even triangulation could have been another idea that Willing had lifted from elsewhere. He would think on this. Then he did think on this. To conclude that this was not a time when originality was of the slightest importance.

Willing did resolve to give his mother no grief. Yet he was unable to make himself want his cousin in his room because open-armed hospitality would be convenient. The clothing and toiletries in the splayed suitcase had nowhere to go, creating disarray where before there was a system.

When his cousin lumbered back from the bathroom with a glare, it was the new roommate's mammalian physicality that was hardest to take: the reek of his socks when he took off his shoes, the sourness of his breath because Goog was clearly one of those idiots who only brushed his teeth in the morning, the diaper look of his briefs and having to turn away to keep from seeing a peek of hair behind the fly. The revulsion was animal. Willing had the unpleasant impression of having traded in Milo for a bigger, dumber pet that wasn't even housebroken.

Willing lay rigidly on the very edge of the mattress, atop the spread with a flimsy throw from the sofa downstairs, abdicating the rest of the bed. They didn't talk. Goog appeared to resent his own impingement on Willing's space as much as Willing did. But then, Goog didn't like his cousin, either. Willing wondered if this commonality was sufficient basis for a working relationship.

When his wife proposed their first contribution to the Darkly budget the next morning, Lowell thought the amount insane. Fine, make a gesture of gratitude, but acting too extravagantly indebted effectively increased the debt. Besides, he was grumpy. His back hurt from the soft mattress, and he missed their 650-thread-count sheets. The pillows here were flat. They had no privacy, necessitating a T-shirt and boxers when he'd slept in the buff since he was twelve, and with restless children snoozing on both sides, he'd no clue how he and Avery would ever have sex. Upstairs, nothing to eat but toast—no eggs, no bacon, no semblance of coffee, not even a 90 percent barley blend. He sometimes had trouble tolerating even the company of his own family, and now he'd wake daily as if attending a chaotic conference whose invitations had been indiscriminate. There weren't enough places to sit. So "breakfast" entailed standing in the kitchen getting crumbs on the floor. He dove back downstairs.

The first order of business was another search for open academic positions. He'd originally limited himself to the top-flight schools where he belonged: the Ivies, of course, the University of Chicago, Stanford, MIT. But he'd have to cast a wider net, maybe stooping to Emory or Chapel Hill, where they could sit out the downturn in agreeable enough faculty housing and at least pour themselves a decent-sized glass of wine. Before long, the re-emergence of orderly market forces was bound to include renewed appreciation for classical Keynesian economists. Restore a steady, predictable growth in GDP and say good-bye to gold-bug losers like Vandermire—currently under the ludicrous misimpression that clinging to candlesticks as a rational medium of exchange had been vindicated by the bancor—and incendiary firebrands like Biersdorfer, his field's street-corner evangelist screaming, "Repent!" Lowell rejected his former chancellor's disparagement of his discipline as not being a "hard science," but it was an insecure science, whose practitioners, in the grip of hysteria, readily lost touch with fundamentals.

"*What?*"

Avery folded her arms before his makeshift desk. "I would like you to go with Florence to the grocery store."

"You don't need my help carrying bags if you take the car."

"Not for your powerful biceps," she said, with an insulting edge. "You claim to be interested in economics. *And* you said what I suggested we give Florence was way too much. So go ahead. Do *fieldwork*."

"Maybe another time."

"Right now. I'm not spending another day in this house without demonstrating that we'll carry our weight."

She remained so infuriatingly adamant that he relented. He'd make short shrift of the stupid shopping trip. Women could make such a to-do about a simple stocking up. At least if he went along he could ensure that tonight's evening meal included more than an ounce of chicken. He could grab a six-pack, and a few bottles of Viognier—although if all six adults matched his own average consumption, they'd go through a case every four days. All this sharing was for chumps. He'd have to send Avery out separately to install a private stash.

The most off-putting aspect of the errand was being thrown into the company of his sister-in-law, whom he didn't know quite well enough to firmly like or dislike, and Lowell preferred such matters settled. Despite her worthy calling, Florence exhibited a hard quality, which made her difficult to read. He vaguely associated benevolence with idiocy, but this shelter employee who'd squandered her studies on *environmental* policy wasn't the schmaltzy pushover you'd expect.

Yet after last night's trying dinner conversation, Lowell *had* rounded on a firm opinion of her kid—a smartass pipsqueak who apparently fancied himself a fiscal fortune-teller. Sure, like Goog, the boy was precocious. But having been precocious himself, Lowell was never wowed by teenagers who could recite the periodic table of elements or whatever. He was on to them. Precocious was not the same as smart, much less the same as wise, and the perfect opposite of informed— since the more you prided yourself on knowing already the less you listened and the less you learned. Worse, with application, less glibly gifted peers often caught up with or overtook prodigies by early adulthood, and meantime the kid to whom everything came so effortlessly never mastered the grind of sheer hard work. That was what he was always drilling into Goog, or had done before his elder son was tragically thrown to the *leones* at Roosevelt High.

But this Willing kid had slathered on an extra level of crapola, and unless his performance the previous evening was a one-off display to impress visiting relatives, Lowell could be throttling the little bastard within the week. The boy glowed with divine inspiration, as if he had a personal psychic hotline to the late editor-in-chief of the *Wall Street Journal.* Unoccupied while Avery helped clean up, Lowell had studied his nephew after dinner: He was too comfortable being silent. He had a tendency to stare, and didn't embarrass when you caught him. He did nothing a lot—and he never seemed lost in his own world or mindlessly vegged out; he was present, he was right there. When he did talk, as he had over that wretched couscous casserole, he asserted himself with an untoward conviction that he could not possibly have earned, and he displayed a doggedness, a staunchness, that he must have come by from his mother. He'd been difficult to rattle, and didn't insult easily either; for a kid that age to be able to hide so well that you'd hurt his feelings was unnatural. But really, where did that boy get off, spouting all that economics drivel? Someone was feeding the kid lines.

So it irked Lowell inordinately that the squirt was coming, too.

"Do we have a list?" he asked at the wheel of the Jaunt.

"It's pointless to have a list," Willing said from the backseat, though Lowell had asked Florence.

"I find a list keeps you from getting home and realizing you forgot the Parmesan," Lowell said. "And it reduces impulse buying—"

"There will be no cheese," the Oracle foretold, as if incanting the Old Testament. "It keeps too well. And there will be nothing but impulse buying."

"With so many shortages," Florence explained, "a grocery list ends up being a torturous reminder of everything you wanted and couldn't find."

It boggled Lowell's mind that this neighborhood was supposed to be up and coming, or even up and come. The streets sponsored some of the ugliest residential architecture he'd laid eyes on: poky, improbably narrow rectangular units, some brick, some stone-effect siding, some curling tarpaper, with painted iron grille doors, striped aluminum awnings, and front yards the size of Parcheesi boards. Gentrifiers had extended forward with closed-in, skylighted porches, but no amount of home improvement could disguise the deep dumpiness of the neighborhood's very soul. Original residents were savvier about how to decorate in keeping with the East Flatbush spirit: with plastic flowers, plaster dwarfs, flamingoes, and rooster-topped weather vanes.

At Green Acre Farm—ill-christened, for Utica Avenue was a desolate wasteland of tire and auto-repair shops, without a blade of grass in sight—the parking lot was packed, and he was lucky to find a space when someone pulled out. Inside, the supermarket had the atmosphere of a military encampment where hostile powers had called a wary, temporary truce. Shoppers gripped their carts with white knuckles and never left them unattended, like troop transporters that might otherwise be commandeered by the enemy. They shot sidelong glances but never met one another's eyes, preferring to peer pryingly at the contents of other carts. Some carts were covered in tarps, as if the nature of a pantry haul were a state secret. Customers spoke in hushed, guarded tones. Sent on sorties three aisles over, children undertook their missions with the gravity of carrying coded messages to the front lines.

"My God, Willing, they've got eggs!" Florence whispered. "Quick!"

Willing serpentined the traffic jam, returning triumphantly with a half dozen.

"We're buying for ten people," Lowell objected. "Can't we get more than six?"

"Limit of a half-carton per party," Willing said. "And they're under guard."

"Yeah, why's there so much security?" Uniformed personnel were stationed in every aisle. To Lowell's astonishment, the burly men were armed.

"The shoplifting is unbelievable," Willing said. "Everyone at school brags about slipping cans of baked beans into their coat linings, even with the guards and cameras."

Intrigued, Lowell ambled off to explore. He was accustomed to expansive American emporiums packed floor to ceiling with enticements, where the main challenges were to keep from overstocking because you forgot there were already six cans of tomatoes back home, to avoid chips and chocolates that would thicken your waistline, and to resist falling into a paralytic stupor while choosing between forty-five flavors of soup. But here, whole chunks of the displays were missing, the shelves bare. Remembering Willing's remark that cheese "keeps too well," he picked up a pattern: dried pulses, grains, frozen foods, and canned goods—particularly cans with meat, like chili, Vienna sausage—were the sections consistently ravaged. For those products that were available—canned grapefruit ($19.99) did not seem much in demand—reprinting the shelving's price tabs must have become too much trouble, and many of the labels had been scratched out and scrawled with ballpoint corrections half a dozen times.

"What's with the run on nonperishables?" Lowell asked when he relocated his party. "Everyone's gone all Jarred, preparing for the End of Days?"

"The hoarding has begun," Willing intoned portentously.

"Why do you say it that way?" Lowell didn't hide his irritation.

"It was inevitable. I tried to get my mom to start stockpiling months ago. She wouldn't listen. Now it's much harder to buy twenty bags of flour. They have rules. Not that you can't get around them. Some kids at school spend their weekends going to different stores all over Brooklyn, buying one of this and one of that. Which is how you beat the maximums."

"Willing, I'm tired of your giving me a hard time about that," Florence said. "Whatever would we have done with twenty bags of flour anyway?"

"You could have traded them. You'd have had real currency. Better than your salary. You'd have had power."

"Flour power," Lowell said, but neither had watched enough documentaries about the 1960s to get the joke. "What you mean is, these shortages are artificial?

There'd be plenty of food if people would go back to buying one jar of mayo—"

Their backs were to the cart. After wheeling to survey it, Willing was running after a guy in his fifties who was striding down the aisle with a canister of Quaker Oats. The boy stood in the man's way and demanded, "Give that back."

"I don't know what you're talking about, kid," the guy said.

"You stole that from our cart. It was the last one."

"It's only stealing if I walk outta here without paying for it. Until then it's called *shopping*. Now, push off."

As the man brushed past her son, Florence said, "So, we cross another Rubicon. Shaming used to work."

Lowell should probably have intervened, but he wasn't getting into a fistfight over oatmeal.

In the long lines for checkout, customers rubbernecked each other's loot, sometimes sending kids back to search for products they'd missed. Though their own cart contained little that Lowell found appetizing, the other two exchanged congratulations over their prizes. (Ground mutton—ugh. Chicken gizzards? *Please*. And beets were so yesterday.) Suffering his sister-in-law's glare, he felt comfortable slipping in two Blossom Hill chardonnays only after offering to pay the bill—rashly, for to his consternation the $1,100 he was packing turned out to be not enough.

Loading groceries on the belt, Florence fished out a canister of Quaker Oats. "Willing! You accused that man, and it's here after all!"

"He took it, all right. I found him with his wife in the cereal aisle. While they were on their toes cleaning out the Cocoa Puffs, I swiped it back."

Florence shook her head. "Honey, you don't even like oatmeal. You've got to learn to let this stuff go."

"Uh-uh," Willing said. "You have to learn to *not* let stuff go."

"I refuse to allow this situation to turn me into a petty, greedy, mindless animal."

"Petty, greedy, mindless animals," Willing said, "eat breakfast."

Chapter 11
Badder Bitter Gutter

Florence and her aunt often shared their disgust: the situation in the States was not nearly as bad as the schadenfreude from abroad would suggest. Sensationalist reports on European websites portrayed American cities as *Night of the Living Dead*, with crazed, rampaging looters tearing down the streets with TVs but no electricity to plug them into, while the elderly roasted their cats in the flames of their burning furniture. Okay, there'd been *some* looting, especially of grocery and liquor stores. There were *some* shortages, although it wasn't as if nine million starving New Yorkers were stuffing each other's hacked bodies into upright freezers to serve later with fava beans and a nice Chianti, as the international media would have had you believe.

As for the inflation over which German coverage obsessed, Lowell insisted that America's bore no resemblance to the Teutonic experience after World War I, when restaurant patrons paid for their meals when they walked in, because the bill would be higher once they finished eating. Why, by the end the mark was printed on only one side, because the mint was running out of ink. But had greenbacks changed in the slightest? Didn't dollars sport American presidents on one side *and* IN GOD WE TRUST on the other?

These reassurances aside, they all faced a dilemma. Lowell's unemployment would soon run out. Having been on contract, Esteban never got unemployment in the first place. Kurt should have qualified for welfare, and benefits of every description were jacked up frenetically month upon month; if the Fed was going to print the money madly anyway, what better use for the stuff than bribing the savages to stay home and put their feet up? Yet further hurdles had gone up to new claimants—most of whom were biddable, formerly solvent citizens unlikely to torch City Hall. Only applying because Florence begged him, Kurt simply didn't think of himself as a lowlife ward of the state, and flubbed the interview as a consequence. (Alas, he had a place to live. Someone in the household was working.) Which left Nollie's Social Security and Florence's stressed salary as their sole remaining income.

On the other hand, Lowell and Avery had that lump sum from the sale of their house; their extent obscure, Nollie had those "resources." But these monies would purchase ever less as time went by. Florence resented it more than she could say—now more than ever, they needed to conserve funds for emergencies—but the most sensible policy at the moment was to spend everything they had as fast as possible.

Seizing on Willing's idea that tangible goods would become the new currency, Avery took this strategy too eagerly to heart. For Florence, shopping was a chore; for Avery, it was an entertainment. So Florence learned the hard way that you never gave her sister carte blanche to buy out the store.

Returning from the Home Depot on Nineteenth Street, Avery burst through the front door, arms full, eyes dilated, her complexion mottled with hypertensive purple splotches.

"What's this?" Florence asked, nodding at the bulging canvas shopping bags.

"I really scored!" Avery pressed past with her burdens and dumped the booty on the living room floor. Several bottles of Gorilla Glue—"New anti-clog cap!

Dries 2X Faster!"—clattered from one sack. "And wait—there's more. Goog's watching the car."

When Avery finished unloading, Florence picked diffidently through the swag. She found multiple bags of spline, though why they'd need to rescreen the windows several times over was anyone's guess, and Avery hadn't bought any screening to go with it. There was weather-stripping, two-sided tape, some twenty canisters of Comet cleanser.

"Avery, what will we do with all these L-braces? And where will we store this junk?"

"*Junk?*" her sister repeated, incensed. "These are real goods. Made of metal, and other materials of lasting value. They make things, and fix things, and stick things together. They're not made of paper, and they're not an abstraction—which is more than you can say for dollars. I was incredibly lucky, and wily, and fast, and beat hundreds of other customers to the punch when Home Depot unloaded a warehouse backlog that was all pre-Renunciation, because China won't exchange *real goods* for our money anymore. This was a lot of trouble to snarf, and you should be thanking me. When a goon busts down the neighbors' front door, they'll offer a whole case of long-life milk for replacement hinges, and we'll be the only ones on the block who have the hardware." The speech, Florence inferred, was prepared.

Forcing her sister to sacrifice her family's limited space in the basement to accommodate the preposterous plunder should have discouraged more acquisitions along these lines—for the purchases were driven by the same just-in-case, you-never-know-what-might-come-in-useful reasoning that had buried wackos under suffocating piles of old newspapers and magazines, before the demise of print journalism deprived hoarders of their traditional nesting material. But a separate trip to Home Depot purely to confirm how much more her haul would have cost two weeks later inspired Avery to further extravagance. An expedition to Walgreens netted numerous kits for the treatment of toenail fungus, manifold boxes of denture-cleaning tablets when everyone in the household had real teeth, and herbal remedies for depression that actually would have come in handy, considering how this inundation of absurd consumer goods was affecting Florence, if only the pills worked. They now had nail polish remover but no nail polish, and out-of-date antibiotic ointment that wouldn't have fazed the rage of resistant superbugs when it was fresh. Thanks to a remarkably "fruitful" rampage through Staples, during which, according to Goog, his mother nearly got into a slugfest over the last package of mixed rubber bands, they were now supplied with tens of thousands of Post-it notes, hundreds of felt-tip pens, several boxes of extra-long manila envelopes, and replacement cartridges for a 3-D printer they did not own.

In fairness, Avery was not alone. The entire country, newscasters reported, was on such a feverish buying spree that for a few weeks the American economy registered an uptick in GDP. Yet even the most dentally conscientious reached a limit on how much easy-glide spearmint floss they would squirrel away, and the uptick was brief.

Living in such close quarters with relatives, Florence had promised Esteban not to take after her mother, who tended to suppress grievances and stew in silence, like a can in the pantry that's fizzing with botulism and begins to bulge. Yet it wasn't any abstract policy of resolving conflict in the open air that brought the spending issue to a head, but a delivery truck from Astor Wines & Spirits. Returning from work, Florence recognized its logo at ten paces, and something snapped.

"*What is this?*" Florence exploded on the sidewalk, while the poor deliveryman was still getting a signature in the basement stairwell.

"Stocking up on necessities," Avery said tersely, as the man scuttled to his van.

"Toothpaste is a necessity," Florence spat. "Not a tart, surprisingly supple Cabernet-Shiraz!"

"We mostly drink white, actually," Avery said coolly, pushing a last carton inside. "But assuming that's any of your business, which I doubt, could we not discuss this on the street?"

"You think I haven't known for months what's in those boxes beside the paint cans?" Florence called down the steps. "You could hide them better; pulling that old shower curtain over the top insults my intelligence. Think I don't know why you and Lowell disappear after dinner—the only time you show any interest in spending time downstairs? You don't even share it! You scurry off and get shit-faced in secret!"

"Obviously not in secret. If you want a glass so badly, you can always knock."

"I'm not the one who wants a glass *so badly*. On the contrary, I think it's important right now to stay sharp. Meanwhile, the mortgage has skyrocketed. The utilities are crucifying us. And you fritter away our meager reserves on a private wine bar!"

In Brooklyn, families shouting in the halo of a streetlamp enjoyed a long tradition, and the neighbors wouldn't blink. But they would listen. Diversion was scarce.

Closing the basement door behind her, Avery emerged from the stairwell. "Lowell and I contribute to joint expenses. But I wasn't aware that our money had become everybody's money—"

"Avery—are you an alcoholic?"

"Oh, please!"

"*Are you an alcoholic?* Because that's the only explanation—"

"Our witless *presidente* having renounced the national debt doesn't mean we're on war rations. For me, a glass of wine at the end of the day—"

"Avery, I haven't seen you drink 'a' glass of wine since you were fourteen."

"Strip away all the joys of life, and it's not worth living!"

"Strip away the booze and life's not worth living. That is how alcoholics think. If I'm wrong, prove it, and send the wine back."

"This is out of order." Lowell lumbered up from the basement entrance as well. "Your sister and I are over twenty-one. You may not approve of how we spend our funds, but just because we're guests in your home—"

"I realize you have a lot invested professionally in the notion that this is a temporary 'downturn,'" Florence said. "But we don't know how long this spiral is going to last or how deep it's going to go, and between us we have four children to feed!"

"It's your son," Avery said, "who keeps harping on how we have to convert dollars into hard assets that could be used for barter—"

"Oh, don't be disingenuous!" Florence's voice had hit its less attractive upper register. "Yes, of course I've heard how over in the park alcohol and high-nic e-bacco are used instead of money, but you're drinking your currency."

"Listen, this whole communal arrangement only works," Lowell said, "if we maintain some boundaries—"

"Oh? How am I to maintain any 'boundaries' when the primary asset I'm pooling with Nollie, Kurt, and your whole family is my house?"

"That's what this is really about?" Avery shouted. "You have to have total control over everything we do in *your house*? You're now the big momma bear, and we have to ask permission to drink, or use curse words, or eat nonorganic chicken?"

"*Any* chicken. That's what this is about! ANY CHICKEN!"

Drawn by the commotion, Esteban slipped out the main front door. "Hey, even in my old neighborhood in North Bellport, this sort of shouting match was considered low-rent. What's the *probelma, amigos*?" If the dash of Spanish was meant to inject a note of jocularity, it didn't work.

"You and I only allow ourselves to have sex every two weeks," Florence said, "so we can make a tube of spermicide for my diaphragm last for months. You wouldn't even take ibuprofen for that muscle strain last week, because the bottle's almost finished. Meanwhile these guys are self-medicating their hearts out! Though their investment in the 'necessity' of two bottomless glasses of chardonnay is, I'm informed, 'none of my business.'"

As Florence rarely lost her temper, Esteban seemed uncertain how to kid-gloves her down to earth. "Mmm," he said, waggling his hand. "Whether that's our business is a gray area."

"It's our business the moment they exhaust their savings," Florence said. "At which point, it will retroactively become our business how they wasted that money before they threw themselves on our mercy!"

"Maybe everyone needs a safety valve," Esteban submitted; he'd been missing his Dos Equis himself. "One small indulgence."

"Small? We're not talking an airline miniature here, but cases and cases!"

"Two cases," Avery said scornfully.

"Indulgence?" Florence fumed. "Think I wouldn't like to go out to eat with my boyfriend once in a while, or catch a movie like a normal person? Wouldn't I rather have been able to buy my son a proper fifteenth-birthday present in January, instead of scrawling on a lousy card? Why do you people imagine *I'm* totally fine going without chocolate, and bacon, and real coffee? Why wouldn't *I* miss having wine from time to time? I used to love doing a couple of lines of coke, too, in case you think I'm a party-pooping priss, and I don't buy that either! Any more than I save up my salary to go on vacation in Italy. My name is *Florence*, and I'll never get there, will I, I'll never go! Because every dime I make goes toward making sure nine other people aren't starving to death! Don't you think I'd also like a little whimsy, a little lightness, a little spontaneity in my life? Because I'm sick of everyone acting like I'm tight and stingy and mean and stinting because I choose to be like this, because I'm a killjoy, because I have no sense of fun, and I work in a homeless shelter because I'm grim by nature! I hate my job, you hear me? I would love to quit, and I can't, because I'm apparently some— earth-mother chump!"

"We should obviously move out," Avery said. "All this pent-up resentment. I knew you were keeping things in, but—"

"Don't be ridiculous," Florence said, stamping her foot. "Where do you plan to go, with a husband whose head's in the clouds and three kids?"

"We'll think of something," Avery muttered.

"If you could think of anything, you wouldn't be here." Florence's arms were folded and she was glaring, while Avery's head was bowed and she'd started to cry. Screaming out in the open having been cathartic, Florence couldn't sustain the fury; since childhood, she'd always been a sucker for her sister's tears. Sighing, she crossed the three segments of sidewalk between them, opened her arms, and took Avery to her chest. At length all four effected a rapprochement in the basement over a chenin blanc from upper New York State, one glass of which put Florence off her face after not having had a drink in months. This wasn't their first fight, and wouldn't be their last. But they could all reach giddy heights of rage and vituperation, after which the principals simply stood there and were obliged in due course to shuffle off to their assigned mattresses. It was one more luxury the Mandible family could no longer afford: a permanent falling-out.

It especially rankled Florence that foreign websites made such a big deal over the dryouts. If anything, the city was sending out more water trucks than ever, and post-Renunciation dryouts were no more frequent than before.

Yet they were more distasteful. With ten residents and two bathrooms, the oil drums didn't hold enough rainwater to purge the toilet bowls in a *timely fashion* for more than a couple of days. Thereafter, since modesty proved as dispensable as fresh parsley, they all peed out back; more *substantial business* required a trowel. But it was winter, when the air smacked your bare ass like the slap of a hand, and the ground was hard. Avery had confided that she and Savannah both opted for *self-storage* for as long as mind-over-matter remained feasible.

When the pipes were flowing—which, in defiance of the snide foreign coverage, was most of the time—Willing had adopted an inflammatory habit of standing sentry outside the Stackhouses' bathroom downstairs when the kids took showers. The family wasn't accustomed to water conservation, and considered showers of indefinite duration a Human Right. Since their arrival, the water bill had tripled. So preparing dinner, Florence would typically hear a variation of the following exchange from below:

"Get away from the door, you pervert!" Goog would shout.

"That's four minutes," Willing would announce in a monotone.

"You're keeping an ear to the crack, hoping you can hear me jerk off."

"You may masturbate as long as you like if you turn off the water. Soap is a more effective lubricant when the suds don't wash down the drain."

"You let Savannah shower for ten minutes, I timed it! You were just trying to get a peek at her tits—"

"Five minutes," Willing would say stoically. "I gave you fair warning."

At which point the spigot filling a pot with water for pasta in the kitchen would slow to a drizzle.

"Wilber, you asshole! I've got shampoo in my hair!"

Willing had learned to operate the main shut-off valve to great punitive effect. His purpose was honorable, but his interventions as water policeman were not improving his relationships with his cousins. He may have enjoyed his offices a bit too much.

Then there was the emotionally charged issue of toilet paper. In most major cities, stockpiling of family packs was rife, leading to chronic shortages and gouging. At the shelter, it had become impossible to keep the restrooms supplied, because residents swiped the rolls; the Department of Homeless Services had issued a memorandum withdrawing funding for paper goods altogether, to Adelphi's decided olfactory detriment. Public facilities in the likes of department stores and museums also ceased to provide the means of tidying up after one's ablutions, presumably having suffered the same pilfering from a higher class of clientele.

Florence initially taped a TWO SQUARES PER WIPE notice above both holders, a polite request that, given the continued depletion of this precious resource downstairs, was roundly ignored. She tried discreetly taking her sister aside to suggest that maybe she "peed too often"; if she was capable of disciplining her digestive tract during dryouts, perhaps she could direct a degree of similar grit to her bladder. Big surprise, Avery was offended. Florence had also to take Savannah to task for leaving wads in the trash with red and beige traces: the paper had been squandered on removing makeup. Monitoring her guests on such a tawdry level was embarrassing, but when both expense and sheer availability were at issue, she had no choice. Substitutes like cotton balls, paper towels, and napkins were bad for the plumbing, and soon as hard to come by as the real thing.

Eventually, the inevitable occurred, what Florence had been dreading: repeated shopping trips netted no replenishment, and they were down to their last two rolls. Enraged internet postings established that New Jersey, Long Island, and Connecticut were experiencing the same scarcity. She was aware of neighbors quietly trading their stash one roll at a time for red meat and chicken, which was nothing short of extortion. So she assigned Willing a research project, and called a house meeting.

"I realize this is mortifying for everyone," Florence said. "But until the situation improves, we're going to have to do without in the ass-wipe department. Willing?"

"Before indoor plumbing," Willing said. "Americans used newspaper, or pages of a Sears catalog. But there are no more magazines and newspapers."

"Dad would be so proud," Avery said. "Finally one good reason to rue the downfall of the *New York Times*."

"The Romans used a sponge soaked in vinegar on a stick," Willing said. "Also, that tradition of only eating with your right hand in India? It's not just a ritual, but a biological imperative. Because I knew they wipe with their left hands. I didn't know they do it with no paper."

"Oh, *grossss!*" Bing wailed.

"Nix that," Lowell said. "I'd sooner use the bedspread."

"That's sort of what we're coming around to," Florence said. "I have a bag of clean rags, and I could stand to cull my closets. Anything you also don't wear we can cut into small pieces. With vinegar by the toilet, too, you might find the sanitation a step up."

"But you can't flush cloth," Willing said.

"In megacities like Rio and Beijing," Nollie said, "people haven't put paper down the toilet for years. The sewers are too delicate. They put it in a bin, beside the john."

"We could get used to it," Willing said. "You can get used to anything."

"Well, I can't get used to that," Avery said, standing up. "I'm opting for the American solution: I'm going shopping."

"I'm with Mom," Savannah said. "You people are barbarians."

Avery and her daughter flounced out to the Jaunt, and were gone for hours.

They returned chastened, however. After scouring Long Island and New Jersey while exhausting nearly all the gas in the car—also exorbitant and hard to come by—they scored one package of paper towels (reserved for roll-your-own tampons), along with two bottles of white vinegar, an admission of defeat. Meantime, the rest of the crew had spent a riotous afternoon snipping "ass napkins" from torn sheets, old towels, worn-out socks, lengths of fabric left over from hemming curtains, and Florence's iffier thrift-store purchases.

Harlequin squares piled in sprightly towers like vertical quilts. If and when Florence was once again able to reach for a squishy nine-pack from a grocery shelf, she was bound to feel a curious loss.

Willing might have quit going to school altogether because they taught the wrong things: algebra and state capitals. If he held sway, they'd be learning how to purify water and how to forage for edible plants. How to build a fire when your matches were wet. How to pitch a tent, or make one from a rain poncho. How to tie knots, how to grow potatoes. How to catch and skin a squirrel. How to load a gun.

Students at Obama High studied biology, but teachers did not apply the lessons to the right environment. The urban ecosystem was unusually fragile. It was terrifyingly interdependent. Too many things had to work in order for a city to work at all. You could not count on many things working. You did not count on anything working.

When the Renunciation first began to bite, people shared on social media the best Dumpsters to dive and which supermarkets had breakfast sausage. But city dwellers soon kept such tips to themselves. If Pathmark had thrown out some only-slightly-moldy pre-sliced Swiss, the last thing you did was tell someone else.

Thus Willing continued to go to school because his classmates were excellent sources of information. Their parents would be alarmed to learn it, but kids blabbed. They couldn't keep from boasting about the family stash. Thanks to other students' bluster, he knew the Rosangels on Tilden had laid in two cases of Goya coarse-ground cornmeal. Having run out of room owing to repeated shopping bonanzas, they stacked the boxes on the back patio: easy pickings. The Browns opposite, gentrifiers who'd yet to relinquish vanities like being "lactose intolerant," kept a bottomless supply of Trader Joe's vanilla-flavored rice milk in their basement. Its small upper window over the washer was never locked. The Garrisons on the corner had salted away hundreds of cans of garbanzo beans in a backyard tool shed. The padlock was decent, but the door's hinges were on the outside. Tapping them out was a cinch. Best of all, once the hinges were tapped back in, no sign remained of invasion. As for the Doritos and other salty snacks that lined the average cellar, Willing let them be. The bags crackled, and would give him away.

Naturally his mother had taught Willing not to steal. So inclined, he might have contrived a host of rationalizations for his foraging. In their panic, most families had overstocked. Poorly protected provender fell prey to rats and insects. After a power outage in March, the streets of East Flatbush were lined with trashcans full of reeking meat from overloaded freezers. He never pillaged in quantity; the judicious disappearances were less theft than tax.

But Willing felt no need for rationalizations. He was refining a skill, like purifying water and building a fire—one that would later come in handy when thou-shalt-not-steal joined anachronisms like lactose intolerance. If Willing's descent to thievery signaled a broader corruption of the American moral order, the moral order would decay with or without him. The degradation of his mores was merely a matter of keeping up to date, like downloading the latest operating system on his fleX.

So far, his mother hadn't queried where the mysterious additions to her pantry hailed from. Everyone was pitching in, and she wasn't about to look a gift bag of Carolina long-grain in the mouth. She must have known, really. It was called *disonancia cognitiva*. No one else paid any attention when Señora Perez floated the concept in Social Sciences, but Willing liked the fact they'd given lying to yourself a fancy name.

Other people focused on their wretchedness. But Willing knew that these were the good times, that they were shy of something. And he liked having so much to do. It was useful that he was still, at fifteen, slight, and naturally watchful. Made for stealth, he could penetrate fences and slit window screens in silence. (It was horrifyingly easy to gain access to pretty much any house, especially since the one implement he selected for himself when Avery went on her rampage in Home Depot was a glasscutter.) Besides, much of what he scavenged was from Dumpsters and trashcans. He kept the house supplied with fabric for ass napkins. He scoured as far away as Prospect Park for sticks and small logs, so they could have barbecues out back and also keep warm while they ate, the better to save on natural gas. When his mother decided to plant vegetables in the backyard that spring—nothing pointless and watery, like radishes and lettuce, but crops that provided real sustenance, like squash—he had to remind her that the tiny plot had been used as a latrine. So he spent a solid week filling his bike panniers with dirt from Holy Cross Cemetery and emptying them in the garden, to build a six-inch upper layer uncontaminated by human waste—after which he implored everyone that during a dryout they had to use a pail. He planted the seeds and watered the rows. According to a news report, residential yards were being converted to vegetable gardens all across the nation. Pre-Renunciation, lawn grass was the largest crop in the US—three times bigger than corn, covering an area the size of New York State. But you couldn't eat it. The trend toward beets instead was eminently sensible.

It was an energizing time, an industrious time. It was better than it would be later.

Meanwhile, the news itself made for fascinating study. For months now, anchors had referenced the present with nouns like *crisis, catastrophe, cataclysm,* and *calamity,* and they were running out of *C*-words. They'd already used up the *D*'s, like *disaster, debacle,* and *devastation.* Terms like *hardship, adversity, tragedy, tribulation,* and *suffering* didn't mean anything anymore—they didn't work; they seemed to allude to experiences that were no big deal. The English language itself was afflicted by inflation, and when everything got ten times worse the newscasters would be stymied. There would be no words left to call the next phase. Maybe CBS News would take refuge in understatement: what had happened to America was *a pity, a bit of a shame, rather a waste, pretty unfortunate,* or *something of a disappointment.*

There were already difficulties, of course. When his mother scored a quart of fresh milk, she insisted on reserving it for whitening tea—that's the way she liked it—but she kept it so long that most of it curdled. When the lumps bobbed to the top of her cup, she cried. Bing stole food *in* the house, quite a different matter from foraging elsewhere, and the pilfering was increasingly obvious because the twelve-year-old was the only member of the household gaining weight. Lowell did nothing all day but hammer in the basement on his fleX, writing his "treatise," and Willing was beginning to wonder if his uncle was insane. Esteban had grown surly; standing around hiring himself out for casual labor was too much like what his father did. He didn't kiss Willing's mother as often, or hold her at the sink. Kurt was in such terror of being any trouble that he absented himself most of the day; he came back looking cold and drawn. Aside from spending hours at a time standing on line for food trucks, he probably did nothing but walk around. There was a lot of that. There was a lot of walking around.

Goog and Bing weren't benefiting much from classes taught in Spanish, but going to school did provide the theater of normalcy. Though scornful back home, in school Goog relied on "Wilbur" to translate for him, a dependency he detested. There were more honks in Obama High now, since many other families could no longer send their precious white kids to private schools, but if you didn't speak Spanish, you were going to get beaten up. Willing tried coaching Goog on a few verbs, but his cousin clung to German as his second language, which was immense dumb because to communicate even in Germany you were better off learning Turkish.

Poor boneheaded Bing made himself a further mark by toting his violin to play in his middle school's small, tuneless orchestra. The afternoon on which the usual well-wishers had thrown the instrument over a hedge and broken its bridge, Willing pressed his youngest cousin: "But why study the violin, when the best violinists have already been recorded playing everything?"

"Well," Bing said thoughtfully. "Someone might write something new, and then they'll need somebody to play it."

"But a computer could play it," Willing said. "Better than you ever will, if your practicing is anything to go by."

Bing began to whimper. Sighing, Willing found one use for Avery's Gorilla Glue and repaired the bridge, though he wasn't really doing Bing any favors.

Savannah often vanished, which gave him a queasy feeling, both in regard to what she got up to and the fact that she wasn't there. Everything about the girl should have grated. She was prissy and pointlessly resentful. She acted above it all, and lounged listlessly around the house when she could at least be stealing something, like a productive member of society. Yet she had a secret life, and that was irresistible. She was pretty, and it made him feel weak that this made any difference. Whenever he came home and she was gone, the air went flat. Helplessly, he sympathized with her perspective. She was supposed to be in college. She should have been leaving her stuffy parents and annoying brothers behind for a new life. Learning the hard way not to drink too much tequila, switching her major when she figured out that she wasn't interested in fabric design after all, falling for the wrong guys. Instead she was stuck with her family, in the crowded home of relatives, like a frat house without the booze. It must have been hateful. No wonder she barely spoke to her mercurial fifteen-year-old cousin.

So he was excited when the two found themselves in a rare moment in the living room with no one else around. Any small intimacy in a house so packed was to be cherished.

"We're fucked, you know," Savannah said, lolling on the sofa. "For our whole generation, it's over." She lit a cigarette. A real cigarette.

"Why don't you use a steamer?" he asked tentatively.

"Because they don't kill you." The world-weariness was affected.

"The smell will give you away."

"What will they do, send me to my room? What room? Refuse to pay my college tuition? Put me to bed without dinner? With the slop we're eating, that would be a mercy."

She was beautiful, but a hollowness in her eyes made her less so. He wondered where she got the money for the cigarettes. She was wearing makeup, too—a profligacy most women went without. Willing accepted that he didn't interest her. But it was upsetting that a promising girl of nineteen was not interested in anything or anyone else, either.

The hardest of Willing's duties fell to him because no one else would do it. The others said they were too busy, or they'd go next week, or they wouldn't want to intrude at an inconvenient time. But the truth was that they didn't go because they didn't want to: *cognitive dissonance.* Not Nollie, who claimed she wasn't welcome, not his cousins, neither Avery nor even his mother, which was especially strange. Except that the situation at the shelter was so grim: the job at Adelphi, she said, was mostly about protecting the legitimate residents from the crowds camped on the sidewalk who wanted in. The homeless with an actual room had become the elect; these days, she said, "no one complains about the view." Still more grimness probably presented itself as out of the question. In a moment of honesty, she'd explained, "I can't take care of everybody."

So every couple of weeks, Willing mounted his bike, loaded with a few choice comestibles that the neighbors had *contributed* for the care of the elderly, and cycled to Carroll Gardens. He sometimes used these rides to contemplate how being encouraged—nay, commanded—to call his grandparents "Jayne and Carter" might have affected the way he saw them. More sharply, but less generously—as if warm-and-fuzzy generic monikers might have offered a form of protection. He saw them more clinically. More as separate real people like anyone else, and all this clear-sightedness was not necessarily in their interests. Everyone else at school called their grandmothers, for example, *Nan, Nanna, Gran, Gramma, Abuela,* or *Yaya.* When he referred to his own as "Jayne" in an essay assignment to describe your family tree, his classmates found the usage both bizarre and pathetic. Perhaps irrationally, he felt a loss, as if deprived of the traditional terms he didn't actually have a grandmother and grandfather, but two older acquaintances with whom he had little in common.

In any event, they were not doing well. After enough visits, he'd passed through the phase of everyone pretending to be fine, though he sometimes wished they'd go back to putting on a brave show. The biggest issue was Depends. They long before ran out of adult diapers. While Willing often brought old sheets, bedspreads, and worn-out clothes from the trash of people whose houses had been foreclosed upon, the scrounged fabric was limited. His grandparents had inevitably to wash and reuse Luella's swaddling: unpleasant.

Jayne and Carter kept Luella tied up—either lashed to her chair or on a short leash anchored to a table leg. When Willing mentioned the trussing to his mother, she was aghast. But he thought the policy sensible. On a tear, Luella could wreck the place. Not that you could tell, now—that is, whether it was wrecked or not.

It was as if the dementia were contagious. No one made beds, or picked up, or took out the garbage. They hardly cooked, and there were no mealtimes. Someone would idly open soup and eat straight from the can. Of course Luella had lost the ability to use silverware, but now the other three often ate with their fingers as well. Worse was the loss of the concept of conversation. Dialogue had become a series of random iterations: "There's a new camp of nursing-home refugees on Smith Street," Carter would say. "We're down to our last few smears of cortisone cream," Jayne would say next. Then Great Grand Man would declare, "If Alvarado keeps digging in his heels on the bancor, he's going to forfeit the '32 election." So when Luella chimed in, "My husband will pay whatever you ask!" the disjunction fit right in.

Luella was convinced that she'd been kidnapped—as in a way she had been—and that Great Grand Mimi had plotted the abduction. They must have tired of putting her right—"No, honey, this is Douglas, remember? And this is his son Carter, who's *my* husband, and you're staying in our house . . ." So instead they played along. It bordered on sadistic. Jayne might say, "We've delivered our demands, but your husband is broke. You're on your own." Great Grand Man would toss in playfully, "No, no, ransom's on its way, my dear. Four fat Social Security checks, thousands apiece! Each of which will buy a sandwich."

Willing still liked talking to Great Grand Man (or "GGM," which the paterfamilias had taken a shine to; it wasn't easy to score a hip sobriquet at ninety-nine). But he preferred their discourse by fleXt, in which assertions tremulous in person came across as robust. That spring, their ongoing dialogue had addressed the pervasive view that the "American experiment" had failed. So on a visit in June—which no one called "unseasonably cold" anymore; one advantage to checking up on his elders was getting warm, because with those "four fat Social Security checks" they ran the central heating—Willing resumed the discussion. He felt it was therapeutic to force his three marginally with-it relatives to engage in focused interchanges, the way a clinician might ask them to count backwards from a hundred by sevens.

"But you can't close a country like a business," Willing submitted. They were sitting around the kitchen table, covered in sticky stains and littered with dirty dishes. Imposing implements from the Mandible silver service were tarnished and smeared with butter. His glass of water having a slice of lemon in it meant Jayne had gone out of her way to be hospitable. "You can't throw up your hands and say, too bad, guess 'the experiment' didn't work. People my age have a long time left to live."

"It's up to your generation to rise from the ashes," GGM croaked.

"I'm fifteen. I can't invent a new country from scratch."

"Country's not going anywhere. It's only the economy you have to Humpty-Dumpty together again."

"Oh, no problem, then." Carter had grown flippant.

"Alvarado's trouble is, he still thinks he's *president of the United States*," GGM said, pronouncing the title sonorously. "The fellow who strides in with a retinue, and everybody trembles. Hispanics have a big investment in flag-waving, land-of-the-free exceptionalism. Otherwise, they've merely emigrated from one Spanish-speaking third-world dump to another

Spanish-speaking third-world dump, and what's the point of that?"

Jayne said, "Lots of Lats are going back. Mark my words, we'll miss them."

"Everyone says we're in a 'depression,'" Willing said. "But it's emotional depression, too. Like you guys. Why is the 'American experiment' over because this isn't the greatest country in the world anymore? Maybe it never *was* the greatest country in the world. Lots of other places used to be empires. Now they're not. The people who live there are careless with that. It seems like everyone's being babyish."

"They're going kill me," Luella stage-whispered in Willing's ear. "Tell Mimi that Douglas was unhappy in his marriage before we met! It's not my fault!"

"It's never anyone's fault when you fall in love," Willing told her solemnly.

Perhaps hungry for the coherent conversation that Willing had imposed, Jayne looked annoyed that he was engaging Luella at all. "Americans aren't depressed," she said. "They're in denial. Everyone thinks the crisis is temporary, and any day now we'll all be sipping lattes at cafés again. Every other economic crisis has come to an end. So at the worst you worry about a 'lost decade.' The notion of a lost everything, a permanent, irreversible decline—it's alien to this country's psyche."

"I don't know why," Carter said. "The place has been falling apart since I can remember. Crumbling highways, collapsing bridges, decrepit train tracks. Airports like bus stations. I'll be damned why foreigners have kept piling in here, or why it's taken them so long to think twice and turn around."

"You people have a bad attitude," Willing said sadly. "Maybe you deserve this."

"Whole school of thought agrees with you," GGM said. "Brought this on ourselves. Tried to butter both sides of our bread. Raised our children soft. Took supremacy for granted, with nothing to back it up. Evangelicals in the Midwest claim this is the day of reckoning. Except nobody's being selected for the right-hand-of. We're all chaff."

"You know I'm chaff! I'm chaff! You know it!" Luella sang, to the tune of Michael Jackson's "Bad."

Willing surveyed the tableau. In a dingy striped nightgown, strapped to a straight-back with her wrists duct-taped to its arms, Luella recalled a victim of the early electric chair. Her wide eyes showed excess white, as if the current had been switched on. Her teeth were long and yellow, with the retracted gums of peritonitis. Draped in the floor-length black gown of a fairy-tale witch, his gaunt grandmother was once again tearing at her cuticles until they bled, then dabbing at the red beads with a napkin. In times past, his grandfather had always struck Willing as fairly fit, and boringly normal: considerate, unassuming—everything his sister Nollie was not. But now what seemed to give Carter a workout was sheer animus. He sat there glaring, arms bunched, hands clenched around his biceps. His metacarpal tendons stood out like the strings of a tennis racket. Meeting his eyes was like looking down the twin barrels of a shotgun.

Still exuding a tattered nobility, GGM was at least back in one of his cream suits, but the garb was crushed. His uncombed white hair shocking willy-nilly in arbitrary directions betrayed a fatalism beyond coiffure. It was discouraging how reduced the patriarch became once you stripped away the cravat, the manicure, the props—the crystal decanters, the platinum Mont Blanc fountain pens clipped nattily to an outer pocket. Even his steamer was now filled with a cheaper e-bacco, which smelled like disinfectant. Yet coming up on two years of the Great Renunciation, one thing hadn't changed: Great Grand Man was enjoying it—albeit in that confounding way that adults got a taste for espresso. Willing had a sip of real coffee once. The stuff was vile. But it was clearly the murky liquid's most awful qualities for which the drink was prized.

You could see it, in this kitchen. There were too many old people. They all had a bad attitude. They all relished this ongoing calamity—the implosion, the sucking vortex, the vertigo. They thought they were going to be able to take everything with them, like pharaohs buried with their treasure. Willing stood up. "I'm not chaff."

"Will, don't get the wrong idea," Carter said, though Willing was certain he had the right idea, and he'd never cared for *Will*. "This just isn't the way I pictured my seventies."

"Baby, be honest," Jayne said. "You never pictured your seventies, period."

"Being able to eat, that's important," Willing said. "And having a place to live. But what else is so important that now you can't buy? You guys just seem so bitter—"

"Bitter is better than butter," Luella babbled. "Bitter batter. Badder bitter butter."

"At least you've got each other," Willing finished.

"Maybe that's the problem," Jayne quipped, ripping another cuticle.

"Being robbed," GGM said, "is an emotional experience. One much more intense than suddenly not being able to buy a boat. And we haven't been robbed by marauding outsiders, but by our own government.

The Renunciation has severed the bond between Washington and the American people—which was tentative at best to begin with."

Willing shrugged. "All governments rob their people. It's what they do. Kings and stuff. They did it, too. The president did it all at once this time. Maybe that's better than little by little. At least you know where you stand."

"In the gutter," GGM said.

"The badder bitter gutter," Luella said.

"But you explained to me before," Willing told GGM. "The national debt got too big to pay back a long time ago. You said if it weren't for foreign creditors demanding to be repaid in bancors, they'd have had to inflate the debt away. Which is the same thing, you said. It's still welshing on the debt. It's still a form of default. It's still cheating. It makes you just as 'feckless' and just as dishonest. The Renunciation was what was going to happen anyway, over sneaky years and years, except the scam was fast-forwarded overnight. Big deal. You predicted this. So I don't see why you're upset about it."

"Simply because you see a train coming doesn't mean it can't broadside your car," GGM said.

Mischievously, Willing had also described the conventional erosion of sovereign debt with inflation as "dishonest" to Lowell, and had enjoyed watching his uncle turn purple. Money, Lowell explained scathingly, has no moral qualities but is simply a "fuel," and all that matters about an economy is that its engine turns over. An economy is a set of "mechanisms" that work well or badly, and to get hung up on irrelevant concepts of "justice" or "honesty" or "fairness" is to condemn those mechanisms to working badly. The only "good" that pertains, Lowell said, is the greater good of an efficient machine, from which all cogs benefit. It was one of Lowell's finer moments, and once Willing decoded the tirade to mean that both government and capitalism were fundamentally unscrupulous, his uncle's point seemed well taken.

"I should have clarified," GGM went on. "Alvarado has only stolen from the Americans who saved something, and that excludes over half the country. So, yes, I *am* bitter. I'm being punished for not spending the entire family fortune when I had the chance. For not slugging down a three-grand Lafite Rothschild at every meal. For trying to ensure that the likes of you, my boy, eventually profited from my prudence."

"Pop, an estate in Oyster Bay hardly qualifies you as having led a life of ceaseless self-denial," Carter grumbled.

"A bunch of money for doing nothing might not have done me any good," Willing said.

"It could have sent you to college," GGM countered.

"College might not do me any good. Studying engineering. I think it's more important right now to know how to garden."

"I could've sent you to *gardening school*, then." GGM sounded frustrated. "The best definition of wealth I ever came across is 'money is stored energy.' In other words, since '29 this whole country has been running the air con with the windows open."

"But the Mandible fortune," Willing said. "It only accumulated because one of your forebears was good at designing diesel engines. None of you earned it. You guys were lucky. Then in '29 you were unlucky. But lucky and unlucky have nothing to do with right and wrong. Besides, you're still lucky. You have Social Security. It's pegged to inflation. And you have Medicare. Younger people don't have that. Anyone over sixty-eight is protected. Aside from Nollie, no one at our house is protected."

"Nollie's not protected against a sock in the jaw," Carter grumbled, "if I ever get my hands on her. The prodigal used to have France as an excuse. Now she won't travel five miles to spell us for a night or two."

"Nollie does help out at our place," Willing said. "It's kind of a zoo there, too."

"Enola is a free spirit," GGM said. "And she might find stopping by more enticing, Carter, if you acted as if you wanted to see her, rather than merely wanting free nursing care. I have hopes that coming back to the States will inspire her to start writing again. There's a great book in this upheaval, and she'd be the ideal chronicler of the times. She's always had the eye. For most people, what lies outside our front door is tragedy. For Enola, it's *material*."

"Right," Carter said. "The perfect author for today's Great American Novel is a fallow lightweight famous for a thinly disguised romantic tell-all who hasn't lived in the country for decades."

"But what you were saying, Willing," Jayne interrupted, yanking her first proper conversation in weeks back on course. "I do think Douglas is right about the moral hazard. The Americans who've suffered the deepest losses are the ones who had a conscientious, caretaking relationship to the future. Who saved for the future. Who believed in the future. Who kept reserves on hand, in the expectation that they'd take responsibility for themselves and whatever befell them in the future. The pessimism that's bothering you, Willing, is a result of that sense of betrayal. The people who believed in the future now feel like dupes. Like victims of an enormous practical joke."

His grandparents had been fighting to formulate a way of looking at the incineration of Carter's inheritance that didn't make them seem like ordinary greedy people who were enraged that now they wouldn't get their money. After all, for liberal Democrats to have come into a mountain of unearned cash would have been an injustice in the terms of their own politics. Now they could be aggrieved on behalf of "people who believed in the future." It was clever. He admired the intellectual gymnastics. Performed by ordinary greedy people who were enraged that now they wouldn't get their money.

"One of the primary responsibilities of government is to provide a functional currency," GGM was declaring. Jayne and Carter's averted gazes indicated they'd heard this more than once. "Functionality entails meeting three criteria. It's a *means of account*—for keeping track of who owes whom what. Cross that one off, since with today's rates of inflation, people in hock up to their eyeballs can effectively pay off loans of a thousand dollars with ten cents. Second, a currency is a *medium of exchange*, which the dollar remains barely—although only if you earn the money in the morning and spend it by the afternoon. Because the third purpose of a currency is to act as a *store of value*. The dollar has not been a sound store of value in my lifetime." As he'd aged, GGM had become more emphatic, and almost impossible to interrupt.

Willing raised his palms in dismay. He shouldn't have to play missionary, but someone had to say it. "I don't know how, but you've all got to get over this. Having been 'robbed' is eating you up. It's like letting the government win twice."

GGM chortled. "Put it that way, and the boy's got a point."

"You're a very smart young man, Willing," Jayne said, in a way that made his skin crawl.

"It's not smart to say something that's obvious," Willing muttered.

Right then, Luella got a squeezed look, followed by a beatific smile. "You know I'm chaff! I'm chaff! You know it!"

The smell that always infused the house grew more intense. The other three locked eyes and sighed.

"It's my turn," Jayne said, slumping. "But, Carter, you have to be on hand. Last time she got into the kid-napping thing again and kicked me in the shin."

"Before you go, son?" GGM had pulled Willing aside confidentially and lowered his voice, as if to bestow a final wisdom that might resonate for his great-grandson in the years to come—since at his age any parting could easily be the last. "We can't seem to locate any laxatives. If you come across a box or two . . ."

It was literally a world of shit. Willing promised miserably, "I'll keep an eye out."

On his return home, Willing walked into a face-off in the living room. "I'm nineteen, and it's my business," Savannah was telling her mother.

"Its having become your *business* is just what I'm afraid of," Avery said hotly.

Savannah glanced at her cousin, and seemed to make a decision to be shameless. "You'd be careless with it, Mom, so long as I was giving it away for free? That wouldn't be very smart, under the circumstances."

"Under the circumstances we're managing, and you do not have to debase yourself!"

"We're not managing," Savannah said. "Have you told them yet?"

His aunt blushed. "I don't know what you mean."

"I heard you and Dad talking. Your basement *boudoir* doesn't have any walls. It's gone, isn't it?"

Her mother glanced at the floor, arms bunched.

Turning to Willing, Savannah spelled it out. "The cash, from the sale of the house. It's finished. Kaput.

Pasado. Good-bye domestic *contributions*, hello abject dependency. Of course, we've got a lot of hinges and Q-tips to show for it. Oh, and quite a little stash of wine, though you'd better make it last, Mom. Florence won't be springing for Viognier when she can barely cover the vinegar for our assholes."

"You father is searching high and low for another university position," Avery said. "Meantime I—I've thought about running something from the house. If not PhysHead sessions, cooking, even taking in laundry!"

"Mom, please! Nobody's having dinner parties at all, much less catered ones, and most people wear the same clothes for a month!"

"The only thing I'm too proud to do is what you're doing."

"You're too old for my vocation. And somebody's got to bring some scratch into this house besides Florence. You want to see inflation work to our advantage for once? Because *my* prices are going *up.*" Savannah grabbed her coat and marched out the door.

"Did you know about this?" Avery asked him.

"I wondered."

"Leaving aside the indignity—it's dangerous, and there are diseases. Which antibiotics can't always treat."

"She doesn't have a large *skill set*," he hazarded. "And she's right: my mom can't support ten people. Except there's one main problem with Savannah's chosen *career path*. From what I've seen on the street."

"That is?"

"Too much competition."

Chapter 12

Agency, Reward, and Sacrifice

It would have been around July '31 when Florence first held a $100 bill up to the light and called, "Lowell? Could you come up here, please?"

Her brother-in-law shambled up from the basement in one of his suits, of a sort common at the shelter: creased fine tailoring that hadn't seen a dry cleaner in months. He'd stopped shaving, and unevenly scissored a beard that already grew in tufts. Irregular beard lengths had grown trendy, as had "the DIY" haircut: the results of hacking off fistfuls in a bathroom mirror. The popular self-barbering had put most salons out of business.

She handed him the bill. "This has changed."

Lowell fingered the waxy C-note. "Looks counterfeit. Afraid you've been suckered."

"That's what I thought at first. But these bills are from all over town. Look." She pulled the wad from her wallet—they did not make wallets large enough to carry the bills an average shopping trip required, and this wallet would no longer fold in half—and splayed the cash on the kitchen counter. "It's not the same quality of paper. The ink isn't right, either. It's brighter. Greener. Garish."

"Well, they often change the design to *prevent* counterfeiting."

"But this isn't adding holograms or finer engraving— and Ben Franklin looks smudged, to my eye. It's cheaper."

"And why, exactly, are you reporting this to me?"

"You said. That one of the signs was the physical degeneration of the deutsche mark—"

"I do not run the federal mint. If they've decided to save on the costs of production, good for them. In an era of belt-tightening, it makes no sense to lavish resources on a mere medium of exchange, which has no value in and of itself but only represents value."

As he stalked off, she called behind him, "You know how I know this isn't counterfeit? Because no one would bother!"

She didn't know what she'd wanted from him. An apology, when he hadn't done anything wrong? Or more of his improbable optimism, assurance they'd get their furry, avocado-colored dollars back in no time? Florence returned mournfully to the bills, separating the older notes from the stiff, crass reissue. The new bills were smaller, too, albeit in that cheaty, oh-the-little-dimwits-will-never-notice way that a half-gallon of ice cream had evaporated to twenty ounces. Regarding herself as not especially concerned with money, she was surprised by the depth of her sorrow.

Hitherto, the one-dollar bill had not changed its design in her lifetime. Funny, for an item she handled daily, she'd never looked hard at a single. Her corneas stiffening at forty-six, she located a magnifying glass to examine a buck of the sort she grew up with. The engraving was absurd, really. The bay leaves sprouting around the four 1's and beneath the cameo of Washington. The radiant crisscrossing and minute curlicues around the perimeter. The fine parallel lines shadowing THE UNITED STATES OF AMERICA. The now-dubious contention in crimped print that THIS NOTE IS LEGAL TENDER FOR ALL DEBTS, PUBLIC AND PRIVATE. The multiple numbers and letters and signatures of ambiguous purpose. The reverse was even more grandiose, the crosshatching yet more exuberant. Insistence on printing "one" over the numbers in each corner seemed overkill. The pyramid on the left, with its unblinking triangular "eye of providence" hovering like a levitation trick over the top, lent the bill a mystic air, as if the currency had magical powers (and maybe it did; maybe the fact that you could ply a total stranger with a bundle of green paper and he would give you a doughnut was nothing short of miraculous). The bald eagle opposite, bristling with arrows in one claw and an olive branch in the other, could only remind citizens and foreigners alike which talon had been historically the more persuasive.

A barrage of Latin always imparted pretension, if not also a desire for obscurity. For the first time in her decades of counting these notes into an open palm at checkouts, feeding them into the grinding maw of a MetroCard machine, and fishing their crumples from a jeans pocket, she looked up the translations online. NOVUS ORDO SECLORUM meant "New Order of the Ages," implying that the creation of her country marked a transformative era not only for Americans but for the whole world. Ratcheting up the braggadocio still further, ANNUIT COEPTIS meant "He favors our undertaking"—He being God, of course. E PLURIBUS UNUM she already understood—"Out of many, one"—though in the fractious, factionalized USA of her lifetime E PLURIBUS PLURIBUS might make a more suitable slogan. The Roman numerals not a millimeter high at the bottom of the pyramid decoded as 1776. News to

Florence, the strings of foreshortening bubbles on the perimeter were purportedly thirteen pearls. For only in America was thirteen a lucky number: the pyramid had thirteen layers; above the eagle gleamed thirteen stars; the heraldic shield on the bird's chest boasted thirteen stripes. The poor scrap of paper was so freighted with symbolism that it was amazing you could pick it up off the floor. Yet haul this mighty token into a minimart, and it wouldn't buy a gumball.

Florence rifled the fat wad from her wallet to compare the old one-dollar bill to the new version. She shuffled the stack twice. There were no new singles. Clearly, like the metal coinage technically in circulation but increasingly a form of litter, singles weren't minted anymore.

Comparing hundreds would have to suffice. The C-note was redesigned in her twenties, at which time a hundred-dollar bill seldom crossed her palm; she was living with her parents, unemployed. But her father brought one home for Jarred and Florence to marvel at. The renovated bill had grown only more self-important, with a host of ingenious devices to prevent counterfeiting. It was less scrip than toy—wrapped like a Christmas present, a purple ribbon vertically woven into the very paper. On close examination, the ribbon shimmered with tiny Liberty Bells, which moved up and down on a diagonal trajectory when shifted one way and switched to 100s when shifted the other. The worn hundreds in her wallet weren't as dazzling as that first fresh one, but the holograms still functioned. The Liberty Bell in the inkwell turned from copper to green. Held up to the light, a ghostly reiteration of Ben Franklin's portrait loomed in a rare blank space on the right. Goofy, minuscule 100s in faint yellow freckled the left-hand face, arrayed in the irregular pattern of doodles.

The latest C-note sported no ribbon, only a purple stripe like a slash from a Magic Marker. Poor-quality reproduction smeared Ben Franklin's expression from a gentle grimace of resolve to a sarcastic smirk. The complex anti-counterfeiting devices had been dropped. The paper was thin and slick. This was a mere gesture toward a hundred-dollar bill, a nod, an allusion—an oh-you-know-what-I-mean from a mint that couldn't be bothered with all that tiresome symbolism. The bill looked and felt worthless.

Florence had never before reflected on her unchar-acteristic affection for her country's cash. In defiance of her compatriots' reputation for being uncouth, the design of American bills distinguished itself from more flamboyant currencies with dignity and reserve. Though the new notes' shrinkage drifted alarmingly toward the size of Monopoly money, the dimensions of the originals were attractively modest. For a yet young nation, its notes had a stodgy, antiquated cast. Like the typeface of the *New York Times*, whose masthead remained staunchly archaic to its final issue, or the comfortingly eternal form of a Tabasco bottle, dollars felt storied, grounded, timeless. By contrast, her aunt claimed that the notes of individual European nations had never recuperated their grandeur and particularity after the euro debacle. Florence had seen samples left over from Nollie's travels: the revived pesetas, drachmas, and lire looked plain, stripped down, and interchangeable. They looked embarrassed.

Her relationship with the downy older bills in her wallet was surprisingly emotional. They were primitively associated with her earliest experiences of agency, reward, and sacrifice. In grade school, exchanging a cherished sheaf of ones for a Walkman was a seminal assertion of will. When she was sixteen, these rectangles were the prize after six weeks of repainting the entire interior of the family's house in Carroll Gardens every afternoon after school, while her friends cavorted off to Canal Jeans. Dropping a twenty on the sidewalk in haste drove home the cost of inattention; finding a five buried in a handbag emblemized serendipity; parting with a taller stack of these tokens than she'd planned for her mother's birthday taught the return on generosity. The soft green tender was inextricably bound up with her experience of loss and gain, achievement and inadequacy, caution and imprudence, calculation and abandon, benevolence and malice, taking advantage and being taken advantage of. So the shoddy, coarse pretenders palmed off on her during the last visit to Green Acre Farm made Florence feel robbed, personally insulted, and anxious for the United States, as if in compromising the integrity of its mere emblems of value the nation had devalued itself.

This was the most riveting period for his profession that Lowell had ever lived through. Yet Avery regarded his growing treatise as a child's puttering in a sandbox. Indeed, one of the very regressions he was documenting was the way all cerebral endeavor had been demoted to irrelevance—thereby sending civilization hurtling backwards at warp speed. Had Avery expressed such contempt for her husband's papers in the Georgetown days? No! She would knock timorously on his study door, ask if he wanted a bowl of soup, and apologize, apologize *profusely*, for interrupting. Nowadays, when he was poised over his fleX mid-inspiration, she'd bark that he could at least join the kids in combing curbsides for cast-off furniture they could use for firewood. Rather than cruelly break the flow of his intellection and thus imperil the very future of American scholarship, she could as well have come across him with his dick in his hand.

Lowell had to admit that his wife astonished him. Previous to this reversal of fortune, he'd have described her as spoiled. Now, it wasn't such an egregious thing, being spoiled, so long as you had the wherewithal to cover life's niceties. It was in the nature of niceties, too, that they would slide to needs. Seen from the perspective of plenty, her extravagance had appeared a form of refinement. He had always brought in the larger measure of their income, and had privately considered her "practice" barely a step up from the all-female book club: it was cute.

In the initial stage of this Jobian trial in East Flatbush, Avery had assumed a demeanor he was tempted to call whiny. But something happened shortly after he and Avery mournfully downed the last bottle of chenin blanc. In a tribute to the homonym, once their evenings ceased to be *winey*, her daytime disposition could no longer be characterized by the adjective's crabby twin. She seemed to have made a conscious decision: to be stoic, heroic, and selfless. Incredibly, after having quite reasonably drawn the line at living *without toilet paper*, a few months later his fanatically hygienic wife hadn't given her sister the slightest grief when Florence announced that they couldn't keep snipping up old clothes and linens to wipe their privates, because they were running short of fabric. And get this: Avery *volunteered* to collect the bags of used cloth squares from both bathrooms every weekend, to *run a laundry load* of these noxious "ass napkins," and to restore stacks of fluffy clean ones to beside the toilets! This was a woman who, the first time she had to walk out in public without eyeliner, burst into tears!

Lowell's difficulty was not so much that he was living with a woman he no longer recognized, which might have spiced things up. Rather, they had a yin and yang problem. It was as if Avery had co-opted the sole chair labeled "Valiant Survivor Type Rising to Challenge in Face of Adversity and Discovering Brave Sides to Self Hitherto Unsuspected," and the only other chair left for her husband to assume was labeled brutally "Big Baby." With Avery marching about *seeing to everyone's needs*, mending and chopping and fetching and washing up; soliciting Kurt *whom she didn't even like* to please have some more polenta because the so-called tenant was looking peaked while going without seconds herself; urging Kurt and Bing to play evening concerts in the living room when duets of sax and violin were preposterous, not to mention the fact that *Kurt's saxophone drove her crazy*—all with nary a peep of petulance or confession of fatigue, never the hint of an admission that she reviled living in this cramped, ugly house with people whose company had grown more than trying . . . Well. Someone had to insert a note of peevishness into this hellishly halcyon Keep Calm and Carry On. Generating some reputable resentment, giving voice to the free-floating outrage that imbued their environs like smoke from a burnt dinner—it was a job to do, as Avery's tireless goodwill was a job. With corresponding self-sacrifice, he'd taken on the less glamorous task of reminding the rest that this sucked, it all sucked, it wasn't fair! Savannah should be a sophomore at RISD, Goog should be applying to MIT, Lowell should be giving speeches in Geneva. Lowell was officially the grump, the grouse, the grouch, the Grinch, the grumbler, and he gave himself up to the part heart and soul, thus allowing the others their virtue, their high-mindedness, their this-too-shall-pass-ness. His diligent dyspepsia made all their infernal goodness possible.

Not that he got any thanks. Rather, his housemates seemed to blame him for this whole mess. But writing about inflation doesn't mean you control it. In fact, no one including the Fed really listened to economists about anything. Governments did what suited them,

and in the high-turnover administrations of elec-
tive democracies, that meant whatever suited them in
the myopic short term. Though that sententious pipsqueak Willing Darkly sought always to cast his uncle
as naive, Lowell was savvy enough about the artificial
divide between central banks and national treasuries.
So obviously in printing money like it was going out of
style—which it sort of was—the Fed chief was doing
the president's bidding. Across the board, Alvarado
was taking advantage of what most electorates tend to
shy from: a sovereign state *can do anything, really.* The
reserve-currency coup, the Renunciation, Alvarado's
refusing to play ball with the bancor bullyboys—it was
all politics, and precious little to do with economics.
The next boomerpoop who tossed off the popular trope
that economists were "modern-day witch doctors" he
would deck.

Moreover, no one could posit cogent academic theories that covered the flukish arrival of every deus ex
machina, a.k.a. people from outside the system doing
dumb shit. This bancor nonsense was like being hit by
a comet. The towering eminence of the field having
failed to allow for cosmic annihilation didn't invalidate
Keynes. (The fact that John Maynard Keynes himself
had whimsically coined the inane word *bancor* Lowell
experienced as a slap in the face.) Besides, whoever

heard of loaning in one currency and then demanding to be paid back in another—particularly in a currency you just *made up*?

The truth was, Lowell Stackhouse hadn't been proven wrong, about anything. He remained confident that well into the indefinite future the US could have continued to accumulate a quiet, steadily climbing national debt while keeping a foot on interest rates, which had been so low for so long that ages ago it became standard practice for banks to charge hefty fees for the bother of stashing your cash. For debt is an engine of growth, and fattens the pie for everyone. Why, imagine a world in which you need cash in hand to buy a house: the middle class would purchase a home around the age of eighty. "Neither a borrower nor a lender be" was the motto of a public that swung from trees. Lowell's avoidance of debt in his own life was a psychological problem; perhaps in childhood he'd felt a discomfort with accruing an implicit debt to his scrimping parents for taking care of him that a little boy could never pay back. Because philosophically, he believed in debt— *leveraging*, for the sophisticate—which down through the ages had earned an undeservedly tainted reputation. He didn't even care for the word forgiven in relation to a liability that's been written off, implying that a loan is a sin. What was wrong in America at the moment? Not indebtedness but an inability to borrow: that is, *lack of indebtedness*. However temporarily, the United States couldn't buy a house.

Lowell's reasoned, seasoned positions were the braver for also being unpopular. Yet in what passed for his own home, he got no respect. While even an economist was reluctant to reduce all of life to dollars and cents, people revere work that pays. Presently, the work of the mind didn't pay. In the USA of 2031, scientists, academics, and engineers suffered a lower status than the all-hallowed farmer.

Witness: in August, Lowell's feckless brother-in-law Jarred made a run down to the city, his pickup laden with fruits and vegetables from his kooky dude ranch in Gloversville. Having ridiculed the backwards agrarian project from the start, even Avery treated her younger brother's arrival in Brooklyn like the Second Coming, while the kids jumped up and down and danced around in a frenzy they were all too old for. You'd think they'd never seen a tomato. Not that their uncle's trip from upstate had been motivated by familial largesse. Jarred bestowed on his kin a few potatoes, early apples, and bunches of kale, but the majority of the haul had been reserved for the market at Grand Army Plaza, where the price gouging was criminal. So long as farmers were able to flip the money quickly into hard assets like seed and equipment and other people's foreclosed property, the entire agricultural sector was making profits hand over fist.

Having lost his own house and credit cards, Lowell had to admit that it rankled: depreciation of the dollar had allowed his irresponsible, blowhard brother-in-law to painlessly pay off the fixed-rate mortgage of so-called "Citadel" in full, as well as to dispatch the debt from previous whimsies. Having taught his students at Georgetown that the evaporation of debt was one of the most marvelous powers of inflation, Lowell was comfortable with macroeconomic "injustice" in the service of systemic correction. That he couldn't quite install his own dogma on a private, emotional level probably constituted an intellectual failing: microeconomic injustice, up close and personal, bugged him as much as the next guy.

By contrast, Lowell was purely relieved that their friends Tom Fortnum and Belle Duval were doing all right, even if Tom's fleXts to him and Belle's to Avery emphasized the negative out of discomfiture. Shortly before the Renunciation, Belle's parents had taken early retirement while still in good health. Investing the profits from an app start-up in the naughts, they'd bought a top-of-the-line e-RV, and had plans for a global tour. Cut to the chase, all that was left was the e-RV, parked permanently in Tom and Belle's drive. Yet all misery is relative: unlike Lowell's in-laws in Carroll Gardens, at least Belle's mother still knew the difference between a hairbrush and an aardvark, and the parents didn't exactly live in the house. Tom and Belle's kids were attending second-tier colleges, but they weren't kicking around their aunt's mildewed basement, or worse, turning tricks in town for pocket money, as Avery *claimed* Savannah had. (Lowell didn't kid himself that his daughter was a virgin, but for Avery to mistake the girl's footloose experimentation for whoring . . . *Really.* The gorgeous but aging mother jealous of her alluring daughter—couldn't his family come up with something fresh?) Bottom line: Tom worked for Justice, and Belle's patients were mostly Medicare. When financed by loose monetary policy, government expenditure is most valuable when first spent; high inflation would erode both Tom's and Belle's incomes only as the cash infusion rippled through the larger economy. Both government salaries and Medicare reimbursement rates were now linked to an inflation algorithm that didn't require further action from Congress. Even if a Snickers bar eventually cost five billion dollars, they were safe.

Odiously, Ryan Biersdorfer and his sidekick Lin Yu Houseman were better than safe. While *The Corrections*

couldn't rake in the royalties of the old hardbacks, Biersdorfer had cannily priced the download so low that for
better-heeled foreign buyers it was too much trouble to
go looking for a pirated copy, and the pittances added
up. More substantially, he was much in demand on the
lucrative international lecture circuit. That meant earning bancors (doubtless through an offshore shell company), and the currency *confoundingly* did nothing but
appreciate. So rather than convert his foreign income to
dollars, required for repatriation, Biersdorfer was reputedly buying up real estate in Paris, Tuscany, Hanoi,
and Jakarta. Any American who championed his own
country's collapse as well-deserved payback and promise of socialist rebirth was a treasured performing bear
abroad, since most of the fatuous economist's serious
scholarly competition back home couldn't bankroll air-
fares. Europeans were fascinated by the rare Yank who
had been allowed out of the country, thus moronically
conflating capital controls and controls on freedom of
movement. (On second thought, maybe being at liberty
to go wherever you want so long as you don't spend any
money there is fairly tantamount to house arrest.) Typically, too, Biersdorfer and his sexy Asian yes-woman
spent little to no time in the US these days, which apparently made them ideal interlocutors for explaining
to the rest of the world what it was like here.

Lowell wasn't hung up on masculinity, but it was hard on a fellow, having to appeal to his sister-in-law for the means to acquire a new lip balm and then being abjured to please use a dab of lard instead. So when in October of '31, Georgetown finally came through with his back pay for the summer before last, he felt literally *flush*: his blood vessels dilated, his cheeks ruddied, the tips of his fingers tingled. Determined to be an asset for once, Lowell offered munificently to do the week's shopping.

He shook out some slacks and a stylish shirt, both worn only ten days since their last wash. (The competition for washing loads was fierce, and he tended to cede the two items permitted per resident to poor Savannah.) Grandly, he filled the Jaunt's gas tank to the brim. Outside Green Acre Farm, he relished the ease of parking, since few Brooklynites could manage the costs of running a car. Sashaying through the entrance with a whistle, Lowell found his posture had improved, his first realization that it had ever deteriorated. His pink suede loafers may have been blemished in places, but they still drew glances from afar. He felt like a man, a real man, for the first time in months, a sensation startlingly reliant on trouser pockets that bulged with banded cash.

While imported goods were still out of stock, the shortages of American products the previous year had given way to shortages of income. You could now buy eggs and broccoli and even meat—for a price. Emboldened by the deposit that had only cleared that morning, Lowell refused to check the scribbled price tabs, and bought whatever he wanted. That was how *men* shopped. The mounding cart drew even more envious glances than the pink loafers.

After the last of his swag swept through checkout—where all the trusting self-service machines had been removed, stealing having grown too socially acceptable—Lowell froze. Hands on his padded pockets, he had to ask the girl to repeat the bill; her second iteration was snide. So that's why Ellen Packer had relented when he once more threatened to sue: back pay from one of the foremost universities in the country meant to cover four months of prestigious employ could not now cover one tank of gas and a week's food.

Lowell marshaled his most theatrical indignation and marched coolly from the store, leaving its minions to put the groceries back. The stylish exit meant sacrificing the canvas shopping bags, already packed with flank steak, for which he was sure to get it in the neck from Florence. The least he could get out of the humiliation was a parking space, so he left the Jaunt where it was and launched farther down Utica Avenue. It wouldn't do to return empty-handed. He could pick up enough eats for the next couple of days at the Quickee Mart on Foster.

"Spare some change."

A snatched side glance at an unshaven young man with greasy hair gleaned only that he was wearing the same sort of collarless tunic-style suit jacket in which Lowell had looked so snazzy during his final year at Georgetown. The fellow had sidled so close that the sleeve brushed Lowell's arm.

"No, thank you," Lowell said, a bit insensibly, eyes straight and gait stiff.

"Nice shoes, pal."

The compliment hailed from the opposite side, as a second under-washed gentleman brushed the other arm. He'd noticed both of these young men nearby him in the supermarket, where they'd idly picked up lamb chops and put them down again. Lowell wasn't born yesterday, and inferred some sort of hustle. Yet it took him a beat too long to register that the white guys bracing him weren't swindlers but hoods. Though no one else witnessed this moment of being hopelessly dim, the slow uptake embarrassed Lowell in front of himself. He shouldn't have had to lay eyes on the knife to get it.

A mere kitchen knife but of excellent quality, one of those German-steel numbers of which his wife had bought whole butcher-block sets, all forsaken in their ignominious scuttle from Cleveland Park. Not the chef's but the *utility* knife, that's what the contents list on the box would call it, was pointed at Lowell's gut. Lo, it did seem very useful.

Perhaps their routine was sufficiently established that the duo was bored by it, for rather than focus on the business at hand, Lowell's new friends chatted between them about an all-agricultural mutual fund that was doing improbably well, then commiserated over their favorite sushi bar on Liberty Street in lower Manhattan having finally closed. Were they indeed former Wall Street financiers, the segue from one form of larceny to another could only have been graceful. Keeping their target tightly between them, as the second fellow pressed the knife tip just below the ribs, they steered him onto Avenue D and up East Forty-Ninth. They needn't have bothered to get off the main road; other pedestrians took no more notice of that blade flashing in the sun than they would have of a glinting rearview mirror. His escorts pushed him through the gate of the overgrown front yard and kicked him onto a mound of briars. The thugs would score more handsomely than usual, though as he emptied his pockets Lowell had never been happier that the US Federal Reserve had debased the banded stacks into fancy green insulation.

It was worse that they found his fleX, hidden in Lowell's left loafer. Worse still, they found the fleX because they took the shoes. Wiping beads of blood from his briar-torn cheeks and limping back to Green Acre Farm in socks, Lowell rehearsed the gratitude that he would underscore on return to the Darklys': thank God he'd kept walking toward the Quickee Mart, and they hadn't got the car.

They're only objects," Willing said patiently. "You're confusing the objects with what they mean to you. With objects, you can take the meaning back. They return to being empty things. Cuboids. Heavy cuboids that take up a lot of space."

They were in the attic, to which Willing alone was admitted. This was the warmest room in the house, which wasn't saying much. Though headroom was restricted, his great-aunt commanded more square feet for her personal use than anyone else. No one objected, because she was also the only resident besides his mother who contributed to their tiny economy. Other than by drawing Social Security—and the stipend was too modest to explain her generosity—he was not sure how. He did not know how much Nollie had left or where it came from.

But of course he was interested. Nollie was the only one who didn't spend her money as fast as possible, before it turned to ash. Yet she didn't run out. This, too, was interesting. All the same, she was very particular about what she would pay for. It had to be a strict necessity.

"They're not 'cuboids,'" Nollie objected. "They're my life's work."

She was balled on her mattress like a kid. The laces on her tennis shoes had broken and been knotted back together several times. The bulky red sweater was too big for her. She was wearing gloves, though they all wore gloves indoors. It was gloves that Avery should have bought up in Walgreens. The fingers of his own had holes.

"It's getting cold." He would speak slowly and clearly. She had to be coaxed. "It's only December. It's going to get colder. The natural gas costs too much to use through the whole winter. We have to save it for emergencies. Medical emergencies. Meanwhile, we have to keep warm, and cook, with the oil drum out back. The snow has covered the cemetery and the park. Which have been picked clean of firewood anyway. Even if we found any, the sticks would be wet. You can help."

She was sulking. "Book burning is the end of civilization."

"All your novels are available online."

"The pirated versions."

"Piracy is a compliment."

"Forgive me if I'm not bowled over."

"Your copies." He would push his luck. "They say the same thing over and over. You have boxes and boxes of the same books."

"I save them, to give to special friends. They'll never be printed again."

"They are produced in an obsolete format," Willing said. "Most of these 'special' people would regard a present like that as a burden. They'd take it home and burn it in an oil drum."

"So if I gave you one of my novels, you'd march downstairs and burn it."

"Yes," he said steadily.

"You've never expressed the slightest interest in my work." She sounded peevish.

"No," he said. "Maybe later, on the other side of this."

"Will there be an 'other side of this'?"

"That's up for grabs," he conceded. "But now isn't a time for novels. Nothing made up is more interesting than what's actually happening. We're in a novel."

She seemed to like that.

"You're sort of old," he said, quickly amending, "but not *immense* old. I mean, you're in malicious shape. All those jumping jacks. No one would think you were seventy-four." This was pro forma flattery for her generation. It should have raised a red flag for boomers: obviously the fawning lickspittle plying them with hackneyed compliments wanted something. Yet it always worked. "But you don't live in the past. One of the things I like about you. You seem to be following the plot, more than the others. Lowell not hiding his fleX in a smarter place than his shoe. Avery mooning about how careless it used to be, ordering groceries online. They don't get it. You seem to. Maybe it's all those books you wrote. Maybe you're used to staying a step back, keeping track of the larger arc, aiming for that final chapter. So holding on to these old-format hard copies, when we need them to boil pasta—it isn't like you."

He could feel her relenting. He was relieved. He didn't want to take the cartons by force.

"My father would be horrified by your proposition, you know. Book burning is antithetical to everything the Mandibles stand for."

"But everything important about those books is safe," he said. "The words don't burn. They live forever on the internet."

"So long as there is an internet," she countered.

They thought the same way. They both lived in a world that was provisional. The ground was forever soft. For Willing, flux kept him supple. It toned his balancing muscles. It was like having sea legs on land.

"Besides, you'll die," he said. "When you're not here, you won't care whether anyone reads your work. You won't care whether they used to read your work even when you were here. That's the great thing about nonexistence. It's not that you *don't* care, either. It's not as if you still feel, but you feel apathetic. You *can't* care. There's nothing to do the caring. So you won't care about 'the Mandibles,' or what they stood for. The Mandibles will be the same as every other family. The same as rocks, or dust particles, or the Taj Mahal, or the Bill of Rights, or the Pythagorean theorem. Because you won't be a 'Mandible' anymore, and you won't know what a 'Mandible' is."

Somehow he'd turned the key. "You're right," she said flippantly. "Once I kick it, these boxes are more trash to dispose of, *oui?*"

"*Oui*," he said. "But now they can serve a purpose."

"Only one condition," Nollie said, hoisting a carton labeled "*The Ecstatic*, MM PB, Hungarian" in a show of strength. "*Don't touch the foul matter.*"

When he informed the rest downstairs that Nollie would sacrifice the books for cooking the evening meal but insisted on reserving the loose manuscripts, Avery and Florence fell over each other laughing. Jokes were hard to come by.

"Can you believe," Avery said, training her voice low enough that she wouldn't be heard in the attic, "she's still holding out for her papers to be bought by some highfalutin university library? I mean, *what* university library? What university? They're all going down the tubes! Just goes to show," she added, with a pointed glance at her husband, " the last thing to go is *ego*."

Bundled glumly in a blanket in the kitchen, Lowell shot his wife a black look. "It's still vital to maintain top-flight scholarly research facilities. Her protection of those manuscripts would be more than justified, if only the beastly woman were any good."

The books burned well, though they made a lot of ash. Nollie soon came downstairs and firmly removed the task from Esteban, who was displaying an undiplomatic relish, and insisted on feeding paperbacks to the oil drum herself. Once she got into the swing of the occasion, she seemed to enjoy it. There must be something exhilarating about immolating your own attachments. Trial by fire. That was an expression. When you make glass very hot, it gets stronger. Willing assessed his great-aunt, her face red from the flames. She looked excited. She was having a *tempering* tantrum.

This was real exercise, better than jumping jacks. By the time she finished tossing *Gray*, *The Stringer*, *Ad-Out*, *Cradle to Grave*, *The Saint of Glengormley*, and *Virtual Family* into the drum, she would be stronger.

As dirt clods flickered in the light of the fire, Willing cast a mournful eye at the waste ground of their poky backyard, trying to learn the same lesson. Throughout the spring and summer, he had tended their small crops—potatoes, tomatoes, onions, string beans. He eked out just enough water on the plants during dry spells that the produce wouldn't cost more to raise than it was worth. He had allowed himself affection for the infant vegetables as they developed: as a rule a mistake. Aside from a single tomato and one pot of beans, the harvest was stolen. A gang rampaged through the garden late at night and trampled the plants. The destruction was deliberate. He suspected someone at school. He still attended Obama High to glean intelligence—the spy kind. Other students must have been sniffing around for scuttlebutt also. He may have mentioned the garden once, and should have known better.

No one gave a shit about Christmas. For his sixteenth birthday in January of '32, his mother made Willing a cake out of cardboard.

It was shortly thereafter that he came upon his mother, bowed over her dresser upstairs. She had already been on a rampage in the kitchen.

Before the Great Renunciation, many were the evenings that his mother or Esteban had despaired that there was "nothing to eat." Willing had always known what they meant: Esteban had forgotten to thaw the chicken burgers. Or after a draining day at Adelphi, his mother was running short on ideas for a meal they hadn't already eaten three times that week. But this time, no cans of pineapple in sugar syrup lurked at the back of the pantry; no peeled plum tomatoes lay at hand for a meatless Bolognese. There wasn't a half-used, iced-up bag of corn in the far corner of the freezer, or a long-spurned package of desiccated pork sausages whose packaging had torn. The canisters beside the stove no longer brimmed with flour and sugar and cornmeal. The cabinets were bare of rice and couscous and kasha. His mother had ceased disposing of foodstuffs beyond their "sell-by date," a policy she now ridiculed. So it wasn't a matter of overcoming a reluctance to open a can of stew beyond its prime. There was no stew. Willing felt partially responsible—his quiet thieving through the neighborhood had netted little of late; in the current climate of mistrust, property owners had improved security—but there was no food in the kitchen, at all, anywhere, of any sort.

A matter different but hardly unrelated, there was no money, either. It was the end of the month; per custom, they'd already spent his mother's paycheck. Nollie was meeting an old boyfriend in Queens, and his mother refused to rummage through her aunt's things looking for cash. That would be stealing. Esteban hadn't picked up work as a day laborer for weeks. Thus far, Avery hadn't been able to interest their neighbors in buying or trading her stockpiled toenail fungus kits, replacement door hinges, or window-screen spline—in a variety of widths.

Of course, for professional traders on the stock exchange, money had always been imaginary—just as notional, just as easy come and easy go, as the points in a video game. Wage earners like Willing's mother thought money was real. Because the work was real, and the time was real, it seemed inconceivable that what the work and the time had converted into would be gossamer. They had been promised that they could store the work and the time, later to exchange it, if only for other people's work, and other people's time. But money was just an idea, and most people did not understand that natural forces also acted on the abstract: evaporation; flood, fire, and erosion; seepage, leakage, and decay.

Most people liked the prospect of justice, and confused what was appealing with what was available.

So his mother had spilled a jarful of coinage that had accumulated for years on her dresser. She was feverishly separating the pennies, nickels, dimes, and quarters, then stacking them in what looked like piles of ten. The scene made Willing sad. It wasn't only his mother's desperation. It was the coins themselves. When he was small, a tower of quarters had seemed so precious. Something about the character of metal—hard, shiny, heavy, and immutable—had always made change seem more valuable, more substantial, than paper bills. The jar on his mother's dresser had glinted like the treasure you might unearth in a buried chest, or raise to the surface with pulleys and divers from the timbers of a shipwreck. As a boy, he had walked the streets with a front pocket bulging with change, which would pull down his jeans on that side and thump against his thigh. Even in grade school he knew that the paper five in the opposite pocket was worth more than the coins. But it was the swinging, sagging swag of copper, nickel, silver, and tin that made him feel rich.

Now a coin was a mere disc, like a Tiddlywink—a historical oddity, since metal money was no longer minted. The change his mother was maniacally separating was rinky-dink, and her project was dumb. After spending an hour on this chore, she'd be lucky to assemble enough legal tender for a can of Coke.

Willing swept his hand over his mother's piles, and toppled the towers. Coins rattled to the floor and curled under the bed. He surprised himself. There was anger in the gesture. He seldom afforded himself anger, and he wondered where it came from.

"What was that about?" his mother cried. He wished she wouldn't get down on her knees like that and chase quarters among the dust balls. It was undignified. No one stooped to retrieve a quarter from the sidewalk. "Now I'll have to start all over again."

"You're wasting it." Willing fetched a sock from Esteban's dresser, and checked that it had no holes. By the fistful, he loaded coins into the sock, until the toe sagged as his pocket had in boyhood. Then he knotted the sock above the change.

"Green Acre won't accept that," his mother said. "They only take coins if they've been counted into sleeves."

"I've heard of *socking* money away." Willing swung the pendulum, thudding the coinage against his opposite palm. It had force. It had momentum. "This what they mean?" He launched the sock from behind him and whacked the ball of metal against the bedroom door frame. The cracking sound was loud. The coins made a dent in the wood.

His mother looked frightened.

"It makes a good weapon," Willing explained. "A weapon is worth more than anything this junk would buy."

"You're changing," she said.

"I'm adapting," he said.

"Stop adapting," she said.

"Animals that don't adapt," he said, "die."

Give me the bag." He said it gently, with a tinge of sorrow. The boy could not have been more than ten or eleven. At least he was white, which would make this easier.

They were on East Fifty-Second, a side street, two blocks from Green Acre Farm. As ever, the walk was blighted by human excrement. Interesting, how readily one spots the spoor of one's own species.

"I can't." Intimidated against a fence, the boy gripped the canvas bag to his chest. He would have been sent to shop for dinner. He was slight and red-haired, with a wary, flinching twist to his face that in a few years would grow permanent. His coat was too thin for the weather. "I'll get in trouble."

"Give me the bag now." Willing swung the sock into his opposite palm, as he had in his mother's bedroom. For Willing and the boy also, the motion was hypnotic. "Or you'll get in worse trouble."

The boy glanced up and down the street. It was scarcely bustling, but it wasn't deserted, either. They were in front of a house, from which someone peered, then drew the curtain. When the boy's gaze met the eyes of an older woman down the block, she turned and hurried in the opposite direction. That's the way it was now.

The kid started to run, but there'd been a tell—a sudden feverish glance in the direction he planned to bolt. That gave Willing time to grab his arm. The contact was shocking for them both.

"Okay, okay!" the boy wailed. He held out the bag solemnly, an offering. Willing let go. With another look at the sock as the sagging toe reeled lazily from his tormentor's right hand, the quarry ran.

Willing examined the groceries. Artificially flavored cherry drink, the kind of sponges that fell apart, white sandwich bread, a pound of fatty hamburger. Fatty was good. Fatty had more calories. In all, the haul was poor and not to his mother's taste, but they wouldn't go hungry. Funny, he hadn't thought the change on his mother's dresser would buy anything near dinner, and it just had.

At first he hoped Savannah would be home tonight, so that his commonplace bullying might pass as chivalry. This was the sort of escapade that impressed girls. But he would have to stop himself from bragging, which would sound foolish to his own ears later and would get back to his mother. The most useful skill he'd mastered in childhood was keeping his mouth shut. At sixteen, the aptitude was harder to sustain.

As he walked home with his booty, the thrill of success was muted by melancholy. During previous exploits, he had shied from verbs of thievery; the stashes stacked on back patios had been *confiscated*, *raided*, or *taxed*. But this form of borrowing a cup of sugar from the neighbors felt different, and Willing was aware of having crossed a line. Others would cross it, too, then. Still others had crossed that line so long ago that they'd lost sight of it, and there was no line.

Thus at dinner—a crumble of ground beef, two slices of bread apiece that were soaked in grease—Willing announced, "We need a gun."

"Are you off your nut?" his mother exclaimed. He would let her sputter through her predictable indignation, but he was bored. "We are not having a gun in this house. I don't believe in guns. Half the time it's the person who owns the dratted thing who gets shot. What on earth would we need a gun for?"

"To protect us," Willing said, "from people like me."

Chapter 13
Karmic Clumping II

Carter accepted philosophically that human life was sacred. He also accepted that in this country all men—women, too, in more enlightened times—were "created equal," even if, as a well-educated and temperamentally more competitive man than his father ever recognized, he had always found the assertion optimistic. All right, he knew what the Declaration of Independence meant really, not that everyone was good at math but that they all had the same rights. Ergo, even Luella Watts Mandible enjoyed the right to life, liberty, and the pursuit of happiness—the most vital being that first item, since he and Jayne were most certainly denying her liberty, and were she ever to pursue happiness she would forget she was pursuing happiness within sixty seconds and come back instead with a parsnip. Carter could marginally credit the possibility that somewhere deep inside that tangle of rhyming paranoia in his stepmother's head remained some tiny glimmer, some infinitesimal remnant—under the size of a pea, even smaller than one kernel of popcorn—of the graceful, stunning, well-spoken, black-only-in-the-sense-of-exotic but comfortably-white-in-all-but-name seductress who had stolen his father's heart in 1992—though Carter couldn't locate an iota of the femme fatale himself. Theoretically, too, what was at issue in the compassionate, respectful day-to-day caretaking of a woman who *through no fault of her own* had COMPLETELY LOST HER MOTHERFUCKING MIND and was nothing but a PISSING, SHITTING, SHRIEKING SHELL wasn't only the physical comfort, sense of self-worth, and feeling of psychic safety of their ward, but perhaps more importantly *their own humanity*, because *obviously* the very *measure of a society* is how it treats its *most vulnerable* citizens, so that to save his very soul and to represent the very best in what it meant to be a real American he was clearly obliged to ruin EVERY DAY and EVERY NIGHT of his WHOLE REMAINING MOTHERFUCKING LIFE.

So. Perhaps his calm, considered, rational, progressive forbearance had its limits. Belonging to the first generation of American men who pulled their domestic weight, Carter had already changed the X-thousand diapers he'd planned to, and at least his infant children hadn't *bitten* him in the process. Yet God forbid his father would lend a hand. Douglas had embraced such a perfect passivity that you'd never know he had any causal link to the presence of this creature in their house.

Deploying the difficult situation to fortify the all-for-one-and-one-for-all of their marriage, Carter and Jayne convened in the kitchen, just the two of them, before bed, in the precious interval before Luella's "night terrors" set in and she began to wail. Together they'd each sip a tiny glass of port. An emblem of better days, the measured extravagance helped to preserve their sanity. (A few luxuries had been facilitated by the sale of the BeEtle—a mere encumbrance now that they never went anywhere, and a liability given that the police may have abandoned investigating burglaries, muggings, and homicides, but were more rigorous than ever about issuing revenue-raising tickets for alternate-side parking violations.) The couple always lit a candle and turned off the overhead to create a semblance of romantic ambience. Ritually, exhaustedly, they would share the indignities of the day.

All the same, Jayne blamed him—their visitors-for-life were his family—and knowing she shouldn't blame him merely buried the resentment into the deeper, more instinctual emotional stratum where the feeling was at its most virulent. Likewise, Carter couldn't help but fume when Jayne threw up her hands, reminded him of how strenuously her doctors had advised against "stress," withdrew to her Quiet Room, and locked the door—deaf to his proclamation that they had now entered a hard-assed era of American culture during which all that gutless guff about *ADHD, gluten intolerance,* and *emotional support animals* was out the window.

Yet the prime target of his enmity wasn't his wife, but Luella herself. Carter had never much cared for the woman when in possession of her faculties. That floating, willowy deportment she'd cultivated, the hypercivilized manners, the too-precise elocution—he'd never bought it. Luella's whole shtick had been an artificial construct, and now, he believed, the surface refinement had been stripped off to reveal the real thing. Deep down, she'd always been a catty, cunning, covetous animal—ferociously determined to get her way; suspicious of others, since calculating, self-centered schemers always assume that everyone else is just like them; shrewd, but not very smart. It didn't surprise him in the slightest that when you set her mind loose it produced rhyming drivel.

He found it telling, too, that the only food she'd eat without its being shoved forcibly down her gullet was anything chockful of sugar. In Luella's heyday, she'd claimed to have no taste for sweets, a pretense that serviced her fashion-model figure. Add a few protein plaques and a smattering of miniature strokes to that mean scrabble of predatory opportunism in her head, and behold: a sweet tooth the size of a mastodon's.

Luella had never liked Carter, either. She didn't find him impressive. He'd overheard her once despairing to Douglas that his only son hadn't inherited more of her husband's *esprit* and *joi de vivre*. But the real reason she was uncomfortable around her stepson was that Carter had her number. She was a fake, she was a social climber, she had plotted from the start to marry Douglas only to outlive him and inherit his fortune, and when it eventually got out that Luella had left for la-la land in her latter fifties, Carter thought that was the best news he'd heard all day. Except now the revenge had boomeranged. She seemed to have deposited herself on his doorstep on purpose, like, *There. You wanted the real Luella? Well, this is the real Luella. Happy now?*

It didn't help, either, that Luella was now a drooling kewpie-doll substitute for his real mother, whose disappearance into Manhattan's anonymous mire of unremarked murders and missing persons had deprived him of any formal mourning of her passing. Only three years ago, the demise of the formidable powerhouse of charity fundraising would have occasioned one of the best-attended memorials of the year. If at last genuinely necessary, most charities had folded in the interim, and the sort of celebrity gala he imagined was unheard of. No one with a sou would flout it.

Carter saw no point in disguising it from himself: he wished Luella dead. While he might not have throttled her with his bare hands, in his personal *Twilight Zone* he'd gladly have thought-crimed the hellion cleanly to the cornfield. Because for all the hype about how dementia sufferers were "still capable of joy" and "still had value as human beings," he detected no joy in their charge; the household hardly sponsored the buoyant sing-alongs and imaginative crafts projects of the apocryphally stimulating nursing home. And lifetime liberal or no, he was inexorably rounding on the view that to have "value" as a human being you needed to be of some earthly use to someone else.

At least Carter didn't wish his father dead, too. Their relationship decontaminated of ulterior motives, Carter continued to feel a bedrock fondness for his father that he'd never trusted when it paid too handsomely. Late-life penury had likewise confirmed that his father's character transcended the two-onion martini. Oh, he railed along with the best of his class, but at length Douglas had accommodated lifestyle demotion with surprising aplomb. So long as they kept him in liquid nicotine, he rarely complained. (In these ravenous times, the newer flavors of e-bacco stuck to the ribs: turkey-and-gravy-with-stuffing, or caramelized-ham-and-red-onion-chutney.) It was only the repetition that had grown unbearable; if Carter heard the three criteria of a functional currency one more time he would scream. Otherwise, Douglas had quietly adjusted to reading digital books and watched loads of TV.

Which was just how he was occupying himself in his room on the third floor the afternoon of March 7, 2032. Douglas was obsessed with the approaching presidential election, and that month would see primaries in Texas and Florida, among others—heavily Lat states that could help the incumbent. Naturally the Republicans were a write-off; the leading GOP contender had branded Dante Alvarado "Herberto Hoovero," an epithet widely decried as racist. Yet the president was battling a serious challenge for the nomination from the leftwing grandee Jon Stewart, who was campaigning to wave the white flag on the bancor. Since the smallest little child could see that boycotting an increasingly entrenched international currency had proved a calamity for the US, the primaries—which, without a viable opposition party, *were* the election—pitted it's-the-economy-stupid against the consolidation of ethnic equality. None of the Lats and white progressives who'd elected Alvarado wanted to see America's first Mexican-born president serve only one term. Carter himself was torn, though he wasn't telling Jayne that.

Not that *Carter* was allowed to divert his energies to the paltry distraction of who would be the next American president, since he was wholly absorbed in the more monumental matter of feeding Luella lunch. She'd been in restraints for two days in a row, and they weren't running Guantánamo. To prevent muscle cramping and pressure sores, they alternated lashing her to the chair with a four-foot leash. This being a leash day made shoving protein down her throat more difficult. Jayne had begged him not to feed Luella cheese. If his stepmother got constipated, in lieu of hard-to-come-by enemas or laxative tablets, one of them would have to dig the shit from her anus with their fingers. But cheese was easier to force her to chew than chicken. With Jayne barricaded in her Quiet Room, Carter, a bit spitefully, chose the cheddar.

This time, however, Luella didn't seem in the mood for her *sélection de fromage*, and after noshing the first chunk into a viscous paste she spewed it halfway across the kitchen, spraying Carter's cheek in the process. Thereafter, she picked bits nimbly off her nightgown with dinner-party fastidiousness.

"You're not worth your father's little finger," she said distinctly.

These moments of lucidity always threw him for a loop, and if the sentiment she'd expressed had been nicer it might have moved him to gentleness. Instead, on the next hunk, he clapped his hand around her mouth to keep the cheese in. Luella reached around and grabbed a fistful of his precious remaining tresses and pulled for all she was worth.

Okay, that was it. Wiping a saliva-smeared palm on a dishtowel, Carter marched from the room. She could starve for all he cared. "Jayne!" he shouted up the stairwell. "You're going to have to watch Luella, because I've been *tearing my hair.* I'm going out for some air."

Marginally becalmed by a well-earned constitutional, Carter returned about an hour later, planning on a couple of Advils for his aching knees. A singe smote his nostrils the moment he unlocked the door. Had Jayne burned a casserole? The formerly passionate recipe clipper rarely boiled an egg. A haze fogged the hallway, and Luella, last left leashed to a table leg, was *too quiet.*

He rushed into the kitchen to find the candle for port-sipping marital debriefings *lit*. Eyes gleaming, Luella was fluttering a flaming paper napkin into the open trashcan. The cheese wrapper on top caught fire. As Luella must have been sticking everything within reach into the candle and tossing incendiary projectiles every which way, Carter's immediate extinguishing of the candle was starting a bit small. The curtains were on fire. The trashcan was on fire. A patch of linoleum was on fire, right around the table leg to which Luella was still attached. As smoke thickened rapidly, the choice was stark: try to save the house or the people in it. Well. All that liberal upbringing proved good for something.

Did I leave them out?" Jayne wondered weakly. "I worry I left them out."

"Whoever did, I should have noticed them," Carter said. "But isn't that our luck. Holds a fork by the tines, but still remembers how to strike a match."

They were huddled across the street in the blankets Carter had grabbed to protect them from being scorched. New York's finest had taken their time, though at this point he was amazed that there *was* a fire department. The blaze wasn't contained. In the glow, Luella danced with pagan glee.

"You didn't have to rescue her, you know," Douglas said heavily.

"I, ah—had a single moment of hesitation," Carter admitted. "It gave me the creeps."

For the better part of the last year, Avery had taken refuge in toil: scrubbing, dishwashing, mending, chopping, and laundry. She arranged neighborhood hand-me-down swaps of children's clothes. To combat Bing's give-away weight gain, she led him in sets of jumping jacks (she got the idea from Nollie), because pantry pilfering was a perfect formula for becoming a pariah. Swallowing her umbrage, she coached Goog on his Spanish. She only panicked when she ran out of tasks. Drudgery was therapeutic. Were she ever to start another practice, she'd have all her patients mop the office floor.

Besides, she had committed to this refurbished persona out of cold calculation. The alternative was to continue to cede the moral high ground to her sister, who would keep laying claim to competence, grit, efficiency, stoicism, selflessness, and her famous *practicality*, so that everyone would feel grateful to *Florence*, and Avery's children would look up to *Florence*, and come to *Florence* with their problems, and her husband might wonder why he had chosen a weepy sniveler over this pillar of fortitude. Petulance, too, could not manifest provender or privacy if it couldn't even manifest toilet paper. Spiked with an acute awareness of how unattractive the propensity looks to others, the experience of petulance was itself a small torture; it was a thin, sharp, needling emotion and ultimately a form of self-abuse. In sum, Avery could not control history. She could only control her disposition while history did its damnedest. Carrying on being a princess was lose-lose. To Avery's delight, Florence sometimes seemed actively annoyed that her sister had become a saint—at points an even *saintlier* saint than the patron paragon of East Fifty-Fifth Street.

Thus it was in the midst of single-handedly cleaning up after yet another big communal dinner that Avery dried her hands hastily to answer the door. Through the peephole, her parents, Grand Man, and Luella were framed in curvature, faces sooted as if fresh from a coalmine, wrapped in blankets like squaws.

"What the fuck!" In her shock on opening the door, she forgot to watch her mouth around Grand Man.

Her father announced with a curious triumph, "Luella burned down the house."

In short order, the news spread, and everyone but Savannah—out doing what her mother dared not contemplate—convened in the living room. Amidst many an aghast "Oh, my God!," hurried inquiries about whether the four disaster victims were all right, and homilies about what really mattered was having escaped with their lives, Avery could detect a collective anxiety murmuring barely below the surface: this untoward turn of events brought this bursting abode's population to fourteen—or, if you credited her father's previous proclamations about how Luella alone was "the equivalent of twenty extra residents in their right minds," to thirty-three.

They ceded seats to their new guests. Lowering himself onto the distinguished claret sofa with which he'd grown up, Grand Man shot a woeful look at the duct tape.

"Our brave troops, gold mining in Brooklyn," Florence said cryptically. "Nollie? I was going to make everyone tea, but if you could spare it . . ."

"Fuck tea," Nollie said, heading with Florence to the kitchen. "I have a new batch of killer hooch that'll take your head off."

"Did you manage to save anything?" Avery asked, rehearsing an array of childhood keepsakes in their attic.

"It's missing a few pieces that were in the sink, I'm afraid," Dad said, flapping his blanket back to reveal a scarred but regal wooden box in his lap. "But I did rescue the silver service."

Grand Man burst into tears. "You didn't tell me!" Avery had never seen him cry.

"I was saving it. I figured on a night like this," Dad said, "I wouldn't have many surprises of a happy sort to spring." He removed one of the dinner knives, with a large scrolled *M* at the base, and the blade caught the light.

"It's magnificent!" Kurt exclaimed. He was the kind of guy who would resist class distinctions on ideological grounds, yet instinctively think more highly of their family for bearing talismans of noble birth. Avery didn't entirely buy into the notion of American aristocracy herself, whereas her sister aggressively rejected elitism as offensive. But Esteban had been right, back when the Stackhouses first moved in: all the Mandibles felt special, if only, in Florence's case, special for refusing to feel special. Like the larger tussle over American "exceptionalism," the family's tensions over are-we-or-aren't-we-special could now be put to rest. All the sumptuous fine craftsmanship in Bountiful House in Mount Vernon—the carved oak paneling, the curling banisters, the storied oriental carpets, the grand piano, the bone china for fifty—was officially reduced to an incomplete set of silverware and a sofa bandaged with duct tape. That should have been a little saddening, even to Karl Marx.

"If you want to head back to Carroll Gardens to-morrow morning and see what's left to salvage," Kurt volunteered, "I'll give you a hand. Unless it's still an inferno, scavengers will be all over that place within the day, and they'll strip it clean."

"You're at least covered by insurance?" Esteban said.

Dad rubbed his neck. "I don't know."

"What do you mean, you *don't know*?" Mom said.

"Our payments are up to date," Dad said. "But I saw on the news last week that Titan Corp. has gone under. It's a legal morass. I don't know where that leaves us, but settling a claim could be messy."

"You'd have a good case, if you haven't been for-mally notified of cancellation," Lowell said. "But Ti-tan's gone into Chapter Seven—total liquidation—and the line of creditors will be out the door. Even if you do get a settlement, it could be years before you see the money."

"And it won't be pegged to inflation," Willing said from the stairwell. "In which case, a check for the con-tents of all three floors will buy you a cheap suit."

"You're just a one-note wonder, aren't you?" Lowell told his nephew sourly.

"Why didn't you tell me our insurance company was bankrupt?" Mom exclaimed.

"I was going to look into it." Dad had that look of trying to control himself in front of other people, as if with no one else around he'd be screeching. "*After* I tried to give Luella a bath without drowning both of us, *after* I cut Luella's nails if only to keep her from clawing my eyes out, and *after* I cleaned up the shards of the platter from Tuscany that we *thought* was on a shelf she couldn't reach. Speak of the devil, someone had better go find her."

Avery slipped off, checking the basement first, because she didn't want her family's few remaining possessions ravaged by a five-foot-ten enfant terrible. In her PhysHead practice, she'd treated patients with dementia. They'd been universally sweet and submissive, if perhaps lost or disconcerted, on occasion very insistent, but never, like Luella, reputedly, violent or destructive. So Avery had been skeptical of her parents' accounts. Now that her own clothes were in danger of being shredded, it seemed prudent to take their version of events at face value.

She located her stepgran in the upstairs bathroom, where Luella was spurting shampoo in great decorative swirls around the tub, walls, and floor. Taking the bottle away from her was like wresting a tennis ball from the jaws of a rottweiler. Avery had found her parents' practice of keeping their charge on a leash a ghastly violation of an adult's civil liberties. Yet the nylon strap was invaluable for tugging the woman downstairs.

"The adventurer returns," Avery announced, trying to sound jolly, then handing her youngest the nearly empty bottle. "Bing, honey? Unscrew the top, and see if you can scoop up any of the shampoo Luella accidentally spilled." Rescuing shampoo was a perfect job for her thirteen-year-old. He couldn't eat it.

"God, what's that smell?" Goog said, glowering on the sidelines. Not fleshy, but with rounded corners—nose snub, shoulders sloped—he was blunt in every sense.

"I think she needs changing," Avery whispered to her mother.

"I have no doubt," Mom said. "But my house just burned down. Why are you telling me that?"

"Maybe Nollie should do the honors," Dad said, accepting an ersatz screwdriver from his sister without saying thank you. "It's her stepmother, too."

"I don't know how," Nollie said flatly.

"I didn't know how to fasten a square of old bedspread on a flailing grown woman two years ago, either," Dad said. "You've always been a quick study. Everyone says so."

"Oh, I'll do it," Florence said. "We have to remember, Luella's not to blame. In a few years, one of us might need the same—"

"I've done it hundreds of times!" Dad cut her off. "Your aunt could do it once!"

Then the powwowing over where everyone would sleep. Kurt abdicated the sofa to the family patriarch and volunteered to doze in the armchair. Willing offered his room to his grandparents, suggesting Goog take Savannah's mattress in the basement. When Mom wondered why on earth her granddaughter would be out all night, Avery pretended she hadn't heard the question.

"And doesn't our own Mrs. Rochester belong in an attic?" Dad proposed. He was seething so at his sister that you'd think it was Nollie who'd burned his house down.

"I'll stay with Nollie," Willing intervened. The suggestion was politic—Nollie wouldn't permit anyone but Willing in her sanctum—but still left up in the air where on earth they'd bed down "Mrs. Rochester," since Luella was the card no one cared to get stuck with in this game of Old Maid. Avery, for one, didn't want their incontinent ward in the basement with a passion bordering on hysteria. After only a couple of hours with that harridan in the house, she now better appreciated the cravenness with which she'd always elected to do laundry in East Flatbush—*anything* but look after Luella so that her parents could enjoy a night off. Even now, guilt over having ducked geriatric babysitting was overwhelmed by a resolve to keep ducking it.

Yet as matters turned out, all the horse-trading over pallets and pillows was pointless.

The doorbell rang. The house was crowded, but with people who knew and, after a fashion (though it could be hard to tell), loved each other, the ground floor teemed with the energy of a big party. So when Avery went to answer the door, she proclaimed over the hubbub, "Are there any more relatives out in the cold we might have forgotten?" She said this gaily. That was the word, *gaily*.

She recognized the family through the peephole as neighbors from a couple of streets over—the Wellingtons, or Warburtons, something with a *W*. The woman (Tara? Tilly?) had participated in Avery's last hand-me-down exchange, and had seemed grateful for Bing's jeans (which, alas, he had outgrown on the lateral axis).

"Hello!" Tara/Tilly cried on the stoop, clasping her three-year-old to her breast. "We need help! It's an emergency, please!"

Never rains but it pours. Having lobbied with unseemly fervor to keep Luella from bedding down in the basement, Avery welcomed an opportunity to act generous, and opened the door.

"My little girl," the mother went on, bouncing the child. "She's awfully sick. We have to get her to the hospital. We can't find a taxi, and the ER at Kings County won't send ambulances to this neighborhood because they're getting hijacked. We're so sorry to interrupt your evening, but I know you have a car . . ."

Avery frowned. "You sure know how to pick your nights. My parents' house just burned down." Naturally competitive, she trumped their heartache with a higher-value catastrophe.

"You know how disasters seem to happen all at once," the father said gamely.

"Yes," Avery said with a quick smile. "My husband calls it *karmic clumping*."

"We could just borrow the Jaunt, if you're busy," the drawn woman said.

Something snagged in Avery's head when the neighbor cited the very make of their vehicle, the sort of fine detail to which parents of seriously sick children would be oblivious. But it was parked out front, so the noticing probably meant nothing.

"No, I guess I could drive you," Avery said. "Hold on and let me get my keys."

"Please . . . ?" the mother beseeched. "Could we have a glass of water for Ellie? She's burning up."

"Sure, no problem." Avery hesitated; she couldn't shut the door in their faces. "Come in for a sec. It's freezing, and I don't want to leave the door open."

The family piled into the foyer. "Tanya, remember?" Clutching the child with one arm, the woman shook Avery's hand. Freckles always made people look friendly.

The husband kept his right hand in his coat pocket and merely nodded: "Sam." He was squarely built with Italianate good looks, but his limbs were spindly. A deferent bearing of earlier encounters replaced by a clenched rigidity, he seemed determined to get his daughter medical attention, regardless of whom he inconvenienced. "And this is Jake." About eleven, the redhead winced into his father's trousers. Avery recognized the jeans.

"Quite a crowd," Tanya said, as her family huddled at the entrance to the living room.

"Nothing like losing the house where you grew up for an impromptu family reunion," Avery said.

Tanya reached to squeeze her husband's left hand. Willing was following the proceedings from his usual perch on the stairs. He met the eyes of the boy, who drew more tightly against his father's leg and glared. Not a polite expression when your parents were shopping for a favor.

Once Avery returned with water, Tanya stood holding the glass as if looking for a place to put it down.
Wasn't Ellie thirsty? Avery dangled the key fob. Sam
withdrew his right hand from his coat pocket and
pulled out a gun.

She wondered why anyone shouted, "Freeze!" when
pointing a firearm. Perfect immobility was instinctive.
"That's not necessary," Avery said quietly. "I said I'd
drive you."

"We're not going anywhere." Sam leveled the handgun at her chest. "You are."

"I don't understand what you want," Avery said.
"What about your little girl . . . ?"

"She'll be fine," Tanya said.

Avery felt like an idiot. She prided herself on having
grown streetwise in the face of hardship. But underneath the broken fingernails from doing her own
cleaning flitted a Washington social butterfly. In terms
of her expectations of others, she still lived in a world
of lunch dates, coffee klatches, and charity runs for
breast cancer—a world in which the worst thing that
arrived on your doorstep was a dinner party guest with
an insultingly cheap bottle of red. The clincher: until
not long ago, that was the same world that Sam and
Tanya W-something inhabited, too. Having moved
in with the wave of moneyed homebuyers that hit the

neighborhood in the last decade, the desperadoes in this foyer were "gentry."

"I'll take that," Sam said, reaching for the key fob.

"I thought you weren't going anywhere," Avery said. Willing had stood up. The bubble of conversation in the living room had died.

"You never know," Sam said.

"Is this a robbery?" Avery used her full voice. The others needed to know what was up. "Because aside from the Jaunt, there's not much to take here. *Hinges?*" she said defiantly. "We have plenty of hinges."

"You have one big item to take," Sam said. "Sometimes the elephant in the room is the room."

"When you're waving that thing around isn't a good time to be obscure," Avery said.

"I'll say I'm sorry, once." Sam panned the weapon across the living room. "In happier days, we'd have you around for a drink. But our house is in foreclosure, and we've been evicted. They've replaced the locks, set the alarm, changed the code."

"So when the police came by to kick you out, why didn't you shoot them?" Avery asked, glowering at the sidearm.

"Police!" Sam said. "What police? The banks all hire private security firms now. Armed to the eyeballs. Thugs."

"What are you, then?"

"I don't care what you call me. Because there is nothing I won't do to put a roof over my family's head. Your roof. I'm afraid you're all going to have to leave."

The room emitted a collective gasp.

"In my day," Grand Man piped up, "any reputable American man facing ruin would shoot his *own* family. And then himself. Tradition was efficient. Like the self-cleaning oven."

"See, we have elderly people here," Avery said. "Infirm people. You can't throw them on the street."

"I can, and will." The gun barrel betrayed a tremble, but it was insufficiently pronounced to guarantee that valiant funny business would succeed.

"For pity's sake, we just lost everything!" her mother cried. "I suffer from debilitating clinical anxiety! High stress levels could bring on arrhythmia—fibrillation—hyperventilation—!"

"*Mom,*" Avery said quietly.

"Yeah, I've been diagnosed with OCD, restless leg syndrome, and an allergy to sulphites," Sam said. "Then I got real problems. Maybe you should take the same cure."

"This is my house," Florence said, pulling from Esteban's protective embrace. "We're not renting, this is *my* house. By law."

"Of which possession is nine-tenths," Sam said.

"How do you know *we* don't have guns?" Florence said furiously.

"You're not the type," he said.

"Honey," Tanya said. "You weren't the type, either."

"I am now, baby." The swagger was unconvincing.

"You'll never get away with this!" Goog said hotly. "My dad'll report you, and you're both gonna get put away until you're a hundred and ten!"

"Not keeping up with the news, are you, son?" Sam said wearily. "The cops have given up. Home invasions are all over town. Where do you think we got the idea?"

"Home persuasion," Luella said, leashed to the lower banister. "Prone occasion. Peroration! Prestidigitation!" She'd once wielded an impressive vocabulary.

"But these are good people," Kurt said over the Greek chorus. "Generous people. I'm technically a tenant, but Florence and Esteban haven't asked for any rent in eighteen months. They've taken in a whole other family, an elderly relative . . . Florence works for a *homeless shelter*, for God's sake—"

"All right, and I was a climate change modeler for the New York Academy of Sciences," Sam snapped. "This isn't a Sunday school contest."

"We can see how badly you all need shelter." Appearing to exert tremendous self-control, Florence had reverted to the methodic, nonreactive mode she must have refined at Adelphi. "Obviously, this is an emergency. So there's no reason why we can't make room for your family, too. We still have water, even hot water, and heating . . . You could all have showers. Long, relaxing showers. And you must be hungry. We don't have much, but I'm sure I could find something for you and your children to eat. You can put down the gun. We can solve this problem together. Come to think of it, Esteban and I could give your family the whole master bedroom—"

"You'd live peaceably alongside a guy who just tried to throw you out of your own home at gunpoint?" Sam said. "Please. You'd bide your time until you could coldcock me with a hammer."

"All the same, honey," Tanya whispered. "The kids haven't eaten all day—"

"She can rustle up something in that kitchen, then we can, too. Between a whole house and one room? I don't feel especially torn."

"Ever hear of the *sit-in*?" Dad snarled, huddled in his sooty blanket like an extra in *The Ten Commandments*. "When I was a kid, college students figured out just how hard it is to remove large numbers of heavy, thrashing, righteously pissed-off people who refuse to leave."

"Yeah, and some of those numb-nuts protesters got *shot*." Sam was growing impatient. "Now, I'll give you fifteen minutes to gather a few things. I don't have to, but I'll let you keep your coats. Take your tooth-brushes."

"Kurt's right about my niece's generosity, but her aunt has a mean streak," Nollie snarled like a crazy old lady who lured little boys with gingerbread, and Jake shrank in terror. "First thing I'll advise Florence to do is cut off your utilities. *So much for those showers.*"

"Go ahead," Sam tossed back, though he looked rattled. "Everybody's jury-rigging hookups to the grid anyway, and tapping into gas lines for free."

"There's only four of you, *hombre*," Esteban said, putting on an accent like the Mexican lowlife whom honks like Sam would fear. "Two are *niños*. How you expect to control thirteen hostages not in the mood for a midnight stroll?"

"Good point. Very helpful—*muy útil, sí?*" His pro-nunciation was faultless. Beckoned, poor Bing edged wide-eyed to within reach, and to Avery's horror Sam took a firm grip on her petrified boy's arm. "Anyone tries anything, I shoot the kid. Think I won't? Don't try me."

Sam was talking himself into this role, but Avery couldn't discount the possibility that he would do so with some success. Released to "gather a few things," they all just stood there.

"Move it," Sam said. "Or I'll take back the offer, and you'll be shuffling Linden Boulevard in socks."

"Why did you pick on us?" Avery asked Tanya as the others slowly, as if in a trance, dispersed. "This house is home to fourteen people."

Tanya explained, "Because you're the only ones who let us in."

Chapter 14
A Complex System Enters Disequilibrium

Willing hadn't the hubris to claim that he'd seen this coming. But something like it, yes. Which was why an assembled knapsack was already tucked under his bed. Its checklist: ID, bottled water, trail mix, first-aid kit, graphene blanket, pocketknife, matches and lighter, gloves, glasscutter, large heavy-duty tarp, cheaper plastic sheeting, duplicate house keys, and toiletries. His mind freed from these essentials, he pulled on two extra sweaters and checked his pocket for the balled-up fleX; its satellite contract was in arrears, but it would work as a flashlight. Ignoring Goog's incredulous disgust—"What, our in-house clairvoyant is *already packed*?"—he marched calmly back downstairs to make a formal request.

From gripping Bing's arm, Sam's muscles must have stiffened. Slumped against the doorjamb, even Bing had tired of looking terrified. The gun was heavy. Only when Sam spotted Willing advancing did its barrel lift.

Willing stopped mid-flight. "I would like, if it's all right, to take my bicycle."

"Tricycle, popsicle," Luella mumbled, still leashed to the banister. "Icicle, capital. Typical, topical. Tropical, mythical, mystical, mandible . . ."

"Can't you shut her up?" Sam pleaded.

"Greater men than I have tried," Willing said.

"Master bin the ties that bind," Luella echoed.

"The bike?" Willing pressed gently. "You have the SUV." It was important to remain unemotional. The man would feel bad, and he wouldn't like feeling bad, which would make him angry. So all negotiation had to be conducted free of judgment. As if it were the most reasonable thing in the world, to ask a stranger from a few streets over if you could take your own bicycle.

"No," the redhead said, arms bunched at his mother's side. "I want his bike."

Willing settled the boy with a steady gaze that said patiently: *a whole bike for a little hamburger and cherry drink is not a fair trade.*

"But you never ride one," his mother said.

"Daddy has a gun," Jake said. "We can take whatever we feel like. It doesn't matter if we use it. We could smash the bike up if we want. And maybe I will," he directed to Willing. "I'll take your bike and smash it."

Willing could see the boy's injunction backfire: *look, already, what we are doing to our son.*

"Yeah, sure, take the bike," Sam said.

"Blah, purr, make a tyke," Luella said.

"Thank you," Willing said. Permission to be dismissed, sir. He almost saluted.

Upstairs, he found his mother and Esteban in their bedroom, surrounded by a disarray of clothes. "He's not that big a guy," Esteban murmured. "I could take him, *ningún problema.*"

"Doubtless, but someone might get hurt," his mother said softly. "I can forgive you for not being a hero. I might not forgive you for getting one of the children shot."

"That pussy's not going to shoot anybody," Esteban said.

She turned to Willing. "Are we supposed to be plotting? Coming up with an ingenious ploy to get these people out of our house? That's what we'd do in a movie."

"We could set this house on fire, too," Willing said matter-of-factly. "They would have to leave. But so would we. The fire could get out of control. Then neither family would have a place to live. It would be spiteful. Like what those intruders did to the garden."

"So, then—what?"

"If we're seriously letting that *cabrón* house-jack us out of our own home," Esteban said, "can't we hang at Adelphi? Has to be some advantage to your drear job."

"The shelter's already at 200 percent capacity," his mother said. "Other staff have tried to sneak in family. They were fired."

"This is my fault," Willing said.

"Lost me there, *muchacho*," Esteban said.

"We should have left earlier," Willing said. "I miscalculated. This city. It's a complex system, which has entered disequilibrium. It's unstable. That is why there's no reason to 'plot.' We have to leave anyway. The people downstairs won't end well. Even if you don't follow through on Nollie's threat to close the accounts, they won't be able to pay the utility bills. The water, gas, and electricity will be cut off. And he's a computer modeler. He won't have a clue how to access a gas line illegally, not without blowing up the whole block. Besides—think how easily they can take this house from us. It will be just as easy for someone else to take it away from them."

"You think we should leave, but go where?" his mother asked. She was frantic. She would have to calm down. "Grand Man's practically a hundred! Luella's a handful at the best of times, and my parents aren't spring chickens, either!"

"For now, to the encampment," Willing said. "In Prospect Park. It's dangerous, but not as dangerous as being isolated. We can barter there. The encampments are self-enclosed economies."

"Barter with what, for what?" his mother said. "Willing, honestly, sometimes you're such a know-it-all! When the only thing you're really proposing is that we all become homeless! I've seen enough of it. There's no romance in it."

He shouldn't take her insults personally. "We'll stay there only as long as it takes to prepare."

"Oh, for Pete's sake. *To prepare.* For what, the Rapture? So we can open our arms in a field to await the lord's redemption, or the landing of an alien space ship?"

They didn't have time for this. "Take warm clothes," Willing directed. "Wear multiple layers so you don't have to carry them. Remember to bring something waterproof. Fill the plastic bottles in the old recycling container with tap water." (The city hadn't picked up recycling—a quaint practice—for a year and a half.)

442 • LIONEL SHRIVER

"Take ass napkins. Plenty, because we won't be able to wash them. If you salvage any food from the kitchen, be discreet. Prefer backpacks to luggage. Luggage attracts attention, and it's too easy to steal. If you have any cash, put some of it—enough to be credible—in your pocket, or an outside compartment of your pack. Put the rest in shoes, underwear, or rolled inside balled pairs of socks. That way, if they ask for our money before we go, we can give them the obvious money. And whatever you do, don't get mad at Sam and Tanya. The more angrily we behave, the more they'll feel justified in acting rash. We can't seem unpredictable. Remember that we were going to have to leave anyway. They're doing us a favor."

In the basement storage area, Willing replenished the inflation of the bicycle tires. He grabbed his toolkit, panniers, and some bungee cords, as Lowell railed in the background that "protection of private property is the primary responsibility of the state!" Willing couldn't help but smile. Some people just couldn't shift their *paradigm*.

He was feeling better, after attending to his previous task. He hadn't checked the rubble behind the furnace for a while, but they were safe. If he said so himself, it was a very good hiding place. Interesting, that his mother never asked about them. She was afraid she'd be arrested. He wondered if they even did that anymore—arrested people.

As he locked the bike to a parking sign outside, Willing saw his grandfather hunch into the basement stairwell. Carter set something on the steps, and stooped over it with his blanket. Looking up, he put a finger to his lips.

It wasn't clear what Carter was up to, but the crazed expression he'd worn since the fire had grown wilder. Willing didn't want to attract Sam's attention, and this wasn't the time for lecturing his grandfather about complex systems entering disequilibrium. He settled for a fervent head shake to discourage whatever half-baked scheme the old man had concocted, while mouthing *NO, DON'T* and crossing flattened hands back and forth—universal code for *Forget about it!* But Willing was merely an underestimated sixteen-year-old grandson, and Carter E. Mandible had been on the brink of killing someone for two solid years.

Darting back to the stairwell, Willing pointed toward the interior: *Get back inside.* Carter pulled the blanket around his neck and glowered. He wasn't coming.

Uneasy, Willing joined the assembly in the living room. Sam looked worn out. He wanted them to leave in that ordinary pooped way that you want guests who've outstayed their welcome to go—so you can get a start on the kitchen, have a nightcap in peace, watch the news.

"Money," Sam said. They emptied their decoy pockets.

"House keys," Sam announced next, extending a basket from the coffee table like a church collection plate. "I don't want visitors."

As the evictees lined up in the foyer, Sam did a half-hearted search of their bags, prodding the nose of his weapon into unzipped compartments with the cursory poking of a jaded museum guard. Unfortunately, he did confiscate the partial loaf of bread that Willing's mother had stashed, despite Tanya's standing sentinel over the kitchen. But he allowed Kurt to take his saxophone. Having lost all she owned, Jayne had no possessions, and hung back in her blanket by the stairs as the others slumped outside one by one. She must have been trying to stay warm for as long as possible. She'd had a long day.

"What the hell is that?" Sam asked as Nollie reached the doorway. The carton looked much too heavy for a woman on the cusp of seventy-five.

"Foul matter," Nollie said.

"Howl fatter," Luella said behind her. "Prowl patter. Mewl fitter, cowl tatter, whole sitter. Peter Piper picked a bowl of beer batter . . ."

"Someone get that hag out of this house," Sam growled. Unwrapping his wife's reins from her hitching post, GGM tugged Luella out the door.

"Manuscripts, of my books," Nollie explained. "They may or may not be worth something to anyone else, but they are worth something to me."

Sam opened the flaps, and sure enough, the box brimmed with rubber-banded printouts. "Jesus, it takes all kinds, doesn't it?"

Sam now hung on to Bing with the habitual clutch of a parent hauling his kid on errands, and Jake looked jealous. Carrying her second son's coat and backpack, Avery wasn't leaving without her youngest. Otherwise, they were down to Willing and Jayne when Sam surveyed the stragglers sharply. "Hey, where's that surly codger who threatened to stage a sit-in?"

Willing's gaze was drawn to a motion behind their captor. To cover the telltale glance, he supposed hastily, "Carter—my grandfather must be in the bathroom."

Looming on the stoop in the open doorway, Carter raised both hands high behind Sam's back. As his blanket flew backwards, he plunged a gleaming foot-long implement into the interloper's shoulder. Sam bellowed. With a concurrent whoop, Jayne flapped her own blanket over Tanya and Ellie's heads, trapping the younger woman's arms, wrapped around the girl. The gun went off. Bing howled.

Yanking the foreign object from his right shoulder, Sam reeled to train the handgun on his assailant. After hurling herself onto the floor, Tanya kicked Jayne off and thrashed from the blanket. She swept up Ellie and retreated behind her husband. Avery rushed to her son to examine his foot. The tussle was over in seconds.

"What the fuck is this?" Sam brandished the two-pronged silver weapon, which came to two delicate points, now dark and wet. It was an elegant utensil, whose exquisite design he didn't seem in the mood to admire.

"Asparagus tongs," Carter declared unapologetically, eyes wide and black. He nodded at the gun. "Go ahead. Make my day."

"Darling, begging for suicide-by-creep is not what that expression means!" Jayne cried, picking herself up. "It's only funny if you're Dirty Harry with a Magnum, not an old man with asparagus tongs!"

"Out, all of you, now." Sam jerked the gun.

"You shot through the toe of my son's shoe," Avery chided. "His foot will freeze out there. At least let me get another pair from downstairs."

"No more Mister Nice Guy. Go." Sam's shoulder was bleeding, and he didn't seem like one of those mythical hard-asses oblivious to pain.

Jayne, Avery, Bing, and Willing filed out to join the rest on the sidewalk, where they could hear the click of the lock on their own front door and the rattle of its chain being secured. The same sounds soon emitted from the entrance to the basement.

"Dad, I know you meant well," Avery said, arm around her whimpering youngest, whose left tennis shoe flapped open. "But that derring-do was dangerous. It's a miracle the bullet missed Bing's foot, and his toes look burned."

"Asparagus tongs?" Nollie said. "Carter, how about a fucking knife?"

"All the knives in the silver service are blunt, and the wife was in the kitchen." Carter picked his blanket off the ground and shook it out snappily. "At least I tried something."

Jayne adjusted her husband's battle robes around his neck. Their exploit had accomplished nothing, yet maybe it was worth the risk: both grandparents stood proudly upright, looking years younger in the glow of the streetlamp. Whereas Esteban was muttering to Willing's mother, "I'd have flattened that *tonto* with a shovel, but I was ordered not to."

"Never mind a knife, why not a hammer?" Nollie badgered her brother. "There's a toolbox in the basement, and our friend Sam there gave you the idea on a plate!" (It was impossible to envision Carter Mandible crushing Sam's skull with a hammer. Funny—Willing could readily picture Nollie doing it.)

Carter shot back, "At least those silver pincers are a damned sight deadlier than a box of lousy first drafts."

"How are we going to carry that, Nollie?" Lowell charged. "It's awkward, and incredibly heavy. You won't be able to manage that blasted box to the end of the block."

"Watch me," Nollie said darkly. It was never wise to question Enola Mandible's athletic prowess.

"I've put up with your egomania my whole life," Carter told his sister. "But this is the limit. Right now, rescuing originals of your *o-o-o-o-oeuvre* would be imbecilic enough if you were Tolstoy. But you're a hack. I read the *Times* review of *The Stringer*—'prose miraculously both pallid and overwritten'—"

"At least a whole *o-o-o-o-oeuvre*," Nollie said, "beats a handful of articles about *hatchbacks* and *condominiums*—"

"Children!" GGM cried. "Enough! Carter, your sister garnered many fine reviews, and no one publishes multiple novels without drawing the odd stinker. Enola, there's nothing ignoble about an article about condominiums so long as it's written with panache. I've listened to this scrapping my whole life, and

I shouldn't have to put up with playground fisticuffs at my age."

"Still, if we're too weighed down, Nollie," Willing's mother said, "we'll be marks. This time of night, gangs rove all over this neighborhood."

"I guess if anyone gives us trouble," Avery said, "we can always threaten them with *foul matter*."

It wasn't fair. They were picking on Nollie because they couldn't take their frustration out on Sam and Tanya, or the Federal Reserve, or the president.

"I'll carry it for now," Esteban offered begrudgingly, though he was already burdened by the largest backpack. "But keep an eye out for a Dumpster."

"No," Willing said. He took the box from Nollie. It was staggeringly heavy; maybe his great-aunt really *was* fit. He fished a sheet of plastic from his pack and wrapped the box, to protect it from the chill mist. He rested the carton on the back of the bike and lashed it to the rack with bungee cords.

"Willing," Carter said, fetching the box he'd left in the basement stairwell. "Do you think you could manage this, too?"

Banded with another bungee cord, the silver service fit neatly in one pannier. Though precious metal would have value as barter, Willing had already consigned one sentimental attachment to functional currency.

So he vowed not to trade those engraved utensils for transient food and shelter unless their lives depended on it. That set of silver was their inheritance. Sam and Tanya had the sofa. The Mandible estate, the fabled appointments of Bountiful House, came down to this one box.

It was only three or so miles to Prospect Park, but the journey took hours. Kurt took responsibility for Luella at first, but Florence had to admit he was too gentle. When Luella lunged in the wrong direction, he wouldn't jerk the leash with enough brutality to get her to heel. When she sat on the sidewalk and refused to get up, he stood over her reasoning and offering incentives, a rational appeal that didn't work with small children, either. Esteban took over, and slung her over his shoulder. But she struggled, kicking and biting, until he dropped her in disgust. Florence's mother was better at managing her than the men. She employed the steady, stolid, unrelenting resolution with which women had pursued their purposes for centuries. As for Florence's father, for the time being he didn't voice his grief over having lost their house, or having lost her house, either. All he did declare, more than once and with vehemence, was that he was "not minding Luella for one more minute."

Grand Man might have been in fine fettle for a virtual centenarian, but his energy was spent, after the fire, and a harrowing second ejection from his sole safe haven. He had to take frequent breaks, leaning against a parking meter, or resting on the rim of an overflowing public trashcan (garbage collection having grown intermittent at best). His cane helped, but he was as handicapped by bewilderment as by old age. It must have been jarring to go from debonair, high-stakes mover and shaker in Manhattan publishing, to retired eminence gris cum day trader in the plushest assisted-living facility in the country, to exiled nonentity shuffling along the dark, litter-strewn streets of East Flatbush. Yet however fiercely Florence summoned sympathy, it was exasperating to walk this slowly.

Goog kept complaining his pack was too heavy, and Bing wouldn't stop crying; the flapping of his left sole on the concrete must have been getting on everyone's nerves. Avery kept stopping to use their only fleX under contract to try to reach Savannah, who alone of the kids had kept her own fleX paid up. But the calls went to voicemail. On her husband's insistence, Avery dialed 911 to report the house-jacking, but a recording about a high volume of calls repeatedly suggested she try again later. Lowell railed with establishmentarian outrage, whereas Kurt probably counted himself fortunate for having put off a move to the Prospect Park encampments this long. The mizzle thickened to a drizzle, and the damp cold was miserable.

Wheeling his bike at the rear, Willing shot frequent glances over his shoulder. It was no longer an hour at which sensible people went for a walk. As Linden Boulevard swished with occasional cars streaking through the area as fast as possible, their only company was huddles of lone homeless people—*fellow* homeless people—scowling protectively, their supermarket carts having grown more enticing than wallets. Florence jumped at the scuttle of mangy, malevolent strays. It was irksome to have to credit her son for the foresight, when she'd thought giving Milo away to Brendan's family was deranged. But sure enough, few people could cover pet food anymore. Cats and dogs had been released by the thousands to fend for themselves.

Florence should have been seething, but she couldn't afford to seethe. Instead she focused on getting their company through the night. Willing had a tarp; she'd found another, left behind by that useless outfit that waterproofed the basement. They had a few blankets. If they could all sardine onto one tarp, and sandwich under the second, they might stay dry; body heat should keep them warm. She'd rescued bags of peanuts and raisins from the pantry, and hoped the city had the sense to supply water in the park. This was the way poor people thought. The long view was a defining feature of prosperity. The destitute planned a single step ahead.

At last, after they'd climbed the long hill on East Drive inside the park, they reached an access point. In the sulking glow of the city's ambient light, the sweep of Long Meadow quilted below. It was a sorry version of the promised land: edge to edge across what was once the site of picnics and games of ultimate Frisbee, a patchwork of plastic tarpaulins, planks, pressboard, Sheetrock, and corrugated iron, many of the materials for these improvised dwellings salvaged from the abandoned construction sites that hulked across all five boroughs. The patter of rain on the metal panels was almost peaceful.

Presumably, to *wake* in a bad mood, Lowell would have to have slept first. He'd positioned himself on their improvised pallet-for-thirteen next to Avery, but she kept the two boys on her other side, which left him snug against Nollie. Intimate proximity to an elderly woman who, like the rest of them, granted, hadn't bathed in days was noxious. And she snored. In the light of day, too, it became apparent why this patch on the edge of the encampment was available.

They were under a tree, at least a handy anchor for leashing Luella. But branches had dripped on his forehead even after the rain stopped. Their communal bedroll was laid over a barren depression, without a blade of grass for cushion. The dip collected water, so the tarps were now sloppy with mud, which had crept up the cuffs of his only pair of trousers. He hadn't been up for brushing with bottled water at 3 a.m. in a shantytown, and his sticky teeth emitted a sour tang.

As he struggled upright, Lowell panicked when at first he couldn't find his shoes. Good God—in this glass-strewn rubble, merely having your shoes stolen could mark you as done for. Probably a good idea to keep them on all night, though the crud between his toes would fester. His clothes were rank and damp, his unshaven chin itchy, his hair lank. The line between owners of swank Washington townhouses and denizens of his sister-in-law's Fort Greene shelter was perhaps thinner than he'd previously appreciated.

Putting Lowell's nose further out of joint, his smarty-pants nephew had already disappeared, absconding with their party's only paid-up fleX. Lowell was determined to pursue the return of Florence's property through proper channels, and internet access would be a start. Her ownership of the house was a matter of public record. He was incensed by how readily the rest of this crowd gave up on standard procedure. It was when you neither believed in systems, nor employed the tools of systems, that systems broke down for good. Look at what had driven inflation, far more than monetary policy: the self-fulfilling social assumption that the dollar was worthless and would be only more worthless tomorrow. The world has a confounding way of fashioning itself in the form of your imaginings. Act as if a city is lawless, and lawless it becomes.

He would have to write this down.

At least the kid wouldn't have traveled far, since he'd left his bike—looped with a lock and laden with that cockamamie box of manuscripts and the incongruous silver service hidden in a saddlebag. Nollie stood watch. What did you want to bet that she was defending the printout primarily, and the silver only as an afterthought?

Before, to Lowell's amazement, *going to work*, Florence distributed a niggardly handful of peanuts apiece as "breakfast," apologizing that there were no more raisins, because she'd come upon Bing polishing off the bag. Everyone picked on that boy. It wasn't his fault that he was young, growing, and hungry. Kurt said some self-appointed bouncer had already threatened their company with expulsion—from a shantytown!— because Luella's "night terrors" had kept nearby squatters awake. With Douglas's permission, Kurt volunteered his only spare pair of socks for a gag. Generous, yes. Nevertheless, Lowell was flummoxed by why the tenant, in arrears for a second year, was still this family's problem. Apparently you have to keep taking care of people solely because you've *been* taking care of them. By inference, you shouldn't take care of anybody, because if you did you'd never get rid of them.

Grabbing some ass napkins, Lowell sought *local inquiry.*

"How do you do?" he introduced himself formally to their nearest neighbor—a grizzled, filthy old lady. But pots and pans dangling from hooks on a crude but sturdy wooden structure suggested established residence. Queasy about a handshake, he settled for a nod. "Lowell Stackhouse, professor of economics, Georgetown University."

She smiled wryly. "Professor *emeritus*, I presume? Deirdre Hesham, air traffic controller. I took *early retirement* myself."

Because she knew the word *emeritus*, he inspected her more closely; the "old lady" couldn't have been fifty. "I gather air travel has halved," he commiserated.

"Worse than halved," she said. "But now that they've decided folks like me are expendable, I wouldn't get on so much as a hop to Hartford if I were you."

He explained that he was new here, and tried to describe his mission with discretion.

"Don't go near the porta potties," Ellen warned. "They haven't exchanged them for a year. Try the woods that way—though watch your step. You won't be the first, if you get my drift."

Once he returned distastefully from a sea of the one thing worse than mud, Lowell mourned the loss of his fleX: he had nothing to read, and couldn't bury himself in his treatise (which *should* have been backed up on multiple servers—but Lowell had finally parsed this era's crucial distinction between *should* and *would*; he'd only rest easy when he laid eyes on the text). When Florence returned from Adelphi much too early that afternoon, the excitement was welcome.

"What happened?" Esteban reached toward but did not touch a red streak along Florence's jaw, the center of which was blistered.

"I was lucky to be wearing the bandana," Florence said shakily, touching its brown singe around her left ear, "or he'd have set fire to my hair. As it is, only a few escaped strands burned off. Smelled terrible."

She backtracked: undeterred by Adelphi staff's standard no-room-at-the-inn, to gain admittance an obstreperous white guy had held Florence hostage with a blow torch—"the upscale stainless-steel kind—that you use to caramelize crème brûleé." To demonstrate he had enough butane to be dangerous, he'd turned it on.

"You are *not* going back there," Esteban said.

"But I bring in our only paycheck," Florence said weakly.

"*Ever*," Esteban said.

"He's right. You've done your part, Mom." Willing had reappeared. With an obscure glance at Nollie, he announced, "We've reached the Final Chapter."

What an insufferable twit. Rounding up his cousins and elders, the kid called a group meeting around the tree. For reasons beyond his uncle, this sixteen-year-old punk was now their Dear Leader. Any day now the boy would start buzz-cutting his hair above the ears, drinking loads of cognac, and executing his relatives.

"I got us protection," Willing said, keeping his voice low. In the cover of his apostles, the boy withdrew an object from his jacket halfway. Metal caught the sun. *Oh, for Christ's sake.*

"How did you get that?" Florence asked, aghast. Only yesterday she would have asked *why.* "Did you steal it? Like everything *else*?"

Something dense passed between mother and son that piqued Lowell's curiosity.

"He thinks he's so careless," Goog grumbled to his brother.

"I bought it," Willing said.

"But we've got so little money—" Florence began.

"With something of value," Willing said. "Which rules out dollars, doesn't it."

Florence murmured, "The goblets," whatever that meant.

"We have one left," Willing said. "But don't say the G-word aloud in this place. Even in a whisper."

As Lowell couldn't imagine why saying "goblets" could be perilous in a public park, he assumed the boy meant G-as-in-gun. The coyness was absurd. It was widely known that encampments like this were armed to the teeth. "You know how to work that?" he charged.

"I read up," Willing said pleasantly. "It's not complicated. That's why stupid people have been getting their way with these things for centuries."

"Wouldn't want to fault your research," Esteban said. "But if anybody's packing in this party—no offense, it should be a grown man."

"Whoever carries has to be *Willing* to use it." The kid did have a knack for delivering punch lines with a straight face.

"You could be a danger to yourself—" Carter said.

"This is a distraction," Willing cut him off. "Stories like ours—and worse—are all over the web. I think we got off lightly. The administration's expression *civil unrest* is misleadingly mild. We're not talking wide-spread insomnia. And the 'unrest' is mostly in big cities like New York. We have to get out."

"Where's any better, in your expert opinion?" Lowell sneered.

"Gloversville, obviously."

"Oh, yeah?" Goog said. "Who died and left you president of the world?"

Willing ignored his cousin, as usual. "There's food, shelter, and a well. I talked to Jarred. He's short of labor he can trust. It's easy to find people desperate for a job. But food is at a premium. Employees get tempted to steal. Organized crime is heavily into the agricultural black market. He'd welcome us all, if we're willing to work. That would include standing armed guard over the fields at night. Thieves are harvesting whole crops while farmers sleep. Jarred has room for us, too. The Mexican migrant workers who've been squatting over the last two winters have moved on."

"If Gloversville is such an oasis," Esteban said, "why would they leave?"

"To go back to Mexico, of course," Willing said. "Mexico signed on to the bancor. It picked up a lot of the trade that the States has lost. The economy is booming."

"He's right," Carter said. "Though it's hard to sort fact from fiction lately—"

"Dad, enough! Give it a rest!" Avery and Florence said at once.

"I was only saying!" Carter snapped. "TV news, webzines, they're in rare accord: immigration's reversed. Mexico's established a huge military presence at the border. Nationals are being let back in, but white Americans are universally denied visas—even temporary tourist visas. Illegal immigrants from El Norte are being deported in droves."

"Gosh," Nollie said. "Hispanics are *undocumented*. Whites are *illegal*."

"Hypocrites," Avery muttered.

"I don't call it hypocrisy," Esteban said. "I call it payback."

"Except the Mexican border police are giving third-, even second-generation Lats a hard time, too," Carter warned.

"Do you have a Mexican passport?" Willing asked.

"Why would I?" Esteban said. "Any more than you would?"

"That's too bad," Willing said. "It would now be much more valuable than one from the American State Department."

"That's a turnabout I could drink to," Esteban said. "About time you honks find out how it feels when folks who happen to be born in a place lord their precious passport over you like they're anointed. Man, at the border right now, I'd laugh my head off."

"Can we please get back to what we're going to do?" Jayne implored.

Willing gestured to the encampment. "We're luckier than most of these people. We have somewhere to go. We have only one problem: how to get there."

"We should sneak back and swipe the Jaunt," Avery said. "They only took my one key fob."

"No," Lowell confessed morosely. "They were way ahead of you. They demanded mine, too, and the spare."

"I've tallied our cash," Willing said. "We can't afford a single bus or train ticket to upstate New York. And even if we had the money—according to Inner-Tube, Port Authority, Grand Central, and Penn Station are mobbed. We're not the only ones who've figured out it's time to go."

"So what are you proposing?" Lowell said. "That we all pile onto your bicycle, like one of those 1950s stunts with phone booths?" (The taunt fell flat. Willing wouldn't know what a *phone booth* was.)

"We'll have to walk," Willing said.

"To *upper New York State*?" Lowell cried.

"It's a hundred and ninety-four miles by car. Somewhat longer, by back roads. Esteban used to lead treks along the Palisades for a living. He can show us the way."

"My, I can't believe Our Lord and King would hand his scepter to someone else," Lowell said, and Avery kicked him.

"The first part is straight-forward," Willing said. "Down Flatbush, over the Brooklyn Bridge, up the Westside bikeway to the GW. All these exit routes are getting crowded, so it can be faster to walk than drive. But it's not like a disaster movie. Zombies aren't rampaging through the streets. There aren't any giant lizards on Fifth Avenue. The Empire State Building is still standing. Midtown isn't on fire."

"Son," Douglas said, having sagged onto the pile of backpacks stacked on the tarps. "It took us four hours to go three miles last night. At my age, that's about as far as I'm good for in a day. Off the top of my head, I reckon that would put us on the road, and preyed upon by the *kindness* of strangers, for over two months. You younger folks might have a chance. But you'll never make it to Gloversville with Luella and me in tow. You should leave us behind, you hear? We've had our day. It was a good day. Better than yours is likely to be, from where I'm sitting."

"We're not leaving you behind," Willing said firmly. "If it takes two months, so be it."

"But what about supplies?" Jayne asked. "We barely have enough food to make it through today. If our cash can't buy a bus ticket . . ."

"The camps don't use cash," Willing said. "It's all barter, some credit, but you pay your debts with real goods, too. We can't carry enough provisions for the whole trip. But we can make a start. Because, Avery? People around here are desperate to lock down what little they've got left. They have to be able to make shutters." He pulled a fistful of plastic baggies with Home Depot labels from his backpack. "So guess what's in short supply?"

Avery smiled. *"Hinges."*

The plan was lunatic. Yet Lowell welcomed an excuse to get out of this cesspit, and accompanied Avery and the boys to the nearest supermarket on Third Avenue, where they parlayed a portion of the cash for nonperishables with a high calorie-to-weight ratio: fudge, salami, halvah—the antithesis of the micro-greens and tuna-carpaccio table they'd laid in Georgetown.

On their return, Willing had traded hinges for raccoon jerky—a local delicacy.

Meantime, Florence helped Lowell convince Avery to stop leaving messages for Savannah. They shouldn't deplete the remaining credit on the fleX. Of the three kids, their daughter had demonstrated the keenest aptitude for living on her wits. The girl had friends in Manhattan, and was at the age when she couldn't abide the company of her parents. They had to have faith, and hope for the best. Avery left Jarred's address, as well as their whereabouts in Prospect Park—locations bound to put their daughter off reuniting with her family anytime soon.

Sure enough, Savannah fleXted late that afternoon: "im nt gnna liv on any fking farm."

If this motley Chosen People were to set off on their exodus the very next day, as their underage Moses had commanded, Lowell thought privately that burdening their party with Douglas and Luella was self-destructive. That dapper old geezer and his mad consort would never manage a hike of two hundred miles—sleeping rough, depending on serendipity for sustenance, probably trudging much of the trip on an empty stomach. Fair enough, they were his wife's grandparents, but condemning the expedition to certain failure merely to express loyalty to elders near death anyway seemed sentimental. They'd be better off leaving the couple at the encampment, since charity often arose more readily among the penniless than among the prosperous. In short order, however, Lowell was relieved to have kept the opinion to himself.

As Willing told it later, in his Oyster Bay heyday the Mandible patriarch had socialized with the hunting and skeet-shooting set, and was no stranger to firearms. In the flicker of their campfire that evening, Douglas had asked to see the protection for their travels that Willing had secured that morning, the better to ensure that his great-grandson understood the safety catch and how to load the weapon. It happened in a trice: Douglas shot his wife in the chest, and himself in the head. At the sound of shots, even Deirdre Hesham opposite simply battened her shutters.

2047

Chapter 1
Getting with the Program

Returning full circle to East Flatbush should have been gratifying. Willing grew up here. His mother had worked hard to buy this house. With ample funds from helping to grow food during what politicians still refused to call a *famine* in the mid-thirties, she had paid off the mortgage. Legal New York property owners in exile were obliged to press their claims by a certain date, or forfeit title to the state. The state—a cyclone that sucked up houses, trailers, pets, and children in its wake. It was better, he would remain calmer, if he thought of it as weather.

Regaining possession of his childhood home was more complicated than he had anticipated. Years before, Willing had traded his surname, handed down from his grandmother Jayne, for Mandible. The rechristening was a tribute to Great Grand Man—like so many tributes, too late for the honoree to receive the compliment—who had sacrificed so that their exodus from a deepening urban sinkhole might succeed. Yet as far as officialdom was concerned, only Willing Darkly could inherit his mother's property, and his New York State identity card cited the wrong name. So the headache took patience to sort out. But Willing was patient.

Asserting his claim to 335 East Fifty-Fifth Street also entailed having its current residents evicted. Now paid handsomely in dólares nuevos linked to the mighty bancor, the NYPD undertook such tasks with forbidding relish. To be the instigator of this violent flinging aside was disquieting. His mother had never evicted her own delinquent tenant, but had folded him into her family. Oh, Sam, Tanya, Ellie, and Jake had long ago been replaced by other usurpers. If the condition of the house was anything to go by, recent residents had been less genteel (and he should thank them: ravaging squatters had so depressed the property valuation that it sneaked in just under the backdated cutoff for inheritance taxes). Maybe the benevolence of taking Nollie with him to Brooklyn compensated for the uncharitable expulsion. Eighty-four when they moved back to town and now ninety, she had a horror of nursing homes. Besides, he was not his mother. He was a thief. He had mugged a boy in the street. In 2032, he had raided gardens, pilfered orchards, and held up convenience stores to feed their bedraggled party on the long trek north. He had not been a nice boy. He was probably not a nice man, either.

He had been sorry to leave Gloversville, but by the end, only so sorry. Working the land at Citadel was never the same after the federal government nationalized the farms. The Mandibles were demoted to sharecroppers. They were allowed to retain a small percentage of their yield for private use. The rest of the meat, dairy products, and produce was confiscated by the US Department of Agriculture. There were even rules about which parts of your hogs you could keep: butts, shoulders, cheeks. Farmers were seen as profiteers. As many of them had been. So when it was first brought in, the policy was wildly popular, helping to secure the Democrats a landslide in 2036. It was less popular with the farmers. Many burned their crops and massacred their livestock—anything but abdicate the fruits of their labor to a government that had savaged the economy in the first place. But as public relations, spite in the countryside backfired with starving city dwellers, who had hoped the nationalizations meant Valhalla: well-stocked supermarkets with reasonable prices. Instead, most of the federal agricultural haul was exported. Washington needed to improve the current account deficit, and China wanted pork.

At least Willing's reasoned intercession successfully discouraged his volatile uncle Jarred from torching his own land. Even so, submitting to Jarred's rages on a daily basis had been draining. Coal-haired, hollow-eyed, and ferocious, it was Jarred who moved Willing to contemplate the geometrical validity of the political designations *left* and *right*. That is, if you turn left, and left, and left again, you end up on the right. Jarred had started out a radical environmentalist, a position only ninety degrees from survivalist. With one small last adjustment in the same direction, he transformed to libertarian gun nut. Willing himself was not very interested in these categories, but they seemed to mean something to other people. What mattered to Willing was that his uncle's wrath was wasted energy. In each political permutation, Jarred needed, or thought he needed, an enemy. The warring left him spent. Meanwhile the enemy, if there was one, remained unfazed. The enemy did not know that Jarred existed.

Willing was grateful to Jarred. Who had saved his own life, and the whole family. It was a shame that for Citadel's owner working the farm as a serf of the nation came to feel so mean, oppressive, and embittering. Like Avery when something in her settled, Willing was able to lose himself in hard work—tilling, sowing, and cutting kale. He had never wanted to "be" anything, to "make something of himself." Why conjure up a fantasy future that was not obtainable? Perhaps he had no ambition by nature, and he could live with that. As an unambitious person would.

He understood that this was a country where individuals were believed to determine their destinies. But a helpless pessimism—pessimism particularly on that previous point, about whether there was anything worth "becoming," anything worth aiming for, anywhere to go—characterized his whole generation. With the exception of Goog, who was galvanized by malice—Goog had become an utter T-bill—his cousins seemed precociously worn out, almost elderly in their fatigue. Willing's girlfriend Fifa also—she was languid, slurring, stretched out, sluggish. It was what he liked about her. If there seemed an element of laziness in her flopping over the sad shredded remnants of Great Grand Man's claret-colored sofa, beneath her reserving and conserving of energy lay something quite other. A belligerence. She said at work she had refined what the old unions called the *go-slow*. She had calculated the exact pace at which she could not be upbraided. She was doing the job. Just. This digging in of heels was growing commonplace. The countless overlords of your life would take so much, but you would hold something back, or you would not even have yourself. Fifa had herself. If he pressed himself on the matter, Willing liked to believe that he had himself as well. But he was not confident of this. It was possible that he was not here. That he had been stolen.

Which is why resuming residence in his late mother's house had not turned out to be all that gratifying.

Return to the city necessitated a proper job. Packing up at Citadel in '41, he already suspected that a job meant being chipped. It was routine; everyone said so. Like applying for a Social Security number. A bureaucratic matter, a relatively painless, pro forma protocol of the modern day. Thus Willing had not considered the inevitability of the procedure with sufficient seriousness. He had been lulled by what was regular, by what was expected and customary. No doubt all ages have their usual things, about which no one at the time thinks twice. Their leeches and bloodletting, their homosexual "cures," their children's workhouses and debtors' prisons. When drowning in the is-ness of the widely accepted present, it must be hard to tell the difference—between traditions like burying your dead and having dinner at 8 p.m. and other, just as mesmerizingly normative conventions that later will leap out to posterity as offenses against the whole human race. Maybe he was letting himself off the hook. He'd had misgivings, after all. Yet it is always challenging to choose otherwise when you are informed in no uncertain terms that there is no choice to make.

When Willing was small, people made a great brouhaha over pedophilia, and sexual abuse of any kind. His mother had taken him aside with a formality that wasn't like her when he was four or five. She knelt with a maudlin solicitation that made his skin crawl. Her voice dropped into a timbre both stern and over-tender. He should never allow adults to touch him in his "private places." That expression was not like her, either. She had always been a straight shooter. If she wanted to refer to his *dick* or his *asshole*, she called them precisely that. Which is how he recognized that her mind had been contaminated by a communicable virus. The "private places" lecture was repulsive. It made him feel dirty. It made him recoil from his mother in an instinctive dislike that was singular.

In those days, playing outside was forbidden. Employees at daycare centers were required to get criminal-record checks. All scoutmasters were suspect. No one ever seemed to care if you were a murderer. Murderers were let out of prison and blended right back into the neighborhood. They could live wherever they wanted. Sex criminals were marked for life—shuttled from hostels to underpasses, and required to report their whereabouts, which were posted on the web—the better for local parents to start picketing campaigns to have the filth evicted. The no-go radius around schools and playgrounds widened every year. It was worse to be a rapist than a killer. By inference, rather than be raped, you were better off dead.

Willing did not want to return to the preoccupation with "private places." It didn't bother him that sex had grown incidental. He and Fifa enjoyed it, but he didn't see what all the fuss was once about, and most of the time they were too tired. Dispensing with the business in private was more efficient.

Yet long after the larger social conversation had moved on, hovering over new fixations like a cloud shadowing other parts of town, he finally appreciated what they'd been talking about when he was a boy. It wasn't, probably, as bad as being murdered—though he'd never been murdered so he couldn't say. But it was horrific all the same. It was like being murdered and living through it. And you could remember not only the violence but the dying part. You have survived your own death but you have still died, whereas usually survival means not dying after all. He was certain this was what had occasioned the hushed tones, the kneeling, the deep warning strangeness from his mother in his childhood. She had kept him safe, for years thereafter, but she was gone now and couldn't protect him, so that when he was twenty-five it happened and all those teachers and counselors and moderators of school assemblies—it turned out they hadn't been exaggerating after all: Willing was raped.

That was the only word he had for it, a word he did not, therefore, use to anyone else, not even to Fifa. The very word, as it applied to the experience, in addition to recollection of the experience itself, was stored in a "private place." The stasis with which he was now afflicted six years later, that pessimism about whether there was even anywhere to go were he to suddenly discover an ambition to get there, this heavy unmoving sameness—he couldn't help but wonder whether it was all related to having been raped. He wasn't sure what he'd been like before. Clinically, as reliable biographical information, he could recall a deep sense of belonging at Citadel. The big round-table dinners. The loamy exhaustion after milking cows and slopping hogs. A gathering fondness for a group of people several of whom were very different from him—which made the emotion more of an achievement. A fondness for each person yet also for whatever the combination of them made together, which was more than the sum of parts. Yet since this numbness had descended, he could summon only the fact of the warmth; he could not inhabit the warmth itself.

He tried not to rehearse it (though the memory would intrude, when he was unguarded, falling asleep or not yet woken). He was still more disciplined about not discussing it. Virtually everyone else had been through the same thing. Thus, or so went the reasoning, there was nothing to say. This most minor of medical indignities was less of an ordeal than getting your teeth cleaned. Any expression of his distress would be interpreted as Willing Mandible being a big baby. Indeed, even newborns were now subject to the same procedure within their first hour in the world. Granted, some parents had expressed concern that infants might find the operation painful, traumatizing, a rude introduction. But physicians had reassured the public. The local anesthetic was skillfully targeted. The foreign object was the size of a pinhead. A mere poke would be more painful, a squeeze, even. Parents were far better off anguishing over male circumcision, now roundly discouraged. Willing envied the newborns. The real trauma had little to do with physical torment. A baby's clean slate would preclude any horror over what the "foreign object" was for.

Since he was eight years old, Willing had understood that most systems worked badly. It was a surprise to discover in his young adulthood that they could also work too well.

He had recently moved back to East Fifty-Fifth Street. Of a lesser order, the return also entailed a violation. The house had been occupied by strangers for nine years. Their alien residue was everywhere—dirty shirts, empty liquor bottles, syringes. More upsetting was the familiar—cups his mother had lovingly washed in gray water salvaged in the plastic tub year after year, now chipped, missing handles. Nary a plate or a bowl he'd grown up with wasn't broken or cracked. Comically, remnants of Avery's raids on Walgreens, Staples, and Home Depot remained. He continued to come across the odd packet of L-braces, a half-used bottle of Gorilla Glue, a scatter of multicolored paperclips in the basement. From the ripped-open packaging, he construed that someone had actually availed themselves of the toenail fungus kits. The closets had been rummaged. The few left-over shreds of his mother's wardrobe were speckled with mildew. Her beloved Bed Bath & Beyond laundry hamper, emblem of Esteban's devotion, had been moved to the kitchen for use as a garbage pail, and smelled. The cleaning job alone was arduous, and underneath the scum and the dust lurked deeper structural issues. A pervasive dampness was ominous. Oh, Florence Darkly—you and your obsession with shabby waterproofing.

From the start, he knew the variety of employment widely available: home health aide placements, health insurance and billing, design and maintenance of healthcare websites, answering healthcare help lines, medical device manufacture, service of medical devices, medical transport, medical research, pharmaceutical manufacture, pharmaceutical research, pharmaceutical advertising, hospital laundry, hospital catering, hospital administration, hospital construction, and work in assisted-living establishments that served every level of decrepitude from mildly impaired to moribund. Like so many his age, he was a high school dropout. That ruled out neurosurgery.

So Willing found an opening listed online at a nursing home facility called Elysian Fields, a short bike ride away on Eastern Parkway. For the scut work going begging—emptying bed pans, mopping—all they required was able-bodied youth. (Youth was the sole resource his small cohort possessed for which there was a seller's market.) So during the job interview, his hiring looked to be rubber-stamped, until he mentioned as an afterthought—if it was a problem, best address the matter now—that he hadn't been chipped.

THE MANDIBLES: A FAMILY, 2029–2047 · 481

The news raised every eyebrow in the room. "That's quite irregular," one committee member murmured. Another whispered, "Is that even legal now?" He might as well have revealed that he was a carrier of gray-squirrel flu. They instinctively pulled back from their interviewee an inch or two. He was informed that chipping was a nonnegotiable precondition of employment, not only here but anywhere in New York State. If he took care of it—"A five-minute business," one of them assured him, "bit more of a sting for an adult than for an infant, but you'll be right as rain by the next day"; another bureaucrat added, "Can get it done in any clinic or ER, on a walk-in basis, and for free! I was an early adopter, and it cost *me* two hundred nuevos"—he had the job.

Back home, Nollie was staunchly against it—an easy stance for her to take, since citizens over sixty-eight were exempt. "A monstrous idea," she said. "You'll be their creature." But then, the elderly always balked at innovation. Had shrivs stayed in charge, everyone would still be getting around in donkey carts.

Granted, Willing could instead have swept up the house as best he could and sold the disheveled property in East Flatbush under value. He and Nollie could have headed back to Citadel. But Jarred had grown irascible. Though farms were gradually being re-privatized now that the worst of the food shortages had abated, he was livid over being expected to buy back his own property. Of the supportive extended family that had filled his younger days with humor and solidarity, only Kurt remained. Nollie might not have believed it herself, but she needed readier access to quality medical care than Gloversville provided. Resistance to a simple prerequisite of living in the modern world seemed at once childish and old-womanish.

Turning a blind eye, then, to a wadding in his stomach as if he'd eaten a double order of dumplings, Willing strode too casually into King's emergency room and stated his purpose. "Goodness," the nurse exclaimed. "You're awfully old to be a virgin! However have you got by? You're not one of those strikers, are you? Lolling about on your parents' sofa?"

"No," he said. He didn't care for her ushering touch on his shoulder—the claiming, the corralling, the collusive inclusion, the welcome-to-the-club—but it was too late now. She had literally got her hands on him.

In the simple white room, he was instructed to lie face down while they ran a quick sequencing of his saliva swab; the chip would forever be linked to his DNA. His forehead fit into a padded cradle, while the nurse adjusted the setting screws until each point contacted his head. The brace recalled the abattoir, where

Jarred had taken veal calves, scarcely worth raising to mature cows for so little reward: a narrow chute steadied the skull, ensuring the bolt at the temple would plunge home. Willing could not move his head a hair. That was the idea. For his protection, the nurse explained sweetly. Otherwise, the slightest twitch "might leave him a paraplegic." She laughed.

He did not like lying on his stomach. The position was sexual, a posture of submission. He fought a rising panic as she swung a mechanism behind him and leveled it at the base of his skull—a soft, tender depression, undefended. Glass and chrome maybe, but the device looked like a gun. When she fired it, a white pain flashed up the face of Great Grand Man, gaunt, and pale, and red on one side, before he pitched beside the fire.

Since that afternoon at King's, Willing's sense of himself had been small and inert. He felt limp, lackluster, lumpen. Fearful. Figures flickered in his peripheral vision that, once he turned to them, were not there. He went through a period of scouring his nape with a washcloth several times a day. He felt desecrated, and contaminated, and invaded—as if what had connived itself into his neck weren't a chip but a tapeworm. He felt watched. He felt ashamed. He

felt the need to cover himself, even in his old bedroom, on his own. For a time, even Nollie maintained
her distance—mumbling, tight-lipped, keeping her
thoughts to herself. She asked warily, "Can that thing
hear?"

He had never put it to anyone else outright. He had
not regarded himself as a seer, a savant. He had not,
precisely, been able to forecast the future. But since he
was about fourteen, the disparate bits and pieces that
he had been collecting, idly, like seashells, had co-
hered. Facts that others hadn't fit together would form
a pattern. He had known things, and the things he had
known had been true, or had come true. Ever since the
chipping, the part of his head that perceived so clearly
had gone dead.

Oh, it wasn't that he trusted the fringier theories
on the net. He did not believe the federal government controlled his mind. He accepted that the chip
performed the functions it was purported to. It registered direct deposits of his salary. It deducted the costs
of any products he chose to buy. It debited his utility
bills. Though Willing had no experience of either, it
recorded investments and received state benefits. It
subtracted local, state, and federal taxes, which totaled
77 percent of his pay. It communicated his every purchase to the agency known until 2039 as the Internal

Revenue Service—what the item cost, when and where he bought it, and the product's exact description, down to model, serial number, or sell-by date. It informed the American tax authorities if he bought a packet of crackers. Were the chip to accumulate an excess of fiscal reserves—an amount that surpassed what he required on average to cover his expenses for the month—it would dun the overage at an interest rate of -6 percent. Should the balance cross various thresholds, that interest rate would progress up to -21 percent. (Saving was selfish. Saving was bad for the economy. Negative interest rates also provided Americans a short course in mathematics from which an undereducated public could surely benefit. At -21 percent compounded annually, $100 was worth $30.77 five years later.) Any additional income, including gift coupons for a birthday, revenue from pawned possessions, bake-sale proceeds, and private-party poker winnings, would also register on the chip, and would also be taxed at 77 percent. Chipping solved the problem of the hackable, stealable, long dysfunctional credit card. Chipped, you *were* a credit card.

Parental protest over the chipping of newborns died down altogether when states began depositing a generous $2,000 "baby bond" in every infant's chip. To the population at large, chipping was promoted as the ultimate convenience, and the ultimate in financial security. No more having to carry a wallet or device that thieves could seize on the street. At self-checkout, the terminal simply scanned your head. No more PINs or unique twenty-five-digit passwords, with numbers and letters and signs. No more biometric verification—the fingerprints, facial recognition, and iris scans that hackers had learned to duplicate as fast as the novel authentications had been brought in, since anything digitized can be copied. Obviating the bank account, with its erosive fees, your chip had its own website, or *chipsite*, for arranging monetary transfers. Its calculation of GPS coordinates precise within a millimeter, your chip communed with your very DNA, thrummed to your very pulse. If anyone contacted your chipsite whose distinctive heartbeat didn't synchronize perfectly with the pounding in your chip, your funds went into lockdown. So no one could pretend to be you, and the account that went everywhere you went was safe from predators. (The feds somewhat oversold this feature in the early versions. In a surge of "chipnappings," individuals were forced to make online transfers at gunpoint. Updates guaranteed that when the chip detected high levels of stress hormones like cortisol and epinephrine, or even heavy doses of tranquilizers that might suppress those hormones, transfers would not go through. The same bio-sensitivity ensured that gamblers could not place rash bets while drunk, which had a distinctly depressive effect on the casino industry.)

You were safe, of course, from all but one predator. For every transaction, it went without saying, was communicated to the Bureau for Social Contribution Assistance, the rebranded IRS. (Willing didn't know why they bothered to change the name. If they'd rechristened it the Department of Bunny Rabbits and Puppy Dogs, within minutes the "DBRPD" would evoke the same terror.) The data storage capacity of federal super computers was now so infinite that the old reporting threshold of deposits over $10,000 had come to seem recklessly steep. Tax authorities were now instantly apprised when a six-year-old received the wherewithal from his mother to buy gummy bears. *Two bags.*

The chipped all seemed thrilled to see the end of tax returns. Rendering unto Caesar was effortless. Though that meant there was no more cheating on their tax returns, either. No furtive rounding up or disguise of personal frippery as business expense. This also went down well politically. For decades, the public had been convinced that a remote elite living the life of Riley paid no taxes whatsoever. Oddly, Willing had never met one of these people. They must have lived somewhere else.

Much the same reasoning had led to the complete elimination of the cash dólar nuevo in 2042. Cash was an antiquated store of value. It created logistical hardship for Main Street small business. It leant itself to counterfeiting. It was the easiest form of wealth to steal. Criminals had long conducted business in banded stacks, in bulging briefcases, in whole suitcases stuffed with greenbacks, and now these cinematic clichés were obsolete. For cash was also one of the only forms of wealth that eluded jurisdiction. Willing remembered the furtive spirit in which his mother had plied the plumber with a rustle of twenties, as if to exchange physical money for services were against the law. Because cash is so hard to track, to trace, to tax, to control, Willing was astonished it took the government so long to get rid of it.

Language, by contrast, did not respond to fiat. Americans continued to communicate with idioms grown insensible. When their chips were down, so to speak, people still claimed to be *low on cash*. A profitable business remained a *license to print money*, and its proprietor might *make a mint*, though all the mints had closed. Fifa continued to offer her laconic boyfriend *a penny for his thoughts*. A tax refund would have been *pennies from heaven* had anyone ever got one. Affronted benefactors cut off heirs *without a penny*, although ferocious inheritance taxes kicked in at such a low level that you were lucky to leave children

your button collection. Jarred didn't regard fully automated farm equipment as *worth a plug nickel*, though
the latest safety features enabled driverless electric har-
vesters to stop *on a dime*. Democrats often described
the economic stability and political disempowerment of
the 2040s as *two sides of the same coin*.

A few optimists still *bet their bottom dollar* that the
United States would rise again to world supremacy,
though a digital construct could not be stacked. The
rhetorical convention persisted, but *making a bundle*
was now impossible. A property owner uneasy about a
purchaser's solvency might yet want to *see the color of
his money*; as of 2042, American currency had no color.
A unit of one hundred nuevos was a *C-note*, slang now
easily mistaken for an allusion to music. However ethe-
real the quantity had become, the country's linguistic
Luddites insisted on regarding money as something
you could roll in, throw at something, enjoy a sufficient
excess of which to burn, or—a disconcerting image
even in the days of the paper dollar—pour down the
drain.

To Avery's delight, secure chipping had restored
the online marketplace. Exhilarated by the prospect of
once more buying a toaster without leaving the house,
his aunt was an early adopter. (It was clever, making
the first wave of guinea pigs pay for the privilege of

implantation. Steep charges turned chips into status items.) Unfortunately for the likes of Willing and his cousins, the rousing return of internet shopping was largely theoretical. They commanded too little discretionary income to buy much. The economy was overwhelmingly powered by the whims of the retired.

Socially, Willing kept any reservations about chipping to himself. Detractors of the liberating fiscal protocol were pilloried as crackpots. Although continuous government access to your exact location might have seemed an infringement of civil liberties, most Americans were long accustomed to having their movements tracked by commercial entities like Google Maps. For decades, bicycles had been chipped. Pets had been chipped. People being chipped seemed inevitable. Buying goods with a mere tap at a terminal went back to smart phones, so the technological leap was minimal, while the security leap was huge. Now no one could appropriate the means of effortless purchase without chopping off your head, and nothing destroyed the functionality of a chip more instantaneously than its host being dead. Yet Willing felt not enough had been made of the chip's location. Its biological safeguards would have worked equally as well had it been embedded in an upper arm. The purpose of installing the thing right up against your spinal column was to keep you from digging it out. Employing shady surgeons, a few refuseniks had tried. They were recognizable for being paralyzed.

Nollie's disappointment that her grandnephew had freely become "their creature" was probably harsh. Nollie herself had an old-fashioned bank account, and made purchases with an ancient fleX. (Because it didn't auto-report, she also had to file old-fashioned tax returns. The dodgy throwback documents were systematically audited with a rolfing thoroughness that led to multiple senior suicides.) But the unchipped constituted a dwindling minority: the elderly, the far-flung and rural, a few expats abroad. Such anachronisms drew an accelerating suspicion and contempt. They couldn't buy a quart of milk without hauling out some *device*. Willing had noticed that customers behind Nollie in supermarket lines would fret. The unchipped inspired the widespread impatience that once greeted holdouts who spurned fleXes or their predecessor smart phones. In short order, the whole population would be chipped, and savings, checking, and investment accounts would be eliminated altogether—at which point it would be impossible to buy anything, sell anything, or possess any monetary wealth whatsoever in the absence of a pinhead-sized spy rammed into the back of your neck. That was certainly the plan, and Congress was unapologetic about this intention—a benevolence portrayed as akin to the nationwide polio vaccinations of the 1960s.

Naturally, the web bubbled with the feverish imaginings of paranoid kooks: chips would turn the American people into an army of hollowed-out robs that would do whatever a mad dictator in Washington commanded. True, research was under way to expand the implant's capacity by directly connecting the brain itself to the internet. This breathlessly anticipated "cognitive access" would obviate the chipsite, allowing you to check your balance by merely calling your bottom line to mind, and to make monetary transfers with a cerebral calculator pad. Perhaps in the near future, then, you would be able to read webzines, play games, and watch cat videos in your very head.

But as things stood at present: after a dip in the thirties, life expectancy had better than recovered. On average, Americans were living to ninety-two. The US sported an unprecedentedly large cohort of senior citizens. In contrast to Willing's passive generation, typified by low rates of electoral participation, nearly all the shrivs voted, making it political anathema to restrict entitlements. Together, Medicare and Social Security consumed 80 percent of the federal budget. The labor force had shrunk. Dependents—the superannuated, the disabled, the unemployed, the underage—outnumbered working stiffs like Willing by two to one. In concert with linking the dólar nuevo to the bancor, Congress had finally passed a balanced budget amendment. Mind control? No one in DC gave a damn what you were *thinking*. They just wanted your money.

So perhaps Willing's fleeing back to Citadel rather than do as he was told on Eastern Parkway would only have amounted to a brief delay. Soon enough being unchipped was sure to be classified as a civil violation if not a criminal offense, at which point even armed mavericks like Jarred would be rounded up and *regularized*. The picture was vivid: the gangly, wild-eyed iconoclast, tackled to the ground, bound and branded by the state like a steer—Willing could almost hear the mooing, wordless cry of impotent defiance. He would bet, as they say, the farm on it: Jarred would rather die than be chipped.

Nonetheless, Willing had never been certain whether his offbeat first name suggested a character who was abnormally headstrong, or abnormally compliant. Alas, his having walked into King's ER of his own accord pointed toward compliant.

Chapter 2
So Tonight We're Gonna Party Like It's 2047

I 'm really sorry," Savannah apologized on maXfleX. "I feel like such a yunk. He asked what I was up to, and it slipped out. Now he knows Bing and I are coming over, you've absolutely got to ask him, too. You don't want to get on his bad side."

"No," Willing said gravely. "I don't want to get on his bad side."

The original fleXcreen had worked as well as any personal digital device possibly could. So to keep customers replacing the product with updated models, the manufacturers had resorted to a time-tested solution: they made it worse. A maXfleX was technically capable of unfolding into a screen the size of a small cinema's. But almost no one used the function, which had necessitated further thinning the molecules. Now a device celebrated for its waddability tended to develop permanent creases. At thirty-five, Savannah was no less vain. She'd not have appreciated the harsh dark line shadowing the side of her nose, which made her look ten years older.

"It's no joke," she said. "He could ruin your life. So it's a small price to pay. You have to invite him to dinner."

"Can't we cancel?" Willing pleaded. "The whole night will be splug. He makes everyone nervous. Including me. We'll only talk treasury."

"You can't risk his realizing you called it off because I ran my big mouth, and then you couldn't stand having to invite him. Hardly a stretch. There's never been love lost. He already thinks it's weird you've asked me and Bing but not him yet."

"I have to invite Goog to come Friday," he told Nollie when he'd signed off.

"Why would he want to come?" she said. "He hates you."

"He enjoys hating me. And he likes to be in on things. It's one of the attractions of his job: the inside track."

"The attraction of his job," Nollie said, "is throwing his weight around and making everybody sweat."

Speaking of sweat: she'd just finished her jumping jacks, and was dressed in athletic gear. Another two inches shorter after all that pounding up and down, she was wearing out her third set of knee replacements. The scars on the joints were the only smooth aspect of her spindly, withered pins. Privately, Willing didn't understand the purpose of his great-aunt's exercises, commonly pursued to look more attractive. There was little enough chance of that.

"He was such an asslick as a kid," Willing said.

"He's still an asslick. I'm sure he brings his minders the limp carcasses of citizens he's destroyed, like cats bring mice to their masters. As a teenager, he always took the party line. It's a type. They side with authority and parrot received wisdom."

"Well, sucking up to the suits has sure worked out for him. One lousy training course. And he makes more money than any of us, by a yard."

"Does that matter?"

"It is noteworthy," Willing said, "that it pays so well to work for the Scab."

"You'd better practice spelling those letters out, and putting the *B* up front," Nollie advised. "You know Goog reviles that acronym."

No one called the Bureau for Social Contribution Assistance anything but *the Scab*, and the migration of *Bureau* to the end of its name was so inevitable that the yunks in DC should have seen it coming. "I'm not the one who renamed the IRS after dried blood," he grumbled.

"Or a strike breaker. But that's before your time."

"You know what perplexes me," Willing reflected, "isn't the fact that the *BSCA* is the largest arm of the federal government. What's perplexing is that it wasn't *always* the largest arm of the federal government."

"Yes . . . ," Nollie said, squinting. "I see what you mean."

I've never stood on ceremony myself," Nollie said that Friday, before his cousins arrived. "But sitting around with communal bowls on the floor—it's the way you'd feed dogs."

"No one has 'dinner parties' anymore," Fifa said, draping her long limbs over the sofa. "They're biggin' uncruel. Lord, I don't know how my mother could stand it. All those glasses. All those spoons."

Willing slopped several cans of kidney and garbanzo beans into a stainless steel mixing bowl and conceded to salt. They would scoop the muck up with flour tortillas and splash vodka into disposable plastic glasses. Grateful as children to be fed anything, Willing's generation had rebelled against their parents' bizarre obsession with food. He made sure to slurp the bean liquor messily up the sides of the bowl.

Obliviousness to presentation had become a presentation in itself.

He streamed some retrotech for ambience. Only with Nollie's assistance had he been able to identify the constituent bars of the music, all drawn from the sounds of bygone mechanisms: the *sshtick-brrrr* of a dial telephone; the *EEE-khkhkh-EEE-khkhkh* of a connecting fax; the *poo-pi-pur-pi-poo-pi-puh* . . . *BEE-di-duh-BEE-di-duh* . . . *kchkchkchkch* of a dial-up internet connection; the oceanic slosh and hum of washing machines that used many gallons of water; the crazed white noise of a boxy cathode-ray TV with no reception; the dementing recording "Please hang up and try again," over and over, of a landline telephone off the hook. The *clap-clap-clap-DING!* of a manual typewriter echoed the *ting* of an opening cash-register drawer, the *ping* of an arriving text, the *doo-di-dring!* of an arriving email, and the default marimba ring-tone of an iPhone when you didn't have enough pride to buy something more interesting. Mixed well, the tones fused into a soaring symphonic rush with a staccato under-beat. The sounds were once so blithely integrated into the audio of daily life that few could remember them when they grew extinct, and their interweaving was both catchy and mournful.

Savannah arrived first. Willing did not understand how women had the patience to mummify themselves in the narrow strips of fabric demanded by the latest fashion of "bandaging," but he had to admit that the gaps where the skin showed through were alluring. The bands across her breasts had an impressive effect on her décolletage. But her choice of red, white, and blue strips could only have been ironic. He'd scheduled this do before he realized "next Friday" was the Fourth of July. A few small towns in the heartland continued to stage fireworks displays for their aging "Old Glories"—throwbacks who burbled about purple mountain's majesty, the dawn's early light, glory, glory, hallelujah, liberty and justice for all. In hipper coastal cities like New York, the holiday had become an embarrassment.

In the wake of so many deaths from antibiotic-resistant bacteria—one of whose strains had killed Willing's mother—social protocols had grown less intimate. Reaching for a handshake was a giveaway that you were a clueless yunk who lived in the past. Pecks on the cheek were equally uncruel, and if you tried to say hello by smacking an acquaintance straight on the mouth they'd probably hit you. Willing touched his cousin's shoulder lightly, and she his. "You buy those bandages," he asked, "or do you lie around nights ripping up sheets?"

"I make too much money lying on my sheets to rip them up," Savannah said, sashaying into the living room with a bottle of Light Whitening. Nostalgia for the crude homebrew that fueled the encampments in the thirties made commercial moonshine chic.

Fifa nodded sleepily from the sofa. She was jealous of Savannah, for whom Willing continued to carry a tiny torch. But Fifa was safe. Oh, he appreciated that Savannah's work as a "stimulation consultant" was now a legitimate career. While he might have expected to discern a clichéd coarsening in her features, her manner, or her spirit, in truth he detected no such thing. Accredited, registered, regulated, and—most crucially—taxed, Savannah parlayed a respectable expertise. She carried business cards. She didn't hide behind any euphemistic "escort" nonsense. She was high end. She'd held her own against the robs—increasingly inventive, cheaper, and programmed to swallow at no extra cost. So she was doubtless very good at it. Still. Willing had a conservative side. You couldn't legislate away that little shiver.

"I think you should take up art again," he said, knowing he was wasting his breath. "It's edgier now. The stuff artists made before the Renunciation was treasury. Empty, and a scam. The new stuff—it doesn't sell for much. But you should see the show on the American slave trade in SoHo. Bigging brutal. And it's not about the nineteenth century."

"Yeah," Fifa said sloppily—she'd already had a shot or two—"ain't nobody claiming 'today's young people' don't have shit to say."

"That doesn't mean anyone's listening," Nollie said, walking in with the beans.

Wizened and no better than four ten, Nollie continued to wear the T-shirts, cut-offs, and tennis shoes she'd worn summers her whole life, and now resembled a gnomish extra from *The Hobbit*. Willing was glad she'd joined them, of course. He liked her, and he could see through the crenulations to the mischievous, scandalizing provocateur of fifty, sixty years before. But Nollie had had no children, much less had she been put in her generational place by her children's children's children. The way she saw herself had never changed. So it would never have occurred to her to leave the "young people" to their own evening.

"Spare us the cheap sympathy, Noll," Fifa said, with a nasty bite. "Long as we stoop down, turn around, pick a bale a' cotton, and you get your Social Security checks, and your specially, individually designed chemo drugs like personalized craft beers. Your face replacements, your brain replacements, your desire and drive and love and hope replacements, well—you don't really care what kind of *artwork* we make in *all our spare time*. Honest to God, I get a good laugh when I remember how my dad used to come home from work and go *running*."

Fifa worked three jobs. She did housework and cooked indifferent meals for a cantankerous Bay Ridge shut-in. She installed residential shower bars and handrails for a thriving online retailer, stayinyourownhome. com. Three nights a week, she distributed crunchy tomato slices in a Williamsburg sandwich factory owned by a magnate in Myanmar. Unskilled labor had always to undercut the robs, so the pay was appalling. Fifa did the work that foreigners didn't want.

Yet it was early in the evening for acrimony. The diffident knock on the screen door was opportune.

"Full faith and credit, man," Bing said, with a biff of solidarity on Willing's shoulder.

"Full faith and credit," Willing returned, with a light biff back. The ritual greeting went over the heads of their elders. Whenever older people tried to appropriate the exchange in order to sound cruel, they never got the tone right—the bone-dry straight face, the exquisite subtlety of the underlying sourness.

At twenty-eight, Bing was a big guy, tall as well as broad. The shortages of his pubescent years had left him with a chronic terror of missing a meal, and if he was anticipating another famine he may have over-prepared. Yet he'd taken to farm work at Citadel, and his frame packed plenty of power. Good-natured and generous, he'd never shed his oddly endearing quality of seeming a little lost.

The latest arrival dangled a baggie. "Brought heroin to snort later, if you're interested."

"How'd you ever manage that?" Savannah said.

"Walgreens had a Fourth of July sale. I was going to go for blow, but they were out. Christ, you ever hit the 'More Info' on your chipsite? The skag itself is dirt-cheap! It's not the product, it's—"

"The taxes," the rest recited in unison.

"I think you should wait till Goog gets here and save it all for him," Savannah said. "But only if you bought enough for an overdose."

Bing's face fell. "Nobody told me Goog was coming."

"You'd have begged off," Savannah said. "And with that thug around, I need my protector."

They settled on the floor, a trendy convention that may have hailed from so few young people being able to buy furniture. The custom was fortuitous. From childhood, Willing had been happiest on the floor.

"Have you thought about renting out the basement again?" Savannah asked.

"I always hated knowing when I walked across the living room I was an elephant over Kurt's head," Willing said. "And when you don't get to keep the rent, really . . . What's the point?"

"What about . . . under the table?" Goog hadn't arrived yet, and still she whispered. "Do it in bancors."

"Risky. Get caught, and . . . I don't want to think about it. Besides, who'd live in that dank, dark space if they had access to international currency?" Willing's murmur was instinctive. However seemingly inane, Nollie's question from six years ago circled back: *Can that thing hear?*

"You'd be surprised," Savannah said. "There's a whole economy out there you don't know about. How else would I pull off this fashion statement without ripping up my sheets? Anyway, just an idea. I might be able to help. But don't bring it up on maXfleX, obviously."

The discussion made everyone anxious. Willing changed the subject. "Nollie's started writing again. I caught her."

Nollie glared. "It's not more of my famous egotism. I've nothing else to do."

"I was glad," Willing said. "It may be free, but there's some brutal writing online now. Like the art. People have better stories. 'Real stories.' The kind you said you only like when they happen to someone else."

"Anyone who remembers what one says that verbatim is a menace," Nollie said.

"I read *Better Late Than*," Willing said.

His great-aunt looked discomfited, and pleased. "A pirated copy."

"Of course. We burned the hardbacks. Some of it was good."

"I'm overwhelmed," Nollie said.

He didn't realize she'd be so touchy. "The story didn't take place immense long ago. But it felt like ancient history. It was hard to identify with the characters. They live in an economic vacuum."

"You mean they're rich?"

"You don't even know if they're rich," he said. "They make decisions because they're in love, or they're angry, or they want adventure. You never know how they afford their houses. They never decide not to do something because it costs too much. The whole book—you never find out how much these characters pay in taxes."

"Great," Nollie said. "I'll make my next novel about *taxes*."

"Good," Willing said, turning a blind eye to her sarcasm. He had accomplished something this evening. She would get it later, when she recovered from feeling injured.

"Hey, how's it going at Elysian?" Bing asked.

"Okay. After all"—Willing nodded at Nollie—"I've done geriatric care most of my life."

"None of your new charges is doing three thousand jumping jacks a day," Nollie snapped. "You've hardly been wiping my butt, kid."

So predictable. He loved getting a rise out of her. "Yes, Nollie's what the orderlies call a *walking shriv*. She can make it to the bathroom, which is all staff at Elysian cares about. Then there are the *blithers*, who are demented. And the *morts*—bed-ridden, comatose, vegetative."

"Not a very compassionate lingo," Savannah said.

"No," Willing said. "It's not."

"So is it mostly toilet duty, changing sheets?" Savannah was groping. The jobs they all did were dismal and repetitive. It was challenging to express interest in other people's work when they weren't interested in it themselves.

"Yes. And cleaning crevices the robs have missed. But the most important thing I do is listen. Especially to the walking shrivs. They seem hungry to talk to someone who isn't a hundred years old. Just because you're ancient yourself doesn't mean you like being around a bunch of relics any more than we do."

"God, I know what you mean," Fifa said. "On the bus this week, the biddy next to me started yakking. Grabbed my arm, really sank her claws in. It was like sci-fi, and she was sucking out my life force through her fingernails. I got off, I felt weak."

"And they stare at you," Savannah said.

"Because you're beautiful," Nollie said, with a rare wistfulness. "Because you're as beautiful as we used to be, and we didn't know we were beautiful at the time."

"I don't feel beautiful," Willing said.

"You're a devastatingly handsome man," Nollie said. "You should."

Willing's cheeks burned. She was his great-aunt, she was ninety years old, and she was flirting with him. "I didn't realize before this job how many Chinese shrivs have been shipped here. At least a third of the residents are from Asia. It's cheaper to get Americans to take care of them than to pay the higher cost of labor over there."

"They have an enormous cohort that's over eighty," Nollie said. "Result of the one-child policy. Their age structure looks like a mushroom."

"They don't speak English," Willing said. "But I listen to them anyway. American residents get cross, and demanding—you know, the way younger Asians are now. But the Chinese at Elysian were raised in another time. They're quiet. They curl up. The problem is, they *don't* ask for anything. You have to check, because they'll sit in their own waste for hours. Last week, one of them died from dehydration. He couldn't lift a glass by himself, but he wouldn't ask for a drink of water."

"Isn't nursing home work getting chancy?" Bing asked. "All those shootings."

"Nothing's happened at Elysian yet," Willing said. "So their security is lax. No X-rays or searches. But you're right. It's a fad. And it's spreading. How many did that last lunatic in Atlanta take out?"

"Twenty-two residents," Bing said.

"Twenty-four, really," Savannah said. "That's the one where a ninety-something veteran tackled the killer into the hydrotherapy pool, and they both drowned."

"The shooter did those useless old coots a favor," Fifa said, "and everyone else."

"Your girlfriend," Nollie said, "is a *misagenist.*"

"Don't worry, I take precautions," Willing said. "I don't advertise it, but I carry the revolver from Prospect Park to work." Technically, his trusty protection was a Smith & Wesson .44 called an X-K47 Black Shadow. For Willing, it was simply the Shadow. True to its nickname, the classic pistol with an amber grip went everywhere he went. His mother would be horrified. A fact that he rather enjoyed.

"Not rusted out yet?" Bing asked.

"Great Grand Man taught me how to maintain it—after which he showed me how to use it." Regarding this aspect of their shared past, Willing preferred to be matter-of-fact. GGM had left this world with a selfless act, and wouldn't want them to avoid its mention. "The real trouble is that I could work at Elysian indefinitely. Same as you guys. We're all at a standstill. There's no trajectory. None of us will ever be flush enough to have kids. We could be frozen, in the same moment. We could be dead."

"Let's have none of this 'dead' business! The United States of America needs its able-bodied to look alive! You'll report to work every morning if we have to prop up your corpse with a stick!"

With dread, Willing rose to unlatch the door. Most of their contemporaries' speech was trailing, wispy. Goog's voice was booming.

"How long have you been eavesdropping?" Savannah asked.

"Long enough to know this is one splug bash. You letting the doomster here prophesy another fiscal Armageddon? When, to our shaman's dismay, everything's turning over tickety-boo."

Goog spurned the floor for the broken-down recliner, the better to hold court. He banged down a bottle
of real cognac. The luxury perk would only partially
compensate for his demolition of their evening. Willing
had wanted to talk further about his sensation of running in place. He'd have liked to canvass his cousins
about whether they thought anything might credibly
happen to them that wasn't terrible. Now there wasn't
much point. Everyone would be careful.

"I take exception, Wilbur, to your claim that 'none of
us' will have kids," Goog said. "I personally plan to sow
the Stackhouse *seed*. Just haven't decided between a lab
job—blue eyes, high IQ—or the old-fashioned route. No
lack of candidates in that department!" Bearded, barrel-
chested, and shorter than he struck people at first meeting, Goog was *almost* good-looking. He only got over
the hump when women learned what he did for a living.

"Poor little tyke," Savannah whispered in Willing's
ear. "I've never felt so sorry for someone who doesn't
exist yet."

"This is new," Bing said respectfully. "And very exciting. You're planning a family soon?" He might have
been talking to his schoolteacher, not his own brother.

"Sooner the better," Goog said. "Somebody's gotta
do it. You're hardly up and at 'em with the ladies. And
our sister's a hole."

"You know I don't like that word," Savannah said.

"I don't like being called a *scabbie*, either," Goog said. "I've manned up about it. You can't honestly expect me to call you a *stimulation consultant* with a straight face."

"I have a degree," she insisted quietly.

"A community college degree in a subject that comes naturally to any slit who can lie on her back. Listen, I know it's asking a lot, but could I have a *real glass?*" The rest were passing the cognac. Bing lunged to the kitchen. "Like I was saying. Seems I'll have to carry the procreative can. And I'll spring for more than one, too. Because having kids is patriotic."

"Seriously," Nollie said. "You'll have children to improve the country's age structure."

"Why's that so far-fetched?" Goog said. "This generation's been biggin' lazy in the reproduction department. The birthrate plummeted in the thirties, fine, but it should have recovered by now. Building into a real problem down the line."

"Yeah, we're lazy," Fifa said. "After fifteen hours of slog on splug jobs, netting the bus fare home for our trouble, we should be fucking all night, just to breed the next generation of little taxpayers." She was slooped. But even sober, Fifa's reaction to her own fearfulness was defiance. Willing would need to watch her.

"So what's up with your parents?" Willing interceded.

"Dad's two years from sixty-eight," Goog said. "Then he'll be sitting pretty."

People used to dread being put out to pasture. Desperate to qualify for entitlements, these days everyone couldn't wait to be old.

"Also," Goog added, "some of those investments he made during the Renunciation, and held on to over my mom's dead body? They've biggin' appreciated."

"That's really great for the country, then," Willing said.

"Why's it not great for my *dad*?" Goog asked sharply.

"Eighty-five percent capital gains." Willing beamed.

"Yeah, well. Everybody gotta do their *fair share*, right?"

"Absolutely," Willing agreed. "Their *fair share*."

Goog scrutinized his cousin for signs of irony. Willing's expression was impenetrably pleasant.

Goog leaned back in the recliner again. "I think Dad's enjoying being back in the department at Georgetown. Even if it's an honorary position, and he only lectures one night a week. Trouble is, his area of expertise— debt, inflation, and monetary policy—has been kind of wiped out. Fucking NIMF controls all that now, why they deep-sixed the Federal Reserve. Fucking country doesn't have a monetary policy anymore—"

"Or debt," Willing added. "Or inflation."

"Point is, it's not his fault—"

"Not his fault having been wrong." Willing should really keep his mouth shut.

"Not his fault having been overtaken by events," Goog said.

"If the US had participated in the bancor from the beginning, instead of negotiating from a position of desperation in '34, we might have avoided the depression."

"*Depression* is just a word."

"I bet for the people who starved to death it didn't feel like just a word."

"So Dad likes being back to teaching again?" Savannah said, peacekeeping.

"Yeah," Goog said, calming down. "I guess you could call the appointment a sinecure. Still, it means something to the guy. This is off the record, but I like to think I had something to do with it. I notified the university that because of certain *irregularities* in all that foreign financing—joint is all backed by Beijing, why the student body is lousy with platefaces—their tax-exempt status was in peril. Administration fell all over themselves to be of service."

"You never told me that," Savannah said.

"I'm telling you that now. But you repeat it, you'll be audited up the asshole." Goog's delivery was jocular. No one else seemed to find the advisory funny.

"And your mother?" Willing had maXfleXted Avery last week. He was plenty up to date on her life. Savannah was right: stick to safe subjects.

Goog rolled his eyes. "Truth is, we don't talk much."

"She didn't want you to join the Scab," Savannah said.

"No, she didn't want me to join the *BSCA*. Which makes her a biggin' yunk. Best idea I ever had. So much for advice at your mother's knee. Anyway, you know she got that do-gooding bug. Only got worse after your mother died, Wilbur. Like she had to carry on the same splug tradition. So she's started some 'youth food bank' in the District. Biggin' wrongheaded."

"Why?" Savannah asked.

"Demotivates," Goog said officiously. "Why does she think we eliminated welfare except for the disabled? Half of them are shirkers, too. Sprained their pinkies."

"The medical exams for disability are pretty grueling," Nollie said.

Goog waved her off and took a slug from his glass. "I don't know what we're going to do about the strikers.

Numbers go up every year. Filthy slumbers, too. Makes my blood boil. I'm not saying it should be against the law—"

"You're just saying it should be against the law," Savannah said.

"Maybe the Scab should start importing black people from Africa in big long boats," Fifa said. "There's enough of them—two and a half billion! No one in Lagos would miss them."

"You got one serious attitude problem, honey," Goog said.

"A bad attitude should be against the law, too, I guess," Fifa said.

"I'm sick of this." Goog leaned down into Fifa's face. "America is not a police state. This is a free country, and you can say whatever you fucking well want. I've had it up to the gills with people like you, always mouthing off about 'oppression' and 'subjugation' and 'tyranny.' So you're expected to do your part, to help keep this economy's show on the road, and what's wrong with that? Nothing wrong with people over sixty-eight getting medical care, either, or drawing a modest stipend from a retirement system they've paid into their whole lives—"

"They didn't pay enough in," Fifa said, "to cover sitting around and falling apart for longer than they *worked*—"

"So just because you have to contribute to the same system," Goog plowed on, "doesn't mean you live under the heel of goose-stepping Nazis, got it?"

"Could have fooled me," Fifa said smoothly. "Didn't you threaten Savannah with 'auditing her up the ass-hole'? So go ahead. Audit my butt off. You won't find anything kicking around my chip but digital dust bunnies."

"I could have you re-chipped. On the premise that yours has been hacked—"

"I thought it was unhackable."

"It can be hacked in the old sense of the word—hacked out. It's not enjoyable."

"Ooh, ooh, go ahead," Fifa said, offering Goog the serrated knife for sawing their stale French bread.

"You're slooped," Goog said disdainfully.

"Gloriously," Fifa said, taking another slug of Goog's cognac straight from the bottle—hygienically, dead uncruel. "Wanna hear some real freedom of speech? I think strikers are heroes. If I had any guts, I'd stop fetching some Bay Ridge bitch her stinky slippers, layering other stiffs' miserable sandwiches, and anchoring guardrails for the walking dead. I'd put my feet up, too. Anything but drudge like a dray horse for scabbies like you."

"The strikers are having the last laugh on you, sister," Goog said. "They're not sacrificing for their principles. They're lounging around their parents' house and sponging off their grannies' Social Security. And the more strikers and slumbers? The higher your taxes go. You're being had."

"So *do* you think refusing to work for only 23 percent of your wages should be against the law?" Savannah said.

"Yeah, maybe," Goog conceded gruffly. "Maybe I do."

"I'm not sure slumbers are in the same category," Willing said. "They've saved up—though I don't know how. What little slumbers cost, they pay for up front."

Just as he didn't understand why it took so long for the IRS to rise from a beleaguered, underfunded agency to the rechristened behemoth it was today, Willing was also perplexed by why slumbering hadn't taken off decades earlier. When recreational drugs were legalized, regulated, and taxed, they became drear overnight. Only then did people get wise to the fact that the ultimate narcotic had been eternally available to everyone, for free: sleep. A pharmaceutical nudge into an indefinite coma was cheap, and a light steady dose allowed for repeated dream cycles. Inert bodies expend negligible energy, so the drips for nutrition and hydration had seldom to be replenished (slumbers were hooked to enormous drums of the stuff). The regular turning to prevent pressure sores provided welcome employment for the low skilled. Slumbers didn't require apartments—much less maXfleXes or new clothes. They needed only a change of pajamas and a mattress. An outmoded designation revived, "rest homes" denoted warehouses of the somnambulant, who were only roused and kicked out once their prepayments were extinguished. Previous generations had scrounged to buy property. Many of Willing's peers were similarly obsessed with scraping together a nest egg, but with an eye to dozing away as many years of their lives as the savings could buy.

"Slumbers cost in productivity," Goog said.

"I've thought about it, if I could raise the funds," Willing said. "Maybe a year? Every time my alarm rings at five-thirty, it seems like bliss."

"Willing, you wouldn't!" Nollie said in horror.

"I'd rather watch my own dreams," Savannah grumbled to Fifa, "than another fucking Korean TV series. Separated twins set up housekeeping after unification, and the Northern twin mistakes a hairdryer for a bazooka . . . Mom and Dad had no idea how lucky they were to watch sit-coms set in Minneapolis."

"Mom says the physio after slumbering is pretty grim," Bing said. "Though that new sideline of hers, Vertical Reconditioning, is doing pretty well. Their muscles are jelly. They get rolled out of rest homes on gurneys, like you move bodies from a morgue. Actually being awake can be scary, too. There's been a lot of suicides. I'd rather emigrate."

"Like where?" Savannah asked in alarm.

"The Javanese in management at IBM seem civilized," Bing said. "Maybe I'd head there."

The Indonesian Business Machines plant in New Jersey where the youngest Stackhouse worked as a manufacturing overseer was producing robs that could be tooled as manufacturing overseers. Willing could see why Bing might be making other plans.

"How are you going to get into Java?" Savannah said. "They don't give visas to much of anybody, and they really don't give visas to Americans."

"There are ways . . ." Bing shot an anxious glance at his brother.

"Getting into anywhere in Asia illegally is a bastard." In her determination to dissuade her beloved younger brother from flying the coop, Savannah was oblivious to Bing's nervousness about Goog. "There's none of that 'human rights' and 'due process' and 'claiming asylum' treasury. They don't give you weekly stipends or put you up in public housing with a flabby little advisory that you're not *supposed* to work. There aren't any polite trials with a free lawyer and then when you're turned down you can appeal, and appeal, and appeal. There's no forgetting all about you even though you're not supposed to be there, because they're too disorganized, and politically ambivalent about their right to throw you out of the country in the first place, and frankly too broke to pay for your deportation plane fare. No, no. They keep track all right, and they never throw you idiotically on your own reconnaissance: oh, it would be *nice* if you showed up for this court date eighteen months from now. They chuck you summarily in detention, with rats and spoiled food, and when they collect enough of a crowd they don't even send you back to your own country. They dump you anywhere: Siberia, France, Nigeria. Wherever's convenient for them. Especially in China, they're bigging T-bills. You might never get back home."

"Oh, it can't be that hard," Fifa said. "China and India are both awash in illegal immigrants. Lots from Africa, too, and they're kinda recognizable."

"But I've got to do something," Bing said mournfully. "Even if they keep me on at IBM, which I doubt, it's like Willing said about Elysian. I'll never advance. All the senior positions are filled by Southeast Asians. And it's not like I don't want to do my *fair share*." As he shot another glance at his brother, his expression curdled like a puppy's after peeing on the rug. "It's not that I mind, at all, you know, *keeping the economy on the road* . . . I'm glad to help the shrivs—I mean, sorry, Nollie, the *long-lived.* It's medical care they biggin' deserve, right? Still. I don't get paid much to begin with. When the chip is finished chewing it up, there's nothing left." He wouldn't look at Goog at all now. "At least if I emigrated . . ."

"Hate to burst your bubble, bud," Goog said. "But one aspect of the US tax code hasn't changed since the Civil War. Americans are taxed on their worldwide income, and that includes expats. You get some credit for foreign taxes. But if Jakarta doesn't suck your chip dry, we take up the slack. So it's fortunate you don't *mind* paying your dues, my brother. BSCA satellites can extract what's owed if you're sprinting across the Mongolian tundra. Not that it would *ever occur to you* to cheat your very own United States government, but now that chipping has taken off internationally? Your ability to get your hands on any readies whatsoever without our knowing about it to two digits after the decimal, well. It'll be *slight.*"

"Wow," Fifa said, flat on her back. "What a great party."

"What about Mexico?" Willing suggested. "You might move up the ladder there. The manufacturing sector is huge. It's got a bigger GDP than the US—"

"That's not saying much," Nollie quipped.

"But Esteban is doing great," Willing said. "He runs his own wilderness expedition company now—"

"I don't know how," Nollie said. "Mexico doesn't have any wilderness."

"Well, nowhere does, Noll," Fifa said irritably to the ceiling. "Maybe he takes groups to a parking lot where there are still some empty spaces."

When his much-missed de facto father struck out for the southern border in 2039, Willing had been moved by the depth of the Lat's reluctance to leave what he regarded profoundly as his country. Esteban was an authentic American patriot. By contrast, in the liberal northeastern tradition, the Mandibles had routinely said mean things about America, as if hating it here made them better. True, Esteban scorned aging honks who were vain about their "tolerance" but who didn't really want him here. Who missed the old days, when they controlled everything. But he never insulted the country itself—the idea of the country, and the way it was supposed to work, even when it wasn't working that way (more or less always). Jayne and Carter, GGM, Nollie, and his mother had sometimes seemed to take a savage pleasure in the downfall of the United States. For Esteban, the decline of what he genuinely believed was the greatest nation on earth was solely a sorrow.

Loads of Lats like Esteban had filtered back to the lands of their forefathers. The loss was greater than one of numbers. They'd been American with the zealotry of converts. Emigration being at an all-time high, the US population was contracting for the first time in its history. The remaining public felt trapped, stranded, left behind. These were often the same people who had vituperated about foreigners piling across their borders. Now that outsiders didn't risk their lives to reach America anymore, the native-born felt abandoned. They missed their own resentment. They felt unloved. Little satisfaction was to be found in clinging to something, holding it close, defending it, when no one else wanted it anyway. Maybe Willing could see how white Americans his mother's age and older had sometimes felt invaded, or alienated, or replaced—though they'd have felt so much less threatened if they'd only learned Spanish. But clearly there was one situation direr than living in the country where the rest of the world wanted to live also: living in a country that everyone wanted to leave.

Esteban had been loyal in a personal sense as well. He stuck by their family at Citadel—though grubbing the land in Gloversville duplicated the mindless manual labor that his father had done, and his grandfather, which he thought he had escaped. But then, after all they'd been through together, he lost Florence to a cut finger. His son in all but name had come of age. You could hardly call it desertion.

Savannah roused Willing from his reverie. "Why would Mexico be any easier to get into?"

"Esteban got across the border," Willing said. "He had to hire coyotes, but that was pretty simple. The same guys who ferried Lats to El Norte had started doing the same job in the opposite direction."

"Esteban slipped across before they finished building the fence," Savannah said. "Which is electrified, and computerized, and 100 percent surveilled, from the Pacific to the Gulf. Esteban has a pedigree, too. He'd have a chance at naturalizing. They don't naturalize any 'non-Lat whites' down there. We're a pest species. Even if Bing were miraculously to make it across the Rio Grande, the discrimination is killing. I know what I'm talking about. My clients are a better source of information than the web. As *Ameri-trash*, Bing would be treated with bigging contempt. Worse, remember that old slag, *mexdreck*? Try *yankdreck*. That's what they call us. It's comical, considering the likes of Fifa here is working three jobs, but they think we're lazy. And they definitely think we're stupid."

"To have that much power and let it go?" Nollie said. "That is pretty stupid."

"It always goes," Willing said. "Whether or not you let it."

"Having that much money and letting it go, then," Nollie revised. "Having that much money and still spending more than you've got. I call that stupid."

"That's the most fatuous version of the last twenty years I've ever heard," Goog said.

"Can we *not*?" Savannah said. Teasing out what had happened, why it happened, to whom it had especially happened, and what it meant was a running conversational obsession everywhere you went. Willing could see how she might be tired of it.

"I'm still shredded we didn't do anything when China annexed Japan," Bing said sadly. "I always liked Japanese people for some reason. With their special ways of doing things. Everything just so. I felt sorry for them."

"When they sank that Chinese destroyer, the Japanese did pick the fight," Goog said, paraphrasing what the president had told the American people at the time. "I think they wanted to be invaded. They were going down in flames anyway. It was one big hari-kari kamikaze go-ahead-and-shoot-me-already."

"It's true, the whole Japanese race has practically evaporated," Savannah said. "So I found the elbow-room argument pretty convincing. With that deluge from Africa and all those refugees from the Water Wars, China's bursting."

"Still, you can't help picturing how badly that fleet would have got it in the neck if the Chinese had gone for an American ally when we were kids," Goog reminisced fondly. "I'm biggin' sorry to have missed that ballyhoo. We'd have buried Beijing so deep that the watchtowers of the Forbidden City came poking out the other side in Omaha."

"Treasury," Savannah differed. "If we'd intervened, we'd have made a mess of it, as usual. Same goes for Taiwan. Thank fuck we finally couldn't afford it."

"After so many fiascoes—Vietnam, Iraq, New Zealand—I'd expect to agree with you," Nollie said. "But our sitting idly by, and making excuses for sitting idly by . . . I thought it was a disgrace."

Nollie's sense of shame was widely shared by her whole generation, and most of Florence's, too. But Willing did not have strong feelings on this point. Around the time that the American money in his pocket disintegrated to so much Kleenex, he deftly decoupled something. The abstraction into which he'd been drafted by dint of having arbitrarily been born here no longer seemed to have anything to do with him. He was American as an adjective. He was no longer an American as a noun. He saw no necessity in taking the US demurral from declaring war on China personally. If it meant that he himself hadn't been forced to become a paratrooper billowing onto the rooftops of skyscrapers in Chengdu, this was a good thing. Otherwise, if he were to feel powerless, the source of the sensation would be closer to home: he was obliged to have a cousin to dinner whom he did not like. That was impotence. But he did not feel implicated by Taiwan or Japan. His country did not help because it could not help. It did not have the money. That was relaxing. This must have been what it had felt like to live in most countries, when the United States was sending bombers and ships and troops and airlifts whenever something went wrong. If there was genocide in Madagascar, they didn't beat themselves up for not doing anything about it in Argentina. That was better life. When Willing was young, it was common to despair that a person had "no boundaries." Friends who had "no boundaries" were embarrassing. They had no sense of what to keep to themselves. So maybe one merit of being in a country at all was its boundaries. They drew a line around what was your business. They helped to maintain the existence of such a thing as your business.

"Listen, have you guys seen that glass house that's gone up on the site of Jayne and Carter's in Carroll Gardens?" Savannah brought up. "It's some Vietnamese palace. Garish beyond belief."

"Well, that's all of Brooklyn for you," Goog said. "Half the brownstones have been razed. Platefaces don't have a preservational bone in their bodies."

"Goog, your pejorative is passé," Savannah chided. "You do realize that women like me are going under the knife to get narrower eyes and flatter noses?"

"I talked to Carter and Jayne last week," Nollie said. "Jayne is still fomenting over not getting the insurance payout. But that couple from Hanoi paid a fortune for the land—more than enough to make up for the fact that, between inheritance taxes and back maintenance fees, my mother's co-op wasn't worth reclaiming. They could still buy what they wanted—or thought they wanted. Maybe that's the problem."

"They're pretty old to be holding down a ranch in Montana by themselves," Bing said. "At least I helped them choose a caretaker rob. Except with the top-of-the-line kind they got, the conversation is splug. The cheaper ones keep picking up on the wrong key words. They're hilarious, and a lot more fun."

"Problem with robs?" Fifa said. "Hurl a skillet at one, and you've only wrecked your own pricey appliance. My Bay Ridge Bitch could afford a primo caretaker rob five times over. But then she wouldn't be able to drive it crazy, or ruin its day."

"I guess I can see how, after living cheek by jowl at Citadel, they craved solitude," Nollie said. "But Jayne was practically a normal person by the time they left the farm. Now their whole acreage is one big Quiet Room. She's back to being a nut. And Carter's regressed, too. Jesus, I thought we hashed it out at Citadel. But now he's worked himself into a lather again about the 'lost years' with Luella that give him flashbacks. I swear, couples cooped up one-on-one are deadly. There's not enough to talk about. So you go back and mine horrid, selfish Enola over and over, if only to keep from going for each other instead. You can't eat *all* day, so you feast on umbrage between meals. Honestly, our conversation was barely cordial. And after I didn't put up a stink, at all, about those two helping themselves to the whole Bountiful House silver service. I didn't ask for one butter knife."

"If you'd stopped by Carroll Gardens more often back then," Willing said, "you'd realize why a little silverware can't begin to compensate."

"I couldn't stand it," Nollie admitted.

"No one could stand it," Willing said.

If Jayne really was backsliding to neurosis and Carter was grudge-farming, that made them quite the exceptions. Across the nation, Americans' mental and physical health had vastly improved. Hardly anyone was fat. Allergies were rare, and these days if people did mention they avoided gluten, a piece of bread would probably kill them. Eating disorders like anorexia and bulimia had disappeared. Should a friend say he was depressed, something sad had happened. After a cascade of terrors on a life-and-death scale, nobody had the energy to be afraid of spiders, or confined spaces, or leaving the house. In the thirties, the wholesale bankruptcies of looted pharmacies, as well as a broad inability to cadge the readies for street drugs, had sent addicts into a countrywide cold turkey. Gyms shut, and personal trainers went the way of the incandescent light bulb. But repairing their own properties, tilling gardens, walking to save on fuel, and beating intruders with baseball bats had rendered Americans impressively fit. Sex-reassignment surgery roundly unaffordable, diagnoses of gender dysphoria were pointless. If a woman leaned toward the masculine, she adopted lunging, angular movements and crossed her ankle on her knee; everyone got the message, and the gesturing was more elegant. As dreaming beat drugs, sexual fantasy had always been a cleaner, sweeter, not to mention cheaper route to gratifying a whole host of wayward inclinations, in contrast to the crude, painfully imperfect experience of acting the fantasies out. No one had the money, time, or patience for pathology of any sort. It wasn't that Americans had turned on oddity; they simply didn't feel driven to fix it anymore.

"Hey, Willing," Bing said. "You're always reminiscing about how brutal it was at Citadel. If Elysian is splug, why not go back? You took to that farm treasury more than most of us did."

"I'd consider it," Willing said. "But I haven't been able to contact Jarred for months. I finally fleXted Don Hodgekiss at the property next-door. He says Jarred cleared off. Left Citadel to the feds. Jarred's gone dark."

"Where do you figure he went?" Bing said.

Nollie rolled her eyes. Savannah intently swabbed a last tortilla around the bean bowl.

"How should I know?" Willing didn't meet anyone's gaze. He was careful both to not look at Goog, and to not seem to be not-looking at Goog.

"It's obvious, isn't it?" Goog said. "You don't all have to play innocent. Who's the real nut in this family? Who's naturally seditious? Who's the asshole renegade, with no respect for authority? Who was opportunistically price-gouging all through the thirties? Who completely ignored the weapons amnesty in '38?"

"He didn't completely ignore it," Bing said. "When they canceled the Second Amendment—"

"No one *canceled* the Second Amendment, you yunk," Goog said. "It was *clarified*. Modern constitutional scholars now believe it was never meant to apply to individuals in the first place. A 'well-regulated militia' means the police and the armed forces. Not some lunatic with an AK in a shopping mall."

"Jarred did turn in a pistol or two for appearances' sake," Bing said. "And everyone ignored the amnesty. All those from-my-cold-dead-hands stand-offs—"

"Also, who regarded his dopey farm as a 'citadel'—a fortress and a territory apart?" Goog carried on. "Who has no sense of loyalty to this country, and who has doubtless suffered the consequences?"

"We can't be sure of where he went," Savannah mumbled. "Besides, that rumor about the self-destruct in the chip. I've never been sure it's true."

"Oh, it's true," Goog said ominously. "Believe you me."

Willing almost blurted that, as far as he knew, Jarred wasn't chipped. Which would have precluded the back of his head exploding like a shot-gunned pumpkin the moment a Scab satellite detected that he'd set foot where he wasn't supposed to. Willing managed to keep his mouth shut. The information might have denied his cousin a malevolent satisfaction, and it was not in their interest to deny Goog Stackhouse satisfaction of any sort.

"I heard they live like, you know, animals there," Bing said. "No internet. So it's like the Stonage, forever. People live in mud huts, or teepees or something. No electricity, no TV, not even any radio, 'cause the US jams it. There's lots of webzines say they have nothing to eat, and the whole place is into cannibalism."

"It has to be a shit hole," Goog said. "It's completely cut off from world trade. Violating US sanctions lands you in prison for so long that even off-chip dirtbags won't risk smuggling. The only country that's recognized the USN is *Eritrea.* Even if you could get past the guards and mines at the border, which you *can't*—defection to those subversive wackos is classified as treason. Which is the only crime left on federal statute books that's still a capital offense. So I hope none of you ever get as restive as Jarred seems to. A whole BSCA unit with maximum-security clearance has been deputized with the authority to press the button."

Willing would obviously feign disinterest around Goog. Yet like most people, he was intrigued by the United States of Nevada, incorporating several Indian nations as well as the original polity, colloquially the Free State (causing much resentment in Maryland, which had laid claim to the moniker since 1864). How could you not be fascinated by such a black box, a trapezium that nothing and no one got out of and nothing and no

one, at least officially, got in? Ever since the state's secession in 2042, any information about the breakaway
republic had been shut down as soon as it went up. The
NSA must have installed internet filters, since to do a
search on the fledgling confederacy you had to use coy,
constantly reconfigured euphemisms like "high-stakes
gamble," which would also cease to work within days.
Willing was glad there had been no second Civil War.
He was glad that the same public enervation, sovereign
destitution, and sour-grapes excuse-making that had
kept the US from coming to the rescue of Japan had
inclined Congress to write off the ungrateful western
dustbowl with a sneering good riddance. (America now
conducted livelier commerce with Cuba than with a
no-go hole in its own interior. In modern maps of the
US, Nevada was spitefully blank.) True, national borders could mercifully exclude as simply immaterial all
that lay outside them. Yet the United States of Nevada
still seemed to have to do with him. Assuming his uncle
had not been shot on the American side while trying to
penetrate its notoriously militarized perimeter, he had
no doubt that this was where Jarred had fled. The moments the USN crossed his mind were the only instants
in his day when Willing felt awake.

It was probably true that the borders were un-
crossable. It was probably true that your chip was

programmed to blow your head off in the unlikely event that you succeeded in crossing anyway. Nevertheless, Nevada was the sole exception to Goog's assertion that there was no getting away from the Scab. It was the one place on earth where millions of Americans weren't paying federal taxes. Accordingly, mere mention of the traitorous malcontents drove Willing's most influential dinner guest into a rage. It would be prudent to change the subject.

"So how's it going at the Bureau, then?" Willing asked Goog brightly.

"What's this," Goog said suspiciously. "*Interest in my work?*"

"Everyone in America is interested in your work." Willing had perfected this poker face in adolescence. His ridicule and sincere esteem were indistinguishable.

"Since you asked," Goog said, "we're bringing in some new reporting requirements that are bound to affect you, Nollie. After all, it doesn't seem fair that most of the country sends in so much data on income and expenditures, while outliers can operate under a cloak of secrecy and obfuscation, does it?"

"Yes, my keeping a purchase of incontinence panty shields to myself seems a rank injustice," Nollie said.

"Starting in January next year"—Goog's voice rang with relish—"the unchipped will be legally obliged to file a same-day report on every purchase and deposit. We've already designed the online forms, and they're quite extensive: address of vendor, federal tax ID number, time and date, serial or product number, purpose of purchase—"

"You mean the federal government needs to know *why* I bought incontinence panty shields," Nollie said.

"Best of all, the forms don't accept cut-and-paste." Goog simply could not stop smiling. "You may find that remaining outside the system will cost you rather a lot of toil and trouble."

"That's harassment," Nollie said.

"Looked at one way," Goog said blithely, "all of government is a form of harassment. But you wouldn't want to look at it that way, would you?"

Savannah puzzled, "Why not just make the shrivs get chipped like everyone else?"

"Coercion is crude, and invites tantrums," Goog pronounced. "This way, the *long-lived* are persuaded to embrace chipping as a welcome salvation from the paperwork equivalent of Abu Ghraib. Think about it: if I wallop you with a cudgel, you'll get mad, and you might even hit me back. If I prick you over and over with a straight pin, you'll thank me when I stop."

"You're diabolical," Nollie said.

Goog accepted the compliment with a gracious nod. "Oh, and we've also started digging into old files, now that Congress rescinded that random seven-year limit on our *curiosity*. Lotta irregularity in the thirties. Like those Tax Boycott crybabies, who refused to file returns in some boo-hoo over having been bankrupted by 'their own government.' With compounded interest and fees, those chiselers will lose everything. It's complicated, converting dollars to nuevos, but we've worked out a formula."

"Toward the end, the value of the dollar was changing every day," Willing said. "Every hour, even. So your formula must be terribly sophisticated."

"It works out roughly to our advantage, if that's what you mean," Goog conceded.

"Yes," said Willing. "That is what I meant." He took care to add, "More patriotic that way. Better for everyone. For the country as a whole."

Goog studied his cousin again, searching for mockery. But he must have been accustomed to civilian pandering. Willing's was pro forma.

"So it turns out other folks were under the yunk impression that they could deduct losses from voided Treasury bonds," Goog continued. "Or they had the impudence to subtract the difference between what they were compensated for gold and its grotesque over-valuation on the open market. Like Dad always said, it's a moronic investment, so they deserved to take a hit just for being nitwits, if you ask me."

"I don't know how foolish an investment it's turned out to be," Willing said, keeping his tone companionable. "Anyone who kept hold of all that glitters in '29 would turn a handsome profit today—even after 85 percent capital gains."

"They'd earn nothing but a prison sentence," Goog said sharply. "Any gold in this country remains the property of the US government. You wouldn't happen to know anyone who's still hoarding?" *Hoarding* remained a synonym beloved of bureaucrats for retaining your own assets.

Willing bore up with a bashful smile. "I was being theoretical."

In the face of the kind of grueling interrogation once reserved for terrorists and now exclusively practiced on alleged tax cheats, the suspect's most commonplace mistake was to assume a range of high-intensity emotions: indignation; flopping, tearful contrition; wrath. Yet the most effective defense against Goog had always been bland geniality. An unruffled happyface drove the scabbie insane, but he couldn't object to it.

"Though if gold is such a yunk investment," Willing added politely, "why does the government want it?"

"The US didn't set up the terms of the bancor," Goog said with contempt. "Speaking of which—I got an advance tipoff on a revolution in the works that's gonna make our lives at the Bureau biggin' easier. The administration's been lobbying for years, and the decision's finally gone our way. So you heard it here first: the NIMF is going to eliminate the cash bancor."

Nollie crossed her legs on the sofa with a demure femininity out of character. Savannah blanched, barely able to get out, "Why?"

"Use your head," Goog said. "The entire black market is conducted in bancors. But the cashless economy is catching on the world over. Pretty soon you won't be able to stash liquidity in a shoebox anywhere. Being off-chip will be the same thing as being flat broke. The complete elimination of cash internationally will dispatch corruption, tax evasion, racketeering, and misconduct of virtually every sort."

"I wonder . . . ," Willing mused, as if having only just thought of this, though he and Jarred had discussed the matter at length. "What do you make of the proposition that the definition of a truly free society is a place where you can still get away with something?"

"I'd say that's a treacherous definition of freedom, Wilbur. The law is the law. You obey it, to the letter.

Freedom is what's left over. If the law doesn't say you can't do it, then you can."

Willing put on a confounded expression. "I'm not sure freedom works for me as a remnant. Like the snippets of material left over when my mother made curtains. Isn't freedom a sensation? After all, you don't have to exercise a freedom to possess it. I don't have to get up for a drink of water. But knowing that I could get up, it changes the way it feels to sit, even if I stay sitting."

"You're talking treasury, kid," Goog said. "You were obviously claiming that in a 'free' society everybody gets to break the law and not face the consequences. So in your deviant little mind, *liberty* is just another word for rampant criminality."

"Sometimes I cross the street against the light." Willing could have let it go, but he didn't feel like it. All the pleasantness had been exhausting. "When no traffic is coming. Correct me if I'm wrong, but I think that's a misdemeanor. I haven't hurt anyone, or violated anyone's right of way. But I have broken the law. Being able to cross the street against the light is important to me."

"Jesus, Wilbur," Goog said. "That's fucking sad."

"If you take that away from me, and every other opportunity to not quite toe the line," Willing said, "then however many amusing things I'm at liberty to do, I don't feel free. If I don't feel free, I'm not free." *I don't feel free,* Willing did not add, *and I have not felt free since you and yours jammed this fleck of metal into my neck.*

"Why should the US government give a shit about your feelings?" Goog charged.

"Why should it care about anything else?" Willing countered. "If it feels splug to live here, what are we preserving and protecting? What is the country for?"

"That is the dumbest question I've ever heard," Goog said. "This bash has seriously deteriorated. I'm going to push off."

"But the bancor," Savannah said. "When does it go cashless, exactly?"

"The announcement's next week. Be a happy day, in our office. Champagne and cake."

"So does the cash become worthless overnight," Savannah said, "by decree?"

"Same as when the dólar nuevo was brought in. Folks will have a month to convert. After which, yeah, cash bancors won't be legal tender—anywhere. It's bound to be fascinating. All these funds suddenly popping up on the chips of the erstwhile strapped. Between the fees, the fines, and the back taxes, this is an epic windfall for the Bureau. Or, as Wilbur so nobly observed, for *everyone.* For *the country.*"

"But why would anyone chip black-market ban-cors," Savannah said, "if you guys will take it all?"

"Because they might get to keep a teeny tiny bit of it as opposed to losing the whole whack, and in my professional experience, you lowlife taxpayers are greedy fucks who'll paw after whatever you can get," Goog said. "But why are you so interested?"

"I'm not!" Savannah bound her arms across her cleavage.

"Plenty of big-spending foreigners roll into this town, looking for *entertainment*," Goog said. "You wouldn't sometimes be paid in international currency, would you?"

"Well, if I were, ever, of course I'd chip the cash immediately!" Savannah looked as if she could hardly breathe. She was a dreadful liar.

"I bet you do," Goog said. "I get paid okay, but it's 100 percent on the record. Where I work, not only do I have to be squeaky clean? My whole family has to be squeaky clean. So I'm putting an alert on your chip. Any sudden spikes in income, we'll be watching."

On that happy note, Goog left the party. He took the last of the cognac.

Chapter 3

Return of the Somethingness: Shooting Somebody, Going Somewhere Else, or Both

Cleaning up after a bowl-on-the-floor party took five minutes. Fifa was out cold on the rug. Willing draped her with a blanket. She had to be up in three hours to install shower grips in Windsor Terrace.

"You went quiet. After Goog left," Willing said.

"Mm," Nollie grunted, drying the stainless steel mixing bowl.

"Going back to when you first arrived in East Flatbush. I've never known you to run out of money."

"Mm," she grunted again.

"I did some research," he said. "Your other books did so-so. But *Better Late Than* sold millions."

Not even a grunt. The bowl got very shiny.

"You brought back bancors, from France," he said. "That 'old boyfriend' you visit in Flushing. Whoever it is, he or she trades currency on the black market."

Nollie stopped drying and glared, eyes popping.

"It can't hear!" Willing exclaimed. "I've experimented! I've said aloud in my bedroom, 'I have secret sources of income that the Scab doesn't know about,' and nothing happened!"

"Very well," she said reluctantly. "But my finances are private."

"I'm only trying to help. Whatever you've got left—if you deposit it, they'll tax it to the wall, and they'll ask questions. You could be open to prosecution. Holding bancors is legal now. But when you brought those bills through Customs, their possession was criminal. They could use that pretext to confiscate the lot. On the other hand, if you don't deposit it, you heard Goog. A date will come and go, and the cash will convert to confetti overnight."

"So, what, I should use it to line a hamster cage? Insulate the attic?"

"I know this violates all your instincts. But the new reporting requirements on off-chip expenditures don't come in until January. So before the public announcement about the bancor going cashless, which is going to flood the economy with bancors, and depress the exchange rate for cash transactions—*you have to spend it.*"

Nollie put the bowl down at last. "I've dodged them at every turn. Now I feel cornered. You're not the only one who cherishes getting away with something."

"Spend it on getting away with something, then."

Nollie dried her hands on the dishtowel with an anxious twist. "Young people want money to buy things. Not only clothes and jewelry, but experience, thrills. Old people want money for one reason and one reason only: to feel safe."

"You can never have enough money to be safe," he said gently. "Money itself isn't safe. We should know."

"And how," she seconded. "But then, *life* isn't safe, at ninety years old."

"Exactly," he said. "The illusion of wealth is that it can buy what you want. Which it can, but only if you want, like, a pretty dress. You don't want a dress. You want not to be old. We haven't talked about it much, but don't you wish one of those hothead boyfriends of yours had stuck around? Maybe you want to still be a famous writer, and you can't buy that, either; there are no famous writers. Or you want to write with the same fire that lit you up when you started *Better Late Than*—the kind of fire that hardly anyone gets to keep. You want the thicker hair in your old snapshots. You pretend you don't, but you want people to like you.

You want not to get cancer. What threatens everything that's important to you isn't a cashless bancor, or currency depreciation, or debt renunciation, or economic collapse, but your own collapse. Other than being able to pick up, you know, a nice bottle of wine, or maybe a chicken, you can't buy anything you want."

"You kids think all we boomers have lived in a delusional bubble," she returned. "Think it's come as a shock I've got old? I'm not an idiot. I've been reading since I was your age about 'elderly women' raped and robbed in their homes, and in the back of my head I've heard a whisper: 'Pretty soon, honey, that's gonna be you.' I've always anticipated becoming a target—defenseless, weak, and on my own. Maybe my parents had a premonition. Ever work it out? *Enola* is *alone* spelled backwards. So there was a discrete period in my forties when I had the opportunity to salt away some reserves, in preparation for a rainy day that might last decades—a monsoon—my own personal climate change. In my mind's eye, I was stockpiling a veritably physical fortification. If I bricked the bills high enough, the barbarians couldn't climb over. Less metaphorically? Maybe I could pay them to go away."

"But that *is* delusional," Willing said. "At your age, the main menace isn't rapists and robbers, or waves of marauders in a second Dark Ages—or anything else from the outside. Every day, you face down the enemy within. So the one commodity that you bigging can't buy, more than any other, is safety. Why doesn't that release you? From trying to protect what you're going to lose anyway? It should make you feel brave."

"You're one to talk about brave," Nollie said bitterly, and her tonal turn injured him; he'd put a big effort into that soliloquy, which he thought had come out rather well. "Were you talking trash, for fun? Or have you seriously considered slumbering?"

"Yes," he said. "I have."

"So if I offered to spend the bancors on putting you into a self-induced coma for five years, you'd take me up on it."

In truth, the proposal was immediately tempting. "You say that with disgust. But would five more years of ass-wiping at Elysian Fields improve on sleep? I love to sleep."

"Willing." Arms folded, she confronted him square on, her back to the counter, trapping him against the stove with that look. She was so much shorter than he was; he was damned how she managed to seem daunting. "I don't often play the elder, and deliver judgment from on high. So hear me out this once. All through the early thirties, you were sly. Resourceful. Inventive. Disobedient. Impossible to intimidate. I used to love watching you stand your ground with that cretin Lowell Stackhouse, though he was three times your age. There was a somethingness about you. Sorry. I'm not as articulate as I used to be. Too many brain cells down. Too much homemade hooch. But the somethingness, it's what fiction writers like me—former fiction writers like me—it's what we always try to pin to the page. We always fail. That doesn't mean it isn't out there, only that it's impossible to capture, like those tiny, nefariously evasive moths you can't grab from the air. Even at Citadel. You worked so hard. You savored the effort. You were tilling fields like an ox, and the somethingness only thrived. But ever since the chipping, you've gone gray. You seem like other people. The boy I knew in 2030 would never have squandered his great-aunt's resources on *sleep*."

"The chip," he said. "I doubt it's messed with my mind in the way you're implying. They're not that clever. It probably is merely a means of accounting. Though a means of accounting that won't let me cross the street against the light."

"Cheating," Nollie agreed, "is restorative. It maintains your dignity. Breaking a rule a day keeps the doctor away far better than a fucking apple."

"In the fields at Citadel," he went on, "we had plenty of time to talk. Avery told me about how hard it was for cancer patients when they got better. She said that when you're bigging sick, making it to the next day is a victory. When you're well again, being alive isn't a triumph anymore. She said patients often got depressed not during chemo, but after it had worked. For me, the thirties. They were exciting. Our whole family—over and over, we almost died. When the fleX service went down on the trek to Gloversville, and we had to rely on Esteban, and on the paper map I stole from a recharging station—there was no guarantee we were going to make it. It was a miracle the recharging station even carried a paper map to steal. Carter could barely walk, because of his knees. Bing had something like trench foot, from his shot-out shoe and wet socks. And then we got to that narrow, unpaved drive and found the tiny label on the mailbox, CITADEL? We *cried*. But now. It's this grinding in place. No horizon, no direction, and no threat. We may not keep much of my salary, but we'll probably be all right, even without your bancors. That's part of the problem. The okayness. The nothing but okayness. So chip or no chip. It's not exciting."

"Well, then," Nollie announced decisively. "We won't buy safety. We'll buy excitement."

Willing discovered the very next afternoon, as he had as a boy, that the most exciting excitement is free.

Nollie frowned. "You're back early. Were you fired?"

"I fired," he said, his breath quick. "It's not a passive construction."

"What?"

"I never really expected it at Elysian," he said, pacing. He was probably disheveled. The way you look after you've squeezed into a linen cupboard. "Nothing happens there. Even when people die, it's more nothing-happening. It's expected. Or not-dying. That's expected, too. I carry because I always have, since I was sixteen. Call it a fetish. A dependency. And I'm not the only one. You need money to feel safe, but I don't trust money. After our whole family was forced from this house at midnight in the rain, I need a gun. I like the fact that, like you said, it's against the rules. For most people, packing is a bigging bad idea. The Supreme Court was right. But it's not a bad idea for me."

"Unfortunately, that's what everyone thinks," Nollie said. "Now, stop. Organize yourself."

"I have no idea whether I killed him."

"An excellent first line for a short story. But even a story would have to back up."

"I don't know the guy well." Willing bombed onto the sofa, to force himself to sit still. "Little older than me, maybe thirty-five. He's on staff—was. Since even if he makes it, well—Elysian definitely has grounds for dismissal now. Always looks under-slept. Probably has a night job, too. I talked to him last week, at lunch. He supports his sister, who's a striker. He tops up his younger brother's slumber account, because it's cheaper to keep the brother in storage than to support him if he's unemployed. This guy, Clayton. His wife got pregnant. They both wanted the baby. Badly. But there was no way they could afford to keep it. She'd just had an abortion. He seemed pretty shredded about it. Looking back, I guess he was twitchy. But those 'warning signs' you're supposed to look out for. They only seem obvious in retrospect. In the present—stressed, angry, having money problems, expressing resentment of shrivs—they apply to everyone I know."

"Your friend Clayton shot up the nursing home."

Nollie was hardly psychic. The protocol had become such a cliché.

"I don't know where he got the gun, but that amnesty in the thirties was a farce."

"Any idea of the body count?"

"Not really. He started with the morts, so that would have upped the numbers. I'm sure you could go online and find reports of casualties anywhere from ten to a hundred and forty. The usual."

"You took him down."

"Does that impress you?" In truth, Willing was in shock. For fifteen years, the Shadow had been a mere mascot—part companion, part lucky charm, a metal version of Milo. He'd almost forgotten what it was engineered to do: something a bit more drastic than "sit."

"I'm impressed that you didn't let him go at it. Your mother told me you advocated 'shooting' Luella well before my father did the honors. She worried that having said that might have made you feel bad later."

"It didn't," Willing said.

"Fifa will disapprove. She'll think you should have joined in."

"I had a clear line of sight from the cracked-open door of the closet where I was hiding. The chance wasn't going to last. I had to make a split-second decision. I think I only hit his shoulder. An orderly pinned him when he dropped. I slipped out in the pandemonium. The trouble is—"

"You're more energized than I've seen you in years."

"So that's the answer. To my malaise. Shoot people."

"Seems a start."

"I might have been seen. That orderly could have noticed it was me."

"But you'll be a hero."

"I don't want to turn in the Shadow. I shouldn't have given away that I have it."

Nollie squinted. "We could hide it. You could claim to have thrown it in the East River in some PTSD revulsion. We could make up a story about how you'd found it in the house, how it was left behind by squatters. How you'd always planned to turn it in. But look at you. Just now, your face fell. You don't want my good excuses. You miss urgency. You like the idea of having to leave. Of being on the run."

She knew him well. And he knew her. So they began talking about what they had been talking about since the previous night, without ever saying so outright.

"I have enough bancors to buy an extremely nice car," Nollie said. "This time, we wouldn't have to walk."

Virtually no one bought a car anymore. Major American cities like New York bore more resemblance to mid-twentieth-century Shanghai than to the whizzing futuristic metropolis of *The Jetsons*. In eerie silence, multitudes of electric bicycles swarmed single public buses like bees around a queen.

"I'm chipped," he reminded her. "They can track where I am."

"If they care. That is, if you were the mass murderer at Elysian and you'd escaped, you'd have a problem there. But you were the good guy. As I understand it, too, the police have to appeal to the Scab to use their satellites, and scabbies are proprietary."

Granted, despite Fifa's conviction that they lived in a police state, the powers of the police per se were surprisingly restricted. The FBI was little more than a website. Movie buffs who watched classic thrillers like *the Bourne trilogy* must have been disconcerted by this mythically demonic organization called the *CIA*, whose sticky fingerprints no longer stained assassinations and coups all over the globe, and whose Langley headquarters, according to Avery, had been taken over by a discount grocery chain from the Punjab. (In a flurry of films and series from abroad in the thirties, Americans were popular villains: schemers from the Federal Reserve out to defraud innocent investors with sales of bonds they knew full well would soon be worthless, or wicked financiers who escaped the economic depredations of the era by absconding with ill-gotten gains. But in the Korean and Vietnamese entertainment of this decade, American characters were mostly walk-ons—incompetent or hapless buffoons played for laughs.) The powers of the Scab, by contrast, were very real, and veritably limitless.

"Is it even possible?" he asked. "To just—not show up for work, and—go? Wherever you want? Without asking, or filling out a form, or notifying some official?"

Nollie's smile was pained. "People used to pick up and drive across the country for weeks at a time. Stopping where they wanted. Doing what they wanted. Generally this was called a *vacation*. Back when wage earners got vacations. But the fact that young people like you think you need permission to career into the horizon, think it must be against the law to quit a scurvy job without asking—that alone is reason to go."

"But if it's true. About the chip. You might get through. For me, it would be suicide."

"So you can sleep or ass-wipe your life away, or you can take a chance. Which I rate at about fifty-fifty. Sixty-forty maybe," Nollie said, reconsidering.

"Which direction?"

"Does it matter?"

"I'll have to ask Fifa to come, too."

"Of course. Although—well, she talks a good game . . ."

"I know," Willing said sadly.

"Let's get out of here. We have a car to buy. Meanwhile, if anyone comes nosing around looking for the savior of Elysian Fields, you'll be out."

Statistically, most people anguish longer over the purchase of a pair of shoes than over whether to buy a house. In kind, two of the biggest decisions of Willing's life had been dizzyingly expeditious. It took under a second to determine whether to stop a fellow staff member from putting more residents out of their misery and instead to put Clayton out of his. It took less than five minutes to resolve to commit treason.

On the way back from the dealer, they swung by Fifa's house. Typically, she lived with her parents. Willing had arranged to meet between her railing installations and her shift at the sandwich factory that night (the holiday weekend being extinct). She'd been relieved to hear from him. The shooting at Elysian was already on the news—though the reporting was blasé, nursing home melees having become so commonplace. To give them privacy on Fifa's stoop in Brownsville, Nollie stayed in the Myourea—*Thunderbird* in Khmer, a much-coveted import from Cambodia. Its sweet hydrogen lines combined with a 1950s teal-and-cream two-tone drew admiring onlookers.

"You mean, practically right now," Fifa said incredulously after hearing him out. Her face was ashen, and she needed a shower. She looked hung-over.

"Tomorrow," he said. "We have to throw some things together. I doubt we'll head out of town until afternoon."

"Oh, well, that's different," Fifa said caustically.

"This isn't out of the blue. We've talked about it before. You thought it would be so cruel. *The final frontier*, we said. Becoming modern-day homesteaders."

"We've *mused* about it. But you've no idea what it's like there. Accounts on the web all contradict each other, and you never hear from people who actually live in the Free State. If anyone lives there. The whole population could've sunk into the desert from another round of A-bomb tests at Yucca Flats and nobody would know about it here."

"I love not knowing," Willing said. "Our future in the old United States is *too* known. Most of what I know I don't like."

"You're not being practical. I've seen pics of the border. It's worse than Mexico's fence along the Rio Grande. The walls are massively high, and massively thick, and bristling with guns and soldiers. How would you get across, even if you successfully tippy-toe through the minefield leading up to it?"

"I'll find out when I get there. Any armor has a chink. And there's supposedly an underground railroad."

"Willing, most of what's on the web is fantasy! Have you ever met a real person in this 'underground railroad'?"

"All right, no." He added staunchly, "But other people have made it."

"All you can be sure of is that other people have disappeared. You can disappear without popping up somewhere else. Have you ever heard from Jarred?"

"No, but they stop communications from getting out. I doubt he'd be able to sail a paper airplane in my direction, much less a fleXt."

"And you're assuming that the chip's self-destruct is treasury. Why would it be? You heard Goog. A whole unit at the Scab, he said. And doesn't it sound like exactly what they'd program your chip to do, if you had the impertinence to throw down your cotton hoe, and the ingratitude to walk away from *the greatest nation on earth*? These people are motherfucking T-bills! Seems biggin' likely to me that instead of allowing you to throw off your chains, they'd rather you be dead."

"I would rather be dead," he said, surprising himself, "than stay here. It's not only the taxes. It's what I was trying to explain last night. A heaviness. I feel watched. I pay up, as if I have any choice. It's splug how little is left, but that's not what gets me down. I feel like a criminal all the time. When I think about it, I'm doing everything I'm supposed to. It's what my mother told me it was like going through airport security—

though I've never been on an airplane myself. She said you always felt like you were doing something wrong. Even when you took off your shoes, and removed your 'laptop,' and raised your arms in a full-body scanner, like surrendering when you're under arrest. But I feel that way walking down the street."

"Of course you do," Fifa said impatiently. "It's called *terrorism*. Which isn't only the ploy of religious lunatics. It's a tool of the state. It works by making examples of a handful of people, and then there's a multiplier effect of scaring everyone else shitless. Terrorism is a money saver. The Scab is a terrorist organization, but so was the IRS—the old initials just didn't have the resources to stick an emotional cattle prod up your ass on the same scale. Nothing's changed."

He took a different tack. "But all the companies are owned by foreigners. Even the old national parks. Elysian Fields is owned by a corporation in Laos. Unless you're a doctor, or a pharmaceutical researcher, the only jobs available are the drear ones you and I do now. What can we look forward to? And then the likes of my aunt Avery and uncle Lowell—you know, like your parents—all they do is talk about how great everything used to be and how splug it is now. So why not come with me? If only for an adventure. The worst that could happen is we get there, we can't get in, and we come home."

"That's not the worst that can happen. They can throw you in jail for *trying* to defect. And talk about working for foreigners—all those commercial prisons are also owned by Asians, and they drive you like dogs, not for 23 percent of your pay, but for dick. You've no idea what you're risking."

Fifa's defiance had always rung hollow. But they'd seen each other for three years. His impassioned appeal was an obligation, and so was hers.

"The shooting at Elysian," she said. "It's left you rattled. That makes sense. Having a brush against . . . Well. It makes you take stock. I'm glad you're okay, though Nollie's right: *I* think you should have let him finish what he started. He was doing God's work. But that scene having fucked your head up doesn't mean you should do anything crazy—"

"Agency," Willing said. "That's what I discovered this afternoon. That I could do something. In the United States, *doing something* generally means either shooting somebody, or going somewhere else. I'm a dropout. I don't know much American history. Still, I do understand that a long time ago we ran out of new land, and the space program was too expensive. It's never been the same here since there was nowhere to go. But it's possible to get somewhere else by going backwards."

"Brutal," Fifa said. "First, you're planning to get shot climbing over the wall into the USN. Now it's time travel."

"Yes. I'm not sure, but I think Nevada *is* time travel."

When they parted, he pressed a set of keys into her palm. "Take the house."

"What happens if you wise up and do a U-turn a hundred miles short of Vegas?"

"Then I'll move back in, you can stay, and we'll find out whether misery really does love company." He kissed her. "I'll miss you."

"Not as much as you think," Fifa scoffed, offhand. "I've always played second fiddle to your real girl-friend."

"Like who?"

"That shriv in shades sitting in the sharp car."

What's *he* doing here?" Nollie said irritably.

In the rare warmth of mid-summer, they'd once more thrown the front door open, with only the screen door latched. After serial declarations of martial law in the latter thirties, American cities had restored the protection of property rights and imposed civic order; New York had a surprisingly low crime rate. For most of the public, the miscreants who posed any serious danger were over-zealous keepers of order—one of whom was standing on their stoop.

Goog could see them through the screen, stacking luggage in the living room. They couldn't pretend they weren't home. Refusing to invite an immediate relative inside would seem weird.

"Going somewhere?" their visitor asked, scanning the bags.

"Taking a tour," Nollie said briskly. "Seeing our nation's sites. Inspired by the Fourth of July."

"What sites?" Goog asked skeptically. "Platefaces bought most of them up."

"They haven't put coolie hats on Mount Rushmore. Yet."

"So what's up?" Willing asked, trying to sound casual, which never worked.

"Heard about that ruckus at Elysian," Goog said. "Seems some valiant, self-sacrificing employee intervened, or the carnage would have been worse."

"I wouldn't know," Willing said. "I spent the whole time crouched in a closet. Made a run for it as soon as the shooting stopped." Irksome, playing to Goog's contemptuous opinion of him, but he'd no reason to care what his cousin thought.

"Funny," Goog said. "The home's administration must have been misinformed, then. Because however grateful those poor souls cowering in Elysian might have felt, seems our Good Samaritan was carrying an illicit handgun. So the NYPD put in a request to the Bureau for tracking. I recognized your name."

"Barking up the wrong coward," Willing said, milking the false humility a bit.

"I'm doing you a favor, bud. Thought we might keep this all in the family. Turn in the sidearm—and we both know we're talking about that forty-four you were always waving about Citadel whenever some skinny wayfarer came near your precious potatoes. What with your benevolent intercession and all, I bet I can get the cops to drop it. They just want the gun."

Nollie's story about the weapon having been left behind by squatters would never wash with Goog, who was present in Prospect Park when the Shadow notched its seminal two fatalities. Nor would he believe his annoying cousin would have pitched his protection into the East River. Willing was debating the best method of stonewalling when Goog's eye was drawn by a battered carton on the floor.

"*Foul matter,*" Goog read from the carton's side, and something clicked. "Only times I've seen you drag along that grubby box, Auntie, are when you're planning a one-way trip."

"I'm old," Nollie said. "Getting dotty. Sentimental. Some writers travel with lucky fountain pens. I need my printouts."

"This is way too much crap for Mount Rushmore," Goog said. "And that new Myourea out front. Yours?"

"Getting rash, too," she said. "You know those dementia sufferers. Irrational. Impulsive. Can't be trusted with money."

"Speaking of money: where'd it come from?" Goog never left his work at the office.

"I earned it," Nollie said with fervor. "I got a good idea, I worked very hard to realize it, I paid taxes on the rewards of my labor—rather high taxes, or so I imagined at the time—and however improbable you may find this now, afterwards I had two cents to rub together."

The entire scenario was bound to strike any scabbie worth his salt as highly irregular. But for once Goog Stackhouse's imagination was inflamed by something other than fiscal malfeasance. "You could hop a U-pod for a fraction of the price. Old ladies don't buy state-of-the-art hydrogen sedans to play tourist for a few days."

"Last I checked, it was legal to drive across the *land of the free* without getting a permission slip from your own grandnephew."

"It's legal with one exception. If I even suspect an intention to defect to the USN, you two aren't going anywhere."

Willing was a master of the impassive. Nollie was less adept. It didn't help, either, that her fleX was stiffened on the coffee table, its open GPS app already programmed for the route to Reno. Pity she didn't do updates. In current versions of Google Maps, a search on "Nevada" brought up the name of a street in Greenwich, England. The state itself was missing.

"Wilbur, aren't you the type," Goog said, after a victorious glance at the fleX. "Intoxicated by an idea of yourself as having a direct line to Jesus, or whoever's voices you've been hearing since you were a maladjusted kid. Just the sort of loser who used to sell his soul to Scientology—since the so-called *Free State* is just another fringy, goofball cult. And always so cozy with that fruitcake rabble-rouser Jarred. Makes perfect sense you'd snuffle the wacko's trail, searching for the pothead at the end of the rainbow. Sorry to poop your pipe dream, but I'll be flagging your chip. Drones from the Bureau will descend from the sky the moment you leave the tri-state area. As for you," he told Nollie. "Conspiracy to defect to the USN is one of the few statutory justifications for forced chipping. So you might start shaving the back of your neck."

"How convenient," she said. "Its hairs are already raised."

"Later, you'll both thank me," Goog said. "No no-nagenarian with writer's block would ever have scaled a considerable improvement on the Berlin Wall. And your head, Wilbur, would have splattered over the sand like a busted watermelon the moment you crossed the border."

"Really? I guess we'll find out." Willing had to admit he felt yunk, pointing an X-K47 Black Shadow at his cousin. It simply didn't feel serious. All the same, in seconds he had ratcheted up the stakes of this encounter in a manner that was difficult to ratchet back down. When you've pointed a gun at someone, you pretty much have to keep pointing it. You can't put it back in your pocket and return to calm, interested discussion of your travel plans.

"Don't be ridiculous," Goog said, with a quaver in his voice. "I'm not only your cousin, which obviously doesn't mean much to you—"

"Or to you," Willing said.

"I'm also a Scab agent." Interesting slip. "Any idea what happens to you if you shoot one of us?"

"Nothing worse," Willing calculated easily, "than if I don't shoot you. The difference between drudging at Elysian for next to nothing and drudging at an out-sourced prison for absolutely nothing? Negligible."

"I came here to be *nice*," Goog hissed.

"You came here to be *disarming*," Willing said. "It always pissed you off that Jarred didn't trust you with the guns."

"But what are we going to do with him?" Nollie said.

"We could tie him up," Willing supposed. "But there's food and water to consider. Unlikely, but he might do something resourceful. And this is the last housewarming present I'd want to leave Fifa."

"Nuts," Nollie said. "You mean we have to bring the prick along. And I *had* been looking forward to this trip."

Chapter 4
Singin' This'll Be the Day That I Die

"They only include a manual setting for emergencies," Willing advised.

"Remember what I told you about preserving your dignity by breaking the rules?" Nollie said, struggling into what no one even called the *driver's seat* anymore. "That goes double for driving your own fucking car."

"People your age insisting on controlling the vehicle are the only reason anyone has accidents anymore. It's two and a half thousand miles."

"You want to drive?"

"I don't know how."

"No one does. It's pathetic."

Willing had always liked his aunt for her obstinacy. So he couldn't object when she wouldn't comply with his wishes, either. He suppressed a tremor of trepidation in the seat beside her. This whole venture was a suicidal careen toward a sheer cliff. If they slammed into an interstate meridian midway, the truncated expedition would simply be more efficient.

They set off with their reluctant passenger in the backseat, de-fleXed, wrists duct-taped graciously in his lap rather than uncomfortably behind his back. They allowed Goog to expend his vexation by listing the many crimes they were committing: abduction, false imprisonment, obstruction of the official duties of a federal employee. Yet as they retraced the route their family had trod in the cold, wet spring of '32— east on Atlantic Avenue, over the Brooklyn Bridge, up West Street—even the captive got caught up in reminiscence. Its personnel much reduced, the second Mandible migration was blindingly swift in comparison to the one on foot. Oh, mobes in gang formation did veer into the road with no warning (crazed blithers on motorized trikes having long ago replaced the comparatively anodyne cyclist as the New Yorker's anathema). Yet a shrunken, flat-lined GDP had done a spectacular job of thinning vehicular traffic. After its fifty-some years of snotty road-hoggery, only grinding poverty coast-to-coast had put the kibosh on the hulking sports utility vehicle by about 2040. When Willing pointed to one up ahead, the sighting was rare.

"Still chugging!" he said. "It beats me where they get the gas."

"Man, the SUV was one of the cruelest American inventions of all time," Goog said. "I fucking loved my mom's Jaunt. When it went out of production, I was all set to snag the latest model."

"Bullying, brutish, and plug-ugly," Nollie quipped. "Guess people recognize themselves in cars same as they do in dogs."

On the GW, the metal grates of the surface rattled, the bridge itself lurching with a subtle sway. "I get the willies crossing these things," Nollie said.

"No kidding," Goog said. "This rusted contraption hasn't had any serious maintenance since the 1990s."

"According to Avery, the federal buildings in DC are just as dilapidated," Willing said. "She said the 'White House' is a misnomer. Congress, the Lincoln Memorial—they're all a dingy yellow dripping with black streaks. She said chunks of the Washington Monument keep falling off. After a girl was killed by one, you can't get within a hundred yards."

"My mom is biggin' exaggerating," Goog sneered. "I looked up pics of the Mall online. Pristine."

"That's because it's cheaper to post old photographs than to pay for steam cleaning," Willing said.

They curved on I-95 and bumped onto I-80 in Teaneck. Willing's mood began to lift. He'd only been
to New Jersey a handful of times, mostly with Jarred
to plow rapidly inflating profits into hard-asset farm
equipment. Besides New York, this was the only state
of the union in which he'd set foot. As soon as they hit
Pennsylvania, it was a brave new world. If these truly
were the last days of his life, they'd be interesting days.

Nollie plugged her fleX into the sound system, crank-
ing up the harmonies of her youth: "Hotel California,"
"The Weight," and some of the yunkest lyrics Willing
had ever heard in a song called "A Horse with No Name."
She played Don McLean, JJ Cale, and Fleetwood Mac,
until Goog exclaimed, "Christ, Nollie! This is like *Tunes
of Cro-Magnon Man.* What's next, Vivaldi?"

"I'm bankrolling this operation. This is my car, and
my road trip," she declared. "Ergo, my music. You're a
hostage, remember? Act like one."

In truth, the moldy soundtrack grew on them. By
the time they'd hit Stroudsburg on the Pennsylvania
state line, both Willing and Goog were driving their
Chevies to the levy at the top of their lungs.

With the late start, the first day was short. Nollie
drove manfully—and pointlessly, since the Myourea

could have done the job by itself—until 9 p.m., when they pulled into a rundown motel in Dubois. The proprietor was none too happy about Nollie's being unchipped—since a chip would have automatically covered him for losses if his ninety-year-old guest went berserk on Jack Daniel's and trashed the room. But he accepted a fleX payment because his operation was clearly hard up.

Nollie sent Willing across the way to fetch takeout. Goog lobbied for a proper restaurant meal, but they didn't want to have to explain a taste for bondage in a diner banquette. He wheedled for them to please cut the duct tape so he could eat without making a mess, and it took discipline to resist his imprecations. Likewise, Willing took no pleasure in binding his ankles to the bedstead in the room they all shared.

For Goog had so entered into the spirit of the adventure that it was hard to remember he was being coerced. Only that afternoon, he'd threatened to restrict Willing's movements to the tri-state area with militarized Scab drones and menaced Nollie with compulsory surgery. Granted, he often made cheerful allusions to the doom awaiting at their destination. So perhaps he'd decided to enjoy the ride, confident that he'd have the last laugh: Willing's brain would fry; Nollie would be picked off by a border-guard sharpshooter. At the least, the duo would be drably arrested, and Goog would figure out how to take the credit.

Be that as it may, Goog's travel history was also provincial. He claimed to have attended a Bureau conference in Cleveland, but being on the outs with Avery, he hadn't even returned to Washington since his parents moved back in '44. Alone of the cousins, he could have afforded to explore beyond his tight New York orbit. But theirs was a crimped, wary, stinting generation, and travel is an acquired appetite. Maybe it never occurs to you to go anywhere in particular on a given weekend when you don't ever feel you're going anywhere in a larger sense.

So with the promise of wider horizons farther west, even Goog the ultimate T-bill seemed energized. His work must have been boring—totals, percentages, and occasional deviations from the norm. He was powerful, but wielded only the clenched power to ruin people's lives, as opposed to the looser, open-palmed power to improve them. Everybody with whom he came in contact hated him, and had to pretend they didn't. A few days' unofficial vacation from being an asshole must have been welcome.

As they rolled through the Alleghenies and entered Ohio the following day, Willing continued to be astonished that this journey was possible. No drone descended and fastened itself to the roof of their car with gecko-like suction cups because he hadn't reported to work at Elysian that morning to do his *fair share*. The chip at the base of his neck didn't glow and heat as it sensed his growing geographical distance from the means of making a *social contribution*.

While the wooded hills rolled past his window and Nollie played the contented *la-la-laah-laah* of "Our House," Willing considered all that data pouring into federal supercomputers. He had previously conceived of the central network as an omniscient, all-seeing overlord, which sorted and stored every minute detail to perfectly reconstruct the smallest infringements of each American citizen. But perhaps instead the data fed a bloated, overloaded behemoth choking on its own information excess and suffering from a sort of digital obesity. Woozy from gorging on a smorgasbord of similar tidbits, maybe the monster was helpless to know where to stuff the fact that Willing Mandible nee Darkly of East Flatbush, NY, had bought a packet of soda crackers for $2.95.

In any event, nothing and no one seemed to care that Willing and Enola Mandible, and even Goog Stackhouse—who might not be as important at the Bureau as he pretended—had gone AWOL. It was exhilarating.

Nollie's having plotted their course with her fleX GPS turned out to be unnecessary. The directions all the way to the Nevada border at Wendover, Utah, came down to: "cross George Washington Bridge, then turn right." To Willing's amazement, I-80 stretched in a virtual straight line across the continent from Teaneck to San Francisco. Granted, the tarmac was degraded, and he felt wistful about those apocryphal days when one could smooth along this route at 85 mph, in which case they might have made this whole trip in a mere three days instead of five. Willing was a fairly proficient economics autodidact, but knew soberingly little else about the country.

Because Nollie claimed that "children in the backseat need toys," they disabled the personal communications on Willing's maXfleX, password-protected the settings, and let Goog play with it. Big on showing off his general knowledge as a kid, he enjoyed pitching out factoids: "The interstate highway system was initiated in 1956. I-80 took thirty years to complete. It closely approximated the route of the Lincoln Highway, the first road across America, and also duplicates much of the Oregon Trail and the Transcontinental Railroad." Clearly, this uncompromising streak of roadway gouged remorselessly through boulders and mountain ranges was a staggering feat of engineering. Willing had harbored a variety of emotions about the United States over his short life: disappointment; anxiety, even fear; incomprehension; a whole lot of nothing. Pride was new. It was nice.

To pass the time, Nollie regaled them with reports from her friends in France, who said Americans' reputation abroad was looking up. The arrogant, loud, gauche, boastful stereotype was obsolete. The few of their compatriots who ventured to Europe were widely regarded as modest, deferent, deflective. They were increasingly renowned for a sly acidity, dry self-deprecation, and black humor. No one tossed off clichés about Americans having "no sense of irony" when their entire country had become an irony writ large. And Yanks told great stories. In Paris, it had grown fashionable to invite lively American raconteurs to dinner parties, much as one might previously have invited the Irish.

Yet as the Myourea sped through Indiana and Illinois, the landscape was blighted on either side with huge, warehouse-style manufacturing plants. These would be abundantly automated and 100 percent foreign-owned. Locals were glad for the few low-level jobs that real people who would work for peanuts could do so cheaply that it wasn't worth the capital expense of buying and tooling up robs. The US had become a popular location for foreign investment: the land was ample and economical. If income taxes were fiendish, DC was desperate to raise the employment rate, and corporate tax rates were trifling. Undereducated, true, the workforce was also cowed, biddable, and grateful. A higher than average incidence of workplace shootings was unfortunate, but Americans mostly killed each other, and the casualties were easily replaced. Willing had recently heard from their old tenant Kurt, who after Jarred went dark had ended up in one of these sprawling, single-story factories in the Midwest. Kurt said employees slept in dormitories—more like mausoleums than the kind that housed college students. By day, you could walk for half a mile along the shop floor without coming across another human being. It was lonely work, which Kurt said was worse than the boredom.

Their progress moderately impaired by Nollie's insistence mornings on doing her *jumping jacks*, they struck Iowa on the third day. Fields of corn stretched to the horizon, rarely interrupted by a farmhouse. The region had always been the country's breadbasket. Now it was the rest of the world's. The harvest also mechanized, nearly all this grain was for export. Two years ago, the global population had crossed the ten billion mark earlier than expected. Disappearing for decades, family farms like Citadel had now been swallowed altogether by single concerns with holdings so extensive that they could have become independent countries. Companies from China and India had colonized American agriculture with a sense of entitlement and no small hint of self-righteousness. Feeding ten billion was supposedly a great achievement. Presumably feeding 10.5 billion in three or four years' time would be an even greater achievement. Willing couldn't see the satisfaction himself. Maybe they'd even succeed in feeding twelve billion, but then what did you have—that you didn't have before? He'd rather build an interstate.

Throughout, the housing stock was a disconcerting patchwork. Disheveled clapboards with blistered paint and broken porch railings sat side-by-side glassy, impeccably kept retirement communities with tennis courts and pools. But plenty of smaller outposts along this route were ghost towns. He wondered where everyone had gone.

It was on the fourth day, in Nebraska. At their motel on the outskirts of Omaha that morning, they'd forgotten to fill up the water bottles. Nollie declared she was parched. (She could have been closer to insane, or hypnotized anyway. Between Lincoln and Grand Island, I-80 was so straight you could have used the roadway for a ruler, the land so flat you could have used the prairie for an ironing board. Mr. Expert in the backseat verified that the route didn't vary in its relentless, perfectly western direction by more than a few yards for seventy-two miles. For once Willing and Goog agreed on something: Nollie's refusal to put the Myourea into automatic along this mind-numbingly monotonous passage was yunk.) She pulled off onto an unlabeled side road that soon gave way to dirt.

"No way you're going to find a minimart here," Goog said. "Turn around."

She might have, had Goog not opened his big mouth. Nollie never took directions from their hostage. "Maybe not, but even Nebraska isn't depopulated. Americans can't be so far gone that they won't give a stranger a drink of water."

The track ended at a low-lying building they almost missed, since it was camouflaged by dust, and banked with windblown sand. A few exposed streaks revealed a surface the dun color of the landscape, as if it were designed to be missed. The hockey-puck structure was round, with a flat top and no windows. The featureless dwelling had only one door, which yawned open.

"Looks deserted," Goog said. "Let's go back. This place is weird."

For Willing, unease battled curiosity, and curiosity won out. He stepped gingerly over the sand-mounded threshold. "Hello!" he called, and there wasn't even an echo. "Give me my maXfleX," he told Goog. "It's dark."

Willing struggled with the screen for a moment. The *old* fleX rolled neatly into a flashlight in a trice, but the *new and improved* conversion was awkward. Even when he got the tube rolled, the beam splayed asymmetrically to the left.

The immediate interior was also full of dirt, with the odd empty vodka bottle on top: they weren't the first to discover this place. Willing swiveled the beam. It found more dirt, a smooth interior black wall, and a hole in the middle: a spiral staircase, with no direction to go but down. The entrance had once been protected by a hatch cover, which leaned at a dysfunctional tilt. Someone had jimmied it up. A smell rose from the opening—stale and dry, with an undertone of corruption. The impression of desolation was absolute. No one was here.

"What is this, *Indiana Jones*?" Goog whined. "We should get out of here."

"I'm surprised at you," Willing said. "There might be something down there you could tax."

"Ha-ha. But I'm not setting foot in that pit with my hands taped."

Actually, they'd grown pretty casual about the tape. It hadn't been replaced since the day previous. Goog could probably have twisted free if he'd tried.

"He can stay up here, then. I locked the car," Nollie assured Willing. "He's not going anywhere. I want to check this out."

As he and Nollie cautiously descended the gritty obsidian stairs, Willing glanced enviously at her older fleX. The roll was sweet, the light beam clean. Though the afternoon sun of the Nebraska plains was baking outside, the stairwell was cool. The foul taint in the air grew more intense.

One flight down, Willing swept his fleXpot to the side. It struck, of all things, a dusty treadmill. Behind it, the wall was lined with metal dumbbells of ascending size. A few feet to the right sat a cross-trainer, and next to that a rowing machine. He had no understanding of why anyone would bother to build a gym underground.

"Stop," he shouted sharply to Nollie behind him, embarrassed by the pound of his chest and the bile that rose in his throat. "If you're at all squeamish, or easily spooked, you should go back up."

"You can't imagine I'm 'squeamish,' much less—" She dropped the complaint cold.

Willing's fleXpot was trained on the stationary bicycle. Rather, on its rider. Slumped over the digital readout as if having set the machine for an overambitious hill climb, the figure was draped in a dusty tracksuit. Skulls always appear to be grinning, though this one had enough leathered skin stuck around the mouth to convey more the grimace of exertion. One of the arms had fallen off.

"This guy's been dead a long time," Willing said. "That probably makes us lucky." Were he pressed to theorize: what made corpses horrifying was moisture. The completely alive and the completely dead, fine. The in-between was the problem.

"You up for one more level?" Nollie gestured to the staircase, which wound farther down. "I'm intrigued."

"Take my hand." She seized it. He wasn't sure who was comforting whom.

The floor below contained an elaborate kitchen: convection oven, microwave, slow cooker, a KitchenAid mixer with a clatter of attachments. Finely tooled ash with stylish brass fixtures, the cabinet doors were flung open. Whatever ruffians had rifled the larder were not culinarily inclined. They'd left behind the bread maker, pasta machine, and food processor, while julienne slicers and olive pitters littered the linoleum. Though the floor was sticky from broken bottles of evaporated goo, several shelves were lined with cocktail onions, caviar, artichoke hearts, anchovies, hazelnut oil, and preserved lemons. What struck Willing about this buried Dean & Deluca Christmas basket was that there wasn't merely one jar of Seville marmalade with Glenlivet. Like all the other chichi comestibles, there were dozens of mar-malade jars—foreshortening two feet deep.

He picked up a jar of candied kumquats, and brushed it off. Mumbling, "My mother didn't believe in sell-by dates," he slipped it into his belt pack.

Nollie was panning her fleXpot over the contents of an open chest freezer, six of which lined a whole quad-rant of this level. Poking at the contents with a long-handled barbecue spatula, she read from the labels. "Sea bass, filet mignon, duck breast, quail, foie gras, smoked salmon—"

"*Eat* your salmon," Willing remembered.

"I don't think so." The airless plastic packets were uniformly an evil black.

Opposite the kitchen, a curved dining table of an exotic wood traced the circular wall of the silo. Three of its residents were propped in chairs. They looked hungry.

"The circulation system must have kept working for quite a while," Willing supposed. "Or the smell in here might be unbearable. What do you say—one more?"

They curled a third flight down—which entailed nudging one of their worse-for-wear hosts out of the way, about whom they became blasé with unnerving rapidity. Willing would have predicted this: a floor-to-ceiling wine cellar in the round. Or that's what he inferred, though it was here that previous tourists had concentrated their pillage. Most of the bottles were missing, and those that remained were empty: drained fifty-year-old Bordeauxs lay amid discarded cardboard canisters of Talisker and elaborate wooden corks of top-shelf cognac.

"I know something about French wine," Nollie said, raising a broken bottle of Châteauneuf-du-Pape. "This was a good year."

"If we're going to rule out a virus, that was their mistake." Willing pointed to a break in the grid of cubbyholes: a tall, empty cabinet whose open glass door nonetheless sported a sophisticated lock. Inside, the sections were long and vertical.

The next floor down was an entertainment center, where three corpses were riveted by a cinema screen of a size that a maXfleX could now duplicate in any teenager's bedroom. Below that, a lounge area, where several socializers seemed a bit too relaxed. The two floors thereafter were all residential units, each with a private sitting room and bath. These, too, had been ransacked, the dresser drawers yanked out, the mattresses flung. If the scavengers had been searching for valuables—jewelry, gold—Willing bet they scored handsomely. But they hadn't bothered to take the cash, scattered willy-nilly around the bedrooms like discarded candy wrappers. He picked up a $100 bill, an original-issue greenback—too small to blow your nose in, not absorbent enough to clean your glasses. When the dollar was replaced by the dólar nuevo, like most people he'd been glad to see the back of the old currency, and hadn't thought to save a sample as a memento. The distinctive flannel texture, the painfully pompous engraving, triggered an unexpected nostalgia. He pocketed the bill.

Including an enormous backup water tank, the bottom level was for storage. Looters had disregarded most of the contents: gluten-free pasta, running shoes, joint supports, and sea-salt truffles, one of whose assortments Willing opened; the glaucous chocolates were brittle and encrusted, like barnacles. Here also was the trash compactor. The dense, variegated cubes stacked beside it numbered under a dozen. This underground summer camp hadn't lasted long.

On the way back up, Nollie spotted a glint amidst the discarded bottles in the wine cellar, and rescued a magnum of champagne, its foil intact. "Whole reason we came here," she said. "I'm thirsty."

When they emerged, Goog was grumpy, and, after their detailed lowdown, jealous. Before sliding into the driver's seat, Nollie popped the cork. "Can't remember the last time I needed a drink more," she said, and took a slug.

"If you're going to hit the bottle, you have to put the Myourea in automatic."

"Willing, you're such a pussy drag." But she conceded, and once she bumped back to the mesmerizing straightaway on I-80 put her feet up. Bruce Springsteen's *Nebraska* played for atmosphere while they round-robined the warm champagne.

"So was that some nuclear bunker, then?" Goog asked.

"I checked the dates on the food," Willing said. "It was all bought in '33. So they were hiding from worse than nuclear holocaust: other people. Unfortunately for them, they let some of the other people inside."

"Were they attacked, then?" Goog wondered. "Robbed?"

"Nah," Willing said. "This is *America*. There was a gun cupboard. Better than even odds they killed each other."

"Lived high beforehand, though," Nollie said.

"They were rich," Willing said. "And they were old."

"Rich, obviously," Nollie said. "But how can you tell if a corpse is old?"

"By their products thou shalt know them," Willing intoned. "The exercise equipment is a generational giveaway. The bathrooms were stocked to the ceiling with anti-aging creams, tooth-whitening gel, and caffeine shampoo. Medication for hypertension, cholesterol, erectile dysfunction—and not only a vial or two. Hundreds. Wish I could have told Great Grand Man—we finally found out who cornered the national market on laxatives."

"And your poor mother," Nollie said to Goog, "hoarded Post-it notes."

Rumors had long circulated about the "über-rich." In folklore, these pampered fiscal vampires had retreated to fortified islands of sumptuous abandon, paddling in pools, propping piña coladas, while their countrymen starved. To discover that they hadn't all escaped unscathed—that, if nothing else, they may not have escaped one another—was satisfying.

Attempting to cross into the Free State on I-80 seemed a little obvious. Opting for the road less traveled by was the whole reason they'd chosen a northerly entry point into Nevada in the first place: most subversive emigrants would take I-70 to Las Vegas. If the degree of fortification along the border varied, Immigration and Customs Enforcement would surely concentrate its discouragements near the renegade state's largest and most famous city in its far south.

So Nollie exited the interstate for the secondary parallel roadway, US Route 58, which led into the town of Wendover, whose original municipal boundaries straddled the Utah-Nevada border. At first glance, Wendover seemed buzzier than similar communities en route. Hitherto, motels had been ramshackle, with bedraggled bedspreads and cracked, recycled plastic glasses. Here, more upscale hostelries looked new, with names like Pilgrim's Rest, Pilgrim's End, and Pilgrim's Pillow. They didn't seem to be referring to religious refugees in wide-brimmed hats. As their party drew farther into town, gaudy restaurants, casinos, and shops proliferated: The Turncoat Inn, The Deserter Sands, and Traitor Joe's. Multiple establishments made droll allusions to what visitors like Willing most feared: Fission Chips, or Chip Off Ye Olde Block. The Last Chance Bar advertised concoctions christened *Brain Freeze* and *Stroke in a Glass*.

Goog mewled that he was famished. They all were.

"What about his hands?" Willing asked his great-aunt.

"This town is so barmy," she said, "nobody's going to look twice at duct tape." Goog's titular bondage was already loose enough to qualify as a bracelet, and Willing had seen him more than once shove the stretched bangle back on.

So they stopped at a family restaurant called Final Feast. In reception, a five-year-old was whooping it up in a replica of an electric chair, which gyrated and vibrated and shot real sparks. The menu was designed around the last meals requested by inmates on death row. The John Allen Muhammad: chicken with red sauce and strawberry cake. The John Wayne Gacy came with KFC (Korean Fried Chicken) and shrimp. Or you could choose lighter fare: the John William Elliot was a cup of hot tea and six chocolate chip cookies; the James Rexford Powell, one pot of coffee.

"This is completely tasteless," Nollie said, surveying the entrees.

"How can you tell without ordering something?" Goog said. She rolled her eyes.

"I'm going for the Ron Scott Shamburger," Willing determined: nachos with chili, jalapeños, picante sauce, grilled onions, and tacos. "This guy cut out in style."

"Howdy!" Like her coworkers, their waitress was kitted out like a prison guard, with a shiny badge on her breast that said BETSY. "What can I get you?"

"I'll start with a Lethal Injection," Goog said.

"Great choice!" Betsy exclaimed, though the brandy, moonshine, and grenadine drink sounded vile. After taking the rest of their order, she asked companionably, "You folks defectors?"

"If we were," Nollie said, looking at the girl askance, "why would we tell you?"

"Only making conversation, honey. Don't you notice," Betsy directed to the men, "how these old dears tend to get paranoid?"

"Is there any good reason to be paranoid?" Willing asked.

"I know what you're asking, sweetie," Betsy said. "It's what you all want to know. But the crossers never come back. Make of that what you want. We do get repeat customers, but it's mostly folks who got cold feet at the last minute. Sometimes puts them in a right pickle, 'cause they'll have used up the reserves on their chip in a big casino blowout. You see them on the street, panhandling for chip transfers to get back home."

"You get a lot of these defectors?" Goog asked suspiciously, like the scabbie they sometimes forgot he still was.

"Oh, the pilgrims have really picked up the economy round here! I'll be right back with your grub."

After their late lunch, they returned to the highway and then pulled over. About a mile down 58, straight like the interstate it paralleled, Nollie's fleX indicated the border with Nevada. Sure enough, some sort of edifice rose at the end of the road—it was hard to tell from here how high, or to discern whether guards with snipers' rifles crouched atop it. Willing and Nollie agreed that getting any closer in a populous area was a mistake. Better to steer farther south on small, local roads, and explore the nature of federal defenses in the middle of nowhere.

"Look, I know we haven't always got along," Goog told Willing from the backseat, as dust rose around the car. "That doesn't mean I want your brain to burn out like a light bulb. Can't we call a truce? This trip has been a hoot. Turn around, maybe we can dip into Colorado on the way back. I'll even pay the larcenous fee the platefaces charge to see the Grand Canyon. Really, it's on me, for all three of us. I promise I won't turn you guys in. I won't report the abduction. I'll even let you keep your yunk pistol."

"That's incredibly generous," Willing said.

"I can *never* tell when you're being sarcastic," Goog snarled. "Listen, why risk mental meltdown? The US—it's not so bad!"

"Isn't that what the founding fathers had in mind," Willing said. "A country that's *not so bad.*"

"Not so bad is better than splug!" Goog implored. "I know it's rough going for a while, but once you hit the age of sixty-eight it's a free ride! Just put in your time!"

"Why don't you come with us?" Willing said.

"No way," Goog said. "You don't know the Bureau like I know the Bureau. These guys are not joking around. You think they wouldn't stroke out *noncompliant taxpayers*? In a *heartbeat*. Hell, it's amazing they're not already staging public executions. And not because we're goons. The regular public—they've got no appreciation for how desperate things are. The budget. It's a biggin' catastrophe. A miracle we can keep the Supreme Court in sandwiches."

After they'd traveled far enough out of town, Nollie cut west again. The pitted dirt road resembled the one that had led to the underground silo. Associations: not good. Goog made unfunny cracks about Nollie's homing instincts for corpses.

Yet as they approached what the GPS identified as the end of the world as they knew it, no Great Wall rose up to meet them. Their vehicle did not explode from tripping a landmine. Where Nollie stopped the Myourea and they all got out, two strands of rusted barbed wire stretched limply across the road between listing, poorly anchored posts. The fence continued along a north–south axis in both directions. On the other side, a hand-lettered sign read, "Welcum to the United States of Nevada."

Hands on hips, Goog surveyed the notorious border with disgust. "I can't believe this."

"That fence," Nollie said, "wouldn't keep chickens out."

Ten yards beyond the barbed wire sat a small red clapboard house. On the porch, an old man tilted back in a rocker, smoking. Rarer these days than an SUV, his rollie looked like a real cigarette. Willing waved. The old man waved back.

Willing advanced to the right-hand fence post. The ends of the wires were looped, and hooked around up-tilted nails.

"STOP!" Goog shouted, as his cousin reached for a loop. "It makes total sense to me now! They're happy to let unchipped shrivs like Nollie totter out of the country. Grateful, even. They cost a fucking fortune. But as for all-give-and-no-take taxpayers like you, Wilbur—there's only one possible reason there's no wall, and no guards, and no mines: *they don't need them.* If you want iron-clad evidence I'm right about the self-destruct, this sad-ass fence is it."

Willing unhooked both wires and walked them out of the way of the car—staying in the US of A. Nollie resumed what she insisted on calling the driver's seat, glided into the land of treachery and secession, and parked.

The line was now drawn literally in the sand. A dare.

By God, it was touching: Goog covered his face with his hands. "I can't watch this."

With no further ceremony, Willing stepped into the Free State.

Chapter 5

Who Wants to Live in a Utopia Anyway

The loud cackle from the red clapboard's porch was startling. Willing had been fairly sure, but that wasn't the same as certain. So he had stood there for a moment, sizing matters up, doubtless wearing the expression of patting his body down after an accident: being here, and continuing to be here, with an intense awareness of one point in time connecting to the next that one seldom appreciates. Maybe from the outside it looked funny.

The old man slapped his thigh. "I swear," he cried, "no matter how many times I watch, it still cracks me up."

Despite protestations that he didn't want his cousin's head to detonate, Goog looked consternated that it hadn't. "Okay, then," he said, only two feet away but still in the USA, "what about the cannibalism?"

Willing nodded at the old man. "That guy doesn't look like he's about to eat me. *Now* are you coming?"

"I can't." Goog looked shredded. "Where you just stepped—it's the new Wild West. Whatever it's like, it has to be primitive. And I have a good job—"

"I wouldn't call it a *good* job."

"A lucrative job, then. Perks. Nothing to complain about. And over there—they must lynch people like me."

"What's the young man do?" the old man shouted. He was eavesdropping.

"Scabbie," Willing shouted back.

"Tell him he's right!" the old man said.

Ceremonially, Willing took out his pocketknife and severed the sagging duct tape looped around his cousin's wrists. He rooted in a pocket for Goog's commandeered maXfleX, and fetched a bottle of water from the car. "If you really have to go back," he said, handing over Goog's survival kit, "there's an airport a few miles from here. You could probably walk."

"It's hot," Goog grumbled. The fetching of a second bottle didn't matter. He'd meant, *It's lonely.*

"Tell Savannah, Bing, your parents, and Jayne and Carter I said good-bye. And spread the word that this border scare is treasury."

"Nobody would believe me," Goog said glumly. He was probably right.

They knocked each other's shoulders with rare warmth. Willing restored the two barbed wires to their nails. With a wan wave to Nollie, Goog slouched off toward Wendover, where perhaps another Lethal Injection could dull his disappointment—in his country. In himself.

Meanwhile, Nollie was shooting the breeze with the man on the porch. His old-timer folksiness seemed hyped for effect. He'd got plenty of sun, but up close looked perhaps only a few years older than Lowell, which these days was nothing. The denim overalls were too crisp to be anything but an affectation, and the floppy hat looked crushed on purpose. Given the fields planted behind the house and the cattle beyond, he didn't spend all day jawing with new immigrants. Sitting sentry at this entry point must have been what he did for fun.

"According to our friend here," Nollie told Willing, "that big barricade on US 58 is only plywood."

"The town can't have tourists dancing back and forth over the border in plain view and their heads don't blow up," the codger explained. "Ruins the mythology. Which is a money-spinner. Nobody's ordering a gi-normous *final feast* at lunch if they're planning on supper."

"If I wanted to find someone over here," Willing asked, "what's my best bet? Vegas?"

"Where most folks head. Save yourself some trouble, try the internet."

"I thought you people didn't have any internet."

He chuckled. "Got our own server. Oh, the Outer Forty-Nine block us from the world-wide-whatever. Don't think you'll get all of Google books. But there's plenty local advice on growing alfalfa. Sites for finding loved ones. If they want to be found."

As Goog had warned, the technology was primitive. Their adoptive homeland provided neither satellite connection to http://usn nor the public radio-wave access that blanketed much of the US—a country whose territory began a few yards from here, but which Willing was already starting to think of as far away. Their good-old-boy guide was kind enough to provide the password for his private Wi-Fi. It was unbearably slow.

"Got it," Willing announced after an excruciating five minutes. "Jarred Mandible, 2827 Buena Vista Drive, Las Vegas. That was easier than I expected. Though I don't understand the site I found him on. Something about cheese."

"It's after four o'clock," Nollie noted restlessly, "and Vegas is three hundred miles from here."

"Before you two hit the road," the geezer said, with a glint of mischief in his eye, "might try a local parlor game while you're still by the border."

Curious, Willing followed the gatekeeper's instructions, extending his maXfleX over the barbed wire into the land of his old life. The device could immediately contact http://www.mychip.com again. Once more, the codger hooted. "What's it say?"

"Zero-zero nuevos," Willing read. "And zero-zero cents."

That earned a second thigh-slap. "Another drama I never get tired of! Only part of that fairy tale about the chip that's dead on. But they don't suck the life from your head. Put one foot in the Free State, they suck out the money instead."

"Displays a certain grim consistency," Nollie said.

"Don't matter," the man said. "Nobody use a chip here anyways. Think of it as shrapnel from the Income Tax Wars. But better get used to it, kid: you're broke."

"What about bancors?" Nollie asked warily.

"The USN don't trade, with nobody," the man said, enjoying himself. He had a sadistic streak. "Part philosophy, part practicality—'cause ain't nobody will trade with us. So if you can't make it, mine it, fix it, grow it, or invent it in Nevada, you can't get it. Which means, ma'am, a *bancor* is about as useful for the purchase of provisions as a drowned rat."

"Do Nevadans use money at all?" Willing asked.

"What do you think, we use beads? We're not *savages*. Carson City issues continentals. First currency of the original thirteen colonies. But it went to hell pronto in the late 1770s. 'Cause it wasn't backed by nothin'. We fixed that."

"Don't tell me," Willing said. "You're on the gold standard."

"Ain't you quick! Before we cut loose, the Free State produced the majority of American gold anyways. But supply of continentals is real restricted. Learned our lesson from the thirties. Everybody round here pretty much agree that on the face of it the gold standard's dumb. *Arbitrary*, the governor calls it. Not much to do with the stuff but wear it around your neck. Can't eat it. But for currency, it works. Even if we don't quite know why. One continental buy you a whiskbroom today? One continental buy you a whiskbroom tomorrow. So it's not that dumb."

"Well, thanks for the advice," Willing said, by way of getting a move on.

"I don't recall dishing out any advice," the man objected. "Though I worry you're not focused on your *sichiation*. You got no money. Even if you do find refueling stations for that fancy jalopy of yours, how you going to pay? Here's your advice, and I hand it out free to all the dewy-eyed newcomers who duck through that fence: *Nevada ain't no utopia.*"

"Did I say anything to imply I thought it was?" Willing asked.

"You all think so," the man dismissed. "But your friend there. A *lovely* lady, I'm sure—"

"Watch who you're calling *lovely*," Nollie barked.

"But she ain't exactly fresh off the conveyor belt," he went on. "You bring in old people, you pay for old people. No Medicare here. No Social Security. No Part D prescription drug plans. No Medicaid-subsidized nursing homes. No so-called *safety net.* Every citizen in this rough-and-tumble republic gotta walk the high wire with *nada* underneath but the cold hard ground. Trip up? Somebody who care about you catch you, or you fall on your ass."

They struck out on the two-lane US 93. The land was flat and dry, with a rumple of low mountains on the horizon. Tufts of scrub pilled the plain like the puff of cumulous clouds overhead, the terrain a perfect reflection of the sky.

"You seemed pretty confident, when you crossed the border," Nollie said.

"More than your 60 percent confident anyway," Willing said. "When Goog talked about the condition of the Washington Monument, something fell into place. It's more economical to monitor photographs online than to clean the buildings in real life. So when I saw the fence, I got it. They don't have dogs, or sharpshooters, or a huge concrete barrier around the entire perimeter of Nevada. But not because the chip is coded to self-destruct. They're too *cheap*."

Nollie chuckled. "Same reason they weren't interested in fighting another Civil War in the first place."

"Rumors are free. They spread themselves. Hiring people to post a lot of nonsense about the USN costs next to nothing. It's what Fifa said about state terrorism. Policing by propaganda is a *money saver*. And honestly, Noll," Willing added as an afterthought. "It's the United States. It's not what it once was. But they still don't assassinate you for tax evasion."

They got their first lesson in Nevadan brass tacks that very night. They were running low on natural gas, and wouldn't make it to Vegas without refueling. While the small town of Ely did have a motel and a diner, they hadn't the money for either. So they pulled off 93, locked the doors, and wrapped up in the sweaters that only Nollie had thought to pack in July. After sundown in the desert, it got cold.

Willing didn't care. He'd been colder. During the winter of 2031–32, when his mother wouldn't set the thermostat above forty-three—barely high enough to keep the pipes from freezing. Hunkered down in a trickling culvert on the way up to Gloversville, unable to sleep, waiting for the sun to rise. Freezing his fingers on the handlebars as he pushed the bike up weedy riverbanks, struggling to keep the cycle upright, Nollie's and Carter's boxes making the load top-heavy. The tacos from Final Feast may have run out long ago, but this was hardly his first skipped meal. Avery had taken a year or two to disentangle luxuries from requirements. Willing knew the difference as a kid.

He hit the pavement early, and offered to fry up short orders at the diner. Begrudgingly, the proprietor agreed, but only through the breakfast rush. He heard mutterings about "illegal immigrants"—a slightly bent usage, since what made Willing and Nollie illegal wasn't being denied permission to enter this new country, but being forbidden to leave their own. After also cleaning the bathrooms, he earned his first continentals—their arcane colonial design in sepia even hokier and more retro than the old greenbacks.

Were the prices on the menu any guide, his wages were splug—lower than his post-tax pay at Elysian. Yet it felt better to make less money and keep all of it than to net more money after the income had been plundered. The fact that the diner's owner didn't request the web address of the metal in his neck was heady. These were his first earnings in six years that hadn't been automatically reported to, and neatly evaporated by, the federal government. *Dear Goog, Wish you were here.*

Next, he collected dried cowpats to be sold as manure for a ranch near the highway. He spent the afternoon mending the rancher's fences—the very quotidian chore that killed his mother. Willing took care to wear gloves, even in the heat. The work gave him flashbacks: Florence's forefinger, at first merely sausage-plump, with a halo of red around the cut. She tried to be mindful, soaking the laceration in warm salt water, which afterward the doctor said was futile. Within two days, the hand ballooned into an unmilked udder, and red streaks striped her sturdy forearm. Supposedly, the result would have been the same had they whisked her to the hospital the moment the finger began to swell. "Drugs that don't work," the internist announced forlornly, delivering the respectfully folded bandana like a miniature American flag at a military funeral, "don't work early any better than they work late."

Meantime, Nollie did jumping jacks beside the car, earning no end of rubbernecking hilarity from passing locals. Willing would never have called it to her attention, but her form had decayed. Her hands no longer met overhead, but rose only as high as her ears, then descended to the level of her waist. The result was a weak, dying-butterfly motion. The jumps, too, were ineffectual. She used to click her heels. Now her feet lifted off and dropped in the same place, about shoulder width. When briefly airborne, she hovered only half an inch from the ground—you could hardly even call it a jump. The deterioration pained him. The lunatic regime always had a comical side, but this feebler version would only amuse strangers.

Even Enola Mandible couldn't do calisthenics all day, however lamely articulated. By their second day, she was scavenging for odd jobs herself: shelving canned goods in the minimart, swabbing floors. After which, back aching, she didn't need to do jumping jacks.

It was a poor area, made poorer because tourists from the likes of Boise and Portland were no longer passing through on the way to Vegas. Worse, like Willing, soon after secession the state's entire population— albeit with an unchipped sector vastly larger than the national average—had their chips zeroed by Scab satellites. Nevadans dubbed this punitive farewell fleecing "the Petty Larceny." The cumulative extraction was not insubstantial. The term alluded less to meager takings than to small-mindedness.

As the pittances locals could pay their migrant visitors added up, the community's hostility broke down. Willing worked hard and well. He kept his mouth shut. By the end, more than one Ely native had invited them both for a meal. After five days of living out of the Myourea, they rustled up enough spare continentals to refuel the car.

Nevada had always been a magnet for kooks. Misfits, outcasts, miscreants, mavericks—the malcontents, the fantasists, the seekers of shortcuts. Born of mining boom and bust, the economy was founded on vice: prizefighting, loose women, drunkenness, gambling, and marital fecklessness. Even before going it alone, the state was an outlier, making it all too easy to get married, easier still to divorce. Alcohol was plied twenty-four hours a day. A lenient relationship to prostitution well predated the era in which Savannah was able to earn an accredited community college degree in stimulation therapy. Real cigarettes—or giant smelly cigars, for that matter—were legal in casinos. A prohibition against state income tax was enshrined in its constitution. In 2042, Nevadans had merely formalized that they were a people apart. Thus the mutinous new nation-within-a-nation was tailor-made for Willing's eccentric, ceaselessly outraged uncle. But with what or whom would an iconoclast shadowbox here? The image was discordant: Jarred Mandible, perfectly happy.

Willing had known his mentor as a far-sighted landowner, who had appreciated before the rest of the family the primacy of the need to eat. He always pictured Jarred in muddy gumboots, with a shovel. Surely in the USN Jarred would already have procured a farm—Citadel resurrected, liberated from the humiliating requirement to sell nearly all its meat and produce, at scandalously low fixed prices, to the US Department of Agriculture. Yet the urban address on http://usn should have challenged this rosy, pastoral vision of his uncle's circumstances.

Willing couldn't suppress a bubble of excitement as Nollie crossed the Las Vegas city limits. He had never been interested in gambling—with money, that is. More broadly, he was very interested in gambling. He was gambling now.

Besides, he instinctively responded to the city's reputation. Its wildness, abandon, and incaution naturally called out to a young man whose childhood was constricted by wariness and vigilance. The institutionalized recklessness of a town where many an individual blew the entirety of his assets in a single whirl of the roulette wheel couldn't help but appeal to a chronically parsimonious Brooklynite who had measured out exact three-quarter cups of rice for his mother, that the bag might last the week. He savored the city's obliviousness to the tut-tutting opprobrium it had always attracted from the tight, the prim, the rectitudinous. It cared nothing for virtue. It was crass, it was loud, it was heathen. It was silly, and it was fake—honestly, admittedly fake, which gave it a genuineness of a sort. It did not apologize for itself. Over time, the city had made scads of money for its residents on the very back of what was wrong with it.

Las Vegas was the Anti-Willing. Everyone is drawn to what they are not.

Yet as the sun began to set and Nollie drove past the storied strip, his heart fell. Casinos like the Wynn, the Venetian, the Bellagio, and the Singapore were hulking and dark. The fabled main drag had grown funereal. A sprinkling of neon spangled only farther out. More traffic coursed the freeway than in Manhattan, but the preponderance of vehicles were haulage trucks; extravagant motors like their own were scarce. The immediate touch and feel of downtown was disappointingly serious.

Jarred's address was located on the very outskirts in the far southeast. As they drew from the center of town, sprawling white stucco ranch houses with manicured cactus gardens gave way to smaller, cheaper-looking dwellings with no landscaping—rows of identical homes plunked on barren red dirt. Jarred's development, Aloe Acres, had been left half-finished. Terracotta roof tiling its sole cursory nod toward Spanish Modern, the bleak white house numbered 2827 was surrounded by abandoned, partially built rectangular walls rising waist-high. They'd either run out of money, or the developers had hightailed it when the famously renegade state grew more insubordinate than investors were prepared for.

Jarred was not expecting them. He answered the door wearing boxers and a rifle.

"Christ Almighty, it's my right-hand man! And one of the only old ladies I can stand!" Abjuring social protocol, Jarred threw medical caution to the winds and embraced them both in a bear hug, the rifle cutting uncomfortably into Willing's chest. "Full faith and credit, *mi hermano y mi tía*! I was hoping you'd make it! And what do you make of that treasury at the border, huh? I actually bothered to kayak across the Colorado, when I could have driven the fucking pickup on I-70 without so much as a wave good-bye. Felt like such a yunk! Come in, come in."

Inside was stark: a small laminated table, two straight-backed chairs. Everything but the concrete floor was white, and nothing hung on the walls. As the last of the crimson sunset winked through a stingy window, Jarred switched on a dangling bare bulb. His wild black curls were if anything longer, escaping a careless ponytail. Before his uncle left to throw on a robe, Willing noted that at fifty-three Jarred had finally grown a potbelly. Whatever he was up to, it wasn't tilling, planting, and slopping out hogs.

As if realizing what Willing was thinking, Jarred said on return, "Man, you've got even skinnier."

"Slavery is slimming," Willing said.

Jarred fetched a plastic stool, a bottle of tequila, and three mismatched glasses. "Smartest self-starter around here is the guy who decided to plant blue agave after secession," he said, pouring. "No good having Patrón headquartered in town if they're cut off from their Mexican suppliers. Now this local harvest stuff is all over the Free State, and the guy who makes it is stinking rich. Cheers! To the indomitable Mandibles, may we forever flourish!"

"So there are rich people here?" Nollie asked.

"Better believe it," Jarred said. "This state needs practically everything. Figure out what hole to fill, and you can make a killing. What's more, you keep it. Flat tax of 10 percent. And that's not 10 percent plus sales tax, property tax, state and local, Medicare tax, and Social Security. Ten percent, period. Fucking hell, nobody even resents it."

"I can't picture you, my boy," Nollie said, "not resenting anything. You must be desolate."

"I could always resent," Jarred posited, "not resenting anything."

"Do some people not pay the 10 percent?" Willing asked.

"Oh, probably. But the police force is biggin' small, overstretched, and easily annoyed. I wouldn't cross them. Justice is pretty rough. They'd probably show up at the door, take whatever continentals they could find, and beat you up. If only for being a nuisance. With no, I mean *no*, welfare—no unemployment checks, no disability payments, no aid to dependent children, zip—there are some seriously down-and-out lowlifes in this town, and the crime rate is monumental. Hence the rifle at the door, sorry. You still have that sexy little Black Shadow?"

"Naturally," Willing said, patting the pack on his hip.

Nollie looked edgy. "It's sounds as if we shouldn't leave our things in the car."

Willing frowned. "There's not much out there that's worth anything." He didn't want to immediately pile their luggage into Jarred's house, as if they were moving in—especially if that's just what they were doing.

"Maybe not to you." Nollie scuttled out the door. She returned laboring with a box, and Willing leapt up to take it from her.

Jarred guffawed. "Not the *foul matter!*"

He didn't want it to be true, but Willing worried that his great-aunt was starting to lose it. Yes, the elderly had their attachments. But she had dragged those old manuscripts into every hotel room on the road trip here. She'd plunked the box beside her in the booth when they ate at Final Feast. She'd even kept it beside her doing odd jobs in Ely, where she'd also arrived at locals' houses for dinner, arms wrapped around its failing cardboard like a toddler clutching a stuffed bunny. Fair enough, the documents were totems of her lost life as a professional author. Yet the ferocity of the clinging was off. Willing and Jarred locked eyes with shared embarrassment.

After breaking out corn chips and salsa, Jarred extended the bottle for refills, and Willing put a hand over his glass. "Since when are you so abstemious?"

"I'm not. I'm sentimental." Willing unzipped an outer pocket of his belt pack. Delicately, he withdrew a bundle of fabric. He unwound the sock. It was the same knee sock he had once packed with coinage, and used to threaten the red-haired boy into abdicating his fatty ground beef. Willing placed the object inside daintily on the table. "Pour the next shot into that."

"Hey, I recognize that!" Jarred exclaimed. "It was my sister's, God rest her. She had a fucking fetish about those things. Biggin' unlike her, too. Charming, in fact. Don't take this wrong, but your mother could be a drear. For her to be infatuated with one pair of thingamabobs that were frivolous, and fancy-schmancy, and preposterous—it was a huge relief."

Even in the crude glare of the bare bulb, the cobalt stem gleamed like the windows of a cathedral. The tiny cup was warm and loving. "I always meant to give it back to her," Willing said. "I was keeping it safe. This is all we've got left of Bountiful House. It's our inheritance."

Jarred poured, and they toasted: "To our inheritance!" Hygiene be damned, Willing insisted that they all have a sip from the goblet, which passed between the three like a Communion cup. The ritual sanctified the evening. It seemed to bind them in a pact of some sort. To do what wasn't clear.

To crown the festivities, Willing brought out the ridiculous candied kumquats. When you saved symbolic gestures for too long you could miss your opportunity. If they did not eat the goofy fruits now, he might own the pointless jar in perpetuity. He explained its provenance.

"Now I believe in fairies. You found a colony of the über-rich!" Jarred said. "I always figured the feds promoted the myth of this loaded elite to justify draconian tax rates. Presidents always rail against 'billionaires and trillionaires,' and then the top bracket conveniently kicks in, not at a billion, but 250K."

"They're not fairies," Willing said. "More like an endangered species."

"Say, your mother was right about those sell-by dates." Nollie licked her fingers. "Little sweet for me. But not bad."

"So do you know what it was like here," Willing asked his uncle, "when the USN declared independence? After the border last week, I don't trust anything that was on the news in '42. The massacres, the anarchy. The paramilitary confrontations between patriots and secessionists. Was any of that real?"

Jarred loved to pontificate. He'd only vanished from Citadel six months ago, but that was ample time for Jarred Mandible to become an expert on a new country—if his authoritative air was undermined somewhat by the bathrobe and the plastic stool.

"That was all CGI," he declared. "There were no paramilitary battles—because there weren't any 'patriots.' Everybody had fucking had it with DC, and anyone feeling swoony about America the Beautiful was welcome to leave. From what I've been told, '42 was the most graceful revolution in history. Municipal governments were already in place, and they stayed in place. Ditto the state government—which simply became the national government, bingo, overnight. So people woke up. Sun rose. They went to work. Nothing changed. After all, ever think about what the federal government does? Takes your money and gives it to somebody old. That's about it. Oh, and then the feds do expend an awful lot of energy interfering with anything you want to do. Really miss that."

"There's the Census Bureau," Willing said. "I don't know how much good they do, but it's pretty benign."

"The American Battle Monuments Commission!" Nollie posited. "Harmless."

"The *Coast Guard*," Willing remembered victoriously. "Actively good."

Jarred laughed. "Okay, I'll give you the Coast Guard."

"Remember back when Republicans had the numbers to let Washington run out of funding?" Nollie said. "The federal government pulled down its shutters, and nobody noticed."

"Only one thing made folks cross," Jarred remembered. "The closing of national parks. And now the feds have sold off Yellowstone. So much for that."

"Hey, what's happened to the Las Vegas Strip?" Willing asked, hoping to pull his uncle out of an all-too-familiar sourness. "I've seen pictures of that neon boulevard all my life. Now it's *dark*."

"Well, early in the Renunciation," Jarred said, "Vegas made a killing. Foreign tourists swamped the casinos. With the exchange rate in their favor, drinks, hotel rooms, big shows, and buffets were practically free. Trouble was, at the tables, all you could win was dollars. Alvarado wasn't letting more than a hundred bucks out of the country, so you couldn't take the cash back home. And even if you spent it, in situ? Once inflation took off in earnest, in no time a big win wasn't worth any more in real terms than the stake you'd started with. Didn't make for a satisfying experience. Ironically, with all its early associations with the Mafia, Vegas stayed safer than most American cities in the thirties. The flood of foreign money seeped through the cracks and damped down desperation. So what really destroyed the Strip wasn't mayhem. It was order. The sort of order that fired that lump of tin into your neck, you poor bastard."

"The windfall tax of '37," Nollie recalled. "It applied not only to property sales, but to gambling earnings."

"*Ninety percent*," Jarred said. "So a two-to-one win nets a tenth of the bet. The risk-to-benefit ratio went to hell. All very well, long as Uncle Sam was relying on your *upstanding character* to report that bucket of nuevos from the slots. But then they brought in chipping, and taxing at source at the casinos, even for foreigners. For the pros, it was a death knell. No one could make a living, even if they were biggin' sharp. Then the kibosh: they eliminated the cash nuevo. The feeling of physical money—being able to thumb a stack of hundreds, or heft five pounds of quarters from a one-armed bandit—it's always been crucial to the whole gaming gestalt. When you only got credit in abstraction, most of which was immediately extracted . . . Well. It was the end of fun. If you want a single explanation for secession, that was it. Locals say the public outrage was so palpable that the air turned red." Jarred sounded wistful. He'd missed the party.

"Their motto, as I recall," Nollie said, "was *No Taxation*. That's all. They didn't give a shit about representation. Feisty buggers. I was impressed at the time. Like Hungary rising up against the Soviets. Not an auspicious analogy, either."

"By and large, I think Nevadans were relieved not to fight a civil war," Jarred said. "But they would have put up a fight. Nobody but nobody in this state handed in their arms after the *reinterpretation* of the Second Amendment."

"The Strip could have revived after independence," Willing said.

"Not with the embargo," Jarred said. "The big casinos could never survive on locals, who are mostly low-stakes players. They need tourists. That's been the biggest blow to this economy: no more tourists. Only a steady stream of strapped wetbacks like us. Washington won't grant Nevada-bound planes the right to enter American air space. I hope you realize the scale of what you've done. There's no air travel in or out. And while it may be dead easy to get into the Free State, I'm pretty sure they do arrest you if you go back. At the least, they do you for back taxes—with interest and penalties, compounded; so in either a real prison or a de facto debtors' prison, it's a life sentence. Especially if you're chipped, Willing—this Brigadoon is for keeps."

"So are there any casinos left?" For Willing, it was a matter of atmosphere. He wasn't yearning to play craps. But he didn't want a city for which he'd permanently sacrificed his house, most of his extended family, and a far-better-than-serviceable girlfriend to be just like everywhere else.

"The old downtown dumps like the El Cortez are limping along. Hate to admit it, but I've been hitting their tables myself. I don't know how else I'll amass any capital. You remember those long cold nights at Citadel: I'm ace at blackjack."

"Have you won big, then?" Willing said.

"Haven't lost much," Jarred grunted. "An achievement."

Nollie crossed her legs and propped her feet on the foul matter box.

"DC has clearly expected," Jarred said, "that by choking off trade, collapsing tourism, blocking communication and transport links, and throwing a state notoriously short on water totally on its own devices, they'll bring the USN to its knees. So the parallel is less Hungary than the Siege of Leningrad. Thirsty, poor, isolated, and frantic for fresh peaches, Nevadans will beg to be let back into the union—or so goes the theory. Meantime, the Army doesn't have to fire a shot. No one in Washington had the appetite for American troops mowing down other Americans on maXfleX. As a strategy, it's canny, frugal, and politically cunning. The Chelsea Clinton administration quietly assumed that the USN would crumple into a whimpering, remorseful heap within months if not weeks. Except it's been five years. Nobody's crying."

Jarred exuded an infectious local pride that he may have caught from his neighbors. Yet there was a conspicuous disconnect between Jarred's gung-ho and this dismal, Spartan dive. Willing hadn't noticed any transport parked in Jarred's drive. The bare bulb glared, and Willing was preparing for another night in the Myourea. The corn chips and kumquats were finished, and he wasn't counting on more to eat.

"Is this so-called country working?" Willing said tentatively, trying to be tactful. "Or are people here just bigging stubborn?"

"This state is a riveting social experiment, and maybe the vote's still out," Jarred said with gusto. "All Western social democracies have traveled the same arc. They start out decent and quiet and kind of careless, but eventually they get puffed up with their own virtue. Infatuated by *fairness*. Of course, in a perfectly *fair* world we'd all have a big, malicious house and mounds of food. Unlimited access to state-of-the-art medicine, free childcare, biggin' brutal education, and plumped pillows for the *long-lived*—"

"Fresh flowers every morning," Nollie added. "A cup that infinitely runneth over with tequila." She held up her glass for a refill.

"Exactly," Jarred said, obliging with another shot. "All in exchange, it goes without saying, for doing dick. Socially? An easy sell. Economically? Bit tricky. So the state starts moving money around. A little *fairness* here, little more *fairness* there. But it's like shuffling cargo in the hold, and you have to keep shoving trunks left and right, the boat always lurching in one direction or the other. Eventually, social democracies all arrive at the same tipping point: where half the country depends on the other half. It becomes an essentially patrician funding system. It's no longer contribute—" Jarred had had his share of tequila, and stumbled. "Contributory. Which is divisive. Everybody's unhappy. The lower half don't get flowers. The patricians feel robbed. And all that *fairness*, all that shifting cargo, the taking from Peter to pay Paul—"

"High transaction costs," Willing donated.

"Right. So what started as a reasonable, straight-forward arrangement, whereby everyone throws in a little something to cover their modest communal re-quirements, like roads and a cop on the corner—it's morphed into one of those *complex systems* you're always harping on about, Noll, the kind that courts 'catastrophic collapse.' Government becomes a pricey, clumsy, inefficient mechanism for transferring wealth from people who do something to people who don't, and from the young to the old—which is the wrong di-rection. All that effort, and you've only managed a new unfairness."

"I don't see why you wouldn't have the same prob-lem here," Willing said.

"Lotta shrivs—sorry, the *long-lived*—left at seces-sion. Couldn't face life without Medicare. And I'll be honest with you, Noll. The oldsters who've stuck it out—usually native-born Nevadans; the blow-in retirees fled in droves—well, they're getting sick. Nevada doesn't have any pharmaceutical plants, and the drugs ran out years ago—for hypertension, cholesterol, angina. So they're dying sooner. I've seen it plenty on an anecdotal level, but if anyone bothered to assemble statistics here I bet you'd find a sharp drop in life expectancy. I'm not sure that's such a bad thing. An opinion broadly shared in this part of the world, but scandalous in the Outer Forty-Nine. If you're frail or ailing in Nevada, you have to rely on someone else, and I don't mean collectively, on an institution. A relative, or a neighbor."

"Isn't it interesting that seems so weird," Nollie said.

"The Free State is an experiment in going backwards," Jarred said. "Even technologically—there don't happen to be any rob plants within its borders, yet. So as the existing robs break down they're replaced by human employees. It's not an answer in the long run—someone's bound to manufacture the bastards in due course—but in the short term, loss of automation has really helped the labor market. You'll see, there's plenty of work here. Though it's either biggin' low skilled and often physical, or it requires a level of education you and I, Willing, don't have anywhere near."

"We've gone to some trouble to get here," Nollie said, glancing around a room far more depressing than the cozy home in East Flatbush they'd left behind. "I want to be optimistic. But what makes the USN so much of an improvement?"

"It's what I said to Goog on the Fourth of July," Willing said. "Freedom is a feeling. Not only a list of things you're allowed to do. I *feel* better." He might have just taken his own temperature. "I feel better already."

"Tax forms in this state, believe it or not," Jarred said, "are *one page long*. That's pretty much the way it is with everything. You don't get a business license or a marriage license, an entertainment license or a liquor license. You do business, get married, entertain yourself, and drink."

"However," Willing said. "*Nevada is not a utopia*."

"No, no, no!" Jarred agreed vehemently. "It sure isn't. This town is filthy with losers and T-bills, scammers and swindlers. And people really do starve. Nobody helps you here unless they want to, and what's worse they have to like you. Just being needy doesn't cut it. Native Nevadans are apt to give each other a hand, but we interloping Outer Forty-Niners are on our own. Nobody asked us to come here, so we're expected to make ourselves useful or go away. Right at secession, folks were worried only the hardcore would stick it out, and the state would rapidly depopulate until it wasn't viable. Now the prevailing fear is just the opposite: that refugees from Scab persecution will pour into the Free State in quantities Nevada can't absorb. That's a big reason people don't try harder to get word out that it's not so bad here."

"So maybe some of the more outlandish rumors in the USA," Nollie said, "about cannibalism and genocide, are actually propagated by the USN."

"I wouldn't be surprised," Jarred said. "I'm getting reluctant to spread the gospel myself."

"But if everyone here is a maverick," Willing said. "Doesn't that make you a conformist?"

"Very funny," Jarred said. "Problem is, mavericks rarely get on with other mavericks. And you'll find out soon enough how much stuff you simply can't get: replacement parts for your maXfleX. Lemons. Realize how few dishes you can make without lemons? The Chinese takeout is splug, because there aren't any more water chestnuts, or bamboo shoots, or shiitakes—not even in cans. You're entirely dependent on some entrepreneur who's had the bright idea to manufacture wooden salad bowls, or you can't get wooden salad bowls unless you carve them yourself. Nevada has started to generate its own media—TV shows, movies—which sounds cute, but they all suck. People write their own books, but they're awful."

"Glad to hear it," Nollie said. "No competition."

"I can't overemphasize, though," Jarred said, "how leery locals are of new arrivals. They're not touched by your eagerness to convert. They're not impressed by your bravery in coming here. Obviously, a lot of Lats drained south of the border when Mexico's economy went ape shit. After secession, Nevada lost a fair number more. With all the holdout Republicans around Reno and Carson City, Lats were edgy that an independent state would turn into a racist repeat of the Confederacy. Well, everyone needs a cat to kick, and that's us. We're the new *undocumented workers.* Forty-Niners show up with unrealistic expectations, no education, and worst of all, no assets. They get chip-stripped at the border. You're unusual; most of us don't realize we could have brought in a car."

"Most of us wouldn't have cars," Willing reminded him.

"I kick myself for not crossing in the pickup. I've been getting around on a ramshackle bicycle that isn't even electrified. In the heat of summer, it's insufferable. As for this place, I know it's not much to look at. But it's a miracle I have somewhere to live. Plenty

Forty-Niners are homeless. I only stopped dozing in doorways at the beginning of May."

"What kind of work are you doing here?" Nollie asked.

"I work at a cheese factory," Jarred announced shamelessly. "Separating curds and whey—the whole Little Miss Muffet nine yards. Nevada's had a dairy industry for ages, but they didn't make much cheese. Couldn't top a taco anymore, and everyone freaked. The market for Monterey Jack is biggin'. Casa de Queso is thinking of expanding into a knockoff Parmesan. I know guys who are quasi-suicidal because they can't get Parmesan."

"It's crazy," Willing said, "but I pictured you owning another farm."

"How would I do that? No capital, *mi amigo.* You'll see. I mean, you and Nollie are welcome to crash here. But even in the land of self-reliance with a negligible flat tax, it could take you a while to swing your own place."

"I'd hate to part with it," Willing said. "But selling this goblet might raise enough for a security deposit on a small apartment. The top part is solid gold."

"But what you complained to me about, when you moved back to Brooklyn?" Jarred said. "The *no trajectory* problem? Here, in that respect, nothing's changed. Man, this is the first time in my life I wish I'd earned a degree. Nevadans don't really need another fifty-something yunk to press, cut, and schlep cheese. They need chemists, and engineers."

"What would you do," Nollie said, "if you did have capital?"

"Waste of time to fantasize."

"Wrong answer," Nollie said.

Jarred indulged her. "I'd build a gigantic greenhouse. I'd grow *lemons.*"

"That's better," she said, turning to Willing. "What would you do with capital?"

This house was ugly. With its partially constructed rectangles of waist-high walls, the whole development was ugly. But the sunset had been stunning. On the drive into Las Vegas, looming red mountains to the west were impervious to whatever government came and went. The cityscape was goofy; the land on which it sat was austere. The balance was good. A lightness leavened Willing's body that hadn't percolated through his limbs since before the Stonage. He personified a favorite chocolate bar when he was small, its muddy cocoa solids pipped with hundreds of air bubbles, so what had been heavy and indigestible became fluffy and almost weightless. He didn't know what he was doing tomorrow, and he liked that.

"I would earn a degree in hydrology at the University of Nevada, Las Vegas," Willing said. "I would research how people like Jarred can grow lemons without the USN siphoning so much water from the Colorado River that Arizona brings in the National Guard, and Mexico's objections to reduced flow over the border create a diplomatic crisis. Only five million people lived in Nevada before secession. Washington can live without the tax take. What will endanger the USN's independence is water. Tensions with adjacent states over drainage of Lake Tahoe, the Humbolt River, and Lake Mead."

"My," Nollie said. "You've thought about this."

"I've thought about this," he said. "I would find some way of contacting Fifa, because it can't really be that hard. I would get her, and Savannah, and Bing to emigrate here, too. Maybe even Goog, who wouldn't be such a T-bill if he didn't work for the Scab. We would live together with Jarred, like Citadel in the old days. But it would be big and airy, not tight and frightened, the way it was in the thirties. Savannah would go back to being an artist and stop being a prostitute. She'd find a man who's more attractive than I am, and I'd feel jealous. Bing would discover some other calling aside from being a nice guy. Avery and Lowell could retire from Washington to a separate cottage on the same compound. Economists like Lowell don't believe the USN can work. It would be very enjoyable to watch Lowell live in a place that's impossible. Jayne and Carter would come down from Montana. Jayne would stop being crazy, because she thinks she wants solitude and really she wants companionship. You would have your private office. Where you can write new books for other people to read because otherwise it could start to get boring here. Then you would die. I would be sad. It would be a good sadness, because it's not-being-sad when someone dies that's sad. I would marry Fifa. We would plan to have three children but not be very careful and end up with five."

"Right answer," Nollie said, lifting her feet from the box. She peeled off the tired packing tape, folded back the flaps, and removed the top stacks of banded printouts to the floor. She fingered up a pool of candied kumquat drool from the laminated tabletop and moved the Bountiful House goblet out of the way. Struggling even using both hands, from the middle of the carton she withdrew a boxed manuscript titled *Better Late Than*. When she plunked it on the table, the tequila glasses rattled. She slipped off the top of the mimeo-paper box and removed about fifty pages. "There," she said. "Capital."

The box was filled with gold bars.

"I thought you only brought in bancors," Willing said.

"I didn't have such unfettered faith in a new currency," Nollie said. "Any currency. I learned from my father to diversify. I backstopped with precious metal in 1999. The yellow stuff was down to $230 an ounce. You must have some appreciation for what's happened to the price since."

"That looks like a large enough trove to interest the USN mint," Willing said. "The population is rising from refugee Forty-Niners. Larger gold reserves will allow Nevada to gently expand its monetary base without inflation. But I don't understand how you got this through JFK in the first place."

"The feds had just nationalized gold," Nollie reminded him. "No one in their right mind was bringing it *into* the US. So Customs wasn't looking for it."

"The house-jacking," Willing said. "Now it makes sense. You gave Sam some mouth, but otherwise you were *cowed*. It wasn't like you."

"Took some powerful self-control," Nollie said. "But I had to get the box out; it was worth far more than Florence's house. Still, 'Maxwell's Silver Hammer' played in my head the whole walk to Prospect Park.

"Now, my only condition is that you remember this is not manna from the sky. I earned it. By staying up late at a keyboard when my friends were carousing in bars. By reading the same manuscript so many times—in multiple edits, copyedits, first, second, and third passes, and galleys—that I came to hate the sight of my own sentences. By appearing in public events and saying the same thing over and over until I was senseless with self-hatred. By catching seven a.m. flights to literary festivals when I'd rather have slept in. Remember, too, that if I'd not already paid taxes on that metal, there would be twice as much of it. But what's left I would like you to have. It should stake you for an education, and a home, and a marriage—with enough left over for lemon trees."

Since he was a boy, Willing had been very interested in economics and not very interested in money. When he learned the value of his great-aunt's gift in continentals, he was abashed.

He considered what Jarred had said about fairness. His uncle seemed to imply there was no such thing. There were only competing unfairnesses. As Nollie charged him to remember, she had worked hard—harder than some people. So even a one-for-you-and-one-for-me fairness wasn't exactly fair. The Mandible fortune once destined for his grandfather Carter, and presumably for Nollie as well, though she clearly didn't need it—that wasn't fair, either. Which meant the fortune's evaporation in 2029 wasn't unfair. Though not-unfair was not the same as fair. So perhaps his endowment from his great-aunt was not-unfair.

In his embarrassment, all he came to understand was the one reliably sound thing to do with money: spend it on someone else. Nollie had enjoyed bestowing her assets on her nephews. His great-great-great-grandfather Elliot, toward the end of his life, would also have husbanded his resources to hand them on.

Willing had rescued the Mandible clan once. It could get to be a habit.

There was indeed an underground railroad—which was neither a railroad, naturally, nor a sequence of safe houses. It was a hodgepodge of unaffiliated freelancers: unchipped codgers in Nevada who knew how to drive—since locals believed, not without reason, that the guidance systems of vehicles set on driverless automatic could be taken over by satellites. Carrying fuel and provisions for the journey, the codgers did runs across the continent for a price.

Willing commissioned a van for a three-pointed round trip. Its first port of call was New York. It picked up Fifa—later she said it was like being kidnapped; Willing preferred the term *Shanghaied.* The story would come to seem romantic. The van driver scooped up Savannah and Bing, and after a great deal of argument, their older brother. In DC, Lowell staunchly opposed going anywhere until he got word that, after his son's resignation from the Scab, his lectureship at Georgetown was rescinded. Avery was sad that her Vertical Reconditioning therapy would be superfluous in Nevada, though she was glad of the reason for that. The van returned to Las Vegas by way of Montana. Jayne was terrified, but Jayne was always terrified. Not wishing to repeat the mistake that Nollie had made with their mother, Carter wanted to reconcile with his sister before he died. There was enough room in the van for their caretaker rob and the Mandible silver service, whose restoration to the larger family would make possession of sixteen iced-tea spoons seem much more sensible. It all worked out quite nicely.

The one personal indulgence Willing purchased with Nollie's treasure was having his chip fried. The procedure was common in the Free State, and safer than surgical extraction: a blast of high-frequency radio waves frazzled the implant's satellite communications. Though the technology's inventor had grown wealthy, Willing knew no Nevadans with neutered chips who'd trusted the procedure enough to try crossing into the USA proper. So maybe the process was a load of hokum. But Willing felt cleaner after, like a sexual assault victim having numbly submitted to swabs, examinations, and photographs who was finally allowed to take a shower.

Once he earned a high school equivalency and graduated from college, Willing confirmed the wisdom of having focused his studies on water: he would never lack for work. Yet to avoid becoming a hydrology killjoy, once a year on his mother's birthday he and Fifa took a gloriously wasteful fifteen-minute shower with the eco-setting disabled. The annual ritual cost over a hundred continentals, and it was worth it. Symbolically, he'd framed the original-issue C-note from the underground silo in Nebraska and hung it over the toilet in the bathroom, where once a year condensation from their sinful shower fogged the greenback's glass.

As she grew older herself, Fifa softened on shrivs, and her business installing hallway railings and electric stairway lifts achieved a reputation as compassionate. The biggest favor she did the elderly during her installations was to bring along a selection of rambunctious Mandible children—Bing's, Savannah's, Goog's, or their own.

Unfortunately, the excessive water required made the operation economically unfeasible, and Jarred and Bing dolefully allowed their lemon orchard to wither.

Jarred was philosophical, reminding his frustrated farm workers that all men were endowed by their Creator with an inalienable right only to the *pursuit* of happiness. At least they nursed a few potted lemon trees at Citadel Redux, where there were always wedges for tequila shots. Assembling for ritual cocktails on the veranda at sunset, the adults wrangled good-naturedly over who got to drink from the remaining Bountiful House goblet, until Goog's youngest hellion shattered the legendary keepsake. To quell his temper, Willing remembered what he'd told Nollie about the books that they burned in the oil drum: with objects, you can take the meaning *back*. Presto, the storied goblet became a crummy old glass. Willing wondered if he should learn to take his own advice more often.

Savannah's fabric designs grew as renowned as cloth could get in an embargoed state that was mostly desert—which, admittedly, wasn't very. Avery concocted yet another marginal therapy that attracted scads of cuckoo clients to her practice at Citadel, whom everyone else got to make fun of when they went home. Lowell spent his retirement hunched over another treatise explaining why, with a "medieval" monetary policy, the USN would collapse any day now. Haranguing packed audiences, he became Nevada's most famous iconoclast, while Jarred embraced the mainstream as a solid, patriotic citizen. For the sheer variety at first, they both seemed to relish swapping roles, though over time Jarred found pom-pomming as an establishment cheerleader who promoted the status quo a little dumpy-feeling. Jayne was disallowed a Quiet Room, even if the sprawling Spanish Modern compound had the space. Though better adjusted, she never stopped mourning Great Grand Man's sterling asparagus tongs, gifted pointedly, if you will, to an ungrateful house-jacker. Keen to keep himself gainfully occupied in his nineties, Carter started a newspaper. It ran at a loss, but it seems that Nevadans had missed the *Las Vegas Sun*. Everything in Carter's newspaper wasn't accurate, but the odds of a given factoid being at least sort-of-true were better than fifty-fifty, which beat the internet by a yard.

In due course, Kurt limped through Citadel's gate under his own steam. He'd suffered an industrial accident in Indiana, and wasn't an appreciable addition to the USN workforce. The Mandibles not only took him in, but pooled their resources to replace his teeth with implants. Perhaps the caprices of kindness were no reliable substitute for a welfare system, but a face-to-face meeting of honest need and spare capacity felt better. Kurt was warmly beholden, not militantly "entitled," and benevolence freely given was not begrudged.

To start with, Goog successfully applied to become the sole enforcement officer for the USN Revenue Service. His primary remit was to send out effusive yearly thank-you notes to taxpayers considerate enough to file, and generous enough to share the proceeds of their industry with their neighbors. He was also charged with issuing profuse, prostrate apologies—preferably in person, should time and distance allow—for those all-too-frequent instances where the USNRS had miscalculated a tax bill or lost a citizen's return. Alas, groveling and remorse weren't Goog's strong suits. Worse, the legislature in Carson City had issued strict guidelines to his department, admonishing that it mustn't seek to foster "a social atmosphere of fear, intimidation, and predation," and Goog's enthusiasm for his more punitive duties soon lost him the post. He took up coaching the debate team at their local high school, teaching precocious teenagers how to be show-off know-it-alls who tested adult patience. He was very popular with the kids.

In 2057, an immigrant Forty-Niner arrived with the news that Australia had been invaded by Indonesia. The president of the United States sent Canberra a special communiqué to say that he was sorry.

More news: there was finally a Palestinian state, and nobody cared. Russia had annexed Alaska for its natural gas resources. The Speaker of the House pointed out that "Alaska was always pretty far away anyway."

Nollie lived to 103, collapsing just short of her daily three thousand jumping jacks, which by then she was virtually executing on all fours. Beforehand, she'd written several more novels for a captive audience. Even on http://usn, piracy inevitably grew rife, and most of her readership accessed the books for free. After she died, the University of Nevada library bought the foul matter.

In 2064, Nevada's flat tax was raised to 11 percent. Of course.

About the Author

Lionel Shriver's novels include the London *Sunday Times* bestseller *Big Brother*, the National Book Award finalist *So Much for That*, the *New York Times* bestseller *The Post-Birthday World*, and the international bestseller *We Need to Talk About Kevin*, adapted for a feature film starring Tilda Swinton. Her journalism has appeared in the *Guardian*, the *New York Times*, the *Wall Street Journal*, and many other publications. She lives in London and Brooklyn, New York.

HARPER LUXE

THE NEW LUXURY IN READING

We hope you enjoyed reading
our new, comfortable print size and found it
an experience you would like to repeat.

Well – you're in luck!

HarperLuxe offers the finest in fiction and
nonfiction books in this same larger print size and
paperback format. Light and easy to read, HarperLuxe
paperbacks are for book lovers who want to see
what they are reading without the strain.

For a full listing of titles and
new releases to come, please visit our website:

www.HarperLuxe.com